MRS BARLOW

£ ban

KIRK	LENTON	CARVER
-5 DEC 2000	12 JUN 2001	04 FEB 2002
ALLEN D3	DAVIES	Parker A
-4 JAN 20		-1 MAR 2002
WORTHEY	HARRISON	ALLEN 113
-1 FEB 2001	-4 SEP 2001	
	James	
WALTER		COUPLAND
16 FEB 2001	Spink	16 APR 2002
	-3 OCT 2001	Williams G1
SENIOR	FAGAN	14 MAY 2002
-2 MAR 2001	3 0 OCT 2001	CARROL
WILLIAMS	STARLING	3 0 MAY 2002
16 MAR 2001		TANN
BRYCE	GRAHAM	-9 JUL 2002
-1 MAY 2001	13 DEC 200	SMEDLEY
LINLEY	DERBYSHIRE	24 JUL 2002
15 MAY 2001	31 JAN 2002	Mortimer
		7 AUG 2002

-2

THE KEYS TO THE GARDEN

THE KEYS TO THE GARDEN

SUSAN SALLIS

COMPASS PRESS

★ OXFORD ★ MELBOURNE ★

First published in 1999 by Bantam Press
a division of Transworld Publishers Ltd

Compass Press Large Print Book Series; an imprint of
ISIS Publishing Ltd, Great Britain, and Bolinda Press, Australia
Published in Large Print 2000 by ISIS Publishing Ltd,
7 Centremead, Osney Mead, Oxford OX2 0ES,
and Bolinda Publishing Pty Ltd,
17 Mohr Street, Tullamarine, Victoria 3043
by arrangement with Transworld Publishers Ltd

British Library Cataloguing in Publication Data
Sallis, Susan
    The keys to the garden. –
    Large print ed.
    1. Mothers and daughters –
    Fiction
    2. Large type books
I. Title
823.9'14 [F]

Australian Cataloguing in Publication Data
The Keys to the Garden/Susan
    Sallis
    1. Large print books
    2. Mothers and daughters –
    Fiction
    3. Domestic fiction

ISBN 1–74030–132–3 (hb) 1–74030–133–3 (pb)
(Bolinda Publishing Pty Ltd)
ISBN 0–7531–6272–5 (hb) 0–7531–6278–4 (pb)
(ISIS Publishing Ltd)

Printed and bound by Antony Rowe, Chippenham and Reading

For Sabrina and all her friends

CHAPTER
ONE

The marquee was heaving. People had finished eating but not drinking. They were regrouping themselves, glasses held like talismans as they leaned over to make themselves heard.

"Lovely wedding."

"Lucy looked practically edible."

"An English rose in every sense of the word."

"Roses have thorns, remember. And she'll need them, marrying across-county as it were."

"That's one way of putting it."

"Got to be careful these days how you do put it."

"You can understand the attraction though, can't you? What a contrast. Blonde against his darkness."

"Absolutely. Couldn't agree more."

"It's when the children come along of course . . ."

"They'll be all right. His parents have gone through it — there's a brother, you know. Both he and Len are fine. No chips on anyone's shoulders!"

"I didn't know about the brother. Is he here today?"

"Somewhere abroad. Works for famine relief."

"And in any case, Len is in showbiz. It's a different world."

"Absolutely. Couldn't agree more. And dammit, this is 1985! We're a bit more broad-minded these days."

"I'm sure you're right."

"I am. I am. Match made in heaven. Have some more wine."

"Yes. As you say. Match made in heaven. Pity about the old buffer in wellies — who *is* he, for God's sake?"

"Some God-forsaken relative. They always turn up for weddings and funerals."

"Martha's holding up . . . She will be really on her own now, won't she? So sad losing Clem like that . . . She and Lucy all-in-all to one another."

"I remember Clem — do you remember Clem? He would have loved it."

Martha, hearing this with her right ear while her left ear attended to the Rector, thought grimly: Oh no he wouldn't. Clem would have hated everything about it: the tent, the clothes, the ridiculous top hats. She smiled brilliantly at the Rector as he told her about the plight of poor little Miss Darcy, adjusted the smile quickly at the words "gently dying" and thought again: But he would have loved Uncle Bertie in his wellies.

The Rector said, "Now you have a little more time, perhaps you could visit her? She can cope quite well with a single caller and you and she have always got on well."

"We used to do the flowers. Before Clem died." She remembered Clem saying, "How you can put up with that little woman, I do not know. She reminds me of a mouse. And she'll run up your legs one of these days, just you see."

She chuckled. "We used to laugh together." She saw incredulity writ large on the Rector's broad face and added defensively, "She can laugh, you know."

"Of course." He was unconvinced. "It's just so hard to imagine." But, thank goodness, he laughed. And then she was claimed by Mrs Travers, Lennie's mother, whom she must remember to call Toto ("I couldn't manage Thomasina when I was a baby and Toto has stuck and as we're going to be related — well, practically — it would be lovely if you would call me Toto").

"Is everything all right?" Martha asked nervously as Toto drew her away conspiratorially.

"Dear Marty. It's the best wedding I've ever been to — and I've attended some, I can tell you!" Toto gave her huge laugh and then sobered. "Lennie says Lucy is ready to change. And I thought you would like to go with her. Have a private word. You know."

For a second Martha could have cast herself on the broad chest and howled like a dog. How wonderful that Toto knew how she felt. How wonderful that they were "practically related" because Toto was Lennie's mother and Lennie was now Martha's son-in-law. What did that make Toto and George?

She said simply, "Oh Toto."

And Toto squeezed her arm and said, "Bear up a bit longer. It'll be better when the photographs arrive."

"How?" Martha asked, bewildered.

"You'll see it properly then. Now . . . hopeless." Toto had to raise her voice to be heard. George joined them. He really did look ridiculous in his grey morning suit. The topper had ruffled his thin hair and it stood on end.

His face was pallid against Toto's Afro-Caribbean glory. Martha thought: A lily and a marigold. No wonder Lucy loves them all.

George mouthed something, cleared his throat and yelled, "It's the best wedding I've attended, Martha. You've done wonders. Thank you."

Again she wanted to weep. It had been such hard work and last night she hadn't been able to find the precious list which had ruled her life for the past six months. It had been under her pillow all the time.

She said, "Oh George."

"I'm getting a drink for Clem's Uncle Bertie. See you again in a mo."

He was gone, Toto trailing behind him like a galleon under full sail, her mouth of wonderful white teeth a light in a dim world. They had not known Clem but they spoke of him constantly, so that he was here, with all of them.

Martha felt her eyes beginning to water and moved past the Rector and towards Lucy. Dear Lucy, unfamiliar in her yards of tulle. She really did look edible but in a spun-sugar way: a delightful way. Not as Jennifer Bowles, her so-called best friend, had meant, Martha suspected. Jennifer had implied a cream bun; an apple turnover; something stodgy. Jennifer was witty and amusing and tall and svelte and Lucy and she had been friends since playschool, but Lucy was kind and Jennifer was not. She appeared from behind four men at that moment and rushed up to Martha. "Are you all right? Oh Marty, it's been wonderful. Didn't she look lovely? Were you able to enjoy it?"

4

"Of course." Martha's voice was calm, slightly amused, as befitted an honorary aunt, though Jennifer had stopped calling her Aunty some time ago. She wished people wouldn't call her Marty. It had been Clem's name for her. No-one else's.

She said, "And yes, she did look lovely. Edible in fact."

Jennifer looked at her sharply and then smiled. "Candy-floss. Yes. And I'm a cucumber. Cucumber and candyfloss!"

She laughed and Martha knew why Lucy loved her. No-one would have thought of Jennifer as a cucumber in her green silk wrap-around dress unless she had mentioned it. Now she had, it appeared very apt. Martha laughed with her.

Jennifer said, "Should I suggest to her that it's time to change? The taxi will be here in an hour."

"I was on my way." Martha hesitated. It was Jennifer's duty as bridesmaid to help Lucy change from candyfloss to traveller.

Jennifer said, "Listen, I'm getting on rather well with Uncle Clem's something-or-other cousin. D'you think you could manage?"

Martha definitely felt her eyes mist over this time. She put a hand on Jennifer's long arm. "Yes. Yes, I think I could," she said. "Thanks, Jen."

Jennifer watched Martha forge a path through the guests; her face went very still as it so often did when she was hiding thoughts she knew to be wrong. Was it possible to love someone as she loved Lucy, and still envy them? She envied Lucy practically everything, even her dead father. Especially her dead father, because when he had been alive he had often been quite unreasonable with his "house rules" as he called them. Now he was dead he was something unique and special, and his house rules were interpreted by his widow, Martha, who was far more relaxed, though she did not realize it. Jennifer envied Lucy her mother; she envied every little bit of her, piece-meal. The small capable hands that could cook and sew and play the church organ and rest on one's arm like butterflies conveying understanding and gratitude. Jennifer had appreciated those fingers on her arm; they had acknowledged the long-standing relationship between them. Once, when they were eight years old, Lucy had said to her mother, "I want Jennifer to be my sister." And Martha had replied reasonably, "Well, she is in a way, isn't she?" Those fingers had acknowledged that. Jennifer Bowles was half-way to being the "second daughter" she had always pretended to be. So she need not envy Lucy her mother . . . perhaps. The roundness of her, the neat short curls, the ordinary face lit by the unexpectedly blue eyes . . . they were Jennifer's as well as Lucy's. In fact if only Linda Bowles would drop dead during one of her bloody dancing classes, or her aerobic sessions or her ski-ing holidays or her bonking weekends, Jennifer could be taken completely under Martha's wing. But, of course, no such luck. Linda's hectic physical life probably meant she would live to ninety-four. Oh God. One blessing: she hadn't come today. There had been a meeting she couldn't get out of. Of course. A meeting in a luxury hotel somewhere; a meeting with a chairman and one other.

6

Martha was still wending her way through the various small knots of people. Jennifer realized Lucy had not seen her and was talking to one of Len's gorgeous relatives. She might as well be stapled to Len; he was turning away from her to josh his father and Uncle Bertie, but Lucy did not let go of his hand. She must have released him to eat her meal: Jennifer wondered whether, beneath the trestle, their legs had been intertwined. The thought made her weak at the knees. She had fallen for Len the moment Lucy introduced him — "My new boss, Len Travers" — but she had known him in a way before. As one knew radio voices. He was a local newsreader and he chaired programmes about race relations in Bristol and Birmingham. He was what Jennifer and Lucy would have described once as "drop-dead gorgeous". He should have fallen for someone who was tall and sinuous with an air of mystery, but he had fallen for someone small and blonde and very obvious; one of his researchers in fact. It was all pretty obvious when you came to think about it.

A voice behind Jennifer said, "I can see where you've been sunbathing. Looks rather sore just below the neckline of your dress. Would you like me to rub in some cream?"

It was that second cousin once removed again, thinking he was being so bloody daring. Jennifer turned with a slight smile, about to annihilate him, but the sun was catching his blond hair and spinning it into a halo, and his pale blue eyes had a look of the desert and the sea and huge open spaces. And he was a relative of Lucy's.

She widened the smile. "It sounds a very attractive suggestion."

He took her glass from her hand and put it on the nearby table with his, then he stood very close to her. Their eyes were on a level; she could feel her heart suddenly start up exactly the way the pump started for the central heating every morning at six a.m., with a kind of churning sound. Then he said something that people only said in films.

"I want to make love to you. Desperately."

She swallowed convulsively but forced herself to stand still, not let her eyes widen, certainly not allow a flush to ride up her long neck. In spite of university, in spite of working in Birmingham, both she and Lucy had stayed country girls. Martha and Clem had been pillars of village life and eventually so had Lucy. And Jennifer had tried. All right, she had experimented with various young men, but no-one had ever been so direct, so honest, before.

She held his gaze while she counted ten. Then, just before she fell to the ground in a puddle of sweat, she said coolly, "That sounds an attractive proposition too."

He said urgently, "When? Where?"

She was suddenly loving it. She smiled so that he would see every one of her perfect teeth, and said, "Ten minutes. The garage."

He turned immediately and she began, like Martha, to make her way through knots of people towards Lucy. She smiled all the time, feeling so alive she could hardly contain herself. She was conscious of her individual beauty: her black shining hair done up on top and encircled with flowers, her green silk sheath wrapping her around like a tulip leaf and showing every curve of her body. She was twenty-four, bridesmaid to her best friend, and about to creep up the ladder at the back of the garage into the old loft, draw it up after her and make passionate love until it was time for Lucy and Len to leave.

She reached Lucy and kissed her cheek. "Marty is going to help you change. Don't go without me, darling," she whispered. "I'll be back to wave you off."

Lucy looked startled. "Where —?"

"Ask no questions!"Jennifer said mysteriously, her eyes glinting.

But Lucy still said, acutely, "Who?"

It was then that Jennifer realized she did not know his name. And what was more, unless he'd done his detective work elsewhere, he did not know hers. It made the whole thing more outrageous than ever. She almost chortled. "I haven't the remotest!" she said.

Martha fielded people expertly. She had been President of the local Women's Institute twice and Group secretary last year, so she knew how to deal with a host of people all wanting to talk at once. The curate's wife wanted help with the pram service next week and Martha was going to stay with Toto and George for a few days.

"My dear, would you like to water the church flowers for me so that they will last tomorrow and the Sunday after?" she forestalled her.

"Martha! Do you mean we can keep all those beautiful flowers?"

"Of course. I think perhaps the cottage hospital might like the vases either side of the screen. Otherwise . . ."

She turned on the ball of her foot. "Albert, I'll need you to come in daily while I'm away. Is that possible?"

Albert Davis, who had helped Clem in the garden and now did most of it, said dourly, "Course. 'Oo else would you get?"

"No-one," Martha agreed and seeing a small space open towards Lucy, made for it.

She was annoyed to be physically held back by a perfect stranger.

"Martha! You don't recognize me, do you?"

"I'm afraid not. But all Len's family are staying on for tea later, so we shall meet then —"

"I'm nothing to do with the Traverses!" He was not much taller than her; stocky; dry, curly hair receding from a wide forehead; snub nose; darkly fringed grey eyes that were strangely familiar . . . disturbing. He smiled. "Oh Martha, you were my first sweetheart! Surely you remember."

The turmoil inside was beginning to ferment. She said coldly, "I'm afraid not. Now, if you will excuse me, I have to have a word with my daughter —"

"Martha," he said again, deeply reproachful. "Behind the bicycle sheds. Your eighth birthday. Then you went to Norton Grammar and I went to the Secondary Modern and I never saw you again. Till now."

Vaguely, oh so vaguely, she remembered. He had kissed her and she had hated him and run home crying and her father had escorted her to school the next day in case the "nasty boy" had lain in wait for her.

He saw that she was remembering and tipped his head back to laugh loudly. Then he held her shoulders and pushed his face against hers and kissed her a second time.

She was so appalled that for a moment she let it happen. And then, unforgivably, she felt his tongue try to open her lips and she drew back sharply.

"How dare you!" She was going to hit him or walk away or something. But then she remembered that it was Lucy's wedding and that, after it, she had to live in the village alone. She smiled and said through her teeth, "I didn't like you then and I don't like you now and you certainly were not invited here. Kindly leave." And she went on towards Lucy, still smiling, her stomach churning uncontrollably.

Lucy, dear, dear Lucy, drew her into the folds of tulle.

"Oh Ma, it's just perfect! Thank you, thank you, thank you! A million times!"

"Dearest. It went well because everyone wanted it to go well." Martha was flustered out of her usual calm matter-of-factness. She sounded almost irritable. She tried to adjust her voice. "Jennifer suggested that I should help you to change, darling. And I thought it was nearly time."

"It is." Lucy grinned. Jennifer has other fish to fry. She really is awful, Ma. I'll tell you later. D'you want to go on ahead? I'll have a word with Len and be with you in a few minutes." She kissed her mother's forehead. "My God, you're hot, darling! Listen, I'll make you a cup of tea. Lie on my bed. Like old times."

Old times. Obviously old times did not come round again, but because Lucy had still been at home when

Clem died, they had lingered. Now there would be a sort of repeat of the whole bereavement thing. A new bereavement. Lots of new times emerging from the old times. Martha felt the words whirl in her head; she kissed Lucy quickly and turned for the entrance.

It was better outside. She paused and breathed deeply. Then she looked around for a familiar foothold, a point of reference. The garden spread before her. The sweep of lawn leading to the drive, the borders full of hollyhocks and delphiniums rising from beds of natural geraniums. Albert had said it would be a picture for this first week in July and it was. And the house behind, rosy brick and wide stone window ledges; a passion-flower winding over the porch and stone tubs everywhere dripping flowers on to the gravel. A few people stood in the sunshine; the caterers moved back and forth carrying trays. Perhaps they made the familiar seem strange and unfamiliar. Or perhaps this was how it would always look now . . . New times. Empty of Clem and Lucy and Lucy's friends, it would, of course, be different.

She thought: If only Clem were here . . . if only, if only, if only . . .

And then an unwelcome voice said behind, "If wishes were horses, beggars would ride."

She almost spun around; it was good to be angry, so much better than wallowing in melancholia. "I cannot remember your name, but I know damned well you were not on the guest list! Now will you please leave!"

His arch smile died and he looked hurt. "Martha! I'm no threat if that's what you're thinking! I thought you'd be pleased to see me! I've known all along that it was you but I haven't made myself known — I realized you'd be up to your eyes. But now everything is so successful, well, I thought that the least you would do would be to thank me!"

She frowned slightly. "What are you talking about?"

"The marquee! I'm William! Tatham! Tatham's Tents. Surely you realized when you phoned . . . surely it wasn't coincidence?"

She stared. "Tatham's Tents. You are Billy Tatham. My God. Billy Tatham." She swallowed. "It was coincidence. I looked in the *Yellow Pages*. And someone from Littleford Parish Council recommended you. How could I possibly know —"

He regained his confidence immediately. "Don't apologize. Really. And I don't believe in coincidence anyway. Our meeting was ordained." He jerked his round John Bull head skywards. "I've always kept tabs on you, Martha. Knew you'd married Clement Moreton. Knew you'd done it to please your parents, too. All very suitable, Methodist minister's daughter and local solicitor. I even knew you'd changed to C. of E. And I knew when Moreton died. But I'd never have got in touch — I'm beneath you, always have been. I liked to know what you were doing . . . things like that. No more. And then you asked me to supply the marquee for your daughter's wedding. I thought you'd chosen me."

She made a sound and spread her hands helplessly.

He said again, "No, really. Don't apologize. I'd rather it this way. You know . . . meant. Meant to be. There's no escape from fate."

He was still nasty. A truly horrid little man. She had no intention of apologizing for anything, but she had plenty of regrets. She should have got some quotes like Lennie had advised her to do. Tatham's were not cheap and Lennie said the Midland Marquee Company had an offer — three days for the price of one or something.

She said in her W.I. President's voice, "How quaint! Well, everything seems to have gone well. I must thank you for that, Mr Tatham. And now, if you don't mind, I have to help my daughter. Excuse me."

She cut across the lawn and jumped the flower-bed onto the drive so that there was no way he could cut her off. But when she closed the front door behind her and looked through the spyhole he was standing exactly where she had left him, looking almost tiny in spite of his stockiness. She had cut him down to size and felt a pang of self-disgust. But there had been no other way. Billy Tatham. He had been one of the wartime evacuees from Birmingham. Yes, she remembered him well now. For a year, until she got her scholarship to Norton, he had pestered her unremittingly. She had hated him then; she hated him now. She would pay his bill — write a cheque from George and Toto's house — and be done with him. Kept tabs on her, indeed!

She went upstairs and into Lucy's room. Snowball, the white Persian, was asleep on the three-foot-six bed camouflaged by the tissue paper which had wrapped the tulle so lovingly on its hanger. She trailed a finger between his ears and he turned his head and revealed one green eye. They surveyed each other; he closed the eye.

14

"Right," she said. "I get the message. You don't care. About Lucy getting married or Billy Tatham. OK."

She switched on Lucy's Teasmade and began to tidy up. When Lucy came flying in ten minutes later tea was poured and her linen suit, violet blue to match her eyes, was laid on the bed well away from Snowball.

Lucy hugged her. "How do you do it? You're so calm, so in control! My God, I feel as if my head will explode at any moment!"

"Headache?" Martha asked.

"No. Too much happening. Too many impressions. Too many people . . . you know." She flung herself into the spoon-back chair that had been old Mrs Moreton's. Her dress spilled everywhere. "I thought I'd be so conscious of Dad but I haven't been able to think of him! Not once! Oh Mummy!" She began to cry simply because she did not know what else to do.

Martha ignored the tears, went behind her and began to unhook everything. "No tea until this dress is on its hanger," she decreed.

Lucy sobbed and let herself be undressed. "How do you do it? Shall I be like you later? Oh, I hope so. Look at you! You were a bit white in the marquee, but now you're positively glowing!"

Martha began to tell her about Billy Tatham. The bicycle sheds. The hated, unwanted kiss. And now — Tatham's Tents.

Lucy was incredulous. "Mummy! How amazing! And you honestly had no idea it was one and the same Tatham?"

"Of course not! I couldn't even remember his name till he told me!"

"My God. What the strangest coincidence! And is he really so awful?"

"Ghastly. Let me peel your stockings . . . Shall I keep this blue garter for now?"

"Yes, please. That's why you're glowing. Seeing your courtier after all these years — how many years?"

"Darling, I am not glowing. At least not in that way. I'm angry. With him and with myself for being as horrid as he was. And I can't work out how long ago —"

"Well, you said you were eight. And you're fifty now, so it's forty-two years ago!"

"Thank you, darling." Martha grinned and rolled the stockings into a ball for the laundry basket. "Come on, drink your tea. Then we'll get you into your suit."

"And then . . . Oh Ma, it will be time to go."

"Yes. And we've got to remember that you're going to the Caribbean and it will all be wonderful, and I'm staying with George and Thomasina who will make sure we all enjoy ourselves. And when you come home we shall be getting together often."

"I know, I know. I wonder if Lennie is feeling like this?"

"Of course not. Lennie is looking forward to being alone with you, to starting this new life —"

"Yes, well, it's different for him. Because of living in the flat for the last ten years. And he's still got his father. You and me, we've been on our own now for five years. It makes a difference."

"I know." Martha went to the window. Billy Tatham

had gone. She said briskly, "I'm going to the bathroom. Won't be a minute."

She marched along the landing; below there came a sudden surge of voices from the kitchen. She was horribly conscious that the house was not hers until all this was over. But at least the bathroom was free. She locked the door and went to the basin. The mirror showed her with unflattering clarity. Her hat, a pillbox swathed in net, had slipped to the back of her head and looked like a bird's nest settling into her grey curly hair. Her eyebrows, plucked for the occasion, made her look supercilious. Her lipstick had disappeared and her mouth was thin and old.

She leaned on the basin and lowered her head. She never thought of herself as old: people had told her regretfully how young she was to be widowed. But age was relative and she was no longer a young widow; simply a widow. She was thankful Lucy had found someone so special to love, more thankful that he loved Lucy. Her life had been built around Lucy for so long and now, after today, it had been returned to her. It was her life, no-one else's. She had to learn to live it.

She said, "Oh God . . . oh God . . ."

In the bedroom, Lucy sat motionless in the spoon-back chair, her tea untouched. When she moved at last, it was to put the teacup carefully on the mantelpiece above the tiny wrought-iron grate which her father, thank goodness, had refused to remove.

She looked around at Snowball. He eyed her morosely, knowing full well that as she stood above him in her underwear she was about to pick him up.

17

However, instead, she picked up the hanger and stared at her brand-new blue linen suit suspended from it. Slowly she carried the outfit to the wardrobe and hooked the hanger on to the top then stepped back. The skirt of the suit was fashionably short, the jacket so long that only six inches of skirt would show beneath it. Her father would have hated it. He had liked her in maxi skirts and nipped-in jackets. He had said, "You've got your mother's hour-glass figure. Make the most of it."

She said aloud, "What am I doing? Why am I doing it? When Lennie said he couldn't live without me, did I mean it when I said the same?"

She stared at the suit as if expecting an answer. And then she turned suddenly and cast herself on Snowball.

"Oh darling, darling Snowie! I don't want to get married after all! I don't want to leave Mother and you and this lovely old house! I want to stay at home for ever!" And she wept. Snowball, after a moment of being completely affronted, licked her salty face and began to purr.

Jennifer, in the loft above the garage that had once been a coach house, adjusted her dress with care and asked Uncle Clem's relative if she looked all right.

"You are more than all right. You are the most beautiful thing I have ever seen. Come back to me. Please."

She looked down at him. She thought he was beautiful too, with his blond hair and his long muscular body.

She said regretfully, "I can't. Really. I must be there when Lucy and Len leave. She is my best friend. More like a sister than a friend."

He stood up and came behind her to fasten her back. He was naked; she was so conscious of him she thought she might faint. He said huskily, "You know you really are sore here. From sunbathing. Put some cream on it tonight. Look after yourself."

She thought he might say "for me". But he did not. She turned within his arms and kissed him goodbye. She waited for him to say he would see her again; waited for him to ask her name or to tell her his.

He whispered, "Goodbye, green girl."

She stopped herself asking questions or making promises. That was what her mother did: "When shall I see you again? I'll love you for ever . . . You are the only one . . ." That was when they ran.

She turned, opened the trapdoor, and pushed down the ladder. She was suddenly desperate to get away; she did not look back at him, his naked maleness was now an affront. She wanted Marty. She wanted to stand by her and wave goodbye to Lucy and Len and then go back inside and help her to clear up. She wished she hadn't gone off with that nameless once- or twice-removed cousin; she imagined him boasting about his prowess. She had been cheap. Like her mother.

As she let herself out of the garage the taxi drew up on the drive. People flooded out of the marquee; Len's colleagues began to decorate the bonnet. Len and Lucy appeared in the front porch; Marty was just behind them, smiling. Lucy looked the complete dolly-bird in her short suit. Her legs couldn't take it, she should have had a long flared skirt. Len looked marvellous, as dark as the cousin had been fair. Full of vibrant life.

19

Jennifer inserted herself behind him and next to Marty. Marty said, "Hello, dear. What happened to your hair?"

Jennifer put up a hand. The flowers that had kept her hair on top of her head were gone; tousled ringlets fell onto her shoulders.

She said, "Oh damn! I didn't realize — Does it look awful?"

"Not a bit, you always look wonderful." She took Jennifer's arm. "Come on. Let's do this together."

Jennifer thought it was the best moment of her life. Together they stood there wearing identical determined smiles. Lucy was screaming at the graffiti which now adorned the taxi windows. Len was beating off the shower of confetti. Lucy turned and held out her flowers. "Catch!" she called to Jennifer.

And then, from nowhere, a leggy figure appeared. Darting between the bride and the bride's mother was . . . Linda Bowles. Jennifer saw with horror that a heel was missing from one of her shoes, her skirt was miles shorter than Lucy's, her hair was in worse disarray than Jennifer's own, her lipstick was smudged, her mascara leaking . . . She looked . . . a tart.

She screamed as the flowers came straight at her, put out a hand and caught them neatly. Then she grinned delightedly at Lucy and round at Jennifer.

"Here you are, Jen! I've had all the men I want!" and she threw them again.

Jennifer stood there, frozen with horror. It was Martha who leaned forward and fielded the bouquet and then stood, clasping it to her bosom and laughing.

20

"Oh Linda," she said. "You made it — the very last guest to arrive!"

And she held out her arms and together they thoroughly crushed the flowers.

CHAPTER
TWO

"The only good thing about today is that there's no bloody evening do," Len pronounced, collapsing into his corner of the taxi as if she did not exist.

Lucy was so affronted, she hardly knew what to say. More than affronted; bitterly hurt. But she wasn't going to show that.

"My mother went to a lot of trouble to give us a really traditional wedding," she informed him. "She's not exactly rolling in money and the whole thing cost a bomb apart from the —"

"Oh, we're back to Mother again, are we?" Len pulled off his tie and wrenched at his shirt collar. She could see he was divinely handsome but it had no effect on her at that moment.

"That is so unfair, Len! The work she has put in is beyond — yes, absolutely beyond — your comprehension!"

He was instantly contrite. "Can't help being a bit jealous . . . You're so close, the two of you." He was kissing her hair, then her nose, struggling with his jacket at the same time. She collapsed all over him, laughing helplessly, and then between them they got him free of the coat and his starch-smelling shirt-sleeves were rolled up and they were in each other's arms, kissing and laughing and kissing again. He tucked his right arm beneath her knees and slid her easily onto his lap. Her skirt rode up to her hips and she struggled with it and he slapped her hand away. "I like it."

"The driver!" she protested.

"He can't see . . ." They snuggled into a familiar position, his chin on her blonde hair, her lips next to his Adam's apple. She ran the palm of her left hand over his shirt-front as if to remind herself of his body. His rib-cage; his heart beneath her right breast thumping so regularly, yet so vulnerably. She thought: This man is my life now, my whole life . . . I have forsaken all others and am cleaving only to him . . . And even as the thought came into her head she had a picture of her mother standing outside the porch, Jennifer one side of her and Jennifer's mother, Linda, the other. And yet . . . alone.

She turned her head into Len's neck and kissed his throat. "Oh Len," she whispered. "Oh my dear . . ."

"What is it? You're trembling. What is it, Lucy? Tell me."

"We're so together. You and me. So together . . ."

"Of course. But that's good, darling. That's how it should be."

"But don't you see, darling? It can't be like that. Not really. We come into the world on our own. And we go out alone."

"Don't you dare go all biblical on me, my girl. Not after everything you've just promised in that church back there! What on earth put this into your head anyway?"

She hung on to him as if she were drowning. "Nothing."

He was silent as if waiting for more. When it did not come, he held her closer, kissing the top of her head. "I know. It's your mother, isn't it? I've watched her a lot today. Smiling and smiling." He tightened his grip more as Lucy gave a small sob. "Listen, honey-bun. She'll be all right. Toto won't let her feel lonely — Toto never lets anyone feel lonely. And when she gets back from Tewkesbury, she'll be up to her eyes in the village again. The whole place would grind to a standstill without her, you know that. And Linda Bowles appearing out of nowhere, catching the flowers — not a bit your mother's type, but she was pleased to see her."

"Yes, Mother always had a soft spot for Linda. Don't know why. Jennifer hates her."

"Rubbish! No-one hates their mother. Not really. Whatever the psychiatrists say!" He scooped her higher and said, "Listen. What was Jennifer up to with that sandy albino type? Don't tell me that at your wedding, when she's supposed to be in charge of things, she sloped off for a quick roll in the hay?"

"Probably." Lucy had thought it was quite funny when Jennifer had implied that she had made a hit with Daddy's relative. Now it seemed . . . well, no better than Linda's antics. She said defensively, "He's blond, not sandy, and certainly not an albino, Len."

"Who was he, anyway?"

They were almost at Birmingham airport and he was patting his pockets for passports, money, tickets. P.M.T. They had all thought that was funny. It was amazing how unfunny a lot of wedding and honeymoon jokes were.

"Someone from Daddy's side. He came to the funeral. I can't remember his name."

"I thought you wrote the invitations?"

"Yes. Almost a hundred of them. I can't remember every name. There was someone called Aubergine — can you believe that?"

"Friend of Toto's. It's a sort of trade name. She's a chef."

They were silent, holding each other, watching the suburbs roll away. Len had told her once that she was the only woman in the world with whom he could enjoy silences. And she had told him about communicative silence.

"You mean we're saying things to each other even when we don't speak?" he'd asked, indulgently humorous.

"Yes. Bits of body language. Bits of space consciousness. Shared relaxation."

"Body language. OK. But space consciousness?"

"The sense of space between us. Or lack of it. Its . . . significance. Tension."

He'd said. "Hang on. Am I going out with the wise woman of Warwickshire? I need to know."

"Don't you remember that psychologist you profiled? Shepfield? Professor Shepfield? I read him up for you. He was great on sexual tension."

Not that the Shepfield tome had said anything about silence. But Len had been strangely reassured. She had already gathered that he liked her smallness; her blondeness. He hadn't batted an eyelid when Jennifer

25

had made a play for him. He needed to be the protector. And later she had realized he did not want her to be original either. She could be funny and sweet but she could not be deep or thoughtful. She didn't care. She loved him unequivocally and she would be whatever he wished her to be. Just as her mother had moulded herself to Clem, so Lucy would mould herself to Len . . . forsaking all others.

She was back to square one. Which was, in essence, that she had left her mother.

Len's parents had wanted to stay with Martha at the Old Rectory that night and help her with the clearing up but she had refused their offer as gently as possible.

"I'd like to he by myself — only for a few hours," she explained. "I'll drive over to Tewkesbury first thing on Sunday morning . . . I can go to the eight o'clock Service. But I'd like to sort out the kitchen by myself."

"The catering people brought their own stuff," Toto reminded her. "There shouldn't be any clearing up to do."

"Just cups of tea for the lingerers." Martha smiled. "And I must lock up carefully. You know how it is."

They didn't, not really. Len had not lived at home for some time and they frequently closed the Tewkesbury house and went to Bridgetown to spend time with Toto's family. Whereas Martha only ever left the Old Rectory for a weekend at a time to visit friends or take a coach party on a trip and then Lucy would stay at home and probably Jennifer with her. The house was rarely empty.

But George nodded. "It's better to be on your own. Walk around the place. Make sure everything is all right."

So by six o'clock the caterers had gone and by seven the Tatham Tent people had dismantled the marquee — thankfully without their boss — and the grass, crushed by the carpeting, was already unfolding itself arthritically. Martha went around picking up a few missed napkins and cigarette ends. "A spot of dew and you'll be as good as new," she said and then smiled because her words had rhymed. She must tell Lucy — She stopped her thoughts there. Of course she must tell Lucy; but not for a while and by then the whole story would have lost its point.

She went to the rear of the house and dumped her gleanings into the overflowing dustbin. Then she checked the garage; her car sat there in solitary state as it had done since Thursday when Lucy had taken her Mini round to Len's flat. The loft ladder was down and she climbed it just high enough to peer into the wedge-shaped loft. Lucy and Jennifer had used this space as a den when they were small, and sometimes still sat up here and talked together. The dusty boards looked as if a boxing match had just finished; in the corner was something white and green; Martha peered, frowning. It was Jennifer's coronet of flowers. Her hair had been sculptured around them: no wonder it had been hanging everywhere when she'd appeared from nowhere to wave goodbye to Len and Lucy. Only, apparently, she had not appeared from nowhere; she had appeared from the loft.

Martha climbed back down slowly and pushed the ladder into its housing. Then she closed and locked the garage and walked back to the front door and stood in the porch, staring across the broad sweep of lawn to the lane that led to the church. Clem's grave was just over the wall; so close. From this porch she had watched Clem's body leave the house; from here, today, she had watched Lucy. She checked her thoughts sharply before they became maudlin. She was a lucky woman: Lucy had married a good man and they were all-in-all to each other. She was strong and healthy and she saw no problems ahead. Which was exactly how it should be. Martha recalled — with a wry smile — the pang of real terror that had hit her when she was first introduced to Len. Lucy had seen no need at all to inform her that Len's mother was West Indian; it obviously had not occurred to her to do so. In a split second Martha had foreseen all the difficulties that lay ahead, not least for Len himself. But somehow they had never really materialized. Marcus Goodwin had not refused to marry them; even Miss Darcy, after a doubtful moment, merely sighed and remarked that the world was changing all the time. Jennifer had sighed too, quite differently, and said, "Isn't he absolutely gorgeous?" which of course he was, even Martha could see that. And then Jennifer had narrowed her eyes in the calculating way she had and added, "And the marriage will do wonders for his career." Which was a surprise in one way but not in another because dear Clem had always said there was one set of rules for ordinary people and quite another for arty-crafters. As for Len's family, they had welcomed Lucy with open arms. They had an older son who had married an African girl and lived in Sierra Leone; Len's work was based in this country and so was Lucy; the odds were that this part of the family would stay together. George had fallen in love with Toto when she nursed him through his appendix operation. Toto reassured Martha very frankly that, "I never allowed any kind of criticism and neither will my Len. The divide has very little to do with race and everything to do with money. Did you hear his programme last month? He brings that out every time."

Martha began listening to Len's special radio reports after that and it was true, he did emphasize the poverty gap. Even so, in spite of everyone else "accepting" the marriage, she still had moments of doubt. Now she widened her wry smile into a grin and told herself she was a typical mother-in-law already. Lucy was about to have a wonderful honeymoon in Barbados and when she came back she would visit the Old Rectory regularly and there would be normal things like snaps and sun-tans and stories galore. And in any case the interests they had always shared would still be there. And . . . there would be children. Martha straightened her back. That was a role waiting for her. A grandmother, and a proud grandmother to boot! To think of "losing" Lucy was simply ridiculous. And ungrateful. She angled her thoughts to the absurd: Linda Bowles arriving at the last minute so obviously drunk; Jennifer in the loft, losing her flowers, engaged in some unimaginable boxing match. Before she could stop herself Martha said aloud, "Like mother, like daughter." Then was ashamed again. Neither Linda nor Jennifer had had the advantages she and Lucy shared. A wonderful husband and father, a beautiful home, love, security. Jennifer's father was a mystery, probably even to Linda. Linda had looked for love and security all her life and was still looking. And now . . . Jennifer was probably on the same quest.

Martha turned and went indoors and began to lock up again. With a flutter of panic she wondered whether she would be able to bear this house on her own. There were cottages in the village which would be far more suitable. The one next door to the Bowleses had been empty for some time.

She went into the larder and locked the small window above the slate shelf. Clem had said it was the small windows that were the most vulnerable. And Lucy had reminded her about the larder window only yesterday. "Don't forget that one, Mummy. And the downstairs loo. I wish you were going to Thomasina's immediately."

Martha went upstairs slowly. She was doing everything slowly this evening. She walked into Lucy's room. Snowball was still on the bed, camouflaged by drifts of tissue paper. He looked up at her, his eyes startlingly emerald against the white fur. She scratched between his ears and his neck extended to meet her fingers; he closed his eyes ecstatically. She leaned over to bury her face in his fur.

"Albert is coming in every day," she told him. "You won't miss me."

He rumbled with purrs. For two pins she could have been thoroughly self-indulgent and wept into his flank. She blinked and stood up. "Like daughter, like mother," she said again to the wedding dress hanging ghost-like on the wardrobe door. It sounded wrong. "Like mother, like daughter," she corrected herself. Then smiled. She and Lucy were practically interchangeable after all. It made no difference which way round she chanted the adage. Lucy was Martha and would model herself on Martha: loyal to Len, a good housewife, eventually a loving mother. And Martha would make herself into whatever Lucy needed. Whatever role Lucy needed, Martha would take it on.

She realized she was smiling besottedly at the wedding dress and shook her head as she went out of the room. "There's food in your bowl downstairs," she said over her shoulder. "And the catflap is unlatched."

Snowball curled himself for sleep again. And Martha went to bed.

Len had booked a hotel on the Atlantic side of Barbados, though his grandparents still lived in Bridgetown on the southwest tip of the island.

"Better swimming on the east," he explained briefly. "Anyway we're on our honeymoon. Not a family visit."

"We must go and see them." Lucy's protest was half-hearted. She had agreed to Barbados because of Len's family being there, but more than anything she simply wanted to be alone with Len.

"Of course we'll see them. But not every day."

And it was a whole week before they did. The hotel was from the past: sandy lime-washed floorboards often littered with discarded sandals; an enormous verandah stacked with surf-boards; monstrous bathrooms; a bedroom as big as the whole of Len's flat, filled with cumbersome Victorian furniture but with a terrific uncluttered view of Rocky Cove and the sapphire sea beyond. Lucy could hardly believe it. She felt herself unfolding like a flower, yet she had not known she was folded in the first place! Petal by petal she unfurled, physically, emotionally, spiritually. Sometimes when she swam beyond the line of breakers, lifting and sinking with the swell beneath the ever-present sun, she felt as if she could become part of the elements; sea, earth, air: she was at one with them. When she and Len made love on the enormous mahogany bed, she did in fact become part of Len, knowing his body better than she knew her own.

He said wonderingly, "I didn't know you could be like this . . . I adored you before, I worship you now."

She whispered, "I didn't know I could be like this, either. Len . . . will anyone hear us?"

"I think the dining room is directly beneath us. And dinner will have started."

She laughed. "I don't care."

"Neither do I."

At the end of the first week they took a trip around the island because, after all, Lucy could not come all this way and go home with no idea of what the rest of Barbados was like. They saw the mahogany trees whence came their wonderful bedroom furniture. They viewed the barracuda at Sam Lord's Castle and realized the sea was changing colour from sapphire to cobalt. They swam in the enormous rollers, shouting with delight. They saw a sugar plantation, a selection of chattel houses, St James parish church, and finally the museum in Bridgetown.

"I cannot believe we were actually in Bridgetown and did not go to see Toto's parents!" she said that evening as she sat before her frowning reflection and tried on the earrings Len had bought her that day.

"We were on a scheduled trip, honey. When we go to see the Gampies, we'll hire one of the Mokes and drive down in our own time."

Len called his grandparents "the Gampies". Lucy thought it was the most endearing thing she had ever heard.

"We'll have to do it soon," she said placidly. "We're half-way through our honeymoon." She did not really believe it; and anyway this particular honeymoon would last a lifetime. She smiled at Len's reflection in the mirror. He was beautiful.

He grinned. "Do you realize how decadent you look dressed just in earrings?"

"What about you? You haven't got an earring to your name!"

They both laughed and then were silent, their reflections locked into each other. They watched and kept watching as Len's reflection moved towards her and with great care removed the earrings and put them on the dressing table. He lifted her with ease and carried her to the bed and she had a last glimpse of herself in the mirror, her arms flung up and back in an attitude of total surrender.

That evening, she wept during their love-making. He did not stop; he did not pause. She did not want him to, though she was surprised that he was oblivious to her distress. But afterwards he tasted the salt tears on her face.

"Baby, did I hurt you?"

"Oh no, don't be silly. Of course not!" She was so adamant about this that somehow the reason for her tears was not sought again. And she might have had a hard job discovering it for herself. A surfeit of love perhaps? Or the sudden fear that it might be ephemeral?

They went to see the Yowards the next day, driving across the waist of the island exclaiming over flocks of egrets and sudden disturbances in the banana trees which meant the presence of monkeys. The narrow lanes which criss-crossed from east to west were confusing; twice they passed the same garage and the same bar with the same men drinking outside and waving to them. Then at last they dropped down into St Peter's parish and through Speightstown and along the coast road into the capital. It was after they had skirted Trafalgar Square and were into the grimy little streets around the harbour that Lucy began to feel nervous.

Len hooted. "Luce, what's the matter with you? Toto is your mother-in-law — my God, I never thought of it like that before — I don't envy you! Thank God for Martha!"

"Well, if you must know, I was scared to death about meeting Toto! But that's over and we're friends! This is something else. Your grandparents have never left Barbados and they know nothing of our real life together. Oh God!"

Len did a U-turn in the road. "We'll come another time. Next year perhaps."

34

"For God's sake, Len! We have to go now! They really won't forgive me if they think I held you back this time. Turn the car!"

He eventually did so, but his reaction made her realize that he too was unwilling to face his maternal grandparents. The Yowards. Thomasina Yoward. What a name to give to a tiny baby. Were they pretentious?

"How often have you seen them yourself, Len?" she enquired.

"We came most years till I was fourteen. I was pretty thick with my cousins. We used to come for the cricket."

"Cousins? How many?"

"Christ, I don't know. Dozens. The Gampies had eight kids and, apart from Toto, they all had eight each, so work it out for yourself."

"Oh my God!" She clutched the side of the Moke, but said no more and they bumped along the road which had become a track and led down to a rubble-strewn beach and a collection of shacks. She knew, statistically, that Barbadians were poor and had shocking living conditions, but this was the first time she had seen evidence of the statistics. The old portable chattel houses, preserved for the tourists, were attractive; the beggars who roamed the beaches were dignified by the name of traders. Anyway, poverty was probably much easier to bear in a good climate; sleeping rough would be idyllic. Perhaps. She did not know. But poverty was ugly and so far she had seen no ugliness. This was different. Against the background of sea — strangely, almost shockingly, grey beneath one of the island's rare storm clouds — the gritty beach and tar-paper shacks looked like any encampment anywhere. Sordid. A reminder of the horrid detritus left by the human race. A row of Coca-cola bottles had been set up and a group of children threw stones at them. Women moved back and forth to a communal water tap carrying buckets. Men slept at the side of the shacks or sat in small groups playing cards.

Len reversed the Moke out of sight among some trees. "They'd strip it if they saw it," he said. He glanced at Lucy. "Well, Luce. What do you think? Are you surprised Toto got herself over to England and trained to be a nurse?"

"I'm surprised by a lot of things Toto does . . ." Lucy was going to prevaricate more, then added soberly, "No. I suppose not. Thank goodness we came, Len."

"Yeah. I suppose you're right."

He led the way past the playing children. One of the bottles had broken and he stooped to pick up the pieces. "Watch your feet," he warned them.

"Who says?" asked one of the boys. And Len said grimly, "I'm one of the Yowards, all right?"

The children crowded around, instantly respectful. But they had none of the grace Lucy had so admired in the children she had seen before on the island: crocodiles of them walking solemnly on school trips, uniformed, serious with the weight of learning. These children should have been at school and were not. On closer inspection their damson skins were blotched and scabbed. Lucy wondered whether her previous belief that the wonderful sun and sea made poverty much easier was true. If these children were wrapped against

the cold and rain, their plight would be obvious and —
surely? — some kind of care would be forthcoming.

They trailed across to the last of the shacks, waiting
for Len to part with some money. Lucy was surprised he
did not. Instead, as they approached the blank rear of the
shack, he turned suddenly and shouted at them to go
away. They went with a kind of sullen resignation.

He sighed at Lucy and shrugged, then took her hand
and led her around this last shack. It was like a
transformation scene: on the other side a small garden
had been made and railed off. In tubs and old milk
crates, all kinds of vegetables were growing. Tomatoes
spilled out of a black plastic bag, there were lettuces in
a trough, even kidney beans winding along a clothes
line. Further down the shore, a decrepit rowing boat was
pulled above the tide line and an old man was busy with
tar and a brush. A woman emerged from the door of the
shack.

"What's that racket?" she called to the old man.

"It's me, Gampy." Len tucked Lucy beneath one arm
as if making her part of himself. "It's me, Lennie."

"Good Lord Almighty!" She turned and flung up her
arms at the same time. Then her face split into a smile of
welcome. "Ah, Lennie. Lennie, my boy. Lennie the
television man!" She surged forward and took them both
in those gesticulating arms and called back, "Look here,
Henry! It's your grandson come to call — and you
covered in tar!"

There was a great deal of exclaiming and smiling.
"We knew you were here but we didn't think — your
honeymoon and all . . . Henry said to me, You mustn't

expect to see the boy this time . . . ." And Henry, wiping his hands on a rag, laughing. "You said that to *me*, woman! I knew he'd come. It was me said to you, He won't leave the island without showing off his wife! And here she is! Pretty as a picture, just like Toto said!"

Through it all, still hugged breathlessly to Len's side, laughing with the sheer spontaneity of it all, Lucy had time to look at the two people who had brought up Toto and, apparently, seven other children. The family likeness was very obvious: Toto had her mother's ready smile, her long neck, the graphic sign language with hands and arms which accompanied her bursts of volubility. She also had her father's wide, strong shoulders, doubtless developed through nursing, his long, patrician nose and very flat ears. Len had those characteristics too; it was fascinating. Lucy wondered whether Len had ever tried to trace his ancestry: Moorish?

"Gampy" had had time to draw back and separate the two entities of Len-Lucy. "Yes . . . you are the bride! And as pretty as you like! Henry, you're right for once in your life! She is more than pretty, she is beautiful! And very English!" She clapped her hands delightedly. "We like George — we always liked George, didn't we, Henry? But he is not handsome!" She laughed, throwing back her head like Toto did, exposing that wonderful throat. "Now you, child, you are handsome!"

They were ushered inside and two armchairs were cleared of books and knitting so that they could sit down. "You call me Floss, please, Lucy. And Henry is Henry. Lennie always calls both of us Gampy which is very difficult." She began to make tea at a little oil stove in the corner while Henry asked Len about his job and Len asked about his various cousins. Eventually the tea was passed around almost ceremoniously. It was in bone-china cups and saucers taken from a glass-fronted cabinet at the back of the room. The garden outside and the china cabinet were just two of the many anomalies in this curious settlement. Yet Henry and Floss seemed unaware that they had neighbours. When Len said something about the children and the broken bottle, Floss shrugged her expressive shoulders.

"Kids," she said dismissively. "They get worse. But they do not bother us so we cannot grumble."

"Shouldn't they be at school?" Len pursued.

"School's closed for the summer now," Henry said positively. Both Len and Lucy knew otherwise, but said no more. Lucy suggested that the Gampies should come back with them for the evening and sample the hotel's cooking. They were both delighted.

Henry said, "Flossie girl, you go. I will look after the house."

"No," Floss said. "You go, Henry. I will stay here."

"But can't you both come?" Lucy leaned forward eagerly. "Please do. I know how you feel because my mother was doubtful about leaving the house and going to stay with Len's parents. But once you've locked up and left it, you won't give it another thought."

"We can lock up the house," Floss agreed doubtfully.

"But there's the garden," Henry demurred, "and the boat." He looked at Len. "Take Gampy. I'll be all right here."

"I'm not leaving you here on your own," Floss objected.

"And you think I would leave you?"

Len said, "We'll go and shop." He stood up. "Champagne, like we had at the wedding. What do you say, Luce? And some shellfish. A cake maybe . . ."

Lucy nodded. "And some of those frittered flying fish. The kebab things. You know, for starters." She turned to Floss. "We can have the reception all over again. What do you say?"

The Gampies were delighted. As Len and Lucy left they were already putting up a folding table between the hedge of kidney beans and the canes of tomatoes.

Len said quietly to Henry, "Do you never leave the place empty, Gampy?" The old man shook his head and Len went on, "You should get a dog. A guard dog. Even with both of you here, it's not good."

Henry shook his head. "These people are our neighbours, Lennie boy. They've known us all their lives. Besides, you have six very large male cousins, my boy. Everyone knows this!" He laughed uproariously.

"But they also know you've got decent china which would sell for good money."

Henry made a sound of exasperation and pushed them away. "Off you go. Don't see shadows in the sunlight, my boy."

They found the Moke undisturbed and climbed into it thankfully. Len tried to explain. "I suppose it's a bit like living in an old part of town back home and seeing it deteriorate before your eyes."

He backed out gingerly and drove slowly up the sandy road back to town. Lucy said, "They're respected, Len. No-one would harm them."

"Not intentionally perhaps. But what ever the Gampies say, these people are not old and trusted neighbours. When the Gampies moved there first — when they were married in fact — they had the place to themselves. And those people — the equivalent of our squatters — they've got the scavenging instincts of hyenas. And the children are bored. Nowhere to go, nothing to do."

"Oh my God! The sea, the beaches, the countryside —"

"They take all that for granted. They want pool tables and dancing."

They stopped outside a large delicatessen and went around with a trolley just as they would have done in Birmingham. It was fun to get together a celebratory meal; even better to set it out before Floss and Henry, hear their exclamations of delight, and sit down together. Afterwards, Floss went inside to make coffee and Lucy joined her. "Let me help. I want to — to — experience your kitchen!" She laughed at herself but Floss was touched.

"Here are the beans and the grinder." It was like an old-fashioned mincer. "I will watch the kettle."

Lucy ground the coffee beans slowly, enjoying the smell. Floss was taking some of her good china from the cabinet and putting it on a tray. She said suddenly, "Child. Lucy. Do you intend to have a family, you and Len?"

Lucy smiled. Such a question could be impertinent, but not from Floss.

"Oh yes. Len will be such a wonderful father, don't you think?"

Floss lifted thin shoulders. "I hardly know him, child. Not really. But he is my grandson and I suppose has inherited the family love of children." She smiled rallyingly. "You will be all right. He has a good career. Thomasina tells me that. She is right?"

"Yes. He is good at what he does."

Floss smiled, relieved. "Then of course you will be all right." Her smile broadened into a grin. "I have a sense for new life, Lucy. And I think it has started in you already."

"How can you know?" Lucy was astonished but not disbelieving. Nothing was impossible in this magical place.

Floss lifted her shoulders again. "I might be wrong, of course. Say nothing to anyone yet. But if I am right will you let me know?"

Lucy was convinced she was right. It explained certain things. Her physical consciousness was heightened by being with Len in this place, but there was something else too.

She said delightedly, "I didn't think everything could keep on getting better! But it does!" And as Floss poured boiling water onto the coffee grounds they laughed together. Lucy followed her outside carrying the jug and a bowl of sugar. It occurred to her that Floss could have had reservations about another mixed marriage in the family. There was not one reservation in sight! She thought: I must remember this moment, photograph it inside my head, because once we're home it will stop being real.

When they left they discovered both wing mirrors had been ripped from the Moke and the spare wheel was missing. Len's mood changed; he became bitterly angry. "Everyone thinks the problem is only back home. Discrimination and so on. It's just as bad here." He revved the vehicle to a roar as they turned into the hilly central area.

"Not really, Len." Lucy tried to reassure him. "There are no other large cities . . . this is the only time we've seen anything like this."

"We've got it wrong — all our talk about equal opportunities!" He made no attempt to negotiate the potholes; they bumped and staggered across country towards their hotel. "Discrimination has nothing to do with race or colour. It's got to do with money." He took one hand off the wheel to rub his fingers together. "Hard cash, Luce. That's what you've got to have."

She had not seen him like this before. His programmes were about minority issues: gaps in the hospital system, disabled rights. She had always thought him an idealist.

She said gently, "Darling, if you're worried about the Gampies, please don't. They are so *happy*. They wouldn't leave their home. If you bought them a palace —"

"No. But the others would."

"I'm not so sure. Might they find the responsibility of bricks and mortar —"

"For God's sake, Luce! The old argument? They *choose* to live in packs like animals?"

She was silent, knowing suddenly that whatever she said would be wrong. She had seen Len use this aggressive technique when interviewing "hostiles" as he called them. It made good radio. She had always thought it was simply that — a ploy for good listening.

They were high now, in the hills of St Agnes' parish. The moon hung in a purple sky; there were a million stars and as the blackness of the Atlantic came into view, the lines of breakers were like cotton threads strung along the coastline. She wanted him to stop the car and look around with awe. It was a moment — a moment in eternity — which they could share totally. She would tell him what Floss had said, tell him too that she thought Floss was right.

He said, "The argument is that you take people out of slum accommodation and put them into decent housing and within a year they will make it slum accommodation."

She knew this was not the moment to say anything about babies. His voice deepened and quickened. He was almost ranting about wealth distribution. She knew he was right. It was terrible; the whole world was terrible. Yet the Gampies were happy and she had never met anyone happier than Toto. She thought suddenly of her mother alone in the Old Rectory. Would she be able to afford Albert to help with the garden? They had not been able to afford any help in the house since Daddy died but between them that had not been a problem. The garden was another thing.

44

She half heard Len cursing the state of the road as they negotiated the last drop to the hotel in bottom gear. The Moke was roaring like an injured bull elephant. He pulled up behind the kitchen quarters and switched off. Silence settled creakingly around them. He said, "You go on up, Luce. I'll scribble a note for the manager. He'll have a fit when he sees his precious hire-vehicle tomorrow morning."

She said, "It's not your fault, darling," and then wished she hadn't because it was so obvious.

But unexpectedly he said quietly, "In a way it is. He who hath should not show off what he hath, in front of them who hath not!" He laughed as he spoke and she thought gladly that everything was now all right.

She went inside his arm and butted his shoulder with her forehead. "I love you," she said.

"Oh darling, I love you too." He stopped and held her close. "I've been on my soap box. Sorry."

"Don't be. I love your principles too."

"Is that an innuendo?" He was laughing into her ear, kissing her neck; the night sky was above her upturned face; she breathed in euphoria again.

Later, when they were cool enough to switch off the noisy air conditioner, she whispered drowsily, "Len . . ."

"Mmm?"

"Don't let's feel guilty."

"Guilty?"

"About having so much."

He rolled towards her and very gently bit her shoulder. "We haven't got that much, hon! If I don't get my contract renewed —"

She whispered a laugh. "I didn't mean money. I meant this . . ." She swept a heavy arm in an arc around them. "After all, Toto and George are still so in love. You can tell when they're together. And your lovely grandparents — the Gampies — well, they are all-in-all to each other."

He murmured a sleepy agreement. His mouth went slack on her shoulder.

She sighed. "It's Mummy I worry about. So alone. And that big house . . ."

He nuzzled her again then rolled away. "Oh, don't worry about Martha, honey-bun." His voice was drifting into sleep. "She's one of the privileged. She'll always be all right."

Within seconds his breathing settled into the regularity of sleep. Lucy lay, listening to it, hearing again his dismissive words. Of course he had not meant them dismissively; he loved her mother, admired her. He had been expressing his confidence in her, that was all.

She fell asleep a long hour later and dreamed that Martha was shopping in the nearby Tesco. She had a hand basket and there were two items in it. Lucy called to her but she did not hear and when she turned to join the queue at the check-out, she looked at Lucy and did not recognize her. The check-out girl rang up the two items and then said, "And what about the things in your shopping bag?" Martha said, "There's nothing else. I swear." And the girl reached over, grabbed the bag and tipped it out on the counter. Tins of soup, salmon and Gentleman's Relish. All the things Daddy had loved.

"I have to eat!" Martha was saying loudly as they led her away. And Lucy shouted, "Mummy! Mummy!" like a child. But no-one heard her, not even Len who was snoring gently as she sat up in bed.

CHAPTER
THREE

After her late arrival at the Moreton wedding, Linda Bowles had nothing "lined up", as she put it, for the next four weeks. Although she said it herself, frequently, she wasn't a bad little housewife and occasionally she would have a go at the terraced cottage which she secretly loved, but pretended to scorn because Jennifer did. For years now Linda had worked for an escort agency. It was absolutely above-board and businesslike, providing hostesses at business lunches, consorts for opera and ballet visits. Often it boiled down to being a waitress; other times it could be more of an organizer. Linda knew that most of the time it was jolly hard work and the people who engaged her wanted nothing else. Occasionally, especially ten or twenty years ago, it had been different. There had been men who had admired her and wanted to see her "after hours". Linda had never slept with any of them for money, but her affections were easily aroused and since Jennifer had gone to university she had been really starved of affection. She called it being "fond" of someone. She was fond of Martha Moreton. And she was fond of Archie Evans. After all, he had provided her with this cottage. Probably that was why Jennifer despised it.

On the night of the wedding she and Jennifer hung around the tiny parlour, unable to relax, filled with a sense of anti-climax which Jennifer maintained would have been sublimated in the usual evening party.

"Trust the Moretons to be all understated and tasteful," she bemoaned. "A nice cup of tea in the sitting room for the relatives, then — *finito*!" She perched on the arm of the sofa, revealing a split in her dress at the knee. She hadn't realized it was so damned fragile! She made a sound in her throat like a lioness roaring.

Linda knew that Jennifer was furious with her and though, as usual, she refused to show any distress, she was in fact miserable about it, and felt terribly guilty. Jennifer had told her she had ruined Martha Moreton's day, not to mention Lucy's, and, having caught sight of herself in the window of the wedding car, she had had to agree she did not look her best. But then, neither did Jennifer.

Jennifer now vented her own self-disgust on her mother.

"God. I just cannot forget how you arrived! If you wanted to make an entrance there were other ways! You looked as if you've just come off the street! What must Len have thought? And the Traverses? He's some building contractor, oodles of money —"

"She was very sweet to me, actually. Invited me over to Tewkesbury."

"Oh Christ. Don't go. Please don't go. You'd probably get into George's bed by mistake or something ghastly!"

"Jen, don't be ridiculous!"

"Well, what happened to you today? I take it the director's meeting took place in the back of a car! All day?"

Linda denied nothing. "I'm not proud of myself, Jen. But Archie is free so rarely now, and when he is, I can't very well say I'm busy, can I? Especially not for a wedding. If it were a funeral, perhaps —"

"So we'll be all right if Martha dies, shall we? You won't arrive drunk and fall into the grave?"

"Jen, that's unfair! Martha and I have always been friends. Always. She understands!"

"Sorry. I don't."

"Well, you should. Archie has always looked after us. This cottage, your grant supplement . . . He's given us independence."

"*Independence*? That's what you call this?" Jennifer trailed her hand weakly around the tiny parlour. "You call this independence? And having to meet up with him at the drop of a hat! Dress yourself up like a tart! Let him wreck you completely —"

"Darling, what are you talking about? This is the way I always dress, you know that! And of course he didn't *wreck* me! My God, we had a wonderful meal at the country club. He needs to talk as much as anything. He wanted to know all about you — he's lovely. He was going to drop me at the church, but then, well, I admit things got out of hand a bit. If we'd stayed at the club, taken a room, it would have been better. But we didn't actually intend to —"

"Don't dare say make love! Don't dare say that!"

"All right. I won't." Linda closed her eyes. She was bone-tired. "You don't realize, do you? I'm forty-six, Jen. That Archie still wants me — sexually — is a compliment. It helps my morale."

That made Jennifer angrier than before. "What about the gallant Gary? The execrable Ernie? Mr Frodsham? I could go on till bedtime! Let's face it, Linda, you're no better than a —"

"Don't say that either!" Linda's voice was urgent. "I didn't say 'make love' so you mustn't say . . . what you were going to say!"

Jennifer subsided quite suddenly. She had got up from the arm of the sofa and had been pacing around the furniture, swishing against the arms of the chairs with her green dress. She caught sight of another tear, this time in the hem; she sank into the nearest chair in despair.

"Oh God." She rested her forehead on her spread fingers, then raked her hair back almost brutally. "So many things we don't say. I suppose it shows some . . . respect?" She looked up and smiled bleakly and Linda laughed back, recognizing a flag of truce when she saw one.

Jennifer leaned her head back against the cushions and closed her eyes. "You could have told me about my hair. About my torn dress. You didn't."

"Jen . . ." Linda too sat down and removed her shoes. "You look beautiful however you are. That's the difference. You were ashamed of me. I'm never ashamed of you."

Jennifer's eyes opened with a jerk. "Oh Ma . . ." She seemed about to say something else, then closed her eyes again. After a pause she said, "Not ashamed. A bit embarrassed. But Marty didn't mind. I shouldn't have said it ruined her day. She was just glad to see you."

Linda lifted herself high enough to wriggle out of her tights. Then she too relapsed with closed eyes. "Funny how she ended up with Lucy's bouquet," she mused." I wonder if she will . . . sort of . . . look around. Now that she's on her own."

"That's a typical Linda Bowles remark," Jennifer said, irritable all over again. "Marty is not the type to 'look around' as you so inelegantly put it! She probably still thinks of herself as a married woman."

"And anyway . . ." Linda sighed deeply. "If she did look around who would she find? The Rector is Mrs Rector's closely guarded secret and the curate has a wife and Albert Davis isn't exactly Martha's type —"

"She's going to stay with Len's people tomorrow. For a week. Perhaps Mrs Travers has got someone in mind."

"Mmm . . . we'll see. You know, Jen, I thought you and that Lennie Travers would make a match of it. When Lucy introduced him — you know, the first time he came to the village — he seemed much more your type than hers."

Jennifer's eyes rolled beneath her closed lids. "Oh God. Trust you."

"You know what I mean. Lucy will never want to move far from Nortons Heath. Because of her mother. Len is ambitious. He'll want to travel."

"Mmm. Maybe." Jennifer opened her eyes and looked speculatively at Linda's supine form. It was not a pretty sight. The rolled-down tights were hobbling her ankles, and the skirt's top button had provided escape for a bulge of flesh. But the face above the unbuttoned skirt and the tight satin blouse was curiously unlined; the tinted hair dark and glossy.

Jennifer said wryly, "That's one thing, Ma. You and me, we can look after ourselves. You don't have to worry about me and I certainly don't have to worry about you."

Linda opened her eyes too. They were bright and brown as a robin's, curious, interested. She laughed and said, "We're two of a kind, I reckon, Jen."

Jennifer's answering laugh died. She said tightly, "You knew all along, didn't you? All this business of being tactful and not saying anything! And all the time you knew I'd been with someone! It will probably tickle you pink to hear that I don't even know his bloody name!"

But Linda maintained her inquisitive robin expression. "I don't know what you're on about, darling. But anyway, shall we have a drink?"

She began her house cleaning the minute Jennifer left for work on Monday morning. Curtains and cushion covers were pushed into the washing machine; windows and furniture polished with manic energy. As she pegged out her chintzy laundry she found she was singing. She glanced left. The house on the right was empty and the other people in the terrace left early for offices and shops in Birmingham, but it would be just her luck for someone to be at home, ill. Nobody had a good opinion of her but if she were heard singing in the garden, the tale would soon go round that she was batty. She snorted a little giggle to herself. They could all boil their heads as far as she was concerned; so long as she had a friend in Marcia Moreton she needed no-one else. And why shouldn't she go and have a day or two with Lucy's new in-laws? Jennifer only came home to fall into bed each night; and until a job came along, her own social life was going to be nil. Yes. She'd iron all this stuff and then she'd phone the Traverses' number in Tewkesbury — she'd taken it down somewhere — and ask after Martha. A few days with the use of a car and Martha's company would be marvellous.

She began to sing full throttle, but a cough filled the next bar. It came from the grassy lane in which all the residents of the terrace kept their dustbins. She lifted her bedroom curtain which she was just looping over the clothes line, and peered beneath it. A short stocky man stood there. A complete stranger. She smiled with anticipation and fought her way through the other curtains to the little garden gate.

"May I help you?"

He looked nice, sort of chunky with dry curly hair; touchable hair. Linda could imagine ruffling it playfully, hanging on to it desperately at certain times, patting it back into place . . . afterwards. She smiled widely at the thought.

54

He smiled back. "They told me you'd know where Martha is. I called at the Old Rectory and she's not there, so I climbed over the wall into the churchyard —"

"Climbed? Over the wall?" Linda was delighted. "Did Mrs Rector see you?"

"I think it was her. There was a chap with a dog collar behind this enormous woman —"

Linda carolled a laugh. "That's them. I'm surprised you weren't excommunicated! When the children used to climb on that wall she used to tell them they would go to hell."

"Your children?"

"Mine was one of them."

"Perhaps that was why she sent me to your house." He was grinning hugely now. "We're both on the road to hell!"

"Probably. Though I have never committed the mortal sin of climbing the church wall." She paused. "Anyway. Sorry. Martha has gone to stay with the family of her new son-in-law for the rest of the week. Are you a friend?"

"Yes." He looked suddenly downcast, the smile lingering, but sadly. She could feel the familiar sensation of her heart melting.

"Were you at the wedding?"

"Yes."

She said, "So was I. But I was horribly late." She held out her hand; he took it in his rough dry one. She caught her breath. The sensation was merely because her hand was sensitive after all the washing. It meant nothing.

"I'm Martha's friend. Linda Bowles. My daughter was the bridesmaid."

"William Tatham. My friends call me Bill."

"Hello, Bill." She tried to control her expression. He mustn't know how she felt; he was Martha's friend. "Would you like a coffee? I'm just going to take a break. I'm cleaning the house."

"Great!" That wonderful smile appeared again. He opened the little gate and stepped onto her garden path. She could look straight into his eyes. She lowered her own quickly and turned to lead the way into the house. He was still talking. "I've known Martha since we were both in primary school. Has she ever mentioned me?"

"No. No, I don't think she has." Linda went into the parlour. It looked bare without its flowery curtains and cushions. Archie had taught her never to apologize so she said nothing. He, Bill Tatham . . . lovely name . . . like the neighbours, must take her as she was. Or leave her. "Sit down while I put the kettle on."

"This is nice." He looked around. "Minimalist, is it? I've heard of it. Works well."

"Oh. Yes." She shoved the box containing all her ornaments and pictures farther behind the sofa. "I won't be long."

She flew around the kitchen finding decent china and the demerara sugar. In between she checked her appearance in the glass doors of the china cabinet. She stretched her mouth, smoothed her hair, practised a smile. She was glad she was wearing jeans and a halter top. Usually when it was hot like today she wore a cotton frock from the dark ages. She cinched the belt in another

56

notch and pulled her shoulders back. Archie had told her on Saturday that she still had a beautiful body. Thank God for Archie.

"This is an unexpected treat." He took his coffee cup and added three spoonfuls of sugar. "I thought I'd come all the way from town for nowt."

It occurred to Linda that he was not like Martha's usual friends. Mostly her friends had also been Clem's friends. They were gentle, considerate and considering. This man was too . . . immediate. He was rough and ready; direct; not diplomatic.

"Was Martha expecting you?" Of course she wasn't. Martha never forgot anything.

"Yes. She must have forgotten."

"She had a lot on her mind," Linda said, admiring him for lying so convincingly.

"She certainly did." He finished stirring his coffee at last and replaced the spoon in the saucer. "She didn't recognize me at first." He laughed, sipped his coffee, laughed again. "Then I gave her a big kiss, and she remembered!"

Linda was aghast. After all this time . . . Martha had a secret admirer from the past and had let him kiss her? What about Clem? What about Lucy?

"Did you know Clem?" she asked, smiling in spite of her shock. The thought of it: this short, bull-like man had actually taken Martha Moreton in his arms and kissed her? Why hadn't Jennifer said something? Maybe he was lying again . . . that was it, of course. He was lying.

"No." He sounded regretful. "Not personally."

"What about Lucy? Their daughter."

"I saw her at the wedding." He stirred again, sipped, took some more sugar, stirred. He looked up and smiled frankly. "I might as well confess. I can see you're an understanding woman. And Martha's friend too." He drank deeply and put his cup onto the tray. "That was very welcome. Thank you." He leaned forward as if he were about to discuss a business deal. Then he said simply, "Now that Lucy has gone, there will be a gap. I want to fill it."

She could not hide her astonishment. She knew very well that because he attracted her so strongly, he would not appeal to Martha in the slightest.

"Bill! You don't know Martha very well, I'm afraid."

"What do you mean?"

It was impossible to explain the ramifications of Martha's life without making her sound just parochial, which she was not. There was her relationship with Lucy, which would now mean a relationship with Len and with Len's family. She said instead, "What about Clem?"

"He's dead."

"Not for Martha."

He remained unabashed. "I'll make her forget him."

"You won't."

"Want to bet?"

"*Bet*? On Martha's love for Clem?" She was incredulous.

"Sorry. A figure of speech. But you know what I mean. She must look ahead now. And . . . well, there I'll be. Ahead. Her future."

She stared at him; his ebullient self-confidence was as attractive to her as his short strong body. She imagined hitching herself to a man like this; the sheer security to be found with him.

Following this line of thought she said, "What is your line of business, Bill?"

He grinned. "Is this an interview? My suitability as a future husband?" His grin gurgled into a laugh. "Don't worry, Linda. I've got my own business. And it's expanding all the time." He began to edge forward on his seat; he was going to leave. "I provided the marquee for the wedding. Tatham's Tents."

"Ah. I see." She did; Martha had found a way of cutting costs.

She said quickly, "Would you like a biscuit? Another coffee?"

"No, I'd better be on my way."

She made no attempt to get up. "I'm having a sandwich for lunch. Will you join me?"

He looked at her sharply, smiled, stood up. "No thanks, Linda. It's very nice of you, but I'll wait for Martha."

She felt her face become very hot; she knew exactly what he meant but she was forced to say, "But she'll be away until next weekend. I told you . . ." She scrabbled out of the deep armchair and opened the door into the hall.

"Yes." He was close by her, holding out his hand. "Don't worry, I'll do my waiting at home." There were twelve inches of space between them; it seemed charged in some way.

Linda said faintly, "Perhaps that's . . . just as well."

His smile was really lovely; sort of grateful. He opened the front door and stood outside on the path.

There was an enormous car further up the lane which must be his. He said, "You see, I've been married and divorced twice. Other women too — wonderful women. But Martha . . . I've held her in my heart since I was eight years old. I knew one day I'd have another chance and this time I wouldn't muff it."

Linda could have cried. She said, "Oh. Oh how wonderful. How romantic."

"Will you wish me luck?"

"I do. I do."

She closed the door and leaned against it. Her heart was pumping like an engine, but when she closed her eyes and thought about Martha, it began to slow. She refused to be jealous: she just hoped that Martha would see that if she linked herself to this wonderful, certain, strong man, it would be in no way a betrayal of Clem. In fact Clem would be delighted. If Clem was still somewhere, still able to know . . . things . . . then he would be the first to say, "Go to it, Marty. Take this chance. Let him look after you and make you happy . . ." And Martha believed that Clem was somewhere. Linda wasn't so sure, but Martha was. Always had been.

Linda pushed herself upright and went back into the living room. She picked up his coffee cup and held it in two hands. Martha was so lucky, so very lucky. But then, she deserved love. She was lovable. She was almost worshipful. She would never make it obvious to a man that she wanted him. Linda recalled herself saying "will you join me". He must have known. He *had* known. Oh God, he had *known* exactly what she meant.

She took the cup into the kitchen and put it into a bowl. Then she went into the hall and picked up the phone. Luckily it was Martha who answered her call.

"George and Toto had to go to a lunch. Freemasons or Rotary, I'm not sure. It's given me a chance to be by myself, Linda. Think. You know."

"Yes. Yes, I do." Linda thought she could have given Martha something extra to think about. She said, "I'm spring cleaning. No, summer cleaning. I'm going to iron all afternoon!"

"Lucky you." There was a little pause then Martha said, "Linda, I know you're not keen but would you come over? Just for the day if you can't manage longer. Toto is a darling, but I feel such a fish out of water. Or are you busy?"

"Apart from the cleaning, no I'm supposed to have four free weeks at work. I'll ring Maureen at the office and check, but I'm pretty certain there's nothing on. The end of summer. The social scene is dead."

"You'll come, then?"

"How will Len's parents feel about me muscling in?"

"But they asked you! I heard them asking you!"

"They had to when you introduced me as your best friend. They might not have meant it."

"Linda! Your confidence is nil!" Another pause, then, "Please come. I'm feeling dreadful!"

Linda's eyes filled immediately. She said, "I'll be there. I'll get the bus into Worcester and —"

Martha said warmly, "No such thing. I'll pick you up. Tomorrow? Ten o'clock?"

"Oh . . . oh lovely."

Jennifer would be furious. But Linda didn't care. Especially when Jennifer phoned later to say she was staying in the city. Linda told her to have a good time because she would only be young once. Then she lit the gas grill and made some toast. The smell filled the little house. It was a comforting, domestic smell. If she were married to Bill Tatham she would make toast every day . . .

CHAPTER
FOUR

Jennifer was an archivist. She had got a second-class degree and had been lucky to land a job in the County Archive Office after a year spent in Delos helping to catalogue some finds from an archaeological dig. It had been the most boring job of her life, made bearable by swims in the wine-dark sea and a young Greek god she called Adonis but whose real name was, most unfortunately, Berk. Eventually he had lived up to this name and she had been only too glad to come back home, armed with some peculiar certificate from the man in charge of the dig, which had looked much better summarized on her c.v.

In spite of that, she had still kicked around for almost a year, practically penniless, furiously jealous of her mother who was out and about the whole time either working or exhausting her latest craze for aerobics. Jennifer would meet Lucy from the Midland studios once a week and they would go to the cinema or a theatre or have a meal at the Pizza Place and discuss their futures. Lucy was thoroughly caught up in her work at the studio but so far as Jennifer could tell it actually involved more tea-making than anything else.

"Everyone has to start at the bottom," Lucy insisted. "All right, so I'm a gofer at the moment. But I'm finding things out all the time. I tag along to the library with one of the research assistants. I know how to set out a programme." She leaned across the wrought-iron table they were sharing in the Pizza Place. "Last week, Len Travers was doing a piece on Cheltenham — vandalism, mugging —"

"I saw it." Jennifer yawned. "It sort of said that at the end of the day you don't need racial problems to get people fighting."

"I went with him to take notes on some of the interviews —"

"Can't he afford a tape recorder?"

"Of course, idiot. But sometimes a tape is so long-winded. A summary is more helpful to a presenter."

"In other words, you listened to the tape and made a precis."

"Well, yes. But I was there. Len said I'd got an eye for people."

"Len, eh?" Jennifer became alert. "What does he call you?"

"Lucy. Of course."

"D'you fancy him? He looks gorgeous."

Lucy nodded very matter-of-factly. "He is."

"Hey." Jennifer was all ears by this time. "And do you?"

"Do I what?"

"Fancy him!"

Lucy was silent for a long time. "I'm not sure. It's not quite so . . ."

"Why? Because he's black?"

"Oh no. Not a bit. Mother wouldn't care two hoots about that."

"Ah. Mother. Mother Martha."

Lucy took a breath. "I can't imagine leaving her, Jen. Not ever. Not for anyone."

Jennifer shrugged. "Then you're not in love. When you fall in love you'd leave anyone, go anywhere."

"I suppose so."

Jennifer subsided. "You know . . . if ever . . . Well, if ever you do want to fly the nest, I'd always be there for Marty."

"I know. Thanks, Jen. And by the way, don't be offended, but Marty was Daddy's special name for her."

"I know. She doesn't mind me using it." Jennifer was confident about that.

As if to cement this special privilege, Jennifer began to spend more time at the Old Rectory. It was Martha who helped her to fill in the application form for the job in the County Archive Office; Martha who said, "This year in Greece will be an excellent addition, Jennifer. Let's see . . . How can we put it exactly . . ."

When the letter of regret arrived, Jennifer could hardly believe her eyes. She did not tell Martha. She had been certain this job was hers.

And then it was Lucy's twenty-fourth birthday party, 7 April, when the horse-chestnuts around the church were full of candle blossoms, primroses studded the lawn at the Old Rectory and the clematis over the porch was bursting into blossom.

Jennifer wore a lurex pants suit that made her legs look endless. Her boyfriend of the moment was also jobless and, like Berk, was beginning to get on her nerves. She had told Lucy that he wouldn't leave her side, they were "joined at the hip", and when they arrived for the party, Lucy saw what she meant. He seemed unable to take his hands off Jennifer's lurex, his long clinging fingers were on her waist or her shoulder or, embarrassingly, on her buttocks. He grinned at Lucy, congratulated her, kissed her cheek, then immediately turned and kissed Jennifer too, long and lingeringly, as if making a public claim to her.

Lucy obviously thought it was hilarious. Grinning from ear to ear, she said, "How sweet. Martin, will you have a drink?" She tried to put a glass into the hand that was draped over Jennifer's shoulder, but it was no good, he reached over and took it with his free hand. Lucy went on, "Jen, I want to show you Mummy's present. It's a keyboard. I thought we could have sing-songs and things."

They all trailed into Clem's old study, Jennifer walking alongside Lucy, Martin following stubbornly.

"Do you play?" he asked Lucy, realigning himself at the side of the keyboard.

"Oh yes. We had piano lessons when we were kids. And we tried to form a group. D'you remember, Jen?"

"Yes. Ebony and Gold," Jennifer recalled gloomily. "Martin. Darling. Would you mind awfully, you're almost strangling me."

Martin slid his hand down to her waist. "Come on then. Give me a show."

"Don't be ridiculous —" Jennifer tried to wrench herself free.

Lucy, seeing her red face, said, "No time now, Martin. I want you to meet the other people. Ah." She turned to the door. "Here's my new boss. Len Travers."

"Your new boss?" Jennifer was wide-eyed, staring at Len as he advanced towards them. "My God, you never said."

Len took her hand and held it gently. He was wonderfully tall — both Berk and Martin were shorter than Jennifer — and devastatingly handsome. Like a brigand. Like a corsair.

"My researcher went to the BBC. Lucy was the obvious choice." He smiled down at Lucy. "She's been virtually doing the job for a year."

"Well. . ." Lucy temporized.

Martin said excitedly, "You're Len Travers! You do all the controversial stuff. And Lucy works for you? Jen, you never told me!"

Jennifer did not answer: she was trying to analyse how she felt about Len Travers. Sort of . . . gaspy.

Lucy laughed uncomfortably. "It's only just happened. Len, this is Jennifer. And Martin . . . Have you met my mother?"

"I've just arrived." Len flashed a smile at Jennifer and turned away. "Let's go and meet her, shall we? And may I see the house? I had no idea it was so interesting. What about the hidey-hole you shared with your friend . . . ?" Lucy ushered him back into the hall, turned and made a face at Jennifer and was gone.

Jennifer said, "Will you kindly take your hand away, Martin?"

"My hand?" Martin pretended to look for his hand, found his drink, downed it, put the glass on the new keyboard and enveloped Jennifer in both arms. "Honey . . . baby . . . darling . . . where's this hidey-hole? Let's go there and make mad passionate love for the rest of the night —"

She shoved him off unceremoniously. "For God's sake, Martin! Will you leave me alone! Just for one evening —"

"*You* said we were joined at the hip." He pushed himself against her. "Like this?"

She swung at him and actually managed to connect with the side of his head. He reeled back, unhurt and determined to continue with the play-acting. He was still staggering around the study, beating his breast and declaiming that "she loves me no more" as Jennifer left the room. She made straight for the kitchen where Martha and Linda were filling plates with every kind of savoury under the sun.

"Marty! It's all wonderful! The keyboard is great! And Lucy, her new job with Len Travers —"

Linda cut short the eulogy. "Carry these two plates into the dining room, darling. And come back for some more. Where's Martin?"

Jennifer took the plates. "Don't know. Don't care. Marty, why didn't you tell me about Lucy's job?"

"Well . . ." Martha stopped for a moment, filled a glass at the tap and drank deeply. "I thought, you know, in the circumstances, it might be rubbing salt into the wound."

"Oh, I couldn't ever be jealous of Lucy!" Jennifer protested, then paused. "Besides, you never know, the application to the County Archive place . . ."

Martha said, "Oh Jen. I'm sorry — that's what I meant. Linda told me. I really thought you'd get that job. The application looked so *good* . . ."

Jennifer stared at her mother's downbent head. The roots of her dark hair showed grey. She said, "You told Marty then?"

"Of course." Linda looked up, her small face open. "I knew she was interested, she'd been so helpful. I thought you would have come straight round to tell her."

Jennifer's dark eyes met her mother's equally dark ones. She said nothing, then turned away with the plates of food. She guessed Linda would become flustered by the exchange and was not surprised when she heard her say, "I shouldn't have said anything, Martha. I wouldn't have known myself, of course, except that the post comes when we're having breakfast and —"

Martha's voice was soothing. "Linda, it's not your fault Jen didn't get that job. Though I have to admit I am very disappointed myself."

Jennifer thrust the plates all anyhow onto the dining table and made for the French windows into the back garden. If Lucy hadn't taken Len immediately to meet her mother in the kitchen, then it meant they were in the garage inspecting the "hidey-hole". Her spiked heels sank into the lawn, which had had its first cut. She leaned down and whipped off one shoe then the other and ran across the lawn and the vegetable patch to the back of the garage. The familiar sound of the loft ladder made her pause for a moment. What if Len and Lucy were planning the same kind of thing Martin had in mind? Lucy had always maintained she would never "do it' with anyone before marriage, but Len Travers looked a fairly persuasive type.

Jennifer walked quietly in her stockinged feet and peered through the side door into the petrol-smelling interior. The two cars stood cheek by jowl, allowing just enough space for the ladder. There was no sign of anyone, not a sound. Then Lucy's unmistakable giggle disturbed the thick silence and Len's voice said, "I don't believe it! Ebony and Gold? It sounds iffy to say the least!"

Lucy said, "Oh we didn't even know about political correctness! Jen was dark — as you saw — and I was fair. It was just a family thing really. We were so awful!"

"Your musical performance might have been awful," Len said pedantically. "You could never be awful. I don't think I've met anyone quite like you, Luce. I always thought my mother was the most open and generous person in the world. But you — you are quite special." There was a pause. Jennifer imagined them in a clinch and felt a pang of envy. Then Len said prosaically, "I'm very lucky to have you as a researcher. I know damned well that the stuff you give me will be spot on."

Lucy, probably blushing like mad, stammered, "Thank you, Len. I'll try never to let you down."

Jennifer grinned and went to the foot of the ladder. Lucy was hopeless. But in any case it didn't sound as if Len was interested in her that way. "Are you up there, Lucy?" she called. "Can I come up?"

70

Lucy's face appeared in the trapdoor. "Of course. I'm just showing Len where we used to practise singing and dancing." She reached down a helping hand and the two of them stood side by side for an instant, smiling at each other, complementing each other. "Ebony and Gold." Lucy giggled again. "Len thinks we were politically incorrect!"

Jennifer directed her amused look at Len who was crouching under one of the roof beams. "You never take time off, Len?" she asked.

"It's not a question of time off." He refused to joke about this. "It's not a job — not *just* the job. It's me."

She walked towards him and lowered her head beneath the angled beam. "I know what you mean. I want to be like that about work. I want it to be me. Not a role I adopt at nine o'clock each morning and step out of at five-thirty."

Lucy put an impulsive arm around the lurex waist. She did not have to crouch; she stood like a little girl before the two angled figures; she was wearing a frilled Laura Ashley dress and looked like someone who would one day run the Women's Institute and the Parish Council and still be the perfect hostess at her husband's business lunches.

She said, "Jen, I was so sorry to hear about the County Archive job. Mummy was certain you'd get it. She reckons there must have been some fiddling behind the scenes."

Jennifer wondered how many more people knew about her failure. She said wearily, "I wouldn't think so, Luce. I simply wasn't good enough, that's all."

Len said, "The County Archive Office? I know the Archivist. He's one of my father's cronies. I always called him Uncle Arthur."

There was a small pause. Lucy said hurriedly, "Mummy was simply disappointed that Jen didn't get this particular job, Len. She didn't mean there had been anything unfair going on."

Jennifer said nothing; she stared at Len.

He said, "Who got the job? D'you know?"

She said, "No."

"If it were a man of course . . . sex discrimination could have come into it."

She said, "Who knows?"

Lucy said, "Len, we don't want you to get involved. Do we, Jen?"

"No," Jennifer said again.

Len smiled at her. "OK then," he said. "Now. Shall we go down and say hello to your mother?"

Jennifer said, "And mine. They're working their fingers to the bone in the kitchen."

"Let's all go and give a hand," Len said.

It was less than a week later that Jennifer had the letter from Arthur Masonfield himself. It seemed the graduate who had been offered the job of assistant in the Archive office had dropped out and Jennifer was next on the list of applicants. Was she still interested?

Lucy maintained it had nothing to do with Len, and after the first year Jennifer almost believed her. The graduate — male and without a year's experience of cataloguing in Delos — was well out of the County

Archive Office. He had probably known that he would spend six hours of every day transferring the old card index system onto a computer disc and the other hour trying to locate records that had probably been lost during the War. This entailed descending into the cellars of the office and digging into boxes that might easily contain rats or mice but in any case were filthy. One day Jennifer reported a strange gurgling sound and was told that it was probably the sewers. "Our cellars were dug before the sewers," one of the older assistants said proudly. "They had to go around us."

Jennifer shuddered.

She couldn't quite believe it when Lucy announced her engagement. "I thought you couldn't imagine leaving Marty on her own?" she said. What she meant was that she had not thought Len was in the slightest bit interested in Lucy outside the office.

"I still can't." Lucy looked torn. "But I can't manage without Len either. And he can't manage without me. Mummy will. Somehow."

"Yes. Yes, I'm sure she will. And like I said, I'll still be around."

"Oh Jen. Thanks."

But the disbelief remained. In spite of Lucy's assertion otherwise, she was still convinced he had got her the job; and on the few occasions they met she could have sworn he felt something for her. It would only be a matter of time before he made an opportunity to see her alone. She waited, full of anticipation, simply wondering how he would do it, where and when. She had finally got rid of Martin and hadn't been seeing anyone since. A year of celibacy. It was a record. And it made her irritable; irritable with Linda especially.

There was another party, this time at an hotel in Cheltenham. Len's parents lived on the outskirts of Tewkesbury; it was to be just the two families. But Martha invited Linda and Jennifer for supper the week before; she called it a pre-celebration.

"We shall be thinking of you." Linda raised her glass, her bright dark eyes alight with pleasure. "We shall drink a toast at exactly the same time as you will."

"Such a shame everyone couldn't come," Lucy mourned. "But it seemed right to keep it to the immediate family."

Len said, "I don't see why. You four women are so close." He turned to Lucy. "Let's take a decision of our own, darling. Invite Linda and Jennifer. What do you say?"

Martha was cautious. "Hang on a minute, Len. Your mother wanted —"

Linda said, "I can't make it anyway, Martha dear. I've got a dinner that night."

Len said, "Are you popping out of a cake, Linda?" He thought Linda's work was demeaning.

She laughed. "No such luck! I'm skivvying as usual. They want me to make sure everyone's glass is full. So I'm the wine waiter!"

Jennifer felt her stomach tighten. She wanted to kill Len for his obvious condescension. But she also wanted to kill her mother because she did not even notice it.

But Len said, "You come then, Jen. Don't argue. I'll pick you up from work on Friday afternoon. Lucy and Martha are going up in the morning."

She was stunned. So that's how he was going to do it. It was rather late in the day, but he must have suddenly realized he couldn't go through with marrying Lucy . . .

He stopped the car just as she had known he would. He pulled into a gateway along a leafy lane outside Tewkesbury. It was April again and the foliage was young and green and heavy with a recent shower. She found she could hardly breathe. She had wanted this so much . . . so much. And now it was happening. Before he switched off the engine he pressed a button that lowered the two windows. Then he sat very still and let the dripping silence enclose them. She shivered slightly.

"Cold?" he asked quietly.

She said honestly, "No. Excited."

"Why?"

"Because I'm with you."

"OK." Still he did not move. "I won't pretend I don't know what you mean. Nor that I don't feel the same."

"I knew. When we met . . ." She could barely speak, her voice was sibilant.

"You wore a green-gold thing. Lurex. You looked like a serpent."

"Is that good?" She was so thrilled he remembered.

"I don't know. That's how it is, good or not. Lucy is Eve and you are the serpent."

She loved it. She would live in green from this day on. She whispered, "And you are . . . Adam."

He did not look at her; she told herself after that he dared not look at her. He said, "And Adam married Eve. Not serpent." He waited. "Do you understand that, Jen?"

"Of course. I don't like it, but of course I understand it. You want to go ahead and marry Lucy, my best friend. And then you want to have an affair with me." She too waited and realized that his silence was confirmation enough. He wasn't going to cancel his wedding. She felt sick.

If he had turned to her then and kissed her or touched her, or even looked at her, she would have succumbed. She knew that. But he kept his gaze straight ahead, staring at the springing green of the hawthorn hedge with dark concentration. He was leaving the whole decision to her.

She said, "I don't think I can do it, Len. Not in cold blood. Lucy . . . Lucy is a sort of sister."

He said almost coldly, "It is entirely up to you. I love Lucy. Very much. And I want her to be my wife. But an affair with you would be separate. For me."

"You mean you would feel no disloyalty to Lucy?"

"Absolutely not."

She swallowed. "I thought . . . one or the other. Not both."

He shrugged slightly. "You are not the marrying kind, Jennifer."

She was hurt; she was angry. "You know how to make a girl feel good," she said lightly.

"I thought we could be honest."

76

"Yes. Well. Perhaps what you are suggesting needs enormous insensitivity as well as honesty."

"Nobody would know. Ever."

"I would know. You would know. Apparently that does not matter to you. It does to me." She took a deep breath. "It's not just Lucy. It's Martha as well."

He said flatly, "I don't get it. If Lucy and Martha don't know, who is being hurt?"

She cried out, "I am! And of course Lucy would be — she would guess that you were being unfaithful! And if she was hurt, so would Martha be hurt. Can't you see that?"

"If I swear to you that Lucy would never guess — never. Ever."

"Then I would have to think your honesty was very limited. And your sensitivity nil."

He was silent for some time; she knew she had got to him. Then he said, "I am honest enough not to seduce you. Sensitive enough too."

She almost laughed. He was not honest enough to admit he would not take responsibility for a love affair. She would have to do that.

She said, "Let's get on, shall we?"

He started up the car and at last allowed himself to look at her.

"I thought you wanted me," he said as if apologizing.

And she said calmly, "I thought so too."

It was easy to be calm when she almost hated him; but that evening as they sat around the candle-lit table at the Queens Hotel, she felt pang after pang of jealousy as they all toasted the happy pair; she called herself a fool for not having agreed to his proposition. She did not get another chance. Len and Lucy were married that July and because Jennifer had felt so awful she had gone off with that nameless relative of poor old Uncle Bertie and behaved no better than Linda. And then it had been Martha who eventually got the bride's bouquet; Martha . . . who did not want it and would always be faithful to the memory of Clem.

Jennifer vented some of her spleen on her mother during the rest of that weekend and felt even worse for it. In a way it was good when Monday arrived and she could catch the train into the city and walk to the awful dreary building that housed the archives.

She had hoped that she would be sent off to the Inland Waterways office that morning to look through some papers relating to the first plans made for the canal, but Arthur Masonfield had gone himself and she was supposed to be "holding the fort", which meant that she answered all the queries his secretary couldn't. Miss Derry was never going to admit there was anything in the world she could not deal with, so the calls were limited to an invitation from the Chamber of Commerce to speak at their next meeting. Miss Derry said sweetly, "I've explained that Mr Masonfield is away for the whole of August and they asked if his understudy would fill in." Miss Derry refused to call her a deputy or a personal assistant. Understudy indeed.

Jennifer said just as sweetly, "I wonder if you could tell them that with Mr Masonfield on holiday I have to be in the office?"

"It's an evening meeting," Miss Derry said triumphantly. "I'm putting them through now."

Jennifer said a rude word under her breath and then smiled at her reflection in the computer screen. "Good morning," she said in a voice to match the smile. "My secretary tells me you would like me to speak at your next meeting?"

Her smile lengthened gleefully as Miss Derry's receiver wept down with an audible click. It was a wonder she hadn't interrupted to tell whoever was listening that she was certainly not Miss Bowles's secretary.

A voice, vaguely familiar, said, "I certainly would. I mean, we certainly would. I'm awfully sorry it's such short notice and I wouldn't like you to think you are second choice —"

Jennifer laughed. "But I am, is that it?"

She was giving him an opening for repartee: he could say she did not sound as if she would ever be second best. Or he could say that Arthur's holiday was their good fortune . . .

He said, "Not you exactly. Arthur. He did say once that if we were let down at any time he would step in."

"And now he'll be on holiday." Jennifer stopped smiling and closed her eyes. The Chamber of Commerce was probably composed of men like this one. Without an ounce of humour. Dammit, Linda's boss, Maureen, would probably be there! The very idea of talking to them filled her with such boredom she felt tired. She said honestly, "I don't think I'm up to it, actually. I've been here just over a year and so far all I've done is a sort of glorified filing job."

"Tell us about that then." The voice hesitated, then went "And wear something green. And clinging." Then the line went dead.

She opened her eyes, electrified. It was him. Uncle Bertie's long-lost whatever. She buzzed Miss Derry frantically. "Whoever that was, ring him back. I didn't get the date or time or venue or anything."

"The number is —"

"I want *you* to ring him back, Derry dear. He was . . ." She made her voice prim. "He was forward."

Two minutes later Miss Derry said, "Next Monday, seven o'clock, Freemasons' Hall. And he wasn't at all forward with me."

"I'm glad," Jennifer said.

Somehow she couldn't go home that night. She rang her mother and then fingered the key Lucy had given her to the flat in Birmingham. That night, and every night until she gave her talk at the Freemasons' Hall, she slept in Len's bed, hugging his pillow to her. And then, after her talk, when Uncle Bertie's son, nephew, whatever, asked her if she'd got her "own place" in town, she took him back there. She had wondered at herself taking him above the garage during the wedding; now she wondered no more. It was a kind of revenge. One day she would tell Len . . . one day . . .

CHAPTER
FIVE

Lucy and Len arrived home, tired but euphoric. Lucy had said nothing but she was quite certain Floss was right and she was pregnant. She planned to get a test kit and confirm it as soon as life returned to normal. She pushed away the thought that she had to make a new "normal" for herself; the flat, though familiar enough, was not home. She missed her room, the garden, Snowball . . . her mother. It was jet lag. That's all it was. And as her mother had so often said, everything would look better in the morning. Meanwhile they dropped like stones between fresh white sheets and curled against each other with instant familiarity.

"Thought I'd left the place in such a mess," murmured Len. "Looks pretty good."

Lucy said sleepily but gratefully, "It's Jen. Didn't you notice the flowers in the sitting room? They'd be as dead as dodos if you'd left them. Not that you would. You're not a flower person."

"You let Jennifer Bowles have a key?" Len asked.

"Of course. We needed the fridge stocked up . . . et cetera, et cetera . . ." She was already sliding into unconsciousness. But Len, for a little while, was alert again. He propped himself on an elbow and looked around. Yes, someone had been here. Quite often too. He imagined he could smell Jennifer's perfume. He slid his hand around Lucy's waist and cupped her breast, deeply thankful that the foolish attraction he had felt for her friend had not come to anything. And as they both loved Lucy, it never would. He pressed her against him and put his face into her neck. Immediately he'd seen her he had known she would be his wife. She had been born for it. And when she told him falteringly that she was a virgin and would "rather wait if he didn't mind", his feelings for her had intensified into adoration and a near-reverence. He tried now to turn her towards him but she made the small whimpering sound she always made when she was asleep and he smiled and kissed her ear and subsided into his pillow.

They lounged around most of Sunday. He rang Toto and George and she rang her mother and they pieced together that their two families had shared a lot of time during the past two weeks. Linda Bowles had joined them for a few days, then they had all got together in Cheltenham with Jennifer and Uncle Bertie's nephew who had arrived out of the blue.

Len took her for lunch at his local pub where they met other "radio boffs" as he called them. "Not to be confused with buffs, Luce," he instructed solemnly. "Buffs are fascinated laymen. Boffs are scientists."

She laughed. "Maybe they are, in the real world. In media terms they are marketing men — and you know it!"

"They suss out audience reaction, yes. Certainly." He felt himself not so much criticized as . . . somehow revealed. "That's a science. It's called sociology." He kissed her nose. She was pretty. Not beautiful. Entirely unthreatening. "And what do you mean by 'the real world'?"

She held his head and kissed him properly. She had managed to use a pregnancy test and it had been positive. She wanted to tell him, but not yet. "We work in a dream world, don't we, darling? Pedlars of dreams?" She continued to kiss him, his aquiline nose, dark eyes, sharply defined hairline.

He held back somehow. "Are you calling my reports on our troubled world a dream? A fairy-tale?"

She reached his full mouth. "Not those. But you report them. You don't live them. It's all . . ." She kissed him and withdrew slightly. "It's all vicarious."

He held her very gently, as if she were a butterfly that might flutter off at any moment, or could be crushed. "You're going wise on me again." He let her kiss him. Before he made love to her, she had to understand something. He was not sure what it was yet. "You're saying . . . I'm too objective? It's what a reporter has to be, you know."

"There's objectivity and objectivity." Her lips were on his hairline again and she felt his forehead contract in a frown. She leaned back and looked at him. "You're good. You're excellent."

"But?"

"No buts. It's easy to be objective when one is also vicarious." She smiled as his frown deepened. "Darling, I'm not criticizing. I'm *not*! It's simply that when you were involved, totally involved — you know, when you were frightened for the Gampies — then you were not objective."

"Then I was not reporting to the world."

"Of course not." Her smile widened with a hint of incredulity. "You're cross with me!"

"Of course I'm not *cross* with you, Luce! I want your opinion on my work — I need it. You are my average listener, after all."

"No, I'm not. I'm your non-average listener." She began the kissing again. "I'm in love with you. I thought I was before we went to Barbados. I was . . . then. But now . . ." She kissed him harder. "Now, I'm besotted! I think you're wonderful!" She would have told him then about the baby, but he kissed her back and the next minute they were caught in a mutual passion.

On Monday morning she suddenly felt unwell. She told herself it was all in her mind but Len remarked on her pale face and told her to stay in bed, there was no need for her to put in an appearance until the next assignment was planned. She turned over thankfully and buried her face in his pillow and the next thing she knew the phone was ringing and it was midday.

It was Len. "Luce, how are you? I could come home now and get you something, but there's a chap here from St Paul's in Bristol who wants me to do a piece called Bristol's ghetto. What do you think?"

"Sounds OK. Lunch at the Black Boar and lots of discussion?" She hauled herself on to an elbow. She felt ravenous.

"Yes. That sort of thing. Could come to something or nothing. You don't feel neglected?"

She had assumed she would join them and take notes. She sank back into the pillow again. "Of course not. I might go and see Mummy."

"Good. You're better then?"

"It was jet lag. Needed more sleep."

"I know what you mean. OK. See you tonight."

She got up slowly, testing each movement. She was better. She showered, dressed and phoned her mother who was delighted. So was Lucy, in fact she was suddenly excited. She was going home: Mummy, Snowball, Albert and the garden. If she hung on till sixish Jennifer would be back from the Archive Office and they could have time together. She combed her curls and put on some lipstick and a blue sun frock. She felt a bit of a pang as she smoothed the long bodice over her hips. By Christmas her little nipped-in waist would be no more.

The drive out to Nortons Heath seemed endless. She had not stopped for lunch, imagining she would arrive at the Old Rectory by one o'clock to share her mother's midday snack, but the traffic slowed almost to a stop through Edgbaston and she knew she was not going to make it until two o'clock at the earliest. After fifteen minutes of crawling along at five miles an hour, a police notice appeared at the side of the road: "Accident. Slow". As if they could do anything else. She tried to think positively: she was all right and someone else was not; she and the baby were all right. She felt her heart jump at the extra thought. She was responsible for another life. She shouldn't have come, she should be taking care of the baby inside her. She came to a side turning and peeled off, thinking almost seriously of going straight back to the flat. But the road curled round and ran alongside the canal and she was still going in the direction of the hills. And now her physical body longed for them: the air and light and countryside. She skirted Selly Oak and ran through Kings Norton. Then she was on the top road and going through the ford she had loved so much as a child and there, on the very edge of Warwickshire, the spire of the church rose from the trees. She almost sobbed with relief

As soon as she got out of the car Martha was there and they folded around each other, laughing but near tears, thankful when Snowball emerged from the hollyhocks to weave himself around their legs and create a diversion.

"Darling, you look so well!" Martha had meant to rein in her emotion for this first meeting. But then, she had imagined it would include Len and that would have made it easier. It would have been obvious that Len and Lucy were a pair: the base of a triangle of which she was the apex. Now, seeing Lucy on her own like this, unexpected, gloriously tanned, it was as if she were coming home again. The same Lucy. She had to remind herself it was not so.

Lucy said, "Oh darling, it was such an awful drive! I hate being so far away — thought I was never going to get here!" She picked up Snowball and hugged him passionately.

Martha said, "But, darling, you're so used to that drive — and you usually had to do it in the rush hour too."

"I know. But it was awful today. There was an accident. I turned off and came through Selly Oak and Kings Norton. Oh this lovely creature!" She snuffled into Snowball's neck and he gently withdrew himself. "Sorry, Snowie. But that was a lovely welcome." She put the cat carefully back among the large hollyhock leaves. "It was like one of those dreams — you know, where you're running for a train or something and everything stops you. The paving. stones turn to treacle and you can't shout to the guard and —"

"Darling, come on in and sit down. You sound quite desperate." Martha laughed but she was suddenly worried. Not about her own dependence on Lucy any more, but on Lucy's dependence on her. "It's so lovely to see you that I haven't asked why. Shouldn't you be at work today?"

"Yes, but nothing much is happening and I was jet-lagged so Len told me to sleep it off."

They went indoors where it was cool and dim. The sewing machine was by the window and some flimsy material fell in folds from its needle. Lucy went towards it and fingered one of the folds. "You're not making another wedding dress?" She couldn't quite believe her mother's life was continuing as if nothing had happened. There was a tray next to Clem's chair; it contained a coffee cup and plate, both empty. "Damn, you've eaten. I thought we'd have a sandwich together in the garden."

"Then we will. I ate some of the left-over cake from the wedding. Can't bear to throw it away but it's very stale." Martha too went to the window. "You really do look well," she repeated as if to reassure both of them.

Then she laughed. "Wedding dress forsooth. It's a bedjacket for Miss Darcy."

"The old moaner herself?"

"The Rector described her as 'gently dying'. But she's not all that gentle and I don't think she's anywhere near death. I thought a bedjacket might cheer her up."

"Oh . . . Mummy."

"What?"

Lucy looked at the sewing machine and then the window. Outside Albert was staking the tomatoes. She waved her hands helplessly. "Is this . . . how it's going to be?"

Martha said steadily, "It's how it's always been, darling. It's called village life."

"I know. But it was different when we were doing it together. We were . . . sort of going towards something else."

"Of course." Martha's voice was gentle. "We've *found* something else. We got there, Lucy."

"*I* found something else." Lucy glanced up quickly and saw something in her mother's face: something unguarded, akin to despair. She said quickly, "Listen. I've come with some news. It will affect you. Enormously. I'm pregnant!"

Martha's face opened wide; despair was replaced with incredulity and joy. "Darling, you can't know! You've been married less than three weeks! How can you know?"

"Pregnancy kit." Lucy was laughing. "But I knew anyway. Len's grandmother, Floss — Gampy, he calls her — she told me."

"Oh Lucy!" Martha was near tears. "Oh my dear, how wonderful. Your baby . . . I can't believe it!"

"Yours too. He'll be your grandchild."

"Yes. So he will." She took Lucy's hands. Her eyes were full of unashamed tears. "You see? Here's my something else. A new beginning. A new role." She blinked hard, laughed and said, "Grandma. How does it sound? Granny? Nanny?" She drew Lucy to her, gave her a quick hug and then walked away. "What about Toto? What does she want to be called?"

"I don't know. Perhaps Gampy. Like Floss, like her own mother." Lucy swallowed. "She doesn't know. No-one knows. Except me. And now you."

"You haven't told Len?"

"No. There hasn't been . . . opportunity."

Martha said, "I hate to say this, Lucy, but don't tell him I know. He should be the first."

"Yes. Not that he's . . . like that."

"Of course not. But, well, it's a question of priority, that's all." Martha glowed again. "Lucy, it's such good news. Soon, of course. You and Len, you won't have very much time together. As a couple."

"I know. I didn't think it would happen so quickly, I have to admit."

"You didn't take your pills?"

"I thought I did. I'm almost sure . . . I couldn't have, could I?"

"Ah. And you're worried about telling Len?"

"Of course not! Oh Ma . . ." She called Martha Ma when she was teasing her. "It's not a bit like that. Good

Lord, Len's got a terrific job — and an even better future — and we're in love and everything is just perfect."

"I know, I know." Martha laughed at her own caution.

"Come on, let's get some food and sit outside. It'll be shady under the apple tree. We'll talk babies if you like, but not all the time. I want to hear about Barbados."

"And I want to hear about Toto and George."

"And Jennifer's new boyfriend!" Martha grinned roguishly. "I think if only she can get him to propose, she'll realize her basic ambition!"

"What's that?" Lucy followed her mother into the kitchen and perched on a stool watching the familiar methodical way Martha made a sandwich, vowing that she would be just such a housewife.

Martha laughed. "To be part of our family!"

"D'you mean the boyfriend is a relative of ours?"

"Uncle Bertie's nephew, no less. Daddy's cousin. His name is Moreton. Can you believe it?"

Lucy laughed too, incredulously. "Such a coincidence. And yet . . . he must be the one she met at the wedding. She didn't know his name then." She took a tray from Martha and they wandered into the garden. Albert had gone. They walked across the big lawn which still showed the wounds from the marquee's pegs; the grass was pale where the carpet had been laid. Around the other side of the garage was a tiny orchard of apple trees. Lucy went to the garage and brought out two deckchairs. She glanced up at the trapdoor and grinned. Jennifer was so awful, yet so marvellous.

"What's his first name? Where does he live? I take it he's not married?" she asked, setting up the chairs strategically and collapsing into one of them.

"Well, I hope not. Jennifer practically ate him with her starter — Linda apologized afterwards so you can tell. Linda is pretty broad-minded." Martha took a sandwich and held it while she tipped her face to the dappled sun and remembered. "His name is Simon. There were three brothers. Your grandfather was the only respectable one. Uncle Bertie and Uncle Ted were . . . well, disreputable. I mean, Uncle Bertie wore wellington boots to your wedding." She opened her eyes and they grinned at each other. Lucy was wolfing her way through the rest of the sandwiches. Martha went on, "Anyway the three brothers never kept in touch. Uncle Ted died just before your grandfather. Uncle Bertie didn't go to either of the funerals. But he was there for Daddy's." She smiled again. "That was why I wanted to invite him to the wedding. And then he told me that Uncle Ted had had a son. He confessed it on his deathbed practically. He — the son — was at boarding-school when Uncle Ted bequeathed him to Bertie. Anyway, I told Bertie to bring him along. And it seems he did."

"How amazing! What does he do now? Surely he would have said if he had a wife?"

"I would have thought so. He said very little about himself. He must run a shop or something because that's how he met Jennifer again. She gave a talk to the Chamber of Commerce. He was there."

Lucy finished the sandwiches and sat back replete. "A shop. That doesn't sound like Jennifer. Too ordinary."

"Not when he's called Simon Moreton."

"Oh Mummy. You make her sound obsessive. Anyway, I'll pop over before I go back to the flat. Just say hello."

"That would be nice. I'll come and say hello to Linda. Now. Names. If it's a boy . . ."

"I don't know." Lucy knew that she should choose Clement. But she could not imagine her baby called Clement; for her there was only one Clement. "Len's grandfather is called Henry. Henry Travers. Sounds good, doesn't it?"

"Sounds just right. What about a girl?"

"It will be a boy. Somehow I'm sure it will be a boy."

Martha smiled and they went on talking babies until it was five o'clock and time for tea. After that they went across to the row of cottages on the other side of the church and arrived just as Jennifer got home from work. It was like old times. Linda made more tea and they talked across each other and laughed almost hysterically. Lucy told them about the sea and sky and the high and low lands of Barbados. She spoke of the Gampies and how they lived on the beach almost like Mr Peggotty, except that their chattel house was not an upturned boat.

"My God. It sounds like paradise," Jennifer said. Jennifer could not take her eyes off Lucy. She was still so pretty and dainty but she was different. Before the wedding, Jennifer had known that she herself was the more striking, the more interesting of the two of them. Now there was an assurance about Lucy. And something else. Fulfilment? She did not have to try any more. Whatever she did would be all right.

Lucy said, "Paradise. Yes. Poverty, too. But it seemed to me it was much easier to bear, because of the sun and the sea and the — the — containment of it. You know, being an island."

"Perhaps that's why Toto wanted to get away. Containment could become claustrophobic, I suppose."

"Toto?" Lucy queried. "That's the second time you've called Len's mother that. You get on with my in-laws better than I do!"

They both laughed but Jennifer said seriously, "She was so kind to Linda. And to me. She just is . . . kind. Sort of over the top and enthusiastic about everything. She went on and on about a jar of quince marmalade Marty took her. You know, from all those quinces down in the orchard? She made them into marmalade —"

"I know. I helped her." Lucy raised her brows humorously. "I've only been gone a couple of weeks, Jen!"

"Sorry. Seriously, it seems ages."

Martha came in carrying a tray, Linda behind her with the teapot. Linda nodded. "It does, Lucy dear. This is the first time Jen has been home for two weeks. Your mother and I have been grass widows."

Lucy grinned at her friend. "Yes, I've heard about you and my long-lost cousin. Or is he uncle?"

"First cousin once removed?" Martha offered. "He was Daddy's cousin so . . . whatever." She turned to Jennifer. "I take it you and he are what is called an item?"

Jennifer flung her dark head back and laughed. Then she said, "I think we must be. Every night this week. And he's asked me to the Worcester hotel this weekend. I don't think it's for tea and toast."

"The Worcester hotel?" Lucy asked. She felt a small sense of withdrawal somewhere inside her head. Yet Jennifer had always talked like this, been like this. It had never grated before.

"He manages the Huntingford group. They had the Marks Arms in Broadway, then the Avon Bank in Evesham and now this old manor house in Worcester. I think it's called the Manor House Hotel. Sounds great. He's this year's Chairman of the Chamber of Commerce. That's where I met him. Well, met him again." She gave another of her full-throated laughs.

Lucy said, "To think we imagined he ran a shop, Mummy!"

"Imagine," Martha echoed drily.

"Do you think . . ." Lucy began tentatively. "I mean, would you consider marrying this cousin-once-removed?"

Jennifer pursed her lips consideringly. "I don't know. Not sure." She turned her mouth down self-mockingly. "I just can't see myself as a married woman, Luce. You were born to be married. You look absolutely right — absolutely. Besides, you've got the best of both worlds. You share your husband's work too. Simon isn't the least bit interested in archives, not really."

"You'd be marvellous as a hotel manageress."

"At first, perhaps. But everything goes stale on me, Luce." Suddenly Jennifer was very serious. Linda put

94

out a hand and was brushed aside. "I don't need comfort, for God's sake. That's how I am. It doesn't upset me. It's just a fact."

Martha leaned forward and put her cup on the table. "Your friendship with Lucy has never gone stale," she said quietly.

"That's different." Jennifer spoke quietly too, but then laughed. "If I did marry Simon, what would that make us, Luce? Cousins?"

"Sort of cousins. In law." Lucy stared at the face opposite hers and for a moment saw a stranger. It occurred to her that Jennifer did not know — perhaps would never know — what real love was. She said quickly, "Marry him, Jen. There are lots of ways of being happy. Boredom doesn't come into it."

Martha sat back sipping her second cup of tea; for some reason, Linda looked uncomfortable.

Jennifer said, "Well. Your advice has been taken on board, Luce. Thanks."

Linda stood up abruptly. "Come and see the tomatoes. I've grown them in those bag things and they're going mad. I wondered if you'd keep an eye on them for me, Martha? I've got a job next week and I might be away for a few days."

"I'll do it, Ma." Jennifer spoke carelessly. "I'll be around most evenings after the weekend." She watched the two women walk down the strip of garden, Martha so suitable in her linen suit; Linda hopeless as usual in jeans and a suntop that showed her boobs much too clearly. Jennifer put a detaining arm on Lucy's shoulder.

"Seriously, thanks for the advice. I think we both know it won't happen. But it's a lovely thought. Cousins-in-law."

Lucy turned and looked up at her friend; her doubts about her seemed now like disloyalty. She said, "Why won't it happen? Why can't you just . . . let it happen?"

"Don't you think it's what I wanted? From the moment I saw him again? He's great at sex and after that everything else follows. You know that now, Luce, so don't look all buttoned up. It has to start with sex."

Lucy was going to argue and then didn't. Yes, she and Len had been in love before . . . but Barbados had been like a new birth. A revelation.

Jennifer gave one of her sibilant laughs. "You see? Trouble is, I didn't look ahead and play your game, did I? I gave him what he wanted straightaway. There's no need to marry me, Luce. So he won't. So the cousins-in-law bit is . . . redundant."

Lucy's eyes opened wide. "You don't think I — I blackmailed Len into marrying me, do you?"

"No, I don't. I know how you felt. I've always known. Christ, we've talked about it often enough. But I don't think Len would have married you if you'd lived with him first."

Lucy said confidently, "He would. I promise you that."

Jennifer shrugged. "Anyway, that's how it is with me and Simon."

She turned back into the kitchen and turned the tap on in the sink.

Lucy was suddenly so angry she hardly knew what to say. She felt as if Jennifer was deliberately trampling on what she and Len had. She picked up a tea-towel. Her hands were shaking.

Jennifer piled teacups into the sink noisily.

"I'm sorry, Luce. I don't know what I'm talking about. Please don't be angry. I don't think I can bear it if our friendship is spoiled."

Lucy said shakily, "Don't be ridiculous."

There was a silence while they started the routine of washing and drying crockery. When they had nearly finished Jennifer said, "Lucy. Please. I can feel you going away from me . . ."

Lucy opened the door of a cabinet and began to stack cups and saucers. She said, "I'm here. What you said . . . it wasn't good. But I know you didn't mean it. It's OK."

Jennifer had dried her hands and was rubbing cream between her fingers. She said, "You've been different ever since you arrived. Is it going to be like this from now on? Will Len come between us?"

Lucy flipped the tea-towel and tried to laugh. "Stop all the melodrama! Honestly, Jen. I'd better tell you. I'm pregnant. Did a test, and it was positive." She pretended to be exasperated. "Does that explain anything?"

For a moment, Jennifer was still. She stared down at her splayed fingers. She spoke without looking up. "That's what I could do. Get myself pregnant." She looked up and saw Lucy's horrified expression. "Darling — I'm sorry! I meant to say congratulations and it came out all wrong! Lucy —"

But Lucy had pushed past her and was running upstairs to the bathroom and Jennifer stood in the little sitting room and made no attempt to follow her.

"Oh what the hell!" she said to the empty room.

Outside, Linda said. "What a treat! The four of us together like this. Lucy is so sweet, Martha. You must be very proud of her."

"I am." Martha could not prevaricate modestly about that.

Linda's voice dropped into a minor key. "I'm proud of Jen too. But . . . differently. Of course."

Martha glanced at the downbent head sharply. Something about Linda had changed since the wedding. In spite of her peculiar life-style and Jennifer's brashness, there had always been a kind of insouciant happiness about Linda which now seemed dimmed somehow.

Martha said, "Let's go out for a meal tomorrow. Shall we? Get away from the village?"

"That would be nice." Linda looked up and smiled. "I'll have to get along to the hairdresser later in the week. Buy a new outfit. Things like that. Tomorrow would be fine for lunch."

Martha said, "Where is your job next week, Linda?"

"Cheltenham. A convention." Linda drew a deep breath and stood up to face her friend.

"Sounds very posh!" Martha never knew how to deal with Linda's jobs.

"Not a bit posh. Not really." Linda bent her head again, lifted a vine of tomatoes and began picking off the ripe ones.

Martha stared at the grey roots in Linda's dark hair. She did not look up and the way she picked the tomatoes, as if her life depended on it, meant something was wrong.

She said, "Well . . . don't let them take advantage of you. I know you enjoy your work, Lin, but sometimes it seems to be rather . . . well, risky. Just be careful, won't you?"

"I always am. I know how to take care of myself," Linda said stoutly, hating herself for not telling Martha that she was going to work for Bill Tatham. And she wasn't even doing it through her agent, Maureen. This was entirely a private arrangement.

Martha had always found Linda touchingly vulnerable but actually she must be quite tough to take on some of the work she had done, so she sighed and again changed the subject. "How do you feel about Jennifer marrying into Clem's family, Linda? It would be rather special, wouldn't it?" But Linda continued picking as if her life depended on it.

At last she said, "It won't happen, Martha. Jennifer isn't the marrying sort. She's like me. We don't . . . marry."

Len was already at the flat when Lucy let herself in. She sensed his anger; it was a damped-down fire beneath his concern for her.

"You were a long time. I phoned and there was no reply."

For some reason Lucy was quite unable to kiss him. She went to the sink where his breakfast cereal bowl still bobbed in grey water. Her stomach churned.

"Mummy and I went over to see the Bowleses." She stared helplessly at the water. "Darling, I'm so sorry. I can't cook anything."

"No." He was unsurprised. "Jennifer just telephoned. She told me the news. I expect your mother knows too."

She turned. "Jennifer . . . *told* you?"

"She rang to offer congratulations and to say that you misunderstood something she said. She is just so very, very pleased to hear about the baby." His enunciation was staccato-sharp.

To know that Jennifer had not deliberately told tales was something of a relief. She relaxed slightly against the rim of the sink and said in a small voice, "I know. I should have told you first. All sorts of things happened, Len. I had to tell Mummy because she was so lonely and . . . kind of left out. And then I had to tell Jen because she thought I was turning against her." She swallowed. "Aren't you pleased?"

"Of course I'm *pleased*! That's got nothing to do with it!"

She could not hold his dark accusing stare and dropped her gaze to the ground. Jennifer had vacuumed; the carpet had not looked so good since she had gone first to the flat. And suddenly she knew that Jennifer had used the flat. Used it.

He said, "Who do you love best? Me or Martha?"

She was appalled. "Len! You can't ask things like that! It's so different! You know that you are my whole world! But there's room for Mummy — surely you can't be jealous of my *mother*?"

"What if I'd got some news that concerned you and me — a new job perhaps? Something that would take us abroad? What if I went and told George and Toto? Or Jennifer?"

She whispered, "Are we going abroad?"

"Answer my question!"

She said, "Len, I have to go to the bathroom."

"Oh no you don't! You don't get out of it like that, my girl!"

She had never fainted before. It was ghastly. Nausea mounted until she could stand it no longer. And when she came round it was to find him desperate and then, as he was convinced she was all right, loving again. And yes, they were going abroad. They were going to make a film, no less. On the emergence of the Dominican Republic. Finance arranged. Everything.

"But the baby must be born here," she murmured, trying to breathe as he kissed her fervently, frantically.

"The baby can be born at home with the Gampies," he said. She wanted to protest that England was home, then recognized he was determined on this. He kissed her again. "Oh darling, don't frighten me like that again. I'm going to put you to bed and get you some supper —"

"Can't eat."

"Hot tea. Bread and butter. Toto has taught me . . ." He was still kissing her and she knew that they would make love before there was any hot tea. Tears sprang to her eyes. Sex . . . how had Jennifer managed to tarnish it?

He said, "Oh honey, I'm so pleased about the baby. It's what I wanted. To fill you with babies . . ."

Sometime afterwards she whispered, "Len, tell me the truth. Please. If we'd lived together before we got married, would we have got married?"

He laughed. "Is that an Irish question?"

"No. It's my question."

He looked at her and said quietly, "I wanted a wife, Lucy. And you were everything I have ever dreamed of in a wife."

She wept again, silly weak tears. "I let you down today, Len. I'll never do it again."

He propped her while she drank her tea, then he said, "It will do us both good to get away, honey. Away from family. We need to be alone."

She dared not think of her mother because she would have wept again. She smiled instead.

CHAPTER
SIX

Miss Darcy sat up in bed wearing the bedjacket Martha had made for her. Outside her cottage window, autumn was being torn away by a savage November wind. The leaves, which had hung on the trees throughout a quiet October, slapped at the window occasionally and short squalls of rain had made her front garden into a mire.

"Who would think it?" she asked rhetorically. "Only seems like yesterday that you and the dear Rector got me out of bed and over to the church for the Flower Festival."

"It was three months ago, my dear," Martha said, reloading the tray she had brought up two hours before. "We must expect the weather to change in November!"

"Not only the weather," Miss Darcy mourned. "So much has happened in that short, short time. So much."

"Indeed." Martha put the remains of the sponge into a tin. "I'll leave this here, shall I? If Mrs Goodwin pops in after Mothers' Union, you can offer some to her." Truda Goodwin was the daunting wife of the Rector. She did not make cakes because her dear Marcus had to watch his weight.

"All right." Miss Darcy sounded reluctant. She probably knew from bitter experience about Truda Goodwin's sweet tooth.

"I shall be baking again this weekend," Martha reassured her. "Linda Bowles is coming for Sunday lunch. Jennifer and Simon too."

"Oh, you are so lucky!" Miss Darcy said. "I simply dread Sundays. No-one visits, of course. I don't expect it. It's a family day."

"Yes." Martha stood up and went to the window from where she had a perfect view of the graveyard. Albert Davis was raking leaves, helped by the ten-year-old twin girls who had moved in with their parents to the house next, door to Linda's. Linda said they were smashing, really, really, *really* nice. However, Denise Coupland had confided that the Venableses had an "open marriage", whatever that might mean. Also that the girls were completely out of hand and had disrupted the Sunday School the one time they attended. Incredibly, they often turned up at the family service by themselves. The Rector thought they were looking for conformity. Truda commented bitterly they were probably thrown out of the cottage on Sunday mornings.

"The Venables girls are helping Albert with the churchyard," she reported back to the bed. "They seem very pleasant. Teresa and Patience. Lovely names."

Miss Darcy actually chuckled. "That's not what they're called, Mrs Moreton! Haven't you heard their nicknames? Tansy and Pickle. Can you believe it? They come to see me now and then. Bring their homework with them. That's what they like to be called. Tansy and Pickle!" She snorted again.

"I've only seen them at church. And Linda is working so hard lately she hasn't got to know them properly."

104

Martha stared down at the two girls. They were tall for their age, with thick red hair in bunchy pony-tails. "Tansy and Pickle! My goodness! Not something we shall forget in a hurry. Nice of them to come and see you, though."

She glanced round. Miss Darcy was fiddling with the ribbons on the bedjacket and said without thinking, "They turn up here on Sunday afternoons. I've been getting up so that I can make them a nice cup of tea. Their parents like the cottage to themselves on Sundays."

Martha nearly said, "You old fraud!" but told herself sternly that Miss Darcy was using the old-lady equivalent of poetic licence. She was a good actress too: the Rector had described her as gently dying four months ago and it had been something of a triumph when they had got her into a wheelchair and taken her to the Flower Festival in August. Now, it seemed, she was capable of getting up, going down the narrow stairs, making tea and talking to two ten-year-old girls.

She looked up from the ribbons and saw Martha's face. "The parents like their cottage to themselves on Sundays — the children have got nowhere else to go!" Her mouth trembled. "It's a terrible effort. Well, you know how poorly I am, Mrs Moreton. But when it's children — and newcomers too — one has to make an effort. After all, I am the oldest resident in Nortons Heath now. And my parents before me . . . and my dear brother, lost in the trenches . . ."

Martha put her hand over the veined one. "I think you do wonders, Miss Darcy! It must be marvellous for those two girls to be able to discuss their work with you." She

105

picked up the tray. "You know, I think I heard Mrs Coupland say that they were doing a project on the village at school. You could tell Teresa — sorry, Tansy and Pickle what it was really like here. During the War. I remember when I was a girl at Littleford, a bomb dropped on the village green. Things like that. Why don't I bring you up a notepad and pen? You could make some notes for them."

"Well . . . yes. I suppose I could. Actually, Mrs Moreton, I saw a Zeppelin when I was sixteen! That would be something to write down wouldn't it?"

Martha washed up the cups and plates at the shallow yellow stone sink and thought about Miss Darcy's life: born on the same day as the Queen Mother, as old as the century. Miss Darcy had been a wonderful daughter. That had been her career. When both her parents had died, she had had to find something else to do. Being ill brought her visitors and little gifts and an extra bit on her pension so that she could afford some help in the house. Not a bad career change. Martha knew she should be smiling as she tidied up the kitchen and went in search of some paper and a pencil. She wasn't. Her career seemed to have come to a close: or at least part of it. And the other part, the village part, was sterile without Lucy. Certainly Jennifer still appeared now and then and perched on the corner of the kitchen table to say, "Well? What's the local gossip? Apart from my mother, that is!" But Lucy had done her share of talking: about work — which meant, increasingly, about Len; about the traffic; the sales; what they would do at Christmas . . . Martha wondered bleakly just what she was going to do at Christmas.

She found a notepad on the front of which was scrawled, "Meals on wheels. Leave under porch", and took it upstairs with a pen from her handbag. Miss Darcy insisted on kissing her goodbye. Beneath the scent of lavender water lurked a strangely familiar old-lady smell. Martha restrained a shudder with some effort and felt as if she were escaping as she left the cottage. Yet these days she quite enjoyed seeing Miss Darcy and making sure she was "all right". In fact, knowing that she did have other visitors on a regular basis gave Martha almost a jolt. Was this another part of her career that was being eroded?

She should have turned left and gone into the churchyard to have a word with Albert and the twin girls so unsuitably called Tansy and Pickle. This time last year she would have done that sort of thing. "I'm Martha Moreton from the Old Rectory. How are you getting on in Nortons Heath? I expect Mr Davis is glad of your help . . ." or something similar. Now she wondered whether anyone would want to know about the woman in the rambling old rectory that could house three families quite easily. And it might be awkward to invite them for Sunday tea, as if she thought she was Lady Bountiful or someone. When Lucy was there it would have been natural: the Snakes and Ladders would have come out when the tea was cleared and they would all have been laughing together in no time. Anyway, it seemed the two girls were with Miss Darcy on Sunday afternoons and doubtless the parents took the opportunity of having a nap.

She thought of Sunday and seeing Linda. In one way she hoped that Jennifer and Simon wouldn't come. It would be lovely to sit and chat about nothing to Linda. She was so undemanding, yet subtly understanding too. Their friendship was an unlikely one probably based on Jennifer and Lucy's closeness. Yet there was more to it than that. Somewhere, a long time ago, Martha had known girls like Linda: girls who did not have Martha's "advantages" and who scrambled through life with a cheerfulness that only just surmounted . . . pathos. They had come from the middle of Birmingham when the bombs started failing in the War and they had worn pinafores over ragged dresses and had nits in their hair and some of them carried faded snapshots of their parents under yellow vests next to their skin. The village girls had been terrified of them: their harsh Birmingham accents had been incomprehensible; their smell almost unbearable. But Martha's father had gently pointed out their heroism. Martha remembered him saying, "They're not evacuees, they're refugees. And they're unbeatable." There was something about Linda that was unbeatable too. And lovable. She had never been jealous of Jennifer's obvious allegiance to everyone in the Old Rectory. She never envied anyone anything, in fact. And though everyone else thought her shallow, Martha knew she was not. Linda would understand that Martha's loneliness could easily drift into isolation. Of course Linda herself had been on her own for ages: Jennifer was no company. Not like Lucy.

Martha felt her eyes begin to fill and checked her thoughts sharply. Another squall forced her into a run up the gravel drive. She halted in the porch, breathing deeply, feeling in her pocket for the key. On the lawn, where four months before the marquee had blossomed so magnificently, were some spent rockets from Bonfire Night the night before last. They surely had not been there when she went to Miss Darcy's earlier?

She went into the hall cautiously, looking down its length for any signs of occupation. There was nothing. She searched the house. Snowie was asleep in front of the Aga where he'd been when she left. It must be all right. She filled the kettle and collapsed in Clem's old chair. What on earth was the matter with her today? She was seeing horrors everywhere.

She drank her tea which tasted much better than the one she had had with Miss Darcy, and watched the last of the light shrink out of the kitchen. Then it was time to go around drawing curtains and switching on some heat for the evening. She performed each task as slowly as possible, even hanging around while Snowball did his evening recce of the garden; but it was still only six o'clock when she settled down with an early supper. There was nothing much on the television: she would have watched an old film if Lucy had been there, but somehow she could not bother with it on her own. And tomorrow was Friday and there was absolutely nothing to do. She did the church flowers on Saturday and she was cooking on Sunday for Linda, but Friday was empty. It seemed to rise up before her like a featureless wall. She had to get over it but she simply did not know how.

It was when she was getting ready for bed that the thought came to her: she would go to Cheltenham. She'd had a day in Worcester and another in Tewkesbury. Tomorrow she would have a day in Cheltenham. The thought of walking up the Prom and maybe lunching at the Cadena lifted her heart. She had often met Clem in Cheltenham; his law practice had had a branch there as well as in Worcester and Birmingham. They had lunched, usually at Cavendish House. And then in the evening they had gone to the theatre. She wouldn't do that; she would be back home before it was dark so that she could lock up the garage properly and let Snowball out. But she could leave early and get there in time for coffee. There might be a sale at County Clothes. She could do with a new skirt. The sweaters and shirts from last year were as good as new but there was nothing quite like a good tweed skirt for the winter . . .

She went up to bed at ten o'clock, checked that the electric blanket was hot, plumped up Clem's pillow which she would probably push into her back at some time during the night, and peered through the curtains at the November night. The rain had stopped and the sky was clear and full of stars. A frost. Then, down by the gate, she thought she saw figures running down the lane. But though she stared till her eyes ached, she saw nothing else. She adjusted the curtains and told herself she was becoming foolish in her old age.

The garden was sparkling with frost the next day but when she went outside to remove the spent fireworks, the lawn was clear. She frowned and went around clipping off the frozen heads of chrysanthemums and wondering if, in the rain and half-light, she'd mistaken twigs and leaves for fireworks. Albert was coming next week for a final clear-up before winter. She would ask him about the local schoolboys and whether they would think it funny to invade her garden.

Someone was reversing out of a parking space in Oriel Road as she drove into Cheltenham later that morning. She signalled her thanks and slid into it: somehow it was a good omen for the whole day. She knotted her scarf, gathered up bag and gloves and got out opposite the old Gentleman's Club. It was like stepping into icy water: the air hurt to breathe; even the leafless trees seemed afraid to move. Once into the Promenade, it was slightly warmer. The clothes shops were full of velour coats in reds and blues; the jewellers were displaying diamonds outsparkling the frost, the shoe shop concentrated on high boots; Cavendish House had a display of toys and cots and shawls scattered over a nursery mock-up. Martha lingered there, wondering what Lucy's baby would be like. They had gone off to Dominica two weeks after their return from honeymoon and Martha had felt worried about that.

She moved away from the nursery display because it was all pointless; and walked briskly along to the shop where she'd bought skirts before. They were much too expensive; she had known they would be. So she continued into the High Street and Marks & Spencer's. Then it was time for an early lunch which was over much too quickly. She sat over coffee watching people at other tables talking animatedly. There was no-one she knew; the wives of Clem's colleagues used to invite her to join them occasionally, but since she had declined invitations regularly they had stopped issuing them. Obviously. There were things she could join: a theatre club perhaps. It would be good to visit the theatre on a regular basis. She could tell Lucy all about it. Less . . . parochial. Outward-looking. That's what she would do. She would go round to the old Opera House right now and enquire about clubs. It would be difficult at first; getting to know people was always difficult. But she could do it. Perhaps the curate's busy wife would come with her. Denise Coupland was immersed in church work and family; it would do her good to get out now and then. The thing was to get some information. Martha stood up resolutely and went to the cash desk to pay her bill.

"Did you enjoy your meal, madam?"

She honestly could not remember what it was for a moment; then it came to her. Soup of the day and a roll. It had been an indifferent vegetable soup.

"Very much, thank you."

She hoped she wasn't going gaga; first the fireworks and now lunch. She smiled: gaga was an acceptable old-fashioned term. The one to avoid was Alzheimer's disease. She shuddered and turned down the small street that led to the theatre. What would happen to her if she were ill? Oh God.

They were unhelpful at the booking office. There *were* such groups; it made sense because of taking block bookings. One group came from Tewkesbury. Perhaps they were a Women's Institute or something. In fact, perhaps the Women's Institute were the people to contact.

Deflated, Martha turned away. Nortons Heath W.I. had amalgamated with Littleford. Easy enough to make

112

some enquiries. She glanced at her watch: one-thirty. She would take a sharp walk as far as Imperial Gardens and then go back to the car and get home well before it was dark.

There was some sort of exhibition going on in the Gardens. The sign outside the Queens Hotel advertised greenhouse heaters, cloches, insulation. All this, apparently, housed in a marquee very like the one that had been erected on the lawn of the Old Rectory for Lucy's wedding. Martha felt her mouth tighten; it probably was the same one. She thought of little Billy Tatham on the day of the wedding, standing where she had left him on the lawn. She was cross with herself for reacting so strongly and still furious with him for thinking that she might be delighted to see him. The cheek of the man! And he had carried a torch for her ever since they were both eight years old! It was ridiculous. Yet if he had behaved differently, it would have been touching too.

She skirted the guy ropes and went inside the marquee; it was gloriously warm. Grouped around the two main poles were smaller tents: an igloo, a portable shower, a conventional two-man canvas. Around the perimeter a motley of goods were arranged: the promised heaters and insulators, sleeping bags, awnings, folding chairs of every description, cookers . . . She rounded a partition to find a desk covered with brochures and a woman extolling the virtues of winter camping. The woman was dressed in a canary-yellow suit with a very short skirt, black tights and three-inch heels. In spite of a new hair-do and a great deal of make-

113

up, there was no mistaking Linda Bowles. Martha was genuinely delighted.

"My dear! Why on earth didn't you tell me you were working so close to home? I could have come to see you — we could have lunched together! Oh Linda, it's so nice to see you, you're hardly ever home these days!"

"I'm not always here, Martha." Linda deserted her post and came to hug her friend. "We've got another exhibition in Gloucester. And anyway, I don't get lunch breaks or anything like that! My boss is an absolute slave-driver!" Her laugh tinkled falsely. She was flustered. Martha felt herself being shunted behind a pyramid of air-beds, well out of sight.

"When does this job finish then?" Martha laughed too and collapsed into a deckchair. "I mean, really finish? Will you be home for Christmas?"

"I don't know." Linda sat down too; her skirt rode up alarmingly. "It could be . . . sort of . . . permanent. Actually."

Martha stopped laughing. "Well, that's great, of course. But . . . will you always be away? I mean, what about the cottage? And Jennifer?"

"I don't know. My boss is almost a slave-driver!" Linda repeated. She laughed nervously again but she did not look happy. She made a feeble attempt to pull down her skirt. "Not that I mind. Actually, I have to work this Sunday. Were you expecting me?"

"You know I was. Am. I've bought a duck. You always like my duck and orange." Martha felt almost betrayed. "Linda, surely you can come? Jennifer and Simon will be there. Please."

Linda swallowed and suddenly her eyes were full of tears. "Darling, I can't. I think .... I'm almost certain I'm in love. Properly in love. It's casual for him and if I just disappear he'll think it's the same for me. Try to understand."

"Linda." Martha stared. She was so surprised she did not know how to react. She was aware that Linda had slept with her clients in the past because Jennifer had baldly referred to it on more than one occasion. But Martha never thought about it; the Linda she knew was insouciant and frank. She said hoarsely and truthfully, "I'm sorry. I *don't* understand."

Linda waved her hands helplessly. "Like — like you and Clem. I want to be with him. Always."

Martha felt a shrinking of distaste. That Linda could possibly compare this sudden . . . passion . . . with what she and Clem had had, was almost blasphemous.

Linda said, "Forgive me, Martha. Knowing my luck, this will be temporary. But there's just a chance. I can't miss it — I mustn't miss it." She paused but Martha was still silent, her eyes intensely blue with a kind of school-marmish disapproval. "Darling, don't look like that. If you had another chance at happiness — another man came into your life — wouldn't you grasp it? Abandon everything else — every*one* else — and cling to him?"

Martha felt her lips move but no sound came out. It was so absurd, so ridiculous. Linda was younger than she was, probably forty-five now, but even so they should be past that . . . sort of thing.

She managed a single word. "No."

Linda shook her head with a kind of exasperation. "But you under*stand*! You must! Look at the way Lucy has gone with her Len! Nobody, least of all me, thought she would ever leave you. I said as much to Jennifer the night of the wedding. But barely two weeks after they got back from the Caribbean, they were off again. Can't you see? It's the same sort of thing."

Martha felt another wave of shock. She wanted to tell Linda that it wasn't the same thing at all; that Lucy and Len were man and wife and Lucy's baby was also Len's. But she could not because the sense of desertion that had plagued her all autumn was washing over her now in a tidal wave.

Linda heard a voice and stood up abruptly. Martha heard it too. Their eyes met in mutual recognition. Linda said, "Listen, Martha, I have to go. He's bringing some clients to see the new one-man job and I demonstrate it!" She tried to giggle. "That's why I'm in this get-up." She pulled again at the skirt. "He says my legs are selling more tents than the waterproof lining and inclusive ground-sheet!" She leaned down and touched Martha's shoulder. "I'm sorry, my dear. I'm really sorry."

She left abruptly and Martha could hear her greeting people. And then Billy Tatham's unmistakable Brummie accent cut through hers. "Come on then, Linda-love. Let's see you do your stuff"

Martha shrank behind the air-beds. She no longer felt almost betrayed. She felt . . . betrayed.

Linda knew that towards the end of the day her *enfant-terrible* look degenerated into something else. It had been like that when she turned up at Lucy's wedding: though Jennifer had stopped short of saying anything irrevocable, there had been small doubt what she meant. And it was the same now. When Linda scrambled out of the igloo tent to appreciative chortles she knew that her hair was not just in disarray; it was a mess. Her tights had ripped on the zipped-in groundsheet. And her make-up had doubtless slipped because for some unaccountable reason she had wept a little as she lay prone in the dark little tent. She did not know why she wept; it had something to do with Martha.

She wept again in the taxi going back to Bill's house in Pittville. He was genuinely concerned.

"Baby, what is it? I've been working you too hard, is that it? I can't let you off tomorrow — Saturday's our busiest day — but on Sunday we'll lie in bed all day. How does that sound?"

"Lovely." She gave up trying to be brave and sobbed luxuriously. "Can we have breakfast in bed?"

"Whatever you like, baby."

Bill's housekeeper had gone, leaving a casserole in the oven. The house was warm and smelled delicious. Linda revelled in it. She started immediately up the stairs to get out of the ridiculous canary-yellow suit and laddered tights. Bill was pulling off his cap and gloves and suddenly, with one of his wonderful spontaneous gestures, he put his warm hand over hers on the banister.

"Lin, you're a good egg," he said.

She smiled tremulously. "So romantic."

"Not much romance about us, is there? You said you wanted to sleep with me and I said you could. Pretty

117

basic, I suppose. But I want you to know I appreciate you. You're brilliant in bed and even more brilliant when you're selling." He leaned over and kissed her knuckles. The tears started again.

"I feel — in this get-up especially — like a tart."

"That's what I like about you." He grinned up at her cheekily. "You're my tart. My bit of crackling. My bit on the side. My —"

She wailed and he leaped up the stairs and gathered her to him.

"Sorry, baby. I was teasing. You're just right for me. You suit me down to the socks. Does that sound better?"

She said, "I suppose so. Oh Bill, I love you so much."

"I wish you wouldn't." He kissed her. "I really wish you wouldn't. I might have to marry you or something stupid." He kissed her again, laughing, but she was holding her breath and he knew it and stared into her dark eyes, serious at last. "You know I can't, Lin. I've mucked up two marriages. And if I marry again it will be to Martha Moreton."

She whispered, "She'll never marry again, Bill. You don't know how much she loved Clem." She began the kissing again. "And I don't mind about the last two marriages. I don't mind about anything. I want to marry you, Bill. Please . . . please . . ." She interspersed each word with a kiss. He pushed her ahead of him up the stairs and into the bedroom.

They made love satisfyingly and when he said, "There. Is that better?" she no longer wept. And he patted her face as if congratulating her and said, "We'll see about getting married. Give it a few more months. OK?"

118

"Oh Bill . . . " She was ecstatic. She put on a green catsuit that Jennifer had given her. She had shortened the sleeves and legs but of course it hugged her plumpish figure a little too well. Bill loved it. He kept coming around the table to hug her or tickle her or tell her that he liked his women to be ample. Ample. It sounded better than plump.

After their meal they sat on the sofa together and watched telly like any old married couple. She sighed with happiness.

"I wish it were Sunday tomorrow so we could stay in bed all day." She laughed and added unguardedly, "Then I could go to Martha's for lunch the next day!"

"Lunch? You're going to lunch with Martha?"

"No. I was. But not now."

"Lin, of course you must go. I'll come as well."

She looked up at him in horror. "Darling, we can't go together. She'd know. About us. And anyway I've told her I shall be working."

"She'd never guess we were sleeping together. I mean, it's OK for you to work for me, surely? Give her a ring and tell her you'll be coming and bringing your boss."

"I can't do that, Bill. I think . . . she knows about us."

She felt his withdrawal and knew he was angry. "You told her?"

"Of course not. She wandered into the exhibition this afternoon. I told her I couldn't come on Sunday. But I think she heard your voice."

"She still doesn't know that we're sleeping together." He was withdrawing all the time. She shrugged. He said insistently, "Why should she know?"

119

Linda could feel the tears gathering again in her throat. "Because she knows me," she said.

He said something. She did not know what it was but the tone was one of disgust. Then he got up abruptly and went into the hall. A moment later she heard the front door slam.

It was almost dark when Martha put the car into the garage and oh so carefully locked up. The frost had the lawn in a tight grip again and its crystalline sweep had been trampled as if a game of football had been played there. Her heart thumped and she had difficulty in breathing properly. But Snowball was in front of the Aga and the house was exactly as she had left it that morning. While the kettle boiled she went upstairs and stared through her bedroom window across the graveyard and around the lych-gate where she had imagined she saw figures last night. Nothing moved. The silhouettes of the trees were like cardboard cut-outs against the darkening sky. She gave a small sob and went downstairs again to try to reconstruct some kind of normality to her life. The sense of everything slipping into an abyss was ridiculous and, of course, had its beginnings in Lucy's departure last August. The fact that Miss Darcy was getting better and had managed to make friends with two local children who might or might not be trespassing in the garden of the Old Rectory was — surely — a good thing. And if the children were playing on her grass . . . well, they were children and children did that kind of thing. That was nothing. What was something, and yet should not be something at all, was the fact that Linda Bowles was sleeping with Billy Tatham. It wasn't important . . . was it? Linda was not so much promiscuous as . . . kind. She couldn't say no. If anyone wanted to sleep with her she would deem it churlish to say no. Martha knew that — had always known it. But this was different. Billy Tatham made it different. Not that Linda knew that — she had no idea that Billy was someone from Martha's past . . . or had he told her? Had he described their eight-year-old encounter behind the bicycle sheds?

Martha groaned aloud and put her head in her hands. If Linda knew, it would make the affair even more sordid. She gripped a handful of curls until her head ached. She began to wonder what was happening to her. It was some kind of relief when the doorbell ground out its clockwork ring. She almost flew to answer it, praying it would be Denise Coupland. Or even Mrs Rector, Terrible Truda Goodwin. But there was no-one there. Faint giggles came from the direction of the lych-gate: she closed the door quietly hoping Tansy and Pickle — or whatever their ghastly names were — would think no-one was in. Not that it mattered. Nothing *really* mattered.

Then a bright thought occurred and she picked up the telephone in the hall and began to dial the complicated set of digits which would connect her with Lucy. It should be about four o'clock in Santo Domingo. Perhaps Lucy would not be there because she had been helping Len with his interviews and if she had gone with him today . . . Her voice came across the line as clear as a bell. Martha lifted her own voice in response.

"Darling! I had to ring. How are you? What's the weather like? Are you uncomfortable?"

"Mummy, how lovely." Lucy sounded sleepy. "To wake up to you — almost as good as being at home. How is Snowie? Tell him I'd love a cuddle right now."

"Why are you in bed? Aren't you well?"

"We're taking a siesta. We're having tea brought up in a moment." Lucy gurgled irrelevantly. "I'm very well. Wonderfully well now that I've finished with that wretched morning sickness. What's happening at home? What's the weather like?"

Such a typically English question. Martha told her about the frost and the nursery display in Cavendish House and the blackened chrysanths. Lucy described the village she'd visited the day before. It sounded more primitive than Martha had imagined.

"Take care, won't you?" she begged anxiously. "I read up everything I can about the Republic and it all sounds so volatile."

"Volatile?" Lucy was giggling again. "Yes, I suppose you could call it —" She gave a little gasp and Martha suddenly knew what was happening. It was natural, after all. Len was her husband.

She said, "That's all right then, darling. I must go. Look after yourself. I'll ring again next week." She replaced the receiver just as the doorbell rang again.

She whipped to the door; she would catch them this time and give them a piece of her mind. If they went around the village doing this sort of thing there were old people older than she was — who would be frightened out of their wits.

She flung open the door. Billy Tatham stood on the step. He wore a cap with flaps, his greatcoat came

122

almost to the ground and his gloves were the kind motor cyclists wore. He looked ridiculous. But somehow she was glad to see him. He had come to explain — about Linda perhaps. Once she understood what was happening she would be able to accept it, surely?

She said stupidly, "I didn't hear your car."

"I left it in the road. In case you sent me away again." He looked at her. His grey eyes were almost black in the darkness, the lashes pale, as if frosted. She felt that sense of familiarity again.

He cleared his throat. "There were a couple of kids hanging about. I sent them packing. Was that OK?"

Her lips moved woodenly. "Quite OK."

He grinned suddenly. "It's good to see you. I've been frantic driving here, knowing that we've got to talk . . . wondering what to say. And now . . . all I know is that it is good to see you."

She made a movement with her hands; it was a hopeless movement. It said that she could no longer cope with any of this.

He said, "It's a mess, isn't it? And of course, as usual, it's my fault. Can I come in?"

She looked at him for a long moment, then, reluctantly, she stood aside.

CHAPTER
SEVEN

Martha was aware, as she led Billy Tatham through the icy hall and into the kitchen, that something strange was happening to her. She thought afterwards — some time afterwards — that it was as if she became two people. The real Martha, reserved, dignified, wrapped in the security of widowhood and church work, wanted to shut the door in Billy Tatham's face. Would have done. But, as she was about to do just that, another Martha who was vulnerable and frightened and very lonely and also . . . yes, just a bit curious, opened the door wider and stood to one side; then closed it and walked towards the kitchen.

Billy Tatham followed, not removing gloves or the absurd cap. So, thank God, he did not intend to stay.

The real Martha would have stood by the table and asked him his business. But for some reason, the other Martha sat in a chair by the Aga, picked up Snowball and held him close. She said nothing at all. That was odd in itself.

Billy — whose face beneath the peak of his cap was strangely unaltered from that of the boy who had fumblingly kissed her forty-two years ago — stood with his back to the heat.

"Bloody cold in here, Martha. Haven't you got any heat besides this thing?"

"No." She wasn't going to offer excuses. Clem should have left a tidy sum, but in fact there was a small pension from the practice, and the house. And the house was a liability. None of Billy Tatham's business.

He said, "Money's that tight, is it? Why don't you sell up? Get a flat in Cheltenham. Join a bridge club."

She did not meet his eyes. "Because I don't want to," she said.

"Fair enough. I have to admit this place suits you."

There was a long silence. She could feel him looking at the top of her head. She hadn't combed her hair or anything since returning from her disastrous shopping trip. She thought that he was probably sorry for her. Linda with her craziness was his type; poor Martha Moreton with all her heavy — and unnecessary — responsibilities, was not. Snowball tried to free himself from her clutching arms; she had to let him go. She sat there looking at her empty lap, feeling suddenly stripped of all protection. A new Martha, no preconceptions, no guide-lines.

Quite suddenly his face was on a level with hers. He was crouching on the floor, peering at her. She recoiled against the back of her chair.

"It's all right, Mar . . . all right." He ripped off his gloves and hat and threw them somewhere; took her hands. His were warm, hers were cold. All she could think was: Who was Mar? He said, "I know how it seems to you. Sleeping with your best friend. All I can tell you is it doesn't mean a thing. My wives — I've got

125

two of 'em somewhere" — he smiled briefly — "they didn't mean anything either. I've always loved you, Mar. Always."

So she was Mar. Not Martha. Not Marty. Mar. A nasty diminutive.

She whispered, "Don't call me that."

"All right, my darling. Just say you understand."

"I don't understand anything any more. Please go. Please. It's been an awful day and —"

"Why? Because you found out about Linda and me? You must know about Linda. So it was me. You felt I was being unfaithful —"

The real Martha raised her head. "Don't be ridiculous! My god, I don't *know* you! What are you talking about?"

"I told Linda how I felt about you. I assumed she would pass it on."

"Linda has never mentioned your name!"

"Ah . . . and yet you are still miserable. So you must have felt something."

"I'm having trouble with local children. Playing in my garden. When I got back the lawn had been trampled and someone rang the doorbell and ran off. That's all. I'm grateful to you for getting rid of them!" She should have told him to leave again. But his eyes were six inches from hers and she could not.

He held her gaze for perhaps half a minute; it seemed like eternity. Then he withdrew slightly, released her hands and unbuttoned his greatcoat. It joined the heap by the table. Snowball began to knead it with great intensity.

She said, tremulously, what she should have said that half-minute before. "I think you had better leave, Billy."

He flashed a delighted smile at her. "Marty, honey. Nobody calls me Billy any more! You think of me as Billy, do you?"

"I don't think of you at all. And please don't call me Marty!"

He spread his hands. "Why on earth —"

She snapped, "It's what my husband called me."

He was silent again, staring at her. She felt heat rise from neck to face. At last he said quietly, "Martha . . . are you frigid?"

"How dare you!" She made to get up, but he was blocking her way and as she relapsed he moved closer. Her skirt rode up like Linda's. His hands were on her waist; he was wearing a double-knit sweater. She could smell Linda's perfume. She said hysterically, "Are you going to rape me?"

He laughed. "Do you want me to?"

"Please — let me go —"

"I am not going to rape you, Martha. I simply want to kiss you. That's all." He was still smiling, in one way entirely non-threatening; in another very much so. He said, "You've never relaxed and let me kiss you properly, Marty. I think you owe me one kiss. Don't you?" His body was against hers and she could not see past his bulldog head and the treacherous new Martha was saying — as Linda Bowles must say so often — what's in a kiss? If he's been dreaming of a kiss all these years then surely the least you can do . . . So, at first, she simply waited for it to be over.

Jennifer was thankful to drive past the church and see the dark bulk of the row of cottages before her. There was a strange car parked outside the Old Rectory. It was a BMW and the same colour as the Traverses', so probably George and Toto were visiting Martha. She felt a sudden pang as that thought led her inevitably to Len.

She said, "Thank God we're there. One thing about the cottage, we can get it warm in about ten minutes. My God, it's freezing tonight."

Simon had been holding on to the parcel shelf since they left the city. He relaxed and sat back in the passenger seat. "It's great having a country cottage while your mother is working in Cheltenham, but I wish it wasn't such a bloody hairy drive."

"It's not," Jennifer said briefly.

"It is from where I'm sitting."

"Are you going to moan and groan all through another weekend?" Jennifer deliberately swerved up to the footpath and grinned when he gasped. "Makes me wonder if our fling has come to an end."

"You won't say that when we're in bed." Simon got out of the car with alacrity, took the keys from her and opened up. He unloaded the two weekend cases while she went through to the kitchen flicking switches. The cottage was as they had left it last weekend, so Linda hadn't been home. She would not have been able to resist tidying up. Jennifer smiled as she filled the kettle. It was good to have Linda out of the way; it meant she could use the cottage whenever she wanted; and Martha was more especially hers. Without either Lucy or Linda, Martha had seemed to rely on her more and more. And on Sunday, when they went to lunch, she hoped to be able to make an announcement. She looked in the mirror above the sink. She was looking all right; the wild gypsy look — only just contained — was very evident.

Simon said behind her, "The cold weather suits you, baby. You're sparkling."

He paid her compliments for one reason only. She said, "Sparkling or not, I need a cup of tea."

"I don't."

"Right. I'll use just one tea-bag."

He growled in his throat. "Are you trying to drive me mad?"

She did not reply. He stood behind her and took the shoulders of her coat and slid it to the ground. She put a tea-bag into a mug and poured on boiling water. He slid off her suit jacket and she stirred her tea-bag gently and then threw it in the bin. He began to unbutton her blouse and when that joined the other clothes, she reached in the fridge and got the milk and sniffed it suspiciously.

He said huskily, "It's long-life. It'll be OK." He unhooked her bra.

She stood there drinking her tea, apparently not noticing that he was undressing her. When she had finished, she rinsed the mug slowly and put it on the draining rack and then turned to him.

"You're a devil," he whispered. "A she-devil."

"Because I want ordinary things? Like marriage and a home and children?"

"Oh, not that again."

"Yes. That again."

"I'm surprised you don't withhold your bloody favours until I propose, then!"

"That's an idea." She leaned down and reached for her clothes. He grabbed her wrists and kissed her. She stood quite still.

He lifted his head. "For God's sake, Jen! We're not like that! We're great in bed but out of it all we do is bicker!"

"Only because you're so set against a normal life."

"What is normal? I'm male and you're female and together we're the universe! If that's not normal then I'd still prefer it to DIY and telly every night —"

"Don't be absurd. It wouldn't be like that! You'd still be male and I'd still be female!"

"We'd have to domesticate ourselves. House training. Tidying. Laundry. Food. I love you because you're mad and wild and free and —"

"You love me? You've never said that before."

"Is that what you want? Christ, Jen — I love you, I love you, I love you, I love you, I love —" She silenced him with her mouth, melting against him because if he loved her it was one step nearer the announcement on Sunday. And in the silence of their kiss, they heard a key in the door and the next minute Linda stood in the narrow hall.

There was a moment of freeze-frame and then Jennifer swore loudly and grabbed her clothes all anyhow and stood behind Simon. Simon stammered, "Mrs Bowles, we didn't know you were coming home!"

And Linda, recovering herself, lugged a bag through, slammed the door shut with her foot and started up the stairs.

"Sorry," she called back in an artificially lilting voice. "Carry on. I'm going straight to bed anyway. Just carry on."

Jennifer rammed her forehead into the back of Simon's neck and continued to swear quietly but with emphasis. He turned with difficulty and took her in his arms.

"Darling Jen. I'm sorry. Really. If we'd both had a cup of tea like you wanted —"

"Exactly!" She turned her fury on him. "We've been in the house ten minutes — the car is probably still hot out there — and she comes in and finds me naked! My God, she'll think I take after her — she'll think I'm worse than her! She'll never let me forget this; every time we have a row, which is every time we see each other, she's going to bring this up —"

"Jen, don't exaggerate. She's great. She'll laugh about it tomorrow, you see."

She knew he was right but she ranted on for another few minutes until he said, "Look, d'you want me to go? I'll take your car and bring it back tomorrow. Take you and your ma out to lunch at the —"

"You know bloody well we're going to Martha's for lunch tomorrow! That's probably why Linda decided to come home tonight! And you've got to be there so don't try and get out of it!"

"Darling, that's on Sunday. Now just calm down . . ." He tried to kiss her and she shoved him away furiously.

"Go and light the gas fire in the front room. I'll make tea and take a cup up to Linda."

"That sounds sensible. Everything will he all right, baby. In fact, already it's beginning to seem —"

"Don't you dare say it's beginning to seem funny, Simon Moreton! You don't know anything about a mother-and-daughter relationship, so just shut up!"

He disappeared and she could hear him moving about in the little sitting room, doubtless tidying up. She seemed to remember that last weekend they had broken an ornament. She got the dustpan and brush from under the sink, opened the sitting-room door, pushed it through and closed the door again. She made the tea, dressed hurriedly, poured a cup and climbed the stairs. Linda's door was closed. She tapped on it.

"I'm dressed and decent. Can I come in?" She injected humour into her voice, though she still found the whole situation unfunny.

There was a sound from the bedroom and she opened the door. Linda was sitting on the far side of the bed; her head was in her hands. She was weeping as if her heart would break.

Jennifer scraped past the wardrobe and put the tea on the dressing table. She said roughly, "Heavens, it wasn't that bad, was it?"

Linda shook her head violently. Her hair had been chestnut-brown for the past few weeks, glossy as a conker. It looked somehow dull and greasy in the light from the forty-watt bulb overhead. She drew her knees up until her heels were on the bed, then she clutched herself into a concertina shape and gasped out a sob. The tears streamed mascara down her face; she looked choked with tears. Jennifer was anxious.

"Linda. Ma. What the hell's the matter? Come on. Speak to me." She too sat on the bed facing her mother. She thought suddenly: She's small. She's so damned small and vulnerable.

Linda's forehead scraped across her knees as she shook her head again. "You — wouldn't understand —" she gasped.

"I don't care. Whether I understand or not has got nothing to do with it. Spill the beans." Jennifer lifted her voice commandingly. "Now!"

Linda lifted her head, her face looked drowned. "I love him, Jen. Really love him. Not like the others. I just . . . love him. You can't understand."

Jennifer stared at the ravaged face. She said slowly, "No, I can't. And I don't want to if it does this to you."

"It's not his fault. No-one's fault. He told me at the outset that it was Martha . . . I told him then that I didn't care. It didn't matter. I never told Martha that I knew him. That I was working for him. That he'd told me how he felt about her. When she . . . found out . . . this afternoon, I could tell she was — you know — upset." Linda moaned and squeezed her eyes shut. "Shattered. Not upset. Shattered. And when *he* found out — tonight — that she knew . . . he just went." Her voice rose slightly and then her head fell back on to her knees and she began making horrible keening noises.

Jennifer straightened her back and stared down at her mother's tousled hair. At last she said slowly, "This is the tent man, is it? We're talking about the tent man."

Linda nodded, swallowed a sob and said, "Bill. His name is Bill Tatham. He knew Martha at school. He's carried a torch for her ever since."

"That's why you haven't been home for so long. Maureen got you this job with Tatham and you fell for him and —"

"It wasn't quite like that." Suddenly Linda sounded weary, exhausted, finished. She looked up and controlled her sobs somehow. "I met him the Monday after the wedding. He came to find Martha and she'd gone to see George and Toto and . . . I just fell for him. And he knew it." She looked at her daughter, tumbled and beautiful. "Oh Jen. I should have told Martha. I'm a rotten friend. She rang and asked me to go and stay with her at Tewkesbury — she was feeling awful and she turned to me. I could have told her about Bill looking for her. But I didn't. And when things settled down I saw that Tatham's were going to do a big exhibition of their stuff. In Cheltenham. So I rang Bill and offered my services." She tried to smile. Her chin wobbled. "I took it from there."

Jennifer said without rancour, "You idiot."

"I've lost her as well as Bill, haven't I?"

"You don't know that. Let's see what happens on Sunday. Remember we're going to lunch?"

"It's too late, Jen. As the taxi brought me past the Old Rectory, his car was outside. He's been with her since about eight o'clock, I would guess. She hasn't thrown him out. So they're talking."

Jennifer remembered the BMW. She said simply, "Ah."

134

Linda swallowed convulsively again and tried to sound rueful. "Quite." Her voice broke and she crumpled back onto her knees.

Suddenly, involuntarily, Jennifer scooped her into her long arms and held her close. "Listen, Ma. Just listen. You've been a stupid idiot. First of all falling for him quite so hard, and secondly not being open about the whole thing with Martha — Christ, she wouldn't have cared! She'll always be married to Clem and that's that! You went against your own bloody stupid character, didn't you? You've always been up front — that's why the neighbours disapprove! They wouldn't care if they didn't know! Your honesty has been the bane of my life." She rocked the bundle that was her mother back and forth, trying to inject a laugh into her voice. "And now, when it didn't matter, you decided to practise deceit! And you don't know how to do it!"

Linda stopped clutching her knees and clutched Jennifer's waist. "It's done now. Martha didn't like it when she thought I had no idea that Bill was her old school-friend. Now she knows that I've kept it from her all this time — deliberately — oh Jen, it looks as if I was trying to *steal* him!"

Jennifer tightened her hold and said sternly, "Now just listen. Whatever they talked about, it doesn't matter. Because at the end of it all, Martha will send him away. OK? You know that, don't you?" A barely perceptible nod came from the head in her neck. She went on, "He might be annoyed with you for a moment. But, knowing you, you've made yourself practically indispensable, haven't you?"

The muffled voice said, "I've got quite a talent for talking his clients into buying his stuff, I suppose."

"So he's going to ring you and tell you to come back. And then . . . well, he knows Marty isn't ever going to get married, so they'll eventually decide —"

But Linda was shaking her head again and the sobs were choking her throat. "Jen, face facts. You and me, we don't get married. Men like us a lot, but they don't ask us to get married." The sobs broke out of her and she wept into Jennifer's shoulder with a kind of despair.

Jennifer kept hold of her and stared over her head at the bleakly lit bedroom. She thought of the ghastly Martin who had been one in a long line of "experiences". She thought of Len . . . Len had been her sort, they could have married and fought and made love for the rest of their lives. But he hadn't considered her wife material. He had chosen Lucy who was pure and had morals and integrity. And now there was Simon Moreton. Martha's cousin-in-law.

She waited until Linda had cried herself out, then she released herself gently and held the teacup while her mother drank.

"I'm going to fetch a hot-water bottle and another drink and some aspirins. Go to bed, Ma. Sleep on it. It won't seem so bad in the morning."

She went downstairs into the kitchen. Simon appeared, chastened and contrite.

"It's really cosy in the parlour. Is your mother coming down? I've cleared up."

"She's not well. I'm doing her a hot-water bottle. Won't be long." She filled the bottle carefully and

136

screwed down the top. "Simon. I have to talk to you. I wasn't going to . . . but I must."

"OK. But if she's staying upstairs, we won't talk for too long. I want to make love to you on the rug. And on the sofa. And then on the rug again —"

"Just shut up," she advised and ran upstairs. Her mother was already in bed, hiccoughing on her tears like a child. Jennifer leaned over her. "Talk about role reversal." She slid the bottle between the sheets. "We'll get our own back, Ma. In the end. Just you see. Remember, it was you who caught Lucy's wedding bouquet!"

Linda managed a shaky smile. "But I passed it on to Martha," she whispered.

"And it was intended for me." Unexpectedly Jennifer bent and kissed her mother's forehead. "We'll get married, Ma. Both of us. Just you wait and see."

She went back downstairs. She was fighting for something now; she hardly knew what had changed, but something had. It was like a crusade; she was going to marry Simon for her mother's sake as well as her own. She opened the door to the little sitting room and went immediately to the mantelpiece. She leaned one arm along its length and stared down into the pseudo fire. Everything was so neat; Simon had polished the candlesticks which were ranged either end. The toy dog and cat were in their basket — she remembered throwing them at him last weekend and they had hit the picture of the Stag at Bay and skewed it; that was now straight. She smiled slightly; he was trying to please her. And then she saw the whisky bottle by the fireplace behind the cat basket. It was almost empty.

He said hoarsely, "God, you look wonderful. Wanton and wonderful. Did I tear the buttons off your blouse? I'll buy you a new one. Come here."

She said, "No. Sorry, Simon, but no."

"So you *have* decided to withhold sexual favours until I ask you to marry me?" He was laughing, slipping off the sofa and onto his knees, clutching her skirt, pleading, mocking her. She could have kicked him except that her mood was now ice-cold. "All right!" he cried. "You win! Marry me! Marry me tomorrow but sleep with me tonight!" He started to kiss the back of her knee; slobbering, laughing.

She walked away from him and he fell forward onto his hands and knees.

She said, "Simon, I told you. I want to talk to you. This is serious. Just listen. Don't say anything. And after I've finished you can take the car and go."

"What are you talking about? Jen, come on. You know you'll give in eventually. For God's sake, don't make me go through this charade any longer —"

She said levelly, "You told me I've been irritable. You were right. I've been trying to force myself to have an abortion. I'm pregnant. And I know what it's like to be brought up without a father. So I thought: OK, he's not interested in domesticity. I'll get rid of it. But something happened tonight. My mother . . . said something. And I thought: I want this baby. It's mine. I'm going to have it." She went to the window and looked out. Next door the two small girls who lived there were running around with a torch. She wondered whether they'd been there last weekend. She closed the curtains with a jerk and turned to face Simon. He was still on hands and knees in front of the fire.

He said slowly, "Is this some kind of a trick, Jen? Tell me you're lying, for God's sake —"

"Oh, shut up Simon. Just clear off, why don't you? I don't need you any more."

"But you're on the pill —"

"So I am! Isn't that a miracle then? Almost as good as a virgin birth!" She gave a sound not unlike a sob. "Just get up and go. You look ridiculous kneeling there."

He pushed himself onto his heels. "All right. If that's what you want. When shall I see you again? I'll bring the car back tomorrow, shall I? And then I can have a taxi back and drive over on Sunday for this lunch at Martha's place."

"You're not listening, are you?" She leaned forward and enunciated exaggeratedly. "I am keeping the baby, Simon. It was a choice between you. I chose you at first. Now I am choosing the baby. So goodbye."

"For always?" He was incredulous.

"Oh yes."

"But . . . we've been together now since the summer. Dammit, Jen, four months. I've never been with anyone as long as that before!"

"And probably not again."

He stood up slowly. "Are you serious?"

"Oh yes."

"Will you be . . . all right?"

She grinned. "Oh yes."

He went to the door. "Listen. I'll see you tomorrow. When I bring the car back."

She shrugged, went to her bag and threw him the keys. He hovered helplessly for another half-minute and then left. She stayed where she was until she heard the car start up and move away. Then she went into the kitchen and made yet more tea, and after she'd drunk it, she slung her jacket over her shoulders and ran up the road until she could see the gates of the Old Rectory and the BMW still parked there.

"You . . . bastard!" she whispered. And went back to the house to wait. At ten-thirty the phone rang and it was Simon. She smiled, well satisfied.

"Jen. The thing about our rows is . . . it's great making up."

She replaced the receiver and waited again. Next time he blurted, "Don't put the phone down. Please wait."

"I'm here," she replied coldly.

"I asked you a question and you didn't answer."

"I don't remember —"

"I asked you to marry me. I asked you about three times. I was on my knees like you're supposed to be —"

"You were drunk and you wanted me to get drunk with you and make love on the rug. So you proposed."

"I meant it. Jen, will you marry me?"

"No."

He was outraged. "I'm too far away to expect you to satisfy my carnal lusts! I'm asking you — and I'm sober now — to marry me!"

"And I'm saying no."

"You bitch! What d'you want? D'you want it in writing? An engagement ring —"

She replaced the receiver and when it rang again, she picked up the phone and immediately dropped it back. Then she took it off the hook.

During the night she heard Linda crying once. And in the morning she woke to find her standing by the bed with a tray of tea.

"You did it for me last night, so I thought I'd do it for you."

"You're looking better." Jennifer struggled up in the bed. "Thank God for that. You know that what I said made sense."

Linda said, "Yes, I'm much better. My old self, really. Did Simon leave last night? Was it because of me?"

"No. I sent him packing. He got on my nerves."

"Oh well, he'll be back."

Jennifer laughed and sipped her tea. "He certainly will," she agreed.

Linda went to the window and drew the curtains. She was dressed in her jeans and an enormous sweater that made her look smaller than ever. She said, "My God. Those girls next door! They've made a tree house or something in that old beech tree. Almost as if they're trying to see into your room." She turned. "You keep your curtains well drawn, don't you, Jen? I should hate to get complaints from the mother. She's rather peculiar."

"Don't worry about it. We'll soon be the most respectable family in the village!"

Linda smiled. "Oh Jen. Don't kid yourself. I went for a walk while the kettle was boiling. Bill's car is still outside the Old Rectory."

Jennifer was surprised; shocked. "So he spent the night with Martha? Surely not! She'd consider she was being unfaithful to Clem if she slept with anyone else."

Linda shrugged and turned to go downstairs. Jennifer said, "Ma, it's like I said last night. We'll both be married — mark my words!" She started to laugh. "We *will* go to the ball!"

Linda did not say a word.

CHAPTER
EIGHT

Lucy could not pinpoint the transition between feeling sick and then better, then very well, then not quite so well. The morning sickness was bearable, especially as they had had the stress of packing and making arrangements to live somewhere else in the space of two weeks. Flying back to the Caribbean so soon after leaving it had made her feet and ankles swell alarmingly, her ears so painful she had been partially deaf for twenty-four hours after landing, and aggravated the sickness to the point where the local doctor thought it could be food poisoning or even gastroenteritis. She and Len had known better of course, but they had been scared even so. Len knew in his heart that if they lost the baby he would feel a terrible sense of personal guilt. Lucy could have gone back to the Old Rectory and waited for him there. She would have been happy enough with her mother and he could have wangled a couple of flights home; certainly he could have managed it at Christmas.

And then Lucy had a surge of health that took them both by surprise. As October brought the hurricanes across the Pacific and into the tropics, they seemed to blow new energy into her small, sturdy frame. When she talked to her mother on the telephone she no longer had to pretend all was well; she would begin an anecdote and then say, "Too long. I'll write it down. It's absolutely fascinating out here, Mummy. And just outside the capital, there are still really primitive villages . . . No, not witch doctors, darling. That's Haiti . . . No, we're not going to Haiti. The political correspondent is there. I'm talking about villages in the mountains — no roads, no railway . . . Well, we use the jeep, Mummy . . . No, it's not *that* bumpy! And anyway Len is going to start on the mining settlements soon and they have roads and railways . . . Mummy, stop *worrying*!"

She felt wonderful. She and Len were closer than ever; she was able to be with him all the time, taking notes, acting as a sounding board for him to try out his questions, gauging responses, picking up on what he called "the vibes". And although she was pale and blonde, so obviously from another culture, she was also small and unthreatening. Her intuition served her well; she knew when her ready smile was not working and she must step back into the jeep. She could usually spot the one woman in the village who was curious about her; curious enough to cross the divide and return the smile. When they knew she was pregnant, the fences invariably came down.

Len was surprised. "This thing about babies. Is it the universal female bond or something?"

"Well, of course! Idiot!" She laughed at him. They were in bed taking a siesta, enclosed in an old-fashioned mosquito net. Very soon the maid would bring them a

144

cup of undrinkable tea and they would have to get up. In the next room of the hacienda-type hotel, the cameraman's snores were still very audible. Lucy recalled how embarrassed she had been only a few months before at the possibility of being heard through the floor of the hotel in Barbados. Now she hardly ever thought about it. The mosquito net gave them an absurd sense of privacy.

"You're definitely my status symbol," Len chuckled, his hand cupping the slight bump of her abdomen. "Whenever I mention that my assistant is also my wife and that she is pregnant, I get respect!"

"So I've noticed. It's a very macho society." She rolled on to her side and kissed his chin. "Don't let them brain-wash you, darling, will you?"

He laughed and took her in his arms and began to kiss her. The phone rang on the bedside table and he groaned his disgust and fumbled for it through the muslin. "Yes . . . Yes put her through." He made a face and passed over the receiver. "It's your mother. She chooses her moments."

She grinned, her hand over the mouthpiece. "You thought we were going to make love! In the afternoon!" She spoke to Martha. It was bitterly cold there; the first frost. The chrysanths were blackened. She had to force herself to imagine it. "Are you all right, Mummy?" Did Martha sound "all right"? What was all right? Len started to nibble her ear lobe and she moved the phone to the other side. His hand was massaging her stomach, pushing up to her breasts. She giggled inappropriately and Martha said she must go. Len took the receiver from her and replaced it somehow and they clung to each other as if tomorrow they might be parted for ever.

Christmas brought a wonderful surprise. George and Toto were coming over, stopping for a week with the Gampies and then bringing them to Santo Domingo. Lucy went to meet the small Island plane by herself because Len and the cameraman were editing the previous day's film. The airfield was by no means international, the buildings more than iron-roofed sheds; but there were plenty of people meeting the plane and a cheer went up as it landed bumpily and taxied towards them.

It was wonderful to see the four of them clambering gingerly down the steps. George and Toto she felt she knew quite well by now, but the Gampies, met just once last July, were somehow just as familiar. They tried to embrace her in unison and broke apart laughing. Toto came in at her alone.

"A-a-ah, my special daughter!" There were tears in the brown eyes. "How are you? How is the baby? Is Lennie looking after you properly? I felt" — she looked round at George — "we both felt he practically kidnapped you, child!"

Lucy registered surprise at the back of her head. She hugged Toto hard. "I am so well, I can't believe it. And I am so lucky, Toto, to be able to work with him — we are never apart. It's wonderful!"

Floss nodded wisely. "We are the same. Isn't that so, Henry?"

Henry was anxious about the luggage. "The presents, Flossie. We had them in the pink bag —"

146

"They're here, Papa." Toto sorted out a plastic bag from the many dangling from her wrist. "The rest will be in the customs shed. Let's go."

They trooped across the weedy tarmac, unconsciously grouping around Lucy as if protecting her. She had never known a large family and enjoyed the feeling of solidarity. George was trying to get a word in past Toto's exclamations and Henry's continued worrying.

"Your mother sends love, Lucy. We wanted her to come with us so much, but the house is something of a responsibility. She does not want to leave it."

Lucy nodded, unsurprised but regretful. She knew her mother could have found someone to look after the house. It was lack of money that kept her at home. "It's always been like that. Even when Dad . . . but especially since he died. Mummy and I sort of took it in turns to leave the place."

Toto spoke over her shoulder. "George! You're not worrying our girl with all that stuff about the kids, are you?"

"Certainly not!" George looked at Lucy and saw her expression. "Now I'll have to explain, of course!" He rolled his eyes humorously and said, "Don't look like that, Lucy. Nothing to worry about. A new family in the neighbourhood. Twin girls who are a bit rumbustious. I think the Reverend's wife has had to have a word."

Lucy laughed, relieved. Her mother was good with children and the thought of Truda Goodwin having a word conjured up memories.

They piled themselves and their luggage into the jeep. Henry and George were practically buried beneath bags and cases. Floss and Toto squeezed into the front alongside Lucy.

"Apart from these children, you're sure Mummy's all right?" she asked, recalling suddenly that phone call in November when Martha had sounded strangely tense.

"She's better than ever," Toto assured her. And from the back seat George bellowed, "She's blooming, Lucy! In fact if it was anyone else I'd say she was in love!" Lucy wanted to say that her mother would always be in love; but it sounded sentimental even inside her head, so she said nothing.

The two weeks went all too quickly. On Christmas morning, Lucy telephoned the Old Rectory at eight o'clock, calculating that morning service would have finished and her mother would be dispensing drinks in the living-room. There was no reply, so she drank some orange juice and she and Toto swam in the warm sea and lay on the hotel's private beach while Len and George cooked flying fish over a charcoal grill, instructed by Floss. Lucy telephoned before and after the meal and there was still no answer from her mother. In the early evening they went to a special church service which reminded Lucy of her Sunday School days with its simplicity and total faith. The priest was from the mountains, brought up and trained by missionaries. When they sang the familiar carols, holding hands and swaying to the music, he stayed on his knees, praying for all of them, a gaunt figure in front of the crib. Afterwards he joined in the party outside the church and drank rum until he keeled over.

148

"Where is the dignity in that?" Toto asked, outraged. "Where is the reverence?"

Lucy said, "He's drunk on glory. I think his Lord will understand."

Len gathered him up as if he were a child and carried him to the small house next to the church. Lucy felt a renewed surge of love for this man who could so naturally care for others.

"He'll be all right," he said, emerging some time later. He's brought most of it back up and he's sleeping like a child now."

"This would not happen at home," Toto maintained.

But Floss shook her head. "I think it would. There's a church over St Agnes' parish where the priest takes a service in the sea once a month. Now that *is* peculiar."

"Some kind of baptismal thing, though, Ma." Toto shook her head. "And I meant back home in England."

"Ah well. England is perfect, of course," Floss said huffily.

Lucy walked between the two women. "Let's go back to the hotel and have some supper sitting at a table," she suggested. "The barbecue food had a job finding a way down to my stomach!" They all laughed and she went on, "There's such joy in the way he got drunk. Didn't you feel that, Toto? Floss? It wouldn't go down very well anywhere else, but here . . . it did."

The other two were silent for a moment, then Floss leaned forward to address her daughter. "I reckon we're lucky having this girl in our family, Toto. Don't you?"

Toto said quietly, "I do, Ma." She hugged Lucy's arm. "I do."

Lucy tried again to get the Old Rectory. She wanted to tell Martha some of the amazing differences — and the even more amazing similarities — between her usual Christmases and this one. There was still no reply.

"She should be there now." Lucy frowned above the receiver. "It's midnight at home. Mummy is never out after eleven."

"She's with Linda and Jennifer, I expect," Len said.

George nodded. "Jennifer's young man might have invited them all to one of his hotels. Martha was saying they're getting married on New Year's Day. Enormous do apparently. Pity you have to miss it, Lucy."

Lucy had had a solitary letter from Jennifer saying she had "brought Simon up to scratch" but after their last conversation at Linda's cottage, Lucy had not wanted to think about Jennifer very much.

Len, who also did not wish to think of Jennifer, changed the subject abruptly. "Dad, I'm going down to Puerto Plata on Thursday. They're shipping out some gold. I want to interview dockers, the captain, those sorts of people. Then at the weekend I thought of going to Azua. The new oil well. Your sort of thing, probably."

"I'd like that. What about Henry?"

"Count me out," Henry said, shaking his head. "I'll have to catch up on my rest."

"We'll all be doing that." Toto nodded at Lucy. "You'll have to start taking it easy. You're looking tired tonight."

Lucy shook her head. "It's been a long day." She looked at her watch: just past eight o'clock. She laughed apologetically.

150

"Bed," Len commanded and picked her up as he had picked up the priest that evening. He held her close going upstairs as if she were a child again. As if he were standing in for Martha. When he laid her on the bed he kissed her forehead and then slid the straps of her dress from her shoulders.

She said, "Len. I'm sorry. I am tired. Seriously."

He smiled. "Because you can't get hold of your mother? Grow up, Lucy. She's at a party. Raving it up with the poor old Rev."

He was teasing but there was something quite shocking to her in the way he spoke. She began to excuse herself as if she'd done something wrong.

"I've got a feeling. I can't explain it." She let him slide the dress down her legs and onto the floor. "She knows I would telephone on Christmas Day. She would wait in."

"Cut the umbilical cord, my darling. For God's sake."

She opened her eyes wide. "Do you think . . . ?"

"Yes. I do. You're so quiet about it, the two of you, but you're obsessed with each other. It's not natural."

She was astonished. And hurt. "You've never said anything like this before, Len." She stopped him unhooking her bra. "Wait. Let's talk about this. I thought you understood that Mummy and me have been especially close since Daddy died."

"Of course I understand, my darling. Forget it. I wish I hadn't spoken. It's just that your sudden anxiety is illogical."

"But you said yourself that my intuition *is* illogical. But it proves itself right. Time after time."

"That's when you're dealing with strangers, sweetie. You get on with them. They like you, they trust you."

"No, it's more than that. I *have* got intuition. And my intuition is telling me something is wrong with my mother!"

"Oh, please, Lucy. Just forget your bloody intuition for half an hour. Let me make mad passionate love to you and put everything else out of your head —"

"No!" She sat up on the bed, clutching her bra like some outraged maiden. She felt ridiculous but determined. "No, Len. We can't solve all our problems by making love. Sorry, but that's how it is. You've got to accept what I am saying whether you find it unreasonable or not. It — it's a form of trust —"

He said something unpleasant and she gasped as if he had hit her.

"I meant that, Luce. You're acting like a tease. Leading me on. That's what they call women who do that sort of thing."

She looked at him, her face white. Then, slowly, she reached around and undid her bra. He lay on top of her; she had never been conscious of his weight before; now she was. He kissed her very deliberately and she felt tears in her throat because the kiss was empty. She whispered, "Len . . . I'm sorry. I'm sorry. I love you." And later, "Len, please love me."

When he rolled off her she reached up to kiss him and though he returned the kiss she knew he was still angry.

He said, "We're all right. We're all right, Lucy. Stop crying now. We're all *right*."

152

He tucked her body under the thin sheet and adjusted the mosquito net; she waited for him to take her in his arms and cradle her into a forgiving sleep. But he went into the bathroom and she heard him under the shower, and then through the opaque curtains she watched him dress and leave the room.

She swallowed her tears somehow and slid awkwardly out of bed. She could not bear to let him go like this. She tied a kimono around her swollen figure and thrust her feet into mules. She was suddenly conscious that, outside, Christmas night was being celebrated noisily: firecrackers were spitting and a steel band was thumping out a rhythm. By contrast the hotel appeared to be deserted: there was no sign of George and Toto, or the Gampies. She had never felt quite so alone.

She went to the desk and rang the bell but no-one appeared. The old limewashed floorboards were vibrating now to the band, and bonfires lit the interior eerily.

She pulled the telephone towards her and dialled automatically. The ringing went on and on as before, fruitlessly. She could hear her own breathing accelerating. It was one o'clock on Boxing Day morning back home. There were a dozen explanations for her mother's absence but she discounted them all. And then, at last, the ringing stopped and a voice said, "Hello? The Old Rectory here. Who is it?"

Lucy swallowed, panic-stricken. She said, "Where's my mother?"

The voice said, "Ah. It's Lucy. We've just arrived home. She's getting out of the car. Just a mo." The phone was put on the hall table with a clatter and she heard a voice bawl, "Martha! It's Lucy!" And then, thankfully, her mother's voice came across the world into her ear.

"Darling, I'm so sorry. I've been out for the whole day. Such a lovely Christmas. I'll give you details in my next letter. Did you have a good time? Isn't it marvellous that you've got George and Toto with you? I can't tell you how comforting that is."

"Yes. It was very nice. Mummy, who is that man?"

Martha laughed, easily, confidently. "It's Billy Tatham, Lucy. D'you remember I told you about him?"

"The tent man."

"Exactly. He booked us in at a hotel in the Cotswolds and we walked from just above the Devil's Chimney — remember our long walks with Daddy?"

"Very well," Lucy said deliberately.

"I felt as if time was standing still . . ."

"You're all right? I thought you might not be."

"I'm better than I've been for a long time. Since you left, actually. What about you, darling? Is the baby all right?"

"Fine. Absolutely fine. Especially now I've talked to you."

"Oh darling. I'm sorry. Have you tried before?"

"It doesn't matter. You're fine and you've had a nice day."

"Wonderful. Exhilarating. I feel so well — younger somehow."

"George said you were happy." Lucy remembered what else George had said. She had laughed about it.

"I am. There's only one thing. I've had an invitation to Jennifer's wedding. I told you that they seem to have dropped me completely, didn't I?"

"You told me they didn't turn up for lunch one Sunday." Why on earth was her mother talking about such trivialities?

"Back in November. Yes. It's gone on from there. Do you think I should go to the wedding and try to patch things up?"

"I don't know." Lucy wanted to add that she did not care. She felt as if her mother were pushing her out of some cosy nest. "Yes, perhaps you should. Is there something definite to patch?"

"Linda . . . kept something from me. That was all. I expect she was embarrassed. It doesn't matter. Not now."

"Then go. She'll probably be so pleased to see you the whole thing will be forgotten."

"Yes. All right. Yes, I think that's a good idea. Now, darling. How are you?"

Lucy forced herself to tell her mother that everything was grand and that the baby was gently kicking now and then and that Toto had given her the lovely maternity smocks embroidered by Martha, and Henry had made a miniature schooner for the baby and Floss had given her a piece of genuine Bristol blue glass found on the shore from one of the old slave ships. They said goodbye almost awkwardly. Lucy could not believe that she felt jealous. Jealous of the tent man? Was Len right and she needed to cut the umbilical cord?

She went to the little bar in the lounge and made a pot of tea. Outside, hysteria was mounting. She wondered whether Len was there with his family and hoped he was. The alternatives were not good: she did not allow herself to consider them. She knew she could not talk to Len about this evening, not about the tent man and certainly not her terrifying loneliness.

After another hour she went upstairs and lay on the bed. Gradually the sound of revelry died away and she could hear George's snores from along the landing. Much later, Len crept into the bedroom. He undressed and slid next to her. She turned and put her arms around him and he gave a great sob and clutched her to him. She kissed him and tasted salt tears.

"Oh Len. Me and my stupid intuition."

He said, "Luce . . . I'm sorry. I'm sorry." And then he made love to her.

She did not want it. She wanted them to be quiet together, forgiving and kind. But she knew better now and she held him tightly and panted, as if trying to convince herself, "Len, I do love you. I do love you."

But it was from then that she felt unwell. She told herself it was the awful flat time after Len's family went back. The row. But she knew the cause of her lost health. Her mother was having an affair. It was incredible; she could not believe it. Her mother and father had been so close, the heartbreak of losing him had been so awful; Martha had become almost enshrined in her widowhood. This affair was worse than infidelity. It was . . . adultery. Lucy simply could not accept it yet recognized her own

156

complete unreasonableness. She talked to herself; she wanted to talk to Len but loyalty would not permit it. Or was it something less than loyalty? Did she hate the idea of Len saying "I told you so"?

She stopped eating and then found that any sudden movement made her dizzy. She fainted twice while visiting the new mining villages in the hills and she began vomiting again. Len was frantic. He stopped her accompanying him when he worked. She did not argue with this; her interest in all things Dominican had gone. He wanted her to go into hospital but this she vetoed because how could any doctor stop her mother from being unfaithful? He called in the same doctor who had seen her last August. She had no faith in him, he had been wrong then and he was wrong now.

"Rest. This is completely natural. Your wife is tired. Exhausted. The heat, working . . . she must have complete rest."

She liked the idea of that. But soon the canopied bed became a prison, a trap from which her mind could not escape. A packet of photographs arrived from Jennifer. She had been married in skin-tight green velvet; only her glorious hair cascading around her shoulders stopped her looking like an adder. Lucy vaguely remembered Simon from her own wedding. Hadn't he come with Uncle Bertie? Uncle Bertie who had worn wellington boots? He was very blond. Len had called him an albino. But there was something about him. He was taller than Jennifer and she had difficulty in finding boyfriends who were taller than she was; he had very wide shoulders too.

157

Linda was on his other side; she wore a red and black suit and a velvet hat frothing with net. Her skirt was too short, her heels too high. Then came Martha. Lucy hardly recognized her mother; she frowned at the photograph. The dress and coat were from a wedding they had gone to before Clem had died; Martha always wore it to what she called "state occasions". The hat was new, close-fitting for warmth probably. But Martha was wearing court shoes which was most unusual. They made her taller, her head was almost on a level with Jennifer's. They made her legs look good too. Lucy had never realized before that her mother had very beautiful legs. And there was something else; she looked quite solemn, but very confident.

Lucy flipped through the rest of the prints. Linda and Martha were unaccompanied in all of them. No sign of the tent man; no sign of Linda's old flame, Archie Evans. Martha had often wondered whether he could be Jennifer's father, but he probably wasn't tall enough. There was just one photograph showing Linda and Martha in conversation. In all the others they were separated, usually by Jennifer.

Lucy pushed the pictures away and lay down again. She was going to be sick soon, then she might feel a bit better for a while and could look at them again. Nausea swept her to the edge of unconsciousness; she stumbled to the basin and clutched it convulsively. And then a pain gripped her whole body and she knew that something was wrong that had nothing to do with her mother.

The baby was a boy and was dead. The doctor explained to them both, very kindly, that it was nature's way. He would have been deformed, probably blind, definitely no more than a vegetable.

Lucy said weakly, "He must be christened. And buried in the churchyard."

The doctor looked at Len. "There is no-one here who would do it."

Len said, "Darling, he should be cremated. Probably has been already —"

"No!" She looked at the doctor. "Fetch him. Now." She turned to Len, her weakness put aside. "Get hold of that priest. The one from Christmas Day. He will do it. Go for him now, Len. Quickly."

She had never used an authoritative voice on him before. He had been weeping helplessly, ready to take her in his arms and provide some kind of comfort. He wanted to unburden himself; tell her it was his fault for letting her accompany him on those body-jarring jeep rides, for making love to her every night and every morning, for shouting at her, for bringing her here in the first place. Her instructions seemed like a door shut in his face.

She was right about the priest. He arrived within the hour and christened the child Dominic Clement. He explained very simply that the boy was now in heaven whence he had come. That he was with their ancestors. That he was happy and whole. He believed what he was saying and they wanted to believe too. Later that week, when Lucy was strong enough, they took the ashes and buried them in the little church near the hotel and the beach. And then, at last, Lucy wept.

"Darling. I'm so sorry, so sorry." Len wept too, thankful that at last the absolution was to take place. "I shouldn't have brought you here. I shouldn't."

Lucy did not blame him, but she agreed with him. "I shouldn't have come," she said. She dried her eyes and then his. "Let's walk on the beach and talk about him, Len. He was a person. A little bit of us will always be here. That's why I named him Dominic. He is a Dominican . . ."

They spent the rest of the day walking and sitting by the sea. They watched the sudden sunset, the scuttling land crabs, the palms dipping above their heads in the tiniest of breezes. Len said, "I feel . . . a sense of healing. Do you feel it too, Luce? Say you do."

She said obediently, "I do." And she thought that if she had stayed with her mother Dominic would not be born yet and when he was he would have been strong and whole. And her mother would not have been able to betray Clem.

Len whispered, "Can I . . . may I . . . would it be all right, darling, if we made love again?"

He wanted it more than anything. She did not care enough to say no. But she cried with pain when he entered her and felt dismay that he did not hear her. His fierceness bewildered her too and afterwards she said through her tears, "You seemed . . . desperate, Len. Quite desperate."

"I know. I'm sorry, baby. So sorry." He kissed her, contrite again. "I want another baby so much. I want to fill you with babies."

She felt a thrill of horror. If she were pregnant again she would be sick and trapped here until the end of the filming. The muslin mosquito net would wrap itself around her like a shroud. At least, with Dominic safely buried, they could fly home. Tomorrow perhaps.

She wept again, this time with joy at the thought of home.

He said, "What is it, Luce? Was it that bad?"

"Oh no." She sobbed with relief and laughed helplessly. "It's just that . . . my milk has come. Look, my milk has come, Len. And I cannot conceive when my milk is here!"

He cleaned her and then, inflamed with passion, made love to her again. And though it was so painful she kept laughing because she was going home to see her mother.

CHAPTER
NINE

Martha felt as if her life had started all over again. After that Friday night when Billy Tatham had claimed his kiss and so much besides, she had expected to feel terrible guilt and unhappiness. But that had not happened. Instead this new life had begun, and this time around she was subtly different. She was no longer the demure daughter of the village Methodist minister, courted gently but assiduously by the young lawyer who lodged with one of the congregation further down the road, was articled to a firm of solicitors in Worcester and drove a pre-War BSA motorbike. "Such a suitable match," her mother had said doubtfully as his intentions became very obvious. Her father had pulled one of his funny faces and said, "C. of E., too. We might get to heaven yet, Martha!"

Martha had responded to his teasing by blushing and dismissing the whole thing. "He's just a bit lonely, Dad. And let's face it, there's no-one else in Littleford who would go to the Saturday dance with him, is there?"

Her father had pursed his lips consideringly. "Well . . . what about Fred Thompson?" He was referring to the local grave-digger who got drunk every Saturday and could be seen lolloping around the village green claiming to be Fred Astaire. Martha laughed and her mother made disapproving sounds with her tongue against her teeth.

When Clem proposed and was accepted, it was her mother who said, "Are you sure?" Martha was surprised. Why wouldn't she be sure? Clem Moreton was hard-working and had good steady prospects ahead of him. Moreover, he was good-looking without being handsome, and Martha knew full well you could not trust a handsome man. His parents were respectable, middle-class and approved of Martha. Of course she was sure.

"It's just that . . . considering he's been through a war and university and . . . everything, he's quite . . . I don't know . . . staid. Yes, for a man of twenty-eight, he's very staid."

Martha smiled. "That's what's nice about him, Mummy. He makes me feel safe. Like you and Daddy do."

Her mother nodded. "We'll see, darling. You're not twenty yet. Plenty of time."

That was another thing. No-one was in a rush in those days. Old Dr Moreton had been glad his son had taken up with a young girl because she would probably be a virgin. And — obviously — once it was understood they were going to be married at some time in the future, he could be certain that she would stay a virgin. That's how it was in those days. Martha had always determined to save herself for her wedding night and nothing about her marriage had made her think that she might have been wrong.

So they had continued with their courting, she and Clem. And their mutual respect had grown like a sunflower. He bought a sidecar and took her to Weston-super-Mare and they walked to the ferry at Uphill and went across to Brean and lay in the sand dunes, side by side, without touching.

Three years later, when Martha was twenty-two, they married. Clem had got the chance to lease a big old house in the nearby village of Nortons Heath. It belonged to the Church of England and his father knew the Bishop. They rented it for three years, then, when Lucy was born, they bought it from the Church Commissioners for a song as sitting tenants.

Martha still knew that it had been a wonderful marriage. She and Clem had never lost that enormous respect they had had for each other; they were friends, mutual protectors, good parents, co-workers. They shared their interests; Clem talked about certain cases and asked for her opinion. And he was always at her side for church functions and was sympathetic towards the likes of Miss Darcy. They laughed together about Truda Goodwin, alias Mrs Rector, and they both liked the curate and his wife, Roly and Denise Coupland. They were partners in every sense of the word. Which meant — obviously — when the mood took them, they were also lovers. Martha could remember wonderful nights when, in the deep velvety darkness, Clem had whispered his love for her and she had whispered hers back and they had come together so tenderly. Not every night of course; Clem was often bone-tired, especially if he had been in court all day. And she was full of the busyness

164

of her day and, at second-hand, Lucy's day too. But often enough.

Then that November night when Billy Tatham had come with explanations, she had discovered another self: a much younger self possibly known to her mother. The Martha who had climbed trees better than the boys; who had collected shrapnel from the single bomb that had dropped in Littleford and swapped it for some sweet coupons at school; the Martha who had giggled at evacuee Billy Tatham and his Brummie accent and then been so shocked when he tried to kiss her.

That November night she had been vulnerable; frightened by shadows certainly, but more frightened by the prospect of her future. There did not seem to be a future. And then, suddenly, there was. Quite simply, the future was herself: the younger self, the self who took risks and consequences, the self rediscovered by Billy Tatham.

She was honest with him; from that first morning she had "put her cards on the table" just as he'd told her to.

"Come on, Mar. Put your cards on the table," he'd said, coming back from the bathroom to find her struggling into her nightdress. "You've never had sex like that before, have you? Admit it. Come on. You thought you knew everything about men and women and now you know that's just not true."

He had draped her dressing-gown around his shoulders but discarded it and climbed into the bed next to her with such naturalness she was forced to accept his presence with a minimum of shock. It was — all of it — completely out of her ken. Clem and she had rarely wandered around without clothes. Maybe she should have wept tears of shame but she felt so well, so completely in control of . . . everything: her life, her body, everything.

She said, "And you think you know me, Billy. But you don't. I can assure you of that."

"Let me spend the rest of my life getting to know you then, my beautiful stuck-up, pious, wonderful woman!"

She pushed him away, but he evaded her and laughed as he leaned down to kiss her. Incredibly she laughed too. Yet making love had never been a laughing matter with Clem . . . had it? It was something solemn and terribly meaningful. Not like this at all.

She said, "Look. You should have gone last night. And you're still here. People will see your car and there will be gossip. You must leave. Seriously, Billy. Stop it now and I'll make some tea and toast and —"

"I can't stop it. And neither can you. We've waited forty-two year, dammitall, Mar —"

"Oh, stop calling me Mar!"

"If you'd known . . . how it would be . . ." He was kissing her, practically eating her. She laughed and moved her head but he was still there. "If you'd known . . . stay still . . . would you have married me?"

"No! Of course not!"

"But you will now?" Suddenly he held her tightly to him, very serious now. She was terribly conscious of his body against hers; of her body against his. She whispered, "No. No, Billy. I'm sorry."

"Why not? You need me. And I'm bloody sure I need you."

"It's a temporary thing, Billy. We couldn't live like this, can't you see that? Circumstances . . . things happened and last night was a one-off —"

He proceeded to show her that last night had not been a one-off by any means. And she responded, against her will at first and then very willingly, laughing again as he kissed her, suddenly consciously happy that he was so obviously enjoying her fifty-year-old body just as she was enjoying his stocky, muscular one. Last night, that first time, he had not undressed her. He had eased her, weeping and helpless, from the chair on to the pile of clothes hastily vacated by Snowball, and had taken advantage of her before she could find the strength to resist. Resistance had not entered into it. From the moment he had claimed that overdue kiss she had known what was going to happen. By the time they got into bed, she had ceased to worry about stretch marks and drooping breasts.

"One-off be buggered," he remarked as they lay supine again, side by side.

She propped herself on an elbow and looked at him. "You're very sweet, Billy. You saved me from despair. But — cards on the table as you said — you must know that I cannot see you again. You must go away now and not come back."

"I don't know that. Tell me why."

"Because I don't love you. I'd have to love you *enormously* to give up my life — the life I've built with Clem, here in this village. And, frankly, I don't want to do that. Ergo, I don't love you."

"I've been your bit of rough for the night, is that it?"

She flinched. "Perhaps that is it." Then she shook her head. "Or is it that I've been your bit of posh? Come on, Billy. Can you see me as your wife? Linda has been the ideal consort, hasn't she? Your friends like her, they think she's fun. She's a good hostess —"

He interrupted. "None of that matters to me. You see, Mar, I really do love you. So if the whole world was against us, I'd take it on."

She swallowed. "Oh Billy . . . I'm sorry."

He waited. She said at last, "It's no good. I can't do it. Clem would understand . . . this. He would understand that I needed you last night . . . Yes, all right, and this morning. But not anything else."

"Clem is dead, Mar."

"Yes, but Lucy will be home. She is a bit of Clem." She rolled away from him and sat on the edge of the bed. "It's no *good*, Billy," she repeated. "You said cards on table, and that's it."

There was a short silence, then he swung his legs to the other side of the bed. She thought he was angry but she did not know the full extent of his ebullience. "Right. Then it's tea and toast and I'll be on my way." He looked over his shoulder. "I suppose you wouldn't agree to a shower together?" He was grinning and she nearly gave in.

"No. You're right there. And I'll go first then I can get the breakfast."

But by the time she got downstairs he was frying bacon and the tea was made. He looked ridiculous in her dressing-gown which barely met across his middle. The sight of his dry curly hair and bull head emerging from one end of the pink acrylic, and short stocky legs from the other, brought on a rush of tenderness, but she did not dare show it. She trusted neither herself nor him.

"Here, have a bacon butty," he said, offering her a sandwich. He poured hot dark tea and passed her a mug. "Just promise me one thing, Mar. If it gets bad again — like yesterday — give me a ring. Will you?"

She knew she never would but she nodded as she chewed on the bread. She had intended the bacon for rolls around the chicken tomorrow; she could get some more, of course. She glanced at the clock behind his head: she would like to start baking well before midday then she could take some cakes around to Miss Darcy this afternoon.

He said, "You want to get rid of me, Mar."

"No, of course not. Though . . ."

"The car. I know. I should have moved it nearer to the house last night."

"It might have been better. In the circumstances."

"Of course, I didn't know I was going to stay the night." He grinned and she grinned back, but she wished he would hurry. Really they had nothing else to say to each other.

She half expected the awful emptiness of yesterday to return as he drove off. Especially as Jennifer's car passed him as he was doing a U-turn in the lane. But she even managed a wave at Simon Moreton before walking back up the drive and all she could think of as she went into the kitchen was whether to make ginger or chocolate cake. She said aloud to Snowball, "I must be so superficial, Snowie. I've slept with another man —

I've been unfaithful to my darling Clem, and I haven't got the slightest twinge of conscience." She assembled flour and margarine and fetched the egg crock and caster sugar. "Perhaps this is what they mean when they say sex can mean nothing at all." She sieved some flour into a mixing bowl. "But it meant a lot, Snowie darling. It . . . sort of . . . saved me. Yes, it did. When I told him he'd rescued me from despair, I wasn't kidding." Snowie wound between her legs and then made for the chair by the Aga. She went on musingly, "But it was more than that too. It was so different. It made me feel different. Feel myself to be different. Not superficial at all, but deeper." She looked at the cat. "Am I different, Snowie?" The green eyes closed slowly and Martha laughed. "You're right, of course. If I keep analysing it, I shall lose something. I must just accept what I've done, what has happened, and go on from there. Mustn't I?"

The phone rang and she jumped. He couldn't have got home yet; it must be . . . Linda?

It was Jennifer.

"Marty darling, I thought you should be the first to know. Simon and I are engaged. Isn't it marvellous? You and me and Lucy — we're going to be related!"

Martha stared into the hall mirror. Her reflection almost glowed back with sheer defiance: Simon must surely have reported that she was waving goodbye to a male caller just an hour ago.

"Congratulations!" she said, not knowing whether she meant it or not. She hardly knew Simon Moreton but she had not thought he was the marrying kind.

170

Jennifer laughed triumphantly. "Yes. He actually got on his knees to propose! Isn't it the most romantic thing you ever heard?"

"Wonderful, Jen." Obviously nothing was going to be said about the car outside the Old Rectory. "I must get some champagne for tomorrow's lunch!"

"Actually, Marty, we can't make it. I'm so sorry. Linda isn't at all well and darling Simon is going to take us all to the new hotel and make a fuss of us. I said you'd understand."

Her voice was as hard as nails. She knew everything. How her mother had behaved, then how Martha had behaved.

Martha's reflection did not blanch back at her; the blue eyes brightened defiantly. She said, without hesitation, "Of course I understand. Poor Linda. She's been working too hard, I fear. You should make her rest, Jen." She put the receiver down before Jennifer could come back at her, then stood there pressing it hard, waiting for a reaction to set in. It didn't. Her blue eyes gazed out of the mirror with a hint of amusement now. After all, as Billy might well have said, it was no skin off her nose. Linda had already turned down tomorrow's lunch and Martha hadn't been that keen on entertaining Jennifer and Simon on their own. She went back to the ginger cake and, glancing at Snowie who had rolled onto his back in an attitude of complete abandonment, she gave a small giggle, looked up at the ceiling and said, "Well, Mummy, I think that just for last night, I wasn't staid. Was I?"

And so life went on much as it had before except that she was different. Billy Tatham had made her different and she was grateful to him. A little part of her was disappointed when he took her at her word and left her alone, but mainly she was grateful to him for that too. When she saw Miss Darcy, did the church flowers, helped Albert to clear up the leaves, entertained George and Toto to supper at the beginning of December, she was as she had always been; she had a secret of course, but it was wrapped and laid safely away like so many of her private memories.

George hugged her and said, "You are looking particularly well, Martha. When did we see you last — the beginning of November? All Saints' Day? You were a bit down then."

Toto was conscience-stricken. "Is it that long since we were together? How awful. But we've got the most wonderful surprise for you, my dear. I'll help you in the kitchen and then when we're sitting down, we'll tell you."

"I thought we'd eat in the kitchen, actually." Martha had not opened the dining-room door since the night she had searched the house for intruders. It probably looked like Miss Havisham's room, all cobwebs. She led the way across the icy hall and into the cosy warmth of the kitchen. Snowball advanced to meet the guests, arching his back and half closing his eyes blissfully as Toto tickled between his ears.

"Oh, this is nice." George made for the Aga, rubbing his hands together. "It's funny weather for the time of year. Not really cold, but raw."

Toto joined him. "It gets into the bones," she agreed. "That is why it's so marvellous to think . . . Oh, I was going to wait until we sat down."

Martha laughed as she poured sherry and pushed chairs forward. "Sit down now then. Everything is in the slow oven. We can eat when we're ready. Tell me your news first."

So they told her that they were all going to see Len and Lucy for Christmas. "We land at Barbados and then go on with my parents." Toto beamed happily. "It will be such a party! Ninety degrees in Santo Domingo — can you believe it? Len and Lucy will be delighted. We haven't breathed a word to anyone yet. Not until we'd told you."

Martha beamed back. "How wonderful — Len and Lucy will be over the moon! You can bring me back first-hand information on how they are. And you can take the shawl I've crocheted. I copied it from one I saw in Cavendish House window and couldn't possibly finish it in time to post, but now . . . When are you going?"

George sipped and leaned back in his ladder-back chair. "When are *we* going, Martha. We can help you with the fare, no problem at all, we wouldn't have made plans without you —"

Toto said, "The flight is just a few days before Christmas." She gave her full-throated laugh. "Can you finish the shawl by then?"

Martha was amazed and very touched. But also adamant. "George, Toto, I'm so sorry. It sounds ungrateful in the extreme, but I couldn't leave the house all that time. It would get damp, and poor Snowie would have to go somewhere which he would hate. And I'm having a bit of trouble with the local children —"

Toto was aghast. "Vandals? My dear, I thought that only happened in cities. How awful for you! And you on your own here . . . You'll have to move, Martha. You haven't got proper neighbours even." She shook her head. "We must go into that later. For now, all you have to do is to get someone to live in. What about that friend of yours? Linda Bowles."

"Linda is away working. And anyway . . . I wouldn't want that." Martha knew she was sounding like Miss Darcy. She could not very well say that even with help she could not afford such a trip. She laughed. "I'm insular. Worse than insular. I've made a little rut for myself here and I don't want to leave it."

Toto was astonished. "But Lucy . . . to see Lucy . . ."

Martha said seriously, "Lucy is on top of the world lately. It might be the wrong thing to do." She remembered that time she had telephoned and it had been so obvious that she had interrupted their love-making. That had hurt. "And if she weren't feeling too good, she'd want to come home with me." She shook her head. "No, I'm better at home. I'm a sort of reference point here!" She laughed and added, "Honestly."

Toto looked as if she might protest but George said, "Martha knows what is best. For her. And probably for Lucy too. We must accept what she says, Toto."

Eventually they did. And then Martha began to question her own decision. It was crazy: she was like a kid who didn't know what she wanted for Christmas. Often during the next two weeks she almost rang George

174

and asked if it was too late to change her mind. Such indecision eroded her own renewed well-being; she did not finish the shawl and had to go into Worcester and buy feeding bottles and a sterilization kit and black-currant juice and some pure cotton sheets and pillow cases. It was all ridiculous: the "token" presents that Lucy had suggested had already been posted. She simply could not bear to let George and Toto go without sending things that might not be obtainable "out there".

An invitation to Jennifer's wedding on New Year's Day added to her general ditheriness. She had not seen anything of Linda or Jennifer; heard nothing from them since that phone call on 9 November. She tried to ring Linda without success. Obviously she was back in Cheltenham working for Billy Tatham.

Eventually she sent a formal RSVP accepting the invitation. It simply seemed the less damaging of her options.

Miss Darcy said, "Mrs Moreton, have you seen the little tin I use for my gas money? It held Mazawattee tea — a gift tin, you remember it. You were saying how valuable those old containers are these days."

"I remember it well. Didn't you keep it next to the gas meter under the stairs?"

"Yes. It might have dropped down behind the umbrellas and walking sticks. Perhaps you would have a look when you go down to make the tea."

"By all means." Martha tipped the frail body forward on to her shoulder and dealt with the pillows. "There. Is that better?"

"No-one does it quite like you do." Miss Darcy gave a sigh as she leaned back. "I haven't been very well this past week. The twins have been in nearly every day, which has been company for me, but tiring. I shall be glad when they have finished their project on the War. It's really too much for me."

"My dear, I am so sorry. Would you like me to have a word?"

"Would you? Although . . . they're very kind, you know. Twice I haven't been able to come downstairs and they've made tea and brought it up . . ."

"I noticed." The kitchen had been in a mess as Martha walked through. "You're still having your home help, aren't you?"

"She's a moody woman, Mrs Moreton. She said she couldn't be expected to scrub floors and she hasn't been since Wednesday. I've never asked her to scrub a floor in this house! Mrs Davis — Albert's wife, you know — she comes in once a month and does the rough."

"I'll see about that. Don't worry. Just concentrate on getting your strength back."

Martha went downstairs and surveyed the kitchen with some dismay. Obviously Tansy and Pickle had spilled milk all over the flagged floor. It had dried white in the cracks and the smell was sour. There were dirty cups in the sink and biscuit wrappers on the draining board. She went to Miss Darcy's cupboard and found it almost bare. There was no sign of the Mazawattee tin.

She cleaned up as best she could and took tea upstairs. "I'll go down after we've had this. Give you chance to close your eyes for a while. I'll have a bit of a clean-up and search for that tin."

She found it, together with two ancient tennis racquets, discarded in the sitting room. Miss Darcy was lucky to have her windows intact. The tin was empty, of course. Martha put some coins in it before advising Miss Darcy to keep it under her pillow.

She went to Albert Davis's cottage before it was quite dark. Mrs Davis agreed to go round to Miss Darcy's "first thing" and give her a "good going-over".

"Them little devils" — she was referring to the twins — "they drives my Albert potty, then starts on the old lady. Parents got no control. Father no job — girlfriend in there with him most days — Mother working all hours at that hypermarket place in Stourbridge — couldn't care less — takes no notice of the kids."

Martha suddenly funked "having a word" with the awful-sounding Venableses and asked the Rector to deal with it. He seemed unsurprised, practically unconcerned even, by the story of the rifled tin.

"Difficult age, Martha. And their home background is not good."

"We can't let them get away with it," Martha protested. "They've been bothering me — nothing serious — for the past three or four weeks. They should be checked."

"Well, I suppose . . ." Just for a moment the whites of his eyes showed nervously. "Thank goodness you've kept an eye on poor Miss Darcy," he prevaricated. "I don't know how we would manage without you. I'm very glad you decided against going to Barbados with Lucy's in-laws."

Martha was surprised. "How did you know about that?" she asked.

"Mrs Travers rang Truda to see whether she could persuade you to go. We decided it best not to interfere. It was your decision, after all."

"Yes." Martha looked at her hands; there was a liver spot near the base of her left thumb. She was getting old. "To be honest, Marcus, I think I must give Lucy her . . . freedom. Can you understand that?"

"Of course, my dear. Of course. She must never have to think that you might need her."

She smiled fleetingly; he had never had children, how could he understand?

Then he spoke with unaccustomed vigour. "Martha. You can do it. You let Clem go. It will be easier with Lucy, surely?"

Far from being reassuring, his words shocked her. It was so obvious that he and the Gestapo-trained Truda had discussed this very thing. Was she really a possessive mother?

She smiled briefly. "Of course. Oh yes. Of course." She drew a glove over the liver mark. "Getting back to Miss Darcy, Marcus. I really do think you should ask the twins not to visit her again."

He fidgeted for an instant, then smiled. "I tell you what. I'll ask Truda to go. Better coming from a woman, don't you think?"

She nearly laughed. She had planned in any case to start another letter to Lucy this evening; it was a little gem to be recounted. It made her feel somehow a little less dithery. Certainly things were changing; it seemed she had temporarily lost Linda's friendship and Jennifer's adulation, but Marcus and Truda would never change. And she still did the flowers in the church, visited Miss Darcy, kept the house going. Once Lucy came home with the new baby, things would return to normal. And then she remembered Marcus's words. Was she a possessive mother? She frowned, recalling her telephone call to Lucy just before Billy Tatham's arrival. Perhaps she wouldn't write another letter this evening; it was only three days since her last one.

She had been invited to the Goodwins for Christmas lunch but had made her excuses because she could not bear to be seen as "a duty". Miss Darcy was taken into the Willows Nursing Home for a week and she heard from the terrible Truda that Linda and Jennifer were moving into the Worcester hotel until after the wedding.

So she was to spend Christmas at the Old Rectory on her own, and though it was what she wanted her sense of isolation was almost tangible. She told herself the wedding was only a week away and that probably Lucy would telephone, or Toto and George. She would go to church, of course, and then she and Snowie could share the chicken and have a snooze. She shook herself; it was the first Christmas in her life that she had been alone.

And then, on Christmas Eve, Billy Tatham rang. Her heart leaped at the sound of his voice; she would not have believed she could be so pleased to hear him.

"What are you doing tomorrow?" he asked directly.

She should have told him she was going to the Rectory. She said, "Nothing."

"I'll call for you early. The weather forecast is decent. We'll go for a walk and have lunch at a pub. Would you like that?"

She would like it very much, but . . . Even though she knew Linda was with Jennifer and Simon, she still asked, "What about Linda?"

"Don't be silly. How should I know? I haven't seen Linda since November the eighth. You know that."

She hadn't known. She said, aghast, "I thought you would go back to her! Oh . . . poor Linda."

"I meant to show you that I can be celibate because I know you consider that to be faithfulness. It's not, but, well, I can do it for you."

She said quickly, "No. I'm sorry. I can't spend a whole day with you like that. Not when Linda . . . No."

He said incredulously, "Are you telling me you would have come if I had been with Linda? For Chrissake, Mar! I can't understand you!"

"It's nothing to do with Linda. I wouldn't have come anyway."

"Yes, you would. You were in two minds, I could tell. Be honest."

She was totally confused. What was the issue here? Did she want to go? She said hesitantly, "It was just that . . . Clem and I used to walk. Leckhampton Hill. The Devil's Chimney."

"Then that's where we'll go. Don't argue. If you would have come when Linda was with me, you'll bloody well come now!"

180

"Billy! Listen! I can't make the kind of commitment you are obviously expecting."

"Martha, I gave up expecting anything from life a long time ago. Commitment? Forget it. We're going for a walk. OK?,

"And that is all. I can't — do — anything else."

"We'll see about that."

"I'm not coming unless you promise —"

"Christ, I promise. I promise. I promise."

It was the best Christmas she had had for years. Not just since Clem died, but for years before that. Billy had the strength of a bullock and he scrambled up the muddy slopes of Leckhampton Hill along paths Clem would have turned from. His hand, reaching down to haul her alongside him, was always warm and dry. His breath smelled of whisky but probably hers did too because they'd had a generous tipple before starting out. He'd booked a meal at the Dog and Duck overlooking a spectacular view of the Severn valley.

"You booked?" She unwound her scarf. "But you didn't know I would come!"

"It was a chance worth taking. If I hadn't made a booking last week we would never have got in anywhere."

"Why didn't you telephone then? It would have given me time to get used to the idea."

"And find a hundred excuses for not coming."

She smiled suddenly. He was right and she was glad he'd sprung it on her. She said impulsively, "Come back with me and have some tea, will you? I'd like to look at our ordnance survey maps and find out just where we've been."

He looked surprised. "We haven't finished. We cross the Cirencester Road and drop down into Shurdington along Kidnappers Lane. A cup of tea at the Marston Arms and then along to the station where we left the car."

"It will be dark," she protested.

"Not quite. I want you to come to the house in Cheltenham. It was going to be a temporary foothold. I wanted somewhere in the hills. Something grander. But I've grown fond of this little house. And I've got some food. We can look at maps there."

She looked at him. He grinned. "I'll keep my promise. Besides, after you've had a rest, I want to walk you down the Prom and along Imperial Gardens. To see the decorations."

She smiled in spite of herself. She had not been into Cheltenham since that awful day in November. Nortons Heath did not go in for more than a tree outside the Post Office and a string of fairy lights above the War Memorial.

He was so easy to be with. They talked, often rubbish. It didn't matter. After a traditional Christmas lunch they resumed their walk, scrambling down to Leckhampton village and then along a small waterlogged lane to Shurdington and so back to the car. The house turned out to be a narrow slice in a long terrace near Pittville Park. It was very much warmer and cosier than the Old Rectory. The armchairs were soft and deep and the open fire was lit and extinguished by a switch. She told him how lucky he was not to have to clear out an Aga and then, as he poured tea, she found herself talking about Miss Darcy and the Mazawattee tea tin, then Marcus's comment about Lucy.

"He made me feel — the Rector, I mean — sort of holier-than-thou. I mean, that's his role, isn't it? You called me pious before, Billy. Am I pious?"

"Sometimes. Never mind that. Go on."

"Well, he — the Rector — obviously didn't want to have a word with Mr Venables about the twins. And then when he spoke of letting Lucy go, I felt sort of thrown. I questioned my life . . . There doesn't seem to be any point to it any more. The point has been Lucy. And I just don't know what to do about Jennifer's wedding. I don't think I can face them."

He said, "Last things first. Of course you can face them. You've done nothing wrong, Marty. Linda's creased with embarrassment. This is your chance to break through. Chat to her — bring it into the open if you like. But go."

Martha made no objection to him calling her Marty. She nodded. "I think you're right. It will make it worse if I cry off."

"And as for Lucy . . . you're close. Obviously. Mothers and daughter are supposed to be close, aren't they? But you don't interfere with what she does. She's married, having a baby, miles away. And she is still the reason behind everything — for you, that is. And later, her baby will be too. And this old fuddy-duddy vicar-chappie is talking about cutting apron strings? I don't get it, Marty. But then, there's so much about you I don't

183

get." He held up his hand. "And before you start talking about our different worlds, let me just say that I agree with you. We do live in different worlds. But somewhere — and you know this though you won't admit it — we meet. Our worlds — or maybe it's us, you and me, Mar — meet. We touch."

She said warningly, "Billy!"

He ignored her. "You see, Mar, I'm a bit like those awful kids who pinched the old girl's gas money. I used to pinch things. Nobody gave me a decent argument for not pinching them, see. But I learned not to. I learned like they'll learn, through being found out and warned off. If there were two paths I always took the wrong one before the right one — that's how I found out about things. Trial and error. I bet you had nice little talks with your mam. You decided between you what was best for you. Well, you made a pretty good job of your marriage and I didn't. Twice over I didn't. But now . . . now you're not sure, are you? And you're terrified of taking the wrong path." He grinned. "I don't have that trouble, Mar."

She said nothing for a long time, watching him. And at last he said, "Yes. Linda. Linda was the wrong one. But I did what I could, Marty. Laid all my cards on the table. Told her about you. What else could I do?"

"Well, you need not have brought her here to live with you. Linda, being Linda, thought that would come to mean something."

He lifted his shoulders. "I thought . . . differently."

"She is sweet. I mean that, Billy. She has a sweetness of nature that is quite unusual."

184

"OK. Yes, I agree."

"This — this celibacy thing. I naturally thought, when you left me that day in November, I thought you would eventually patch things up with Linda."

"No. When I left you in November I started on the right path. I didn't ring Linda. She didn't ring me. It's over, Marty."

"Billy, she is very much in love with you."

"And if she came back you could file me neatly away with all your other memories? No thank you, Mar." He looked at her. "It's OK. I'm not going to be a nuisance. But I'm not in your past any more. I'm here." He went to the shelf and picked up a book of maps. "Let's drop it. Have a look at this while I make sandwiches."

She took the book from him with a kind of helpless resignation. She would think about it later. Perhaps she could talk to Linda at the wedding next week. Perhaps not.

The walk along the Prom to Imperial Gardens was magical. As far as they could tell they had the roads to themselves and the Park was deserted and eerie. They went on past the hotel to Montpelier and sat on the swings, laughing at nothing.

Billy said, "D'you remember how you used to swing upside-down? You'd stand on the seat and when the swing was at its highest, you'd suddenly flip up and hook your legs into that bit at the top. I knew when you were going to do it because you always tucked your skirt into the legs of your knickers."

"I don't remember. I honestly don't." But as she spoke she could recall the strange sensation of the world tilting

185

and the chains of the swing clanging frantically, and knowing that she must wait until it steadied before she could release her legs from the rings, and just for an instant feeling a stab of fear.

"Don't you remember me crawling along the top of the frame and pulling your skirt out so that it fell over your face?" He was suddenly serious. "Christ. When I realized what I'd done — that you couldn't see a bloody thing — I was worried to death you'd fall! But not you. You swung down like a monkey and chased me right out of the village!" He peered into her dark face. "Don't tell me you can't remember that?"

"I suppose I was ashamed of myself. I block things out sometimes." She took a deep breath. "I block out Clem's death. That's how I deal with it."

"Ahh. Marty." He got off his swing and held out a hand for her. "One day, will you talk to me about Clem? Unblock the memories and tell me about him."

She took his hand but she said sadly, "I don't think so, Billy. I'm sorry. I know now that you are kind and want to help. But . . . I don't think so."

He did not press her. And as they walked back through the empty town, she said quietly, "Thanks, Billy. It's been wonderful."

"Don't block that out, will you, Mar?"

"No. I won't."

Probably that was why she almost gushed to Lucy on the phone that night. It was embarrassing when Billy answered Lucy's call and though Martha was determined neither to explain nor excuse, she tried to cover her confusion with a rush of words. At least Billy could never accuse her of blocking out their wonderful day!

She watched him walk back to the car and drive away, then she locked up and went to bed, still smiling. In the morning, Clem's pillow had not been moved.

CHAPTER
TEN

New Year's Day 1986 was grey and rain-filled but not cold. Martha dressed carefully in her "good" suit which she had worn to Clem's funeral and several others since, and added a pair of court shoes with heels unusually high for her. They made driving difficult, and she arrived at the small church just outside Worcester later than she had intended. The wedding was at midday and she had hoped to find a small hotel where she could have coffee and use the bathroom. There was no time for that. She parked next to a gravestone proclaiming that in the midst of life was death and crouched beneath her umbrella to get to the church porch.

Inside, she scanned the congregation with a quick glance. On Simon's side the guests were all around his own age, probably staff from the various hotels in the group. She had wondered if Uncle Bertie might appear in his wellingtons, but there was no-one over the age of thirty. On Jennifer's side, Linda was peering anxiously around, the sole occupant of the front pew. She looked smaller than Martha remembered; she had lost quite a bit of weight. Her cherry-red and black suit was topped by a black velvet hat frothing net from its crown. She must have noticed Martha's entrance but made sure she did not turn round that far.

Behind her was sitting a middle-aged couple and behind them, a woman on her own. And that was it. Martha took the proffered service sheet and walked down the side aisle to slide in next to the solitary woman, who immediately leaned sideways and introduced herself.

"Amanda Derry. I work with Jennifer, you know." She tapped the shoulder of the man in front. "This is Mr Masonfield, the City Archivist. And his wife."

Whispering, smiling, they all shook hands while Linda studiously ignored them. Martha transferred her smile to the front and right as Simon turned. He sketched a salute. And then, when she was wishing ardently she had not come, the vicar moved to the chancel, the organ's thin pipe played the single warning note of the wedding march and Jennifer was there.

She was on the arm of a portly elderly man; Martha wondered wildly whether it could possibly be her father. But what made the whole thing incredible was the wedding dress. It was green, lime-green velvet, wound around Jennifer's marvellous body like a bandage, leaving nothing to the imagination. No train, no headdress, just that tumble of dark, gypsy hair, apparently uncombed. As she reached Simon's side she reached up to kiss his earlobe and the dress lifted slightly to reveal that she was in her stockinged feet. Martha, trying to register every detail for a later report to Lucy, thought how odd it was that Jennifer had chosen to present herself as at once completely simple

— the words "woodland nymph" crossed Martha's mind — yet undeniably wanton.

During the hymns, Miss Derry insisted on whispering to Martha her belief that she had been the original match-maker. "Mind you, when I booked her to speak at the Chamber of Commerce, I did not dream it would get as far as the altar. . ." Martha smiled, remembering Jennifer's sudden absence during Lucy's wedding. She agreed with Miss Derry; it had been a fling. She stared across at the back of Simon's head; he was so unlike anyone else in Clem's family and hadn't Uncle Bertie described him as a philanderer? She understood his blond attraction very well, he looked Aryan, ruthless. But Jennifer had found a way to tame him. Perhaps Lucy would be able to throw light on it.

The occupants of the front pews began to shuffle into position to go into the vestry to sign the register. Martha prepared to listen to Miss Derry. And then, incredibly, Linda was walking down the side aisle, smiling right at Martha, reaching out a hand for her.

"You're the nearest person to Jennifer and Simon. Aunt-by-marriage? They would both like you to sign the register."

Martha found herself taking Linda's gloved hand and following her to join the others.

"This is Archie Evans. Family friend." Linda introduced the portly man behind Simon. "And Simon's best man, Barry Shaw." She tried to be the old insouciant Linda. "And you know me, of course."

Martha kept her smile in place. She had not reckoned on such a complete reconciliation. When they emerged from the vestry to the triumph of Mendelssohn she was still included in the entourage, and when they put up their umbrellas and hurried to the cars, Linda was by her side still. She hesitated by the driver's door, glancing beneath Linda's umbrella, wondering what was happening.

Linda said, "They're doing the photographs in the hotel."

Martha smiled and nodded. "Very wise. Especially in this weather."

"Shall I travel with you, Martha? I can show you the way. Though I expect you know it, of course. Opposite the Cathedral."

"No, I'm not at all certain. I'd like it if you can come with me. Will it matter though? I mean, should you be with Mr Evans?"

"Not really. I came with Barry Shaw. The best man." Linda closed her umbrella, shook it vigorously and laid it alongside the passenger seat then settled herself with a little sigh. "This is nice. Like old times."

"Yes." Martha started the engine and pulled in gently behind the bridal car. She said tentatively, "Let's do it often — let that be a New Year resolution. Yes?"

"Oh — oh yes!" Linda's small face beamed from beneath the sprouting net and then sobered. "The only thing is, Martha . . ."

"Go on. Be frank. We were always frank with each other."

"Well, I wasn't, was I? Probably if I'd told you what was happening, it would have saved a lot of difficulty. Trouble."

"Why should you tell me?" Martha pulled up at a crossing. "That's all in the past, anyway. Can we sort of . . ." she thought of her words to Billy Tatham. "Can we block that out?"

"That's the thing, you see. That's what I was going to say. I want to see more of you, Martha. But — but I can't face seeing you with . . . him. Bill. I'm sorry."

Martha accelerated slightly to catch up with the wedding car again. She said, surprised, "You won't see him with me, Linda. My God — you didn't think . . ." She laughed. "Actually I thought you and he were together again."

"Oh." Linda sounded completely blank. "No. I haven't seen Bill since that night in November. And I thought — I mean, I knew that he came to see you. To explain . . . Oh Martha, I'm sorry."

Martha kept her eyes on the road. They were driving over a bridge. The Severn, wide and powerful, came into view, the cathedral rearing apparently from its depths. She made no comment about Billy's visit to her last November: Linda must know he stopped the night: or did she?

She said, "You see? We have to block it out, Linda. Start again."

Linda said, "Wait just a moment. I have to ask you this. Are you going to marry him?"

Martha forced a laugh. "No. I am not going to marry Billy Tatham."

Linda said, "He's waited for you, Martha. He must be so . . . persistent."

Martha swallowed. "Not that persistent. I haven't seen him since that night." She had promised Billy she would not block out their Christmas Day together. Yet when she spoke the words, she hardly remembered it. There was a second when she knew she was lying to Linda; then it was gone. She said in a measured voice, "There is nothing between us, Linda. I'll never forget Clem. Surely you realize that?"

Linda was instantly contrite again. "Of course, of course, it's what Jennifer said! I'm such a fool, Martha. Can you ever forgive me?"

"There's nothing to forgive. But oh, it will be good to see something of you again, Linda. I've hated the last few weeks. And I want to be able to talk about the baby, to tell you when it arrives —"

"Oh, my dear! How is she? How is darling Lucy? What's the latest? Are George and Toto back yet?"

"No, not yet. How did you know about that?"

They drew into a car-park. The hotel was black and white mock-Tudor. Beyond the cobbled car-park, lawns led down to the river.

Linda smiled. "The Venables twins. The all-seeing eyes. Miss Darcy used to run the village grapevine but they've taken over."

"Ah yes." Martha wondered whether she should warn Linda about the little girls and decided against it.

They sat in the car and watched staff usher in the bride and groom. Martha thought humorously that at least Jennifer wasn't pregnant; you could not disguise so much as a pimple in that dress.

Linda seemed to be tuned in to the same wavelength. She said musingly, "I just hope I shall be a grandmother soon as well." She sighed deeply. "If not, I don't quite know what will happen."

Martha raised her brows and looked sideways at her friend but Linda said no more and Jennifer was in the porch beckoning to them fiercely. The photographer had arrived.

Jennifer did her best. She had chosen to have a sightseeing honeymoon in Istanbul. She had no wish to lounge around a beach in a swimming costume and sightseeing was fairly strenuous and might be blamed later on for a mythical miscarriage. So she slogged around the Grand Bazaar and the Blue Mosque and insisted on doing the trip along the Bosporus and into the Black Sea, stopping on the way back to look at the summer palace and the harem. It was unexpected good fortune when the hotel food upset her stomach and she spent a day in bed drinking bottled water. Two weeks after their return to Worcester, Simon had to leave early to call into the other hotels on the "circuit'. She waited until he had left, then phoned Miss Derry with her excuses and went round to the doctor's surgery. She told him she thought that she had recently lost a baby.

"My dear girl. Jump up on the bed. I'll call Sister in and I'll have a look at you. Are you still losing?"

"Yes. And I'd rather not have an examination at this stage, doctor. It's just that I am feeling so weak. I wondered whether I should be taking a food supplement."

The doctor, who did not know either of the Moretons and was very busy, said, "I'm going to ask you to drop into the treatment room on your way out and let them take a blood sample. You might be a little anaemic and I can prescribe some iron tablets." He started scribbling on his pad. "But I'd like you to come and see me when you feel able to. It might be necessary for you to have a D and C."

She was in bed when Simon got back that evening. He took the news without surprise or a great deal of sympathy. When she told him she was anaemic and would be taking iron tablets and then going "in" for a small operation, he seemed a little more concerned. He sat on the edge of the bed and smoothed her hair and said, "We've done it once, sweetheart. We can do it again."

She said, "It means so much to you, Si. I'm sorry."

He shrugged. "My parents were conspicuous by their absence during my childhood, honey. The idea of being a father was . . . well, kind of romantic, I suppose."

She said, "I think I understand. I don't even know who my father is. I don't think Ma knows either."

"But you've got each other. The only person I had was Uncle Bertie. D'you remember Uncle Bertie from Lucy's wedding? The old gaffer in wellies?"

They both laughed. He started to tell her, yet again, how he felt about "being a family". He had no idea of course; it was a fantasy he'd cooked up as a lonely schoolboy. But she told herself the least she could do was to show him it was a fantasy. She whispered, "D'you want to try now, darling?"

"For another baby?" He was delighted but surprised. "Shouldn't we wait a few weeks, Jen? What did the doctor say?"

"He said it was entirely up to me. What I felt like. And I feel like . . . trying now."

They tried. They tried on a regular basis until the middle of February and then something happened. Jennifer never knew what it was; perhaps she had talked in her sleep. Whatever it was, he knew. Or rather, she thought he knew. And it was like an insidious poison between them. Whatever their differences, they had always resolved them in the bedroom. Simon had adored her for being so easily aroused, for her complete lack of inhibition, for her sheer appetite. She had loved his directness and his ardour. She would never forget that first meeting. "I want to make love to you. Desperately." And now that ardour had most definitely cooled. He seemed more concerned with Linda's welfare than Jennifer's.

"Why doesn't she come and live here?" he asked after Linda had spent a weekend with them. "I could use an organizer like your mother. And she gets on well with people."

"She has to stay in the cottage because that's the phone number Bill Tatham's got." Jennifer spoke almost wearily. In a way she understood Linda's need to be within call; in another way she was furious with her mother for being so dependent on the man. But she had promised Linda that somehow she would deliver Bill to her on a plate. And she knew how she would do it, too. She would make sure that Lucy — and the baby —

196

would go home to the Old Rectory. Bill Tatham would have to accept then that there was no way he could ever break into that kind of marriage, because that's what it would be. A complete family. Lucy, Martha and the baby. No room for anyone else at all.

The only thing was the timing. She would have to wait for Len and Lucy to come home and for Len to get bored. Then she would be able to take up his "offer" of last year. *I've been considering what you said . . . you were right of course. Simon need not know. And neither need Lucy.* But when it went public — and of course Lucy would have to know — it would mean wrecking her best friend's marriage besides her own. And Martha . . . Martha would hate her for it. Or would she? Martha was as lonely as Linda. Perhaps, eventually, Martha might be grateful to Jennifer.

And her own marriage would go. Simon would throw her out the moment he got wind of what she was up to. She could imagine his ice-blue eyes looking at her with contempt. *It's what you always wanted, isn't it, Jen? You thought it was me. My name. Being a Moreton. And then when you realized how empty that was, that it got you no closer to Lucy and Martha than you were before, you thought you'd destroy them. Poor old Len. Talk about being a pawn in your little game . . .*

But Simon did not know everything and it wasn't quite like that. From the moment they had met there had been something amazing between her and Len. And he had admitted that he was marrying Lucy because she was suitable wife material. He'd implied that Jennifer was the one he really loved.

197

As her marriage to Simon deteriorated, she began to fantasize about Len. Think about him. Plan their first meeting. How she would remind him of his proposition to her. How coolly she would treat the whole thing. And then, when they came together, how different he would be from Simon. His darkness, his warmth and passion. There was a part of her that knew full well that her plan was illogical and ill-conceived. But when she reached this place in her fantasy, she also knew that there would be no stopping her now. She told herself it was fate: they had been made for each other. And so had her mother and Bill Tatham! That was surely the object of the exercise. She was not, after all, and in spite of that small part that said otherwise, behaving selfishly.

Whenever she got to this point in the dream she had to go into the bathroom and hang over the basin because she felt sick. And then, of course, Simon thought she was pregnant and brought home a testing kit so that he would know for certain . . . It was strange that she did not become pregnant. Linda, staying for the weekend and seeing the situation all too clearly, said, "It's some sort of judgement."

Jennifer snapped back, "Oh, don't be so silly, Ma. You've always been superstitious. My God, I remember when you wouldn't let me walk under a ladder or open an umbrella inside the house! You haven't changed!"

"Well, it's true, isn't it? I kept stuff from Bill and he's never forgiven me. That's a judgement, if you like! And now this baby. You lied to Simon. You can't get away from it, Jen." Linda sounded sadly fatalistic. It infuriated Jennifer.

"Oh shut up, Ma! For God's sake. Sitting by that bloody telephone waiting for a call from a man who looks like a bullock and behaves like one too! It's — it's demeaning!"

"I know." Linda had a way of staring through a window rather like Simon did. As if she could see something that wasn't there.

"What's the matter with you?" Jennifer almost spat with exasperation. "You and Marty are as thick as thieves again. Everything is back to how it was before, and you're still looking like a sick cow!"

"I know," Linda repeated. Then she seemed to realize where she was and gave an upside-down smile to her daughter. "See, love, if he's not seeing Martha, why doesn't he get in touch with me? Just about the job, if nothing else."

"Because it's February, Ma. It rains every day and people are not interested in tents. So business is slow. So he does not need you." Jennifer sighed sharply. "Besides, Martha is still on her own. He's still probably hoping she'll phone him."

"Well, she won't. She's refused to see him again." Linda shook her head. "She's still married to Clem. She'll never be free to look at anyone else."

"Cheer up then. I've told you — you will get married."

"Seen it in a crystal ball, Jen?"

"Yes. If that will please your superstitious soul. Yes."

Life, which had seemed so simple, was suddenly not simple at all. But, when all was said and done, that was how Jennifer liked it. When things went well, she invariably became bored.

Linda did her share of fantasizing that cold February. It was the coldest since 1947 and she used this as a reason for staying in the cottage. Martha had wanted her to help with the church flowers, but she usually went to Worcester for the weekend and anyway she couldn't stand Mrs Rector's bossy ways. Besides if she went out too often she might miss Bill Tatham's phone call.

But he didn't call and eventually she swallowed what little pride she had left and rang him at the Pittville house. There was no reply but having done it once she could do it again. And then again. And each time the phone was unanswered, the simmering Vesuvius of her fantasies and emotions threatened to boil over. The only person who could have helped her was Martha, and since Jennifer's wedding the subject of Bill Tatham had been taboo. Martha had assured her that she had not seen him since the night he had explained the Linda situation to her; she believed Martha and that was that. But she simply could not ask Martha's advice; Martha had pride and standards and would not understand — could not possibly understand — that Linda would jettison all her values for Bill Tatham.

She did not realize that Friday was St Valentine's Day until she found the card on the hall floor. It was a cheap thing, illustrated with an arrow-pierced heart and an over-plump Cupid giggling in the corner. Inside was printed "Guess who?" She held it to her chest, feeling her own heart pumping away beneath it. She almost phoned the Pittville number and then something made her look at the card again. She had seen Bill's handwriting on receipts, invoices, labels. This was printed but it was not Bill's hand. She sat down, swallowing frantically. The card was shaking like an aspen leaf between her fingers. She put it on the coffee table and pressed her hands together. This was some kind of cruel joke. It was hateful.

The phone rang and she leaped in her chair, then snatched it up before it could stop ringing. It was Archie Evans. Her heart, jumping about in her rib-cage, settled instantly.

"Hello, old girl. I should have phoned before now. To say how much I enjoyed the wedding. Thanks for asking me to give Jennifer away. It was an honour."

"Oh Archie. It was great to have you. Jen wanted me to do it, you know. I just couldn't. I'm a wreck these days."

"You're certainly not that, Lin. You're as beautiful as ever. My little ray of sunshine. I always used to call you that, d'you remember? My little ray of sunshine."

"Yes, I remember, Archie. You've always been sweet to me." Her eyes filled with sudden tears. "I suppose . . . you didn't send me a Valentine card, did you?"

"Is it the fourteenth? Oh God. I didn't. Sorry, old girl. If I'd thought . . . You know, Lin, when I saw you in that lovely red outfit, it was as if the clock went backwards. Can't we get together again? Weekends? May's often away and now I've retired, time hangs around a bit. Just sitting waiting for the old grim reaper isn't a lot of fun, is it?"

"I'm forty-six, Archie. I'm not thinking of packing up just yet!" But she was laughing because there was something about Archie that had always made her laugh. If it weren't for Bill she'd be flattered into seeing him again -just like she'd been on the day of Lucy Moreton's wedding. And, as she said, it had been good of him to stand by Jennifer last month. On the other hand, Bill might not have sent her the Valentine but one of these days . . . Even so she didn't have the gumption to say an outright no to Archie. "Listen. I've got a job on at the moment and weekends I'm promised to Jennifer. But I'll ring you when I can see the way clear. All right?"

"Will that be soon, sweetheart?"

"Of course, Archie. And thanks for ringing."

She replaced the receiver, then picked it up again and rang the Cheltenham number. No reply. She sat there looking at the card. After a while she began to cry silently and without sobs.

She agreed to go with Martha to Birmingham to buy a cot for Lucy's old room. "When they visit me they can have my room and I'll sleep in Lucy's bed and keep an ear out for the baby." Martha was looking pretty good these days; she was busier than ever, popping in to see Miss Darcy every day and trying to organize a theatre club through the Women's Institute. Linda knew that she herself would look better if she were as busy; when she had worked for Bill Tatham there hadn't been a minute to spare and she had loved that. Now for five days in the week she had too much time on her hands yet found no time to do the essentials. Sometimes she ironed at midnight; showered and dressed after lunch; forgot to prepare anything for an evening meal. It had been good today to get up early and tidy the house before breakfast. It had been good to dress up and do her face and be ready when Martha arrived at ten.

As they walked around Rackhams she said suddenly, "Martha, please let me buy this cot. I don't know what to get the baby — it would be quite a relief to get something useful and pretty. Please say yes."

Martha was surprised and touched. "Linda, it's too expensive. Listen — why don't you do the bedding? Something really pretty . . . Look at those tiny fitted sheets."

Linda eventually bought two complete cot sets and a cat net, Martha bought the cot. They gave the address for delivery and stood at the desk, smiling idiotically at each other, waiting for receipts and wondering why they hadn't done this sort of thing before.

Martha gave Linda her receipt and tucked her own in her bag and they turned for the lift to the restaurant.

"I had a Valentine the other week," she confided. "I've got a feeling it came from those two little girls next door to you."

"Good Lord! So did I! I never thought of them! Yes, that's who it would be. Those little devils!"

They both laughed. Linda remembered how awful it had been that day. She had wept hot tears like lava. But the volcano was quiescent now. She said, "D'you remember when Jen and Lucy sent that anonymous love letter to the music master at school?"

"They should have known better," Martha said, smiling as she led the way to an empty table. "They must have been sixteen then."

"God knows what the Venables girls will be like when they're sixteen!"

They laughed again, both thinking how nice this was. They ate their lunch — Linda would always remember that they both chose a vegetarian dish — then they caught the bus back to the church and went their separate ways. It was almost dark but as Linda let herself in by the front door there was the unmistakable draught that meant the back door was open, and then she heard it close.

She waited a moment in case it was Jennifer. No-one spoke, no lights were on, so it wasn't Jennifer. Petrified, she switched on the hall light, called, left the front door open, reached around the kitchen door and switched on that light. No-one was there but there was movement in the garden. She grabbed the bread knife and opened the kitchen door. The twins were trying to climb the wall back into their garden.

They came back inside at her furious command, and stood drooping in front of her like a pair of tired ponies.

"How dare you come into my house — d'you know what that sort of thing is called legally? Breaking and entering! It's a criminal offence! I can report you to the police! What were you doing? Have you taken anything — are you thieves as well?"

One of them — Linda could never tell the difference — began to cry. The other said desperately, "You won't tell Dad? We haven't taken anything. We looked round, that's all."

"What for? What were you looking for?"

"They say you and Mrs Moreton . . . sort of . . . like someone. You know . . . *like* someone."

Linda began to feel the volcano seething. She said, "You sent Mrs Moreton and me those ridiculous cards, didn't you? Because you thought we had the same boyfriend?"

"Yes." The one twin was doing all the talking. "They said if it was like the old days when people sent Valentine cards, you'd both get a Valentine from the same man!"

Linda kept her hands at her sides with difficulty. The bread knife rasped against her skirt. "Who said that? Your parents? They've been gossiping about me — tell me the truth!"

"No! It was Miss Darcy. Mrs Goodwin said we weren't to go and see her any more but we still go and she tells us all sorts of things and one of the things was that Mrs Moreton spent Christmas with her boyfriend —"

"How did Miss Darcy know that? She was in a home at Christmas. She never goes outside the door —"

She must have brandished the knife without realizing it because the other twin started gabbling frantically. "Mrs Moreton told her! She asked if Mrs Moreton had had a nice Christmas and Mrs Moreton said, very nice thank you, I spent it with a friend in Cheltenham, and that's where her boyfriend lives so it must have been him!"

"Mrs Moreton does not have a boyfriend! You're making all this up —"

"No! Honestly! Everyone knows that her boyfriend came after Bonfire Night! We saw him ourselves 'cos we'd been knocking on her door and he sent us off and we watched and he stayed and — and —"

The other one said, "Listen, we got to go now! Dad will be round!" They began to edge towards the hall. "Really. We'll never do it again. We got to go —"

They turned tail and fled through the open front door.

Linda stood for a long moment staring after them. Then she put the bread knife down and picked up the phone. Almost immediately, Bill Tatham's voice came along the line. She said, "Bill, why haven't you phoned? I've waited day after day. You should have phoned me. Just to tell me what was happening . . . I didn't know — I didn't understand how much she meant to you . . . I said I was sorry . . . You should have phoned. .

His voice, with its trace of accent, was strong and as warm as ever. "Linda. Shut up a minute. I've hurt you and I'm sorry. But this is something I have to do. I have to prove to myself that I can live alone —"

"It doesn't bother you that I can't do that?"

"Of course it bothers me. But I tried to tell you, right at the beginning when you asked for the job —"

"Cards on the table. I know." She took a deep breath and heard it shudder in her throat. "I think I hate you. Did you spend Christmas with her?"

"Yes. Listen, Lin, she wanted me to see you — she tried to persuade me to get in touch —"

"Yes. Oh yes. She would. She's so . . . good. Isn't she?"

She put down the phone and hugged her coat to her, then she walked out into the evening and made for the Old Rectory.

Martha took her gloves off and warmed her hands at the Aga. Snowball had gone out as she came in and she could see the splash of his white fur investigating the beds of snowdrops under the kitchen window. It had been a good day with Linda; they were back on their old footing. And soon — come the spring or early summer — Lucy would be home.

The telephone rang. Len was crying so it was difficult to hear his exact words but she understood instantly what he was saying.

She said urgently, "Is Lucy all right?"

"Yes — yes. Broken-hearted. Wants . . . funeral . . ."

"Len. You're both young and healthy. My dear, try not to . . . Len, just listen a moment. There will be other children. You have Lucy and she has you. Can you hear me, Len?"

"Will you tell George and Toto? Sorry . . . sorry, Martha. My fault. Coming here . . . Oh God . . ."

She forced him to slow down and tell her again. Then she repeated it all back to him carefully so that she would be able to tell Toto.

"You see, Len? It's no good saying it can't have happened because it has. My dear, accept it, be strong. For Lucy. She needs you so much . . ." Martha almost broke down then. If only she could will herself out there somehow. Be with Lucy.

Len said, "Tell Toto I'll phone soon. Tomorrow. Or the next day. I don't know. And we'll be home. Soon. Next month or the one after. Tell her that . . ."

"I'll tell her, Len. Please give my love to Lucy, please —" But the line was dead and, as she replaced the receiver slowly, the bell rang continuously at the front door.

She opened it with a jerk, praying it would be Linda. And it was.

"Oh my dear —" she began.

Linda opened her mouth and screamed. It hit Martha like a shock-wave and she closed her eyes and flinched back.

And then Linda began to talk. She spoke for about three minutes and it seemed much longer. She called Martha terrible names, traitor and Judas among them. She said Martha had been jealous of Bill and Linda and had deliberately seduced Bill. Martha had then lied to Linda about the whole sordid affair.

When at the end of the three minutes she paused for breath, Martha said, appalled, "Linda, I have not lied to you!"

And there was another scream before Linda said, "You told me you hadn't seen him again — Christmas Day — the whole of Christmas Day —"

"Who told you that?"

"Bill!" Linda said with a kind of triumph. "Bill Tatham himself!"

She made as if to hit Martha and Martha stepped back and then immediately said, "Linda, I honestly blocked that out! I'm sorry, I shouldn't have done it! Come in — please come in and let us talk properly —"

"Do you think I'd set foot inside your house again? You're such a hypocrite, Martha! Everyone thinks you're so good, practically a saint! But underneath there's another Martha, isn't there? You pretend not to like Bill Tatham! He's beneath you, isn't he? But you want him all the same! Don't you? Go on, just for once in your life be honest! Admit it!"

There was a terrible silence. Martha thought of Lucy and her dead grandson who had been called Dominic. She thought of Billy Tatham and his down-to-earth common sense.

She whispered, "Yes."

Linda almost ran from her. Down the gravel drive and through the gates and then past the churchyard to her cottage.

Martha closed the door and stood with her forehead against the wood. There was a gentle scratching outside and she opened it again to admit Snowie. She picked him up and wept into his soft fur.

"Oh Snowie . . ."

CHAPTER
ELEVEN

Martha thought her heart might literally break when she saw Lucy first. She told herself they were both — Len and Lucy — suffering from jet lag, but she knew it was much worse than that. Anyway, they had had forty-eight hours to sleep it out and Len looked well; it was Lucy whose appearance was shocking. Thin, drawn, all her prettiness gone, she was like a stranger, looking beyond her mother at something no-one else could see.

They had flown home overnight to find typical British weather; no March winds but plenty of mist and light drizzle. George and Toto met them at Gatwick and took them straight back to the flat in Birmingham, then left immediately. As soon as they got back to their own place in Tewkesbury, Toto telephoned Martha.

"They say they're fine, Martha. But . . . well, none of us are exactly fine, are we?"

"And jet lag," Martha insisted, trying desperately to be "positive".

"That too. It's silly to anticipate . . . anything. They'll be fine. But I wish they had let George and me bring them back here. When all's said and done, I was a nurse. I could have looked after Lucy — got the roses back in her cheeks."

It was such an old-fashioned phrase and Martha had to swallow hard before she said, "They could have come here too. But I sensed . . . they didn't want to."

Toto said quickly — too quickly, "Well, we must accept they want to be together to shoulder this particular burden, Martha. We have to understand."

"Yes. Yes, of course."

So she gave them that forty-eight hours when hopefully they would sleep, then she caught the bus into the city and walked along Corporation Street to the old-fashioned block where Len had lived for the past ten years. It was March and the daffodils blew lustily along the bus route and in Canonhill Park. The flower shops along the city streets were full of them, packed along the front of stalls and backed by the taller statelier tulips. Martha remembered bringing Lucy and Jennifer to lessons at the skating rink and listening to their chatter. Lucy had insisted that the daffodils were trumpeting, unheard only by humans, and Jennifer, so like a tulip herself, had said scornfully, "I wonder you don't call them fairy trumpets! You're so soppy sometimes, Luce!" Lucy had laughed amiably; she had never minded Jennifer's scathing put-downs. Martha stopped and bought half a dozen bunches and stared down into their golden density, wondering whether Jennifer would contact Lucy now, blocking out that awful scene with Linda. That hadn't been difficult when all was said and done. Len's telephone call had put everything else well into the background.

She rang the bell expecting Lucy to appear, but the door opened and, shockingly, Lucy was there. And yet not there. For a dreadful moment neither she nor Martha made a move. Martha was controlling her face with some difficulty and Lucy hardly seemed to register that it was her mother standing there behind the phalanx of daffodils. Lucy was still wearing a dressing-gown and her hair was clinging close to her head in need of a comb or a shampoo. She was, as Toto had warned, absolutely without any roses in her cheeks, but she was not white so much as blue. Her eyes looked smaller than they had been, and almost colourless, and around them the skin was bruised. And her roundness had gone. She was thin and drawn and looked twice her age.

Martha swallowed painfully and then simply held out her arms and they were together, the daffodils crushed between them, Lucy dry-eyed but breathing fast, her fingers clutching at Martha's winter coat as if, just for a moment, she thought her mother might make everything all right again. Martha knew this and wished with all her heart she could do or say something that would help. She squeezed her eyes shut against the pain of helplessness and held Lucy closer, still feeling the terrible lightness of her. The daffodils fell to the ground and were trampled as they somehow moved inside the flat and closed the door. Then Len joined them, haggard but as beautiful as ever, and encircled them with his long arms, resting his head on both of theirs, rocking them gently.

There was the tiniest bit of embarrassment when they broke apart and made for the big living room-cum-kitchen. Martha wondered later how it would have been without Len; he was perfectly sweet, settling them together on the sofa, gathering up the flowers, putting

212

them into vases while the kettle boiled, opening curtains and switching on the fire. But he was there.

Martha said, "Have I come too early? Toto said you were going to sleep -jet lag and so forth."

"Len went into work last night." Lucy sounded slurred and put a hand to her mouth. "Sorry I'm not speaking properly. He went in to make sure the cans of film were there . . . and things . . ."

Len said quickly, "It meant we went to bed late. But our body clocks are probably OK now."

Martha picked up Lucy's left hand in both of hers and massaged it; it was cold, lifeless. "I had to see you. I'll go whenever you say. You must be honest with me."

Len was clattering caps onto a tray. Lucy said suddenly, "All right. I'm glad to see you, Mummy. I didn't think I wanted to. I didn't want to see anyone . . . close to me. But I am glad."

Martha swallowed again, this time with shock. She said, "It will be all right, Luce. You know that really, don't you? It *will* be all right."

"Of course. It is all right. I promise. The trip . . . it was hard. I wanted to come home so much. And yet I didn't. Dominic is . . . there."

Martha closed her eyes. "Oh God."

"I wanted to see you. But then I didn't because we can't go back. Can we? No-one can ever go back."

"Will you come home for a while? A holiday? The flowers are so pretty."

"You're not listening. We can't go back."

"No. Of course not. But we can go on."

Lucy frowned, thinking about it. Then she said another amazing thing. "I would like to see Snowie."

"Well. He'd like to see you." Martha smiled, telling herself that Snowball was a symbol of everything Nortons Heath meant to them both.

Len brought mugs of tea on a tray. The tray was grubby and the coffee table full of clutter. He cleared it by pushing everything together. Lucy sat back watching, making no attempt to help, her flaccid hand still inside her mother's.

"Thank you, Len. Thank you." Martha took her mug and sipped. Len sat opposite them. He gestured vaguely.

"Sorry about the mess. We haven't even unpacked yet. It's going to be difficult to get back into gear. Ma and Dad wanted us to go there — did they tell you?" Martha nodded and he went on, talking loudly and fast as if to cover Lucy's sheer inertia. "I said to Luce: We've got to get ourselves organized again. This is our base — obviously we shall be looking for a house this summer, but until then . . ."

Lucy said, "Jen sent me some wedding snaps. You looked . . . different. You look different now."

"Do I? I feel just the same, darling." Martha sniffed. "I've been very lucky. No illness. Not even a cold this winter."

"George said something about a boyfriend."

Len and Martha laughed together. Martha said, "Not very likely, is it?" and Len said, "You don't know my father very well yet, Luce. He's quite a romantic."

Lucy did not smile. "How is Linda?"

"She's staying at the hotel with Jennifer and Simon. She hasn't been very well —"

"I know. Jen wrote."

Martha felt another little jolt of surprise. She said, "She's much better. It was depression. Something to do with the menopause." Martha looked apologetically at Len, who said something about being the son of a nurse.

Lucy said, "I thought she would come to you. I thought you would take care of her. At the Old Rec."

Martha flushed slightly, memories forcing themselves upon her. Linda had said such terrible things . . . she'd had no idea such hatred could exist. And against her too . . . Did Linda honestly believe that Martha had seduced Bill Tatham? She swallowed yet again.

"I did suggest . . . Obviously she'd rather be with her daughter."

"You know better than that." Lucy did not smile. "Jennifer and Linda never really hit it off."

Len said heartily, "Darling, stop worrying about Linda and Jennifer, for goodness' sake! We're going to concentrate on getting you fit and well, remember?"

Lucy looked up with a kind of mild surprise. "I'm all right, Len. A bit mixed-up, that's all." She withdrew her hand from Martha's and rubbed the knuckles fiercely. "We're not alone with our grief. People all over the world lose babies. It happens."

Len said, "Would you like to go back to bed for an hour or so, Luce? Martha, you wouldn't mind, would you?"

"I told you to be honest." Martha stood up. "Shall I make the bed — change the sheets — or something?"

Lucy looked at her frowning. "I don't need looking after any more, Mummy. I'm a grown woman."

Martha controlled her face with difficulty. Later she wondered whether she should have let her feelings show.

Jennifer had an extra reason now for putting her plan into action. She and Linda were not getting on. Linda seemed to be completely rudderless. Simon had created a position for her — she did two hours on the reception desk in the morning and was supposed to be looking at the cleaning rosters. But her normal energy and vivacity had gone and she merely went through the motions. The computer read-outs on the table in her room remained in exactly the same position as when Jennifer had brought them from the office.

"I can never follow computer stuff," Linda objected. "I've always worked with people, not computers."

Jennifer sighed gustily. "Well, you look bored to death on the desk each morning. I kept an eye on things last Saturday and everyone went to Marlene — they couldn't face your obvious lack of interest!"

Linda had the grace to apologize. "Sorry, love. I've got things on my mind."

Jennifer found herself in the unwelcome position of apologizing to Simon for her own mother.

"She's had a hard life. And this quarrel with Martha—"

"Can't we see Martha? Ask her what happened?"

"No. She's so holier-than-thou. She wouldn't understand what Ma is going through. Ma has changed. She was always so extrovert. Now she's gone inside her head."

216

"It's worse than that really, isn't it? She's so introverted she seems on the brink of implosion."

It was hard to credit; Linda Bowles had been the complete extrovert all her life. It was one of the things her men friends had liked about her; she appeared to live life entirely on the surface; to have no depth at all. It was only Martha who treated her as if she did indeed have a private life that must not be intruded upon. But then, Martha treated everyone with that kind of respect.

It seemed to Jennifer that all roads led back to the same point: Lucy must return to the Old Rectory permanently and then this ghastly little man that her mother so adored would give Linda back her job, and that would eventually lead to something more permanent. Jennifer thought of it all as "reinstating the status quo". Just as it had been before Lucy's wedding when obviously Bill Tatham had known that there was no room for him in Martha Moreton's life.

She imagined herself telling him so: *You got on well with my mother before you got your leg over Martha, didn't you?* It was the sort of language he would understand, he was that sort of man. It was one of the many reasons — Jennifer knew beyond any doubt — why Martha would never consider, for one moment, marrying him. *Now that you know Martha is otherwise engaged, why shouldn't you get on with her again?*

According to Linda, he liked that kind of straight talking; he would admire her for speaking on her mother's behalf. It would work; she knew it would work.

So she called at the flat two weeks after Martha had gone. Like Martha she too brought flowers: freesias and iris; plus a bottle of champagne. It was good that Len was out for this first call. She and Lucy fell into each other's arms, all their previous scratchiness forgotten.

"Your letters . . ." Lucy wept freely, almost happily, into Jennifer's neck. "They kept me sane." She drew them both into the living room. Jennifer saw, as Martha had, that it was somehow forlorn and neglected. Lucy collapsed on to the sofa. "I felt I was losing touch with everyone. Except you. I didn't know Mummy and Linda were had friends. When you told me what Linda said —"

Jennifer said, "I shouldn't have written all that stuff. It helped me to take it, really. But that's selfish."

"You didn't know then about Dominic."

Jennifer had known. Martha had sent for Marcus Goodwin as soon as she had had Len's phone call and for a few days Truda had taken over Miss Darcy. The twins had told her about the baby when she had gone to collect her mother's stuff. It had not stopped her writing to Lucy to tell her that Linda had had to leave the village because of Martha's behaviour.

She murmured, "Oh, Luce. I'm so sorry. So sorry."

Lucy breathed deeply; she did it consciously, not to stay calm — quite the reverse. It was as if she needed to assimilate again and again exactly what had happened to her baby. Her indifference to everything, after the initial agony, seemed like a betrayal of Dominic.

"No-one wants to talk about him," she said. "Len can't bear it. And I think Mummy imagines it will upset me. But he was my baby. He was real. I want to talk about him."

"Tell me then, Luce. Tell me everything. The place, your pregnancy, why he came too soon . . . everything."

Afterwards Jennifer wished she had not invited such complete confidence; it made her course of action even harder. She did in fact try to avoid it by asking Lucy if she could face going home for a while. Though of course "a while" was not really long enough.

"The thing is, darling," she said reasonably. "We were all worried Martha was going to take a foolish step. I think she was simply piqued because Linda had attracted her old boyfriend . . . you know she and Bill Tatham went to school together?"

Lucy nodded; her face was tight with sheer distaste.

"Well, obviously, if you went home, the danger would be gone. She's lonely and has become introspective. It would be good if you were there."

"Sorry, Jen. I can't. I just can't. Mummy and I . . . we were all-in-all. Now we're not. I'm not sure why. I think we've lost each other —"

"It's not that at all. She's cut the apron strings certainly but that's a good thing. She had you so tight, Lucy . . ."

"Did she?"

Jennifer bit her lip; perhaps this was not going to be quite so straightforward as she had pictured.

She said very tentatively, "Listen, Luce. There will be other children. Soon you and Len can start trying again."

Lucy gave a tiny smile. "I can't bear the thought of that, Jen . . . Odd, isn't it? Everyone thinks it's the answer. But you can't replace a child. And there's part of me that never wants to." She shrugged. "I've gone off the whole idea anyway."

Jennifer said directly, "You mean sex?"

Lucy managed another smile. "You don't change. Yes, I mean sex."

Jennifer frowned, thinking what a fool Lucy was. She controlled a shrug; after all it would make her job easier.

"I won't say any more. But darling, I want you to know that whatever happens — however unlikely it might seem — I am always on your side."

Lucy said, with the gentle surprise she often felt these days, "Well. Of course. We've always been best friends."

It all had to be done soon because once Lucy felt better in herself, she might find alternatives to going home. She could start work again and get her own flat. But, Jennifer kept telling herself, at present that was out of the question. When she found out about Len, she would go home to her mother. Jennifer had to believe that. She had to believe that by seducing Len she was being — ultimately — good. She kept using one of the terrible Truda's sayings: cruel to be kind. "I'm going to be cruel to be kind," she said to herself as she whipped past Miss Derry and into her office after one of her many extended lunch hours.

Even so, in spite of all her attempts to justify herself, Jennifer had never found anything in her life as difficult as this particular decision. It meant she would lose Lucy's friendship. It would hurt Martha and, though she told herself that this whole thing was Martha's doing, there was still a nostalgic love and admiration for the woman who had stood in for the family that was missing in Jennifer's life. It would probably mean the end of the marriage with Simon and this was not something to consider lightly. Her lifestyle since she had married him suited her very well. Home life, domesticity, was not for Jennifer and the sheer luxury of life at the Manor House Hotel was perfect. But that was because she had kept on her job at the City Archive Office and had been able to use the hotel as a . . . hotel. Simon had been nagging her for some time to give up her job and take a training course in management. That would be different.

But set against her personal losses — she did not let herself think what it would do to Lucy — was something else. She had always wanted Len. From the moment they met at the Old Rectory, there had been something between them. She accepted that he would never marry her; but she was married and it was dreadful. So in the end the decision was not quite so awful as she had imagined.

She phoned him at work and when he was not there she left an urgent message for him to ring her back.

"Len. Could we meet? I'm anxious about Lucy and I know you are too. I've got an idea."

Len said cautiously, "Can't you tell me over the phone? I don't want to spend any free time away from home."

"All right. It's simply: could you persuade her to come to me for a while? In Worcester? It would be a touch of luxury, Len, yet entirely impersonal. I have this feeling that Lucy does not want to be involved with anyone else for a while. Am I right?"

There was a pause. Then he said, sounding slightly surprised, "Yes. I think you are. She is in a kind of limbo."

"I wouldn't take time off. She would be like any other guest. But when I got home in the evenings, I could see if she would come down to dinner. That means dressing. Getting her hair done. A — a sort of structure."

"I'm with you. It might work."

She forced herself to continue to sound tentative. "It would be worth trying, wouldn't it?"

"Thing is, I don't think she'll agree."

"I might be able to persuade her. But I wanted to hear what you thought first."

"If you can talk her round . . . I don't think you will."

For the first time she felt sorry for Len. He sounded . . . dreary.

"I'll try."

She held on to the receiver and after a while he said, "Thanks Jen."

It was almost too easy. She took another long lunch break and went round to the flat. She heated soup and made toast and served it on trays. Lucy was looking worse, with a yellow tinge beneath her chin. When Jennifer suggested the doctor she shook her head vigorously.

"It's just the cold. I'd forgotten what April was like. Who was it said it was the cruellest month? It is, isn't it? You expect so much, but it cheats."

A wind, funnelling down Corporation Street, rattled the windows in their frames as if in agreement.

"You need a break, Lucy. You're not up to house-keeping and looking after Len." It was obvious Lucy was doing neither of those things but Jennifer swept on

222

regardless. "Come back to the hotel with me. Why don't you? Think about it, darling. Your own room. Complete privacy yet everything you could want within call. I'd be home by five thirtyish. If you felt like it we could have dinner together. Or not." She grinned. "I have a feeling you and Len could do with a break from each other. And this — this would be such a natural thing to do."

Lucy took one of her deep breaths. "I could go to Mummy's if I wanted a break."

"Well yes. But that involves . . . things. Len would come down in the evenings. People would call. The hotel is so impersonal, Luce. Isn't that what you want?"

"Is it? I don't know any more. I suppose I could mention it to Len. See what he thinks."

"I've done that, darling. I wouldn't have asked you without clearing it with Len first. We talked on the phone. He thinks it might be a good thing. But he says you won't agree to it."

"Does he?" Lucy stood up and walked unsteadily to the window. She rammed a rubber wedge into the sash to stop the rattling and then stood looking at the bleak street outside. She said, "I hate it when Easter is in March. There's nothing happening in April at all."

Jennifer waited. She wondered how Len could put up with this every day.

Lucy said, "All right. If you think . . . and Len thinks . . ."

Really, Jennifer thought, when Lucy arrived at the Manor House, it was an ideal arrangement. There was poor Lucy battered and injured and Linda not much

223

better: the two of them found comfort in each other. They sat out in the conservatory overlooking the river and cathedral, like a couple of invalids in a mid-European hydro. Neither of them was really interested in food as such, but they built their days around small routines: morning coffee and afternoon tea were practically sacrosanct; it amazed Jennifer that either of them could stand it. If they went to do a bit of shopping in Worcester they had to be back for these two rituals. They might occasionally lunch out, but they were always back in the conservatory at eleven o'clock in the morning and four o'clock in the afternoon.

Jennifer wondered what Martha made of it all. She must be hurt; mortally wounded that Lucy was finding solace with Linda. Jennifer tightened her lips. Martha had proved to have feet of clay; she was as capable as Linda and Jennifer of lying. Somehow, from her, it was disgusting.

The next part of the plan was easy. She called it the Encounter. She borrowed a key to the flat from Lucy on the pretext of cleaning it up and shopping for Len. It was so above board it was almost pathetic. She did her bit, changed the bed linen and all the towels, dusted and vacuumed and went to the laundrette. That took three days. Miss Derry asked her politely whether she had had a word with Mr Masonfield about her extended lunches. She smiled and said, "Of course."

On the fourth day, when surely Len would be wanting news of Lucy, she told Simon she was working late and went round to the flat at six. She lit the gas fire and laid the table and was on her second glass of wine when Len

224

appeared. It was nothing — really — to do with Dutch courage. Nevertheless her heartbeats reverberated alarmingly throughout her body when she saw him for the first time since the wedding. Nine months.

He was surprised to see her. "Lucy?" he asked immediately. "Is she ill?"

"She's not well. But you knew that. She's no worse and I think she might even be better." Jennifer poured more wine and brought him a glass. "I thought you would want first-hand news of her. And she might like to know I've seen you."

He didn't trust her. She could see his glance darting around the room as if looking for clues. She put her glass down and went around the kitchen counter to take hot plates out of the oven.

"This is from that new place. Salmon *en croûte*. I don't know what it will be like." She spoke over her shoulder, very casually. "What did you think of the devilled kidneys yesterday?"

"Lucy asked you to keep an eye on me, did she?" he asked. He hadn't taken off his car coat. It was as if he were poised to run.

"Yes." She looked up for an instant and said frankly, "Len, I'm sorry it's not working out. Maybe if you give her time . . ."

"What are you talking about?"

She bent to the oven again. "Oh . . . you know. We've talked. She is terrified of becoming pregnant again." She put the dish of puffed pastry on the counter. "There is salad. Will that do? I quite like a combination of hot and cold, don't you?"

"Yes. I don't care." He was at last shrugging out of his coat. "I didn't think that you and Lucy were still . . . close."

"Oh yes. We kept in touch while you were away. And now that we're both married, well, we understand each other."

For the first time he met her gaze; his eyes narrowed. "Have you told her . . . anything about us?"

"Us? There is no us, Len."

He said impatiently, "Have you told her about my . . . proposition?"

She laughed. "Of course not. Anyway, neither of us took that very seriously, did we?"

"No." He was still staring at her. She could almost feel him reconnecting with her. He said abruptly, "It's good of you to get the food. See to the flat. You're a good friend to Lucy. I'll wash and we can eat."

"Yes. Do that."

She took the food to the table and picked up her wine glass and held it towards the bathroom door. "Here's to us," she murmured.

It was not quite so easy as she anticipated that first evening. She had not fully realized the extent of Len's grief for the loss of his child; somehow she had not even thought of the child as Len's. It had been Lucy's baby right from the beginning and it was something of a shock when, one evening three weeks after that first supper, he broke down and tried to tell her how he felt about Dominic. He and Lucy both called him Dominic as if he had been a proper person. Jennifer found this difficult to understand. She tried to tell Len how much worse it would be if the baby had lived for a year or two; become part of them. He agreed with her; it made his grief no less.

She used shock tactics on him and put it to him bluntly that they were both married now so that made any betrayal a more mutual thing, and she would be happy to take him up on his "proposition".

He said, "You're sorry for me, aren't you?"

She thought about it. "Yes," she said honestly, but it was not because of the baby. It was because she knew that he was going to lose Lucy. "I'm sorry for you because I've got a horrible feeling nothing is going to get better." She took a deep breath and said, "I think Lucy has fallen out of love with you, Len."

"No!" He was passionate at first. "She's getting better all the time! You said so yourself! And anyway I can see she is. When I came over last weekend, she told me she was going to see Martha. Martha's called in several times —"

"I know all this, Len."

"She tells you everything!" He sounded bitter. "But surely you can see that by going back to the Old Rectory, she is feeling more certain about things."

Jennifer shrugged. "I don't know. She could be." She looked at him. "Unless she plans to stay there."

"You know something. She's talked to you . . . Tell me one thing. Is she leaving me?"

"I don't know. She talks to me, Len, but she doesn't tell me everything. People don't. They seem to be open and honest, but there's always something." She went to him. "For instance, you want me to think you are broken-hearted. But really, what was there between you and Lucy? When the sun shone you were fine. But then . . ." She took his face between her hands. "Len, is it your pride? If your marriage is on the rocks will it hurt you because you've failed? Or because —"

He shouted at her, wrenching himself free. "Shut up! Shut up, Jen! You don't know what you're talking about —"

She grabbed him and kissed him forcibly. He freed himself again but did not move away. He was breathing heavily.

She laughed. "You're dead when you're with Luce. When you're with me, you're alive!"

He panted, "This is what you wanted all the time, isn't it?"

"Yes. Don't you know why? My marriage is as sterile as yours, Len."

He stared at her; she knew with a little thrill that she was mistress of the situation. For an instant she wondered whether to walk away from it. Just as she'd done with Simon; bring Len to his knees, perhaps literally. But then she couldn't because, in her way, she loved Len.

She took him in her arms.

"It's all right, my darling. It's all right," she whispered.

There was no need for her to find a way of letting Lucy know. The next time Len visited the Manor House, he could not keep it from her. She was not in the conservatory as usual and he found her in her room, sitting by the window, waiting for him.

"Len." She smiled but did not stand up. He found it easier to look at her objectively now. She was thin to the point of being emaciated; he thought with shame that her youth had gone.

She said, "I thought we could talk up here. They'll bring our dinner upstairs later."

He looked at her again; what did she want to talk about? Did she know anything? He leaned over her to kiss her mouth and at the last moment moved his lips to her cheek.

"Bit of a cold," he murmured.

If anything she seemed relieved. She said, "Would you rather not sleep in here, Len? The hotel's not full. Simon will find you another room."

"Well . . . perhaps. It might be better." He tried to tell himself she was rejecting him again, he tried all the time to justify what was happening. It was wonderful with Jennifer; they had been together every moment they could that week. But they were the only times he was happy. Jennifer could not stay overnight of course and he did not sleep. He felt dizzy and longed to see her again. Yet . . . here sat his wife. Even as he asked how she was and whether she was eating her meals, he was wondering how Jennifer would manage to come to him tonight. She had said she would.

Lucy looked at him properly for the first time since that time on the beach in Santo Domingo. She said, "You're thin too, Len. Are *you* eating properly?"

229

He said hoarsely, "Jennifer has been getting me stuff. Did you ask her to do that?"

She could not remember. Jennifer had wanted the key to clear up the flat. Had she said anything about feeding Len every day? She nodded uncertainly.

Len sat down near her but did not take her hand. He said, "What did you want to talk about, Lucy? Have you decided to go and see your mother?"

"I thought . . ." Lucy looked out of the window. Her mother had been to see her every other day and had not been welcomed. Lucy had spoken to Linda and Linda had held nothing back. Now, quite suddenly, in spite of all that Martha had done, Lucy wanted to be with her. Quite simply she wanted her mother.

She said, "You know about it, do you? All the gossip? Mummy and that man?"

"Jennifer's spoken about it," Len said. "I don't believe it. Do you?"

"I don't know. He's not there now, that's for certain. So I might go."

"Please do, Luce."

She glanced at him again. "Yes. All right."

He cleared his throat. "Was there anything else?"

She hesitated. Then she said, "Is it over, Len? Between us?"

"I don't know." Suddenly he was angry. "I think that's a question I should be asking. After last Christmas you started playing hard to get. We haven't been together since — since Dominic."

She looked at him. "After the funeral. On the beach."

"You didn't want me — be honest —"

"I did want you. But all you wanted was sex." She made a face and for a moment he knew why husbands hit their wives. She said, "Tell me something. Is there someone else?" He hesitated too long and she added, "Is it Jennifer?"

"I refuse to be harangued like this! You think you're the only one who is grieving for Dominic! Well, you're not! We could comfort one another, but that, apparently, is not on the agenda! Your mother will comfort you!"

She waited but he said no more. So she said quietly, "I see. You will find your comfort with Jennifer." She took a deep breath. "This explains so much."

He said, "There's still time, Luce."

She looked incredulous and after a while he got up and left the room.

Two days later she moved back into the Old Rectory. Martha was almost frightened to believe in what was happening. Since Lucy had been staying at the hotel in Worcester, Martha had suffered terribly. The pain had been physical; it had affected her breathing like a chronic stitch and she had had to pause occasionally and stand very straight and take deep breaths. She wanted to tell Lucy that Billy Tatham meant nothing to her; that whatever Jennifer had told her she had got the wrong end of the stick. But Lucy was in no state for emotional scenes. Besides this, Martha could not quite block out that time with Linda, when she had admitted that Billy did mean something to her. So she visited the hotel and tried to pretend it was the most normal thing in the world for her daughter to be staying there. The really awful thing was that so often she discovered Lucy sitting with Linda in the conservatory. Each time Lucy immediately got up and joined her mother, but Martha wondered whether that was to spare Linda any embarrassment. Lucy had so little to say, Martha had to fall back on telling her bits of village gossip: Mrs Rector had told the Venableses that they were execrable parents' and they had told her she obviously did not "get enough". At one time this story would have reduced Lucy to tears of laughter; now she murmured, "Oh dear." Martha felt bound to follow these anecdotes with, "I think I should be getting back now, dear." To which Lucy always simply nodded, said her solemn goodbyes and made for the conservatory door again.

And then, as May brought a most welcome heatwave, Lucy telephoned and asked whether she could move into the Old Rectory. And, the day after, she arrived in a taxi clutching a large tapestry holdall that she'd had since schooldays. She looked waif-like, though probably no more than usual, and her face, so small and thin, was not tearful. Indeed, as she put down the bag and gathered Snowie to her, she actually smiled into his fur and let the smile stay on her face as she looked up at her mother.

"It's good to be home," she said, simply.

Martha swallowed. "It's good to have you home, darling."

She had spent the morning removing all traces of baby equipment from Lucy's room, but even so Lucy said, "It smells different, Mummy."

"Sorry, darling. I've used some fly stuff. The heat brought out the midges."

Lucy turned and looked at her mother straightly. Her eyes, so washed-out, darkened. "You made a nursery here, didn't you?"

Martha said quickly, "There were a few things around. Presents. You know." She took one of her deep breaths. "Look, don't think about it, Lucy. Please."

Lucy gave her a look of surprise. "But, Mummy, it's lovely. He was going to be welcomed . . . it's lovely. Really."

Martha felt her eyes watering. She turned away. "It's lunchtime. Shall I make some sandwiches? We could eat outside."

"I'd like that." Lucy sounded quietly pleased. It was the first time Martha had heard that note in her voice since she'd left last August.

She paused by the door. "Darling, will you be able to stay a few days? Because if you can I'll get Denise Coupland to do the flowers for me."

"Oh yes. If she wouldn't mind." There was a little hesitation. Then Lucy unpacked in the way she always had, by tipping the contents of her bag onto the bed. She said, "If you can put up with me, that is."

Martha almost ran to her, sobbing. Then she smiled at the jumbled pile of clothes and said, "Oh I think I can manage to put up with you, darling." And left the room.

But as they established a routine during those first few days, it became apparent that Lucy thought she would still be there the following winter.

She said, "I'll be able to do more quite soon, Mummy. If you like, I could lift the bulbs this year. Then we could have a bed of daffodils in front of the cotoneaster. What d'you think?"

"Why not? Those shrubs always look a bit rusty come spring. It would be lovely to see the daffs against them." She glanced sideways. Lucy had not put on any weight. But then she'd been here less than a week. Martha closed her eyes and planned next week's meals. She'd get some ice-cream. Or make some. There was a recipe she used to have with about a dozen egg yolks . . .

Lucy said, "When I told you we couldn't go back. . . we can in some ways, can't we? Here we are, with Snowie, sitting in the sun. Exactly like it was . . . before."

"Well, yes."

"I want to apologize. I shouldn't have believed . . . what I believed. But, we can go back, can't we?"

"Of course." Martha smiled reassuringly. "You don't have to apologize, darling. There have been so many misunderstandings since you went away. We got ourselves into a muddle. But we're coming out of it now."

Lucy was silent, her eyes closed, her small body lost in the deckchair. Then she said, "Mummy, there's no way of helping you over this. Len and I . . . we're finished. And I want to come back home. To live."

Martha felt her eyes stretch. She took one of her deep breaths.

"You've had a row — people have rows —"

"He's having an affair with Jennifer. That's it, Mummy. I can't live with that."

"Oh my God!" Martha was appalled. "What is she thinking of . . . It might not be true. Are you sure? Listen,

234

Lucy. It's her doing. Not Len's. You have to understand that —"

"Darling" — Lucy opened her eyes and sat up — "please don't be upset. I'm not. It was over anyway. Honestly. I'm relieved for a number of reasons. The main one being, I know now that the things she said were not true." Amazingly, she smiled. "I can come home. I need you, Mummy. It was terrible when I thought someone was here — in Daddy's place. But that's all right now. Isn't it?" Martha still stared and Lucy added quietly, "It is true, darling."

Martha whispered, "I can't believe this is happening. Lucy, you loved him. He loved you — it was obvious —"

"I don't think he did, actually. But . . . perhaps we'll talk about that one day. All I ask you to believe is that now — this present time — I am just . . . relieved. I am so relieved, Mummy. I can come home. Be with you." And at last the pale blue eyes filled with tears. "I have wanted to be with you . . . so much. I can't tell you. I have wanted, quite desperately, to put the clock back. And when I knew I couldn't, I thought I would die. Just . . . die."

"Oh my dear." Martha was on her knees by the other deckchair, folding Lucy to her as if she were a baby again. And so they hugged and rocked, the barriers down, Martha at once appalled and thankful. When they drew apart at last, smiling, Lucy wiping her face with the back of her hand, Martha fishing for a handkerchief, it was Martha who still said, "It can't be over, sweetheart. just give it time. Give everything time. You're not well, you must know that —"

"Oh, I'm well." Lucy took the proffered handkerchief and blew loudly. "I was like this before. With Dominic. Awful for a few weeks and then blooming. I shall bloom again, don't worry. That's how I know I can do the bulbs."

Martha said slowly, "What are you saying, darling?"

"Yes. Cart before the horse . . ." But Lucy was actually laughing. "Oh Mummy, I'm pregnant. I was so frightened and angry and . . . everything. It shouldn't be possible because my milk was coming and I thought it was all right to . . . Anyway, I am. I'm pregnant." She laughed, almost naturally.

Martha stared. "Darling, you can't be. It's too soon . . . it's much too soon."

"That's what I thought. And all the symptoms — well, they were part of the grief for Dominic. I thought. And then when I started feeling sick I thought it was because of Len and Jennifer. I *thought*." She laughed again, this time nervously. "Don't look like that, Mummy. It — it's natural. All the symptoms — they're natural. Not like the awfulness of Dominic." She smiled. "I got one of those kit things — actually there was one in Jennifer's bathroom and I took it. It was positive. So you see I was even more desperate to come home." She shook her head. "I didn't think that it might be . . . well, awfully selfish. I just was so pleased. That you would share it all."

"I still can't believe it." Martha felt fresh tears on her face. "How can it have happened, Lucy? Do you know when it will be — have you any idea of the date?"

236

Lucy said quietly, "I know exactly, Mummy. It only happened once, you see. After Dominic's funeral."

Martha gave an audible gasp. "Oh God . . . oh Lucy!" A tear dripped from the end of her nose. "We must see a doctor. There could be damage . . ."

Lucy shook her head. "I'm sorry, darling. I shouldn't have told you like that. It wasn't . . . awful. Honestly." She leaned forward. "Mummy, if you will help, it could be wonderful. A fresh life for the two of us. I've thought about it so much." Very tenderly she began to dry her mother's face. "D'you think you can help me through this, Mummy?"

Martha could hardly speak. The consequences piled before her mountainously. She heard Lucy say, "Mummy? Are you all right?"

And, at last, she nodded.

CHAPTER
TWELVE

Jennifer would have liked life to continue as it was that early summer. She spent the week in Birmingham living in Len's flat, seeing him every evening, sleeping ecstatically with him every night. At weekends she went back to Worcester, mainly because of her mother, but also because it kept another door open. She was almost certain that Simon knew exactly what was going on; he had a way of looking at her as if she were some kind of entertainer and he was wondering what she was going to do next. His expression said that at present he found her mildly amusing, but that might change. She saw him once looking at the laundry list on the computer so he must know that she brought home Len's laundry as well as her own.

His apparent acceptance of the situation made her feel defiant; she made no secret of the fact that she was seeing Len occasionally. "Len took me for a meal in the week." "It was a good play — Len was there actually, so we sat together."

Simon smiled at these disclosures; it was left to Linda to say, "How is he now, darling? Such a tragic thing to happen."

238

When she did not immediately reply, Simon said gently, "Yes, how is he, Jen? Funny how we've both lost babies, isn't it?"

That made her angry. She was only too aware that Len had turned to her because of his grief; Simon had no idea what he was talking about.

She said, "I think he's coping. Somehow. He's got nowhere to run to though, has he? Not like Lucy."

Simon's small smile disappeared. Linda said placatingly, "Lucy is ill, Jen. I could tell that when she was staying here. And let's face it, her proper place is with her mother."

Jennifer shrugged non-committally. Simon smiled again. "Actually, her proper place is with her husband. Lucy and Len. It's got quite a ring to it, hasn't it? Not quite so amusing as Jen and Len, of course."

Linda looked anxiously from one to another. Jennifer said gaily, "No, I suppose not."

"Better than Jennifer Moreton probably."

Jennifer assumed a little frown as if considering the matter. Then she nodded slowly and said, "Probably."

Simon had been sitting with the two women in the conservatory; he stood up briskly. "Right then, that's settled." He made for the door, then turned. "Your mother is welcome to stay on, of course. But I'd like your room empty by this evening ready to be cleaned tomorrow."

Linda gasped as if he'd thrown a bucket of water over her. Jennifer's expression hardened. She said, "All right. I'll see to it." She maintained her icy calm until he disappeared into his office, then she looked at her mother and quite deliberately started to tell her exactly what she thought of him. Linda waved her arms helplessly.

"Jen, it's absolutely no good going on like that. He's in the right! You've thrown him away, Jen! You're an idiot!"

"Just listen to the wise one!" Jennifer snapped. "What I've done has been for you. Got that? Lucy is now installed at the Old Rectory and likely to remain there. Martha will see it as her life's work to look after her. That leaves the field clear for you, Mother mine! So don't call me an idiot!"

Linda was appalled. "Oh my God! You can't saddle me with this fiasco, Jennifer! I'm supposed to be learning to live without any thought of Bill Tatham! You know what it was like for me in February — that terrible row with Martha and I didn't even know that she'd just heard . . ." She began to weep again just as she had for those first few awful days she'd been at the hotel when Jennifer had seriously thought she was unhinged.

"Oh Ma — Christ, shut up, will you? You've done enough crying to last you for the rest of your life! Pull yourself together. I'm going to talk to your bloody Tatham man and put all the cards on the table."

Linda wailed, "That's what he used to say — all the cards on the table . . ."

"Right. Then that's what we'll do." Jennifer looked at her hands and saw they were shaking. She'd been married less than six months and it was over. All that scheming and work and it was over. And Simon had

240

dismissed her as if she were a chambermaid. "I'd like your room empty by tonight"! Who did he think he was?

She crouched by Linda's chair and put her arms around the heaving shoulders very tightly so that the shaking stopped.

"Listen, Ma. Don't get yourself into a state. I planned this, remember. You said yourself, ages ago, that you thought Len and I had something going for us. Well, we did. And we have. I can help Len through this — he's happy with me. And I am very happy with him. So why are you crying?"

"I feel respon-ponsible," Linda hiccoughed.

"I did what I wanted to do," Jennifer said honestly. "It's presented you with an opportunity. That's all. I'll have a word with Bill Tatham like I said. Then it's up to you. OK?"

After a while, Linda's shoulders relaxed and she said quietly, "OK, Jen." Lucy had said to her not long ago that it did not help to cry; all that happened was that you ended up with a bad headache. Lucy had been right. Linda waited until Jennifer left her then rummaged in her bag for the aspirin.

George and Toto refused to believe what Len told them. He wondered what their reaction would have been had he mentioned Jennifer.

Toto said, "She's ill, Len. *Ill!* Just because she's gone to stay with her mother doesn't mean she's left you! What *is* the matter with you, my son?"

They were sitting around the garden table drinking coffee. It was a perfect day, the Saturday before Whit

Sunday; from across the roofs of Tewkesbury came the sound of bells from the Abbey. Len sat there, looking at the two people he loved so much who had worked so hard to "give him his chance" as they had put it, and wondered what was happening to him. He had been in control of his life; completely in control. And now he was not. When he thought of Lucy, when he was with Lucy, he was unhappy. When he thought of Jennifer, he was also unhappy. But when he was with Jennifer she gave him something he had never known before. He sometimes thought that if he could be with her all the time, he might conquer the world. He hated weekends when Jennifer did not see him. The plan had been for him to visit Lucy at weekends, but that had tailed off quite quickly. There was something about Lucy and Martha together that was indefinably strong. Neither of them were condemning, both of them kept up the pretence that this was a temporary arrangement. But there was simply no place for him at the Old Rectory. When Martha went out — ostensibly to make coffee, but really to give them a chance to be alone — Lucy invariably picked up the cat and held him to her like a symbol of her old self. Len told himself resentfully that she had regressed to the schoolgirl and student she had once been. Quite deliberately she was turning the clock back, pretending he had never happened. He hoped that justified what he was doing. He hoped it would help to make him less unhappy. It did not.

He said, "Ma, forgive me, but you don't know what you're talking about. This . . . split . . . is something separate from her illness. You'll just have to believe me."

It was George's turn. He was less volatile. "We feel we know Lucy quite well, Len. Be honest with us. Has there been a row?"

"Not as such. But there has been this . . . split. We don't need to talk about it —"

Toto exploded again. "So you haven't talked it over? What is the *matter* with you, Len? You are in the business of communication and you haven't talked over the fact that something is wrong with your marriage and you think — you don't even know, you just *think* that she has gone home because she has left you? For goodness' sake, son! I've never heard such drivel —"

George interrupted gently, "You must talk to her, Len. You're ill too. You don't realize it, but you are. You're both suffering from shock after losing the baby. It's worse for Lucy, of course, but it's terrible for you too. You need to discuss these things."

Len saw he was getting nowhere. Of course they were right, he should be talking to Lucy. But the fact that she had moved back to the Old Rectory proved to him beyond all doubt that their marriage was over. So what would he say? "I'm sorry but we were never very good in bed . . ." He couldn't say that when he remembered her in that wood-smelling room overlooking the Atlantic in Barbados. She had . . . how would she put it? . . . she had "given herself" to him then. Night after night there had been this giving. And then, when there had been that tiny ruck during their time in Santo Domingo, she had given into him, but she had not given herself. He had been appalled by her coldness then and had known that it had never been the same since. After Dominic's funeral, when he had wept into her breast on the beach, he had known she had not wanted him. She had wept too, but not with love for him. She had not loved him then, nor for some time before. She had made him feel insensitive, an animal with an animal's desires. He had not made love to her since then. He remembered, with exquisite joy, that first time with Jennifer. She had initiated everything and he had held her and sobbed with gratitude.

He said, "Listen. I've been asked to cover this latest lorry-drivers' blockade in France. They want me to find a personal angle. Like I did in the Republic —"

"When you had Lucy working with you," Toto said significantly.

"I hardly think there will be any pregnant women sitting up in those cabs," he said angrily.

"Why not? It sounds exactly the sort of thing Lucy would have discovered!" Toto came back just as angrily. "There's your personal angle for you straightaway!"

"Ma. Listen. Please. All I'm saying is, when I get back I will talk to Lucy. And I'll let you know exactly what she says."

"And what you say — don't leave that out of the equation." Toto's plumpness quivered with the effort to be sarcastic; it was not her line at all.

George tried to defuse the situation. "Should he take a tape recorder along, Mother?"

"Very funny, George." Toto had another thought. "My God. What is poor Martha going through now!"

Len stood up. "Going on impressions gleaned from my last visit" — he spoke deliberately like a BBC announcer — "she seemed very happy. Things have gone back to how they were before I appeared. That suited her well."

Toto looked up at him and then burst into noisy tears. George gathered her up and said, "There, there." And Len left.

But Len was right in this. Martha was happy. Lucy's pregnancy seemed to make everything all right. Not just all right, but shiningly, amazingly wonderful. It explained so much between Len and Lucy. Martha did not ask any questions but it became obvious during their long talks that Len had not waited more than three days after Dominic's premature birth and death to insist on his marital rights. Martha hardly dared imagine what went on between them. In her mind Len became a grotesque figure and she would shudder at the thought of him. As for Jennifer, who had been married five months, she was the original marriage-wrecker. Martha blocked both of them out of her mind and concentrated all her energies into looking after Lucy. She had a purpose in life again; she could consign Billy Tatham to the back of her head, her indiscretions connected somehow with being a schoolgirl and fancy-free, nothing real. It was as if she and Lucy were safe inside a bubble shining with rainbow colours, protected from the world. When Toto rang and asked if they could call some time, Martha had no difficulty in putting her off.

"You do understand, don't you?" she said. "Lucy is so frail and, after the hurly-burly of hotel life, all she wants to do is to sit and soak up this glorious sunshine

245

and cuddle the cat!" She laughed to take any sting out of her words.

And Toto said sadly, "Yes. Yes, of course. I do understand."

Martha would have liked to tell her about the baby, but then Toto might think it odd that Len wasn't around more often. In fact, Len had not come calling for some time now, which was a relief to both women.

Toto cleared her throat — surely she hadn't got a cold? — and said, "When Len comes back from France, he has promised to come and talk to Lucy. Properly. He won't — he'll try not to upset either of you. But it's so important . . . Lucy will see him, won't she?"

Martha realized with a jolt that Toto knew that they were separated. Len must have told them. So none of it was a figment of Lucy's fevered imagination. Not that Martha had thought for one second . . . She said, "It will be up to Lucy. I can't make any promises for her."

There were sounds from the other end of the connection. Martha knew suddenly that Toto was crying. "I suppose . . . Martha, could I possibly have a word with Lucy? Now?"

Martha lied without difficulty. "She's in the bath, my dear. Perhaps she'll ring you back. But I want her to have a sleep after lunch."

Toto said again, even more sadly, "I understand."

Martha did not mention the call to Lucy. She was in the sitting room using the sewing machine. She was short of summer frocks and Martha had found some gingham in one of the trunks. Lucy was making herself a sundress.

246

Martha called now, "Tea or lemonade?"

"Water please, Mummy. I'm just coming. Shall we sit outside again?"

"Rather." Martha looked at the lemons she had been squeezing when Toto phoned. She added sugar. Much better than water.

She carried the jug and some glasses on to the lawn and settled herself with a contented sigh. The sound of a car passing the gate and making for the terraced cottages opposite the church pointed up the inviolability of the Old Rec. The feeling of being in a fortress was comforting; after Dr Chase had confirmed the pregnancy and told her smilingly he had known only two other cases like it and she must rest as much as possible, Martha had taken her duty as protector very seriously indeed. And Lucy revelled in what she called "sequesterdom".

Martha half closed her eyes and through swimming vision realized someone was turning in at the gate and walking up the gravel towards the chairs. Albert came on a Monday and today was Wednesday. She opened her eyes. It was Billy Tatham.

Linda was back in her old quandary again. Her position at the Manor House Hotel was anomalous, to put it mildly. Simon had long ago given up trying to ease her on to the staff and she hardly liked to suggest it again now, as if trying to make recompense for Jennifer's behaviour. She did try to broach the subject with Simon.

"I don't know what to do, Simon dear. I mean, this thing with Jennifer — it won't last. They never do."

"No. I gathered that. I thought a wedding ring might do the trick, but apparently not."

Linda was flustered; it did not take much to fluster Linda any more. "I didn't mean *you*, dear! Of course not! She will want to come back to you, I'm quite sure of that!"

"Perhaps I won't want that, Linda."

"No, of course you might not. All I mean is . . . it's all my fault, Simon. And this . . . arrangement is so awkward for you. I think I had better go back home."

He said impatiently, "It's not your fault, Linda, for God's sake! And those funny neighbours of yours are still there."

She couldn't tell him that Jennifer had seduced Len to release Billy Tatham from Martha's clutches. For one thing it all sounded highly unlikely and for another, Jennifer was her daughter when all was said and done. So she said, "It's in her blood, Simon. I've always led a pretty hectic life. She gets it from me."

"She spent time with Clem Moreton and Lucy and Martha. She's got reasons to be grateful to them. Look how she's treated them!"

She looked at his pale face and felt a little shiver inside herself. He wasn't particularly hurt by Jennifer's desertion but he was angry. That was another reason for leaving the hotel. And soon.

She wrote him quite a long letter, checking her spellings on the computer, blocking out unnecessary bits, signing it with a flourish, "Linda Bowles", and then wondering whether she should add in brackets, "mother-in-law". Later, when Jennifer told her about the

248

whacking great bill he sent her, she was glad she hadn't. He might have thought she was looking for favours. The taxi from Worcester to Nortons Heath cost quite enough as it was and until she could get to the bank, she had very little cash.

When she saw Bill's car outside the church, she thought her heart might explode. All her resolutions about leading a life without him went to the winds. She almost fell out of the taxi and let the driver struggle with her cases while she fitted her key into the lock tremblingly and let herself in.

Obviously he wasn't there; how could he be? Nevertheless she ran from room to room searching for signs of his presence. Could she smell aftershave in the bathroom? Was that his pen on the flap of the bureau?

The taxi-driver repeated the cost of the fare from his position in the porch. She gabbled an apology and fingered some notes out of her purse. Then she shut the door and leaned against it and let the awful truth seep into her consciousness. Bill was visiting the Old Rec. There was no other explanation. The aftershave smell was the deodorant block she always left in the bathroom; the pen was on the open bureau because she had started to write a furious letter to Martha before she had grabbed the phone and got hold of Jennifer. Bill had not been in the cottage; there was no way he could have opened the door anyway. Linda faced the truth yet again; and again it hurt almost unbearably.

Martha said frantically, "You must go! What are you doing here — you must go straightaway! I mean it, Billy

249

— Lucy is here with me and she is not well and she must not see you!"

He stopped, one foot on the lawn, the other still on the gravel. He was wearing a T-shirt emblazoned on the front with the words "Tatham's Tents" and, even more incongruously, was wearing a panama hat. Martha saw him through Lucy's eyes: he looked ridiculous, a figure of fun; the awful Brummie evacuee who had tried to kiss her at school.

She said again, urgently, "Please go, Billy! I don't want Lucy to see you."

Still he did not move; he seemed incapable of moving. She watched as his ebullience slowly disappeared. As if she had stuck a needle into him and he was deflating. She felt terrible and went towards him waving her hands.

"Billy, I'm sorry. But I told you how it was. You knew —"

"Yes. It's me who should be sorry, Marty. I . . . Actually, I came to ask about Lucy. I didn't know she was here, of course, but when I saw that bit on the telly last night —"

Lucy's voice was clearer than it had been since she arrived. "What piece? We don't often watch the television."

Martha turned too quickly and stumbled. Billy was there, his hand on her arm. She shook herself free.

"Darling. I didn't hear you."

"I know." Lucy's voice was strong as well as clear. "I saw the car parked outside the church and was curious. I take it this is the ubiquitous Billy Tatham."

Martha could have quailed. Lucy was rarely sarcastic unless she was being funny and she was not being funny.

250

Billy stepped forward. "Not that ubiquitous, Mrs Travers." His own voice was sharp. "I think in my life I've seen your mother perhaps six times. And you . . . just the once." He held out his hand and Lucy frowned, ignoring it. He reminded her gently. "At your wedding last summer. You hired your marquee from me." He reached out and took her hand from her side. She was clutching the gingham and he held it against her arm while he shook her hand. Then he took off his panama, produced an enormous handkerchief from the pocket of his flannels and mopped his face.

"I shouldn't have come without telephoning first. But if your mother has advance warning of my arrival, she always puts me off. So I've turned up. And it's the wrong time. I'll leave you."

He turned and stepped back onto the gravel. Martha looked at Lucy. She felt utterly miserable. The T-shirt, the cricket hat. Was Billy Tatham going to spoil everything?

Lucy said grudgingly, "Oh for goodness' sake! You can have my deckchair — I'm in the middle of sewing. And I see my mother has made lemonade. I'd prefer water so please sit down and tell us what you saw on the television and then I can get on!"

Martha had not seen him indecisive before. He hovered and she thought he would lose his balance just as she had; she did not dream he would accept Lucy's awful invitation. But then he turned, gave a small sharp sigh and spoke to Lucy directly.

"Cards on the table, girl. I think the world of your mother and you don't like me. Fair enough. I didn't

251

know you were here, but I do know you've lost your baby. So I'm not surprised, I suppose. Especially . . . Last night they showed the lorry-drivers' business. Further up the coast this time. Britanny, Roscoff. Your hubby was doing a piece. About how the drivers were missing out on their wives and families. Your friend was with him. Linda's girl. Jennifer Bowles."

Lucy said coolly, "Yes. We know about Jennifer and Len. But thank you for telling us."

"That's all right, love." Billy let his Birmingham accent deepen on the term of affection. Surprisingly, Lucy half smiled. He turned again to leave and said over his shoulder, "I've said it to your mum and I'll say it to you. If I can do owt . . . whatever . . . you've got my phone number."

Lucy did not reply and Martha watched, frozen to the spot, as Billy crunched down the gravel and into the road without once looking back.

Then she said, "Lucy, I'm sorry. I felt we were so safe here. Billy Tatham has a way of lumbering in where angels fear to tread."

Lucy had put her sewing on the grass and was settling herself in a deckchair. "So I see." She picked up the lemonade and poured some into a glass. "I really would have preferred water, Mummy. But if you'd rather I had this sugary stuff, that's all right."

Martha looked at her. She knew Lucy was talking about other things besides the lemonade. She said, "That walk. At Christmas. Did it upset you?"

Lucy made a face. "It really is cards on the table!" She shook her head. "There were other things, Mummy. I

252

was going downhill then though I didn't know it at the time. And George told me . . ."

"Yes, I know what George said."

"I suppose I was upset." Lucy gave a wry smile. "I was more than upset, I was . . . bereft! Silly."

Martha took her seat and sipped at some of the lemonade. Lucy was no longer upset. That was good, wasn't it? She was no longer upset because she had seen Billy Tatham for herself and knew that he was not her mother's sort. And that — for some reason — was not so good.

Billy walked back to his car slowly and deliberately. He unlocked the driver's door and threw in the panama hat. He had thought it might make him look more countrified and had bought it for Martha's sake. He looked down at his T-shirt with its self-advertisement blazed across the crimson cotton. He made a face; he had forgotten he was wearing the stupid thing.

He sat down heavily and turned the key so that he could work the electric windows. The car was like a kiln. He took out his handkerchief and mopped his face again. The way the girl had looked at him . . . he hadn't felt like that since Martha, at eight years old, had turned her mouth down in disgust at his kiss. He put the handkerchief away and sat still, staring through the windscreen. The little terrace of cottages looked back at him on the left; on the right the long path that ran parallel with Martha's drive led to the Norman church tower. They were sequestered here; they had deliberately taken up the drawbridge. What was it Linda's girl had said to

253

him? "Face up to it, Mr Tatham. You're in competition with Lucy now. And believe you me, that's no competition." He saw now what she meant.

Someone came out of one of the cottages, hesitantly. Someone wearing a bright red dress that matched his rotten T-shirt. It was Linda Bowles. He had thought she was still with that poor sod Simon Moreton. Silly of him; how could she stay there when her daughter had left?

She waited by the gate; he could feel her uncertainty. He scrambled out of the car and went over to her.

"Linda. How are you?"

She stared at him, he saw her throat moving but no words were coming.

He said quickly, "Linda — love, I had to be straight on the phone. I'm sorry. But I'm no good at being tactful, you know that. I can't really remember — was I that bad?"

She shook her head dumbly.

He said, "Jennifer came to see me, Lin. Did you know?"

Her eyes widened and after a while she shook her head again.

"She told me what an awful time you all had of it that very day. Lucy's baby . . . and you . . . My dear, I'm so sorry."

She found her voice at last. "Not your fault, Bill." She managed a weak smile. "I think, because I'd been on my own here most weeks, I was sort of . . . obsessed. I just flipped."

He frowned. "Doesn't sound like you, Lin. I must have been pretty awful. What did I say?"

"You told me you'd seen Martha on Christmas Day. And she'd already told me she hadn't seen you since that November business." She relaxed suddenly and lifted her shoulders. "I think I felt as if you'd both been laughing about me behind my back. Paranoia? Is that what it's called?"

"Bugger what it's called, Lin. That was rotten." He took a deep breath. "She's ashamed of me, Lin. I've got to face up to it. She's ashamed of me. And why not? Look at me — I went to see her dressed in this and a bloody panama hat!"

She smiled properly. "You look pretty good to me." Then the smile died. "I didn't mean that to sound . . . I've got over it, Bill. Honestly. That's one thing Jen did for me. She cured me of that obsession."

He said curiously, "How?"

"She did what she did — took Len away from Lucy and left Simon in the lurch. She did it for me, Bill, so the field would be clear. For me to move in on you. Like she moved in on Len." She shook her head. "She should have realized that that kind of sacrifice kills what it's meant to save."

He stared at her for a long time. Then he said, "D'you want to come back and work for me? Just work for me? There's going to be a big show in Malvern soon. They want marquees, cooking facilities . . ."

"I thought you wanted to be completely free? For Martha?"

"Just a job, Lin. Nothing else. Seriously."

"I know. Even so . . ."

"If I can cope with it, can't you?"

She noticed the sun for the first time. It struck through her red silk frock and warmed her small body. She said, "Yes. Yes, I think I can cope with it, Bill. Thank you."

June was tropical that year; day after day the skies were cloudless and the main task was to water the plants. There was a hose-pipe ban so the lawn had to manage without any water and there were bald patches here and there. Truda called with an earnest request for Martha's return to flower-arranging. "It's the font," she explained. "Denise does so well everywhere else, but neither of us seems to be able to cope with the font."

Martha told Lucy that she had never ever heard Truda admit to not being able to cope. Lucy said, "Why doesn't she come into the open and say that she misses you! It's so obvious that is what she means."

"Is it?" Martha was stunned. "Well, that makes it better, I suppose." She had felt bound to agree to resuming her place on the flower rota. "You don't mind too much, darling?"

"I could come with you. Except that I don't want to!" Lucy smiled. "But, Mummy, you won't say anything about the baby, will you?"

"Of course not, darling. If you don't want me to. But why? It's going to be obvious soon, isn't it?"

"I don't want Len to know. He might think he should be on the scene."

"Well, he will think that, Luce. Especially after Dominic. This is his baby too." Martha had to force herself to say the words. This baby was so exclusively Lucy's and hers.

"Well, I don't want him to be, Mummy. You know that."

Martha nibbled her lip. "I do know. Of course. I feel the same. But it's wrong, Luce. It's got to be wrong."

But Lucy would have none of it. "If only women could have babies without the help of men!" She said it as a joke, but Martha did not laugh.

Instead she said earnestly, "You must tell Len before he hears of it on the grapevine."

"Not yet, Mummy. And anyway, what grapevine?"

"It won't be long before someone tells Miss Darcy about your regular visits to Dr Chase."

"And Miss Darcy will report back to Truda who will feel it's her duty to —"

"I don't think she would do that. But you never know."

"Then I'll stop seeing Dr Chase. Everything is normal. No need to see him."

"Stop it, Lucy! You have to tell Len!"

Lucy pouted deliberately. "I want it to be you, me and Clemmie."

Martha said, "Clemmie?"

"It's a girl. I know it. It's so different from Dominic. I'm like a warm cat curled up having this baby. All those mood swings, sickness . . . quite different." She smiled right at her mother. "I want her to be named for Daddy. Clementina. It's so pretty. If she doesn't like it she can have Tina. Later on. I shall call her Clemmie."

"Oh, Luce . . ."

"And, Mummy, in case I forget to say this later: thank you. I'll always remember that waiting for Clemmie was the happiest time of my entire life."

Martha said again with a different inflexion, "Luce!"

"I mean it. And *you* know what happy times we've had in the past. So that will show you how content I am now. Utterly content. As if I've left everything awful behind me." She looked up. "Does that make me very shallow?"

"Of course not. Happiness is always something to be thankful for." Martha smiled suddenly. "How wonderful that I can share this time, Lucy. Thank you."

But Lucy would have none of it. "It's down to you," she insisted. "Just think, we've got another two — perhaps three — months of summer. Then lovely autumn and the conkers and looking forward to Christmas. Fires and cosy evenings . . . We'll get out the Snakes and Ladders with the little cannons that fire the dice, and the gales will blow but not us. Never on us."

Martha smiled. It sounded blissful. She realized then that all those early terrors had gone. Jennifer, Len, Linda, Billy Tatham . . . even Toto and George . . . none of them could inflict pain any more. She and Lucy, and later, Clemmie, were safe in the Old Rec.

CHAPTER
THIRTEEN

Jennifer was telling herself — again — that she was happy. What she had with Len was most definitely love. This is what it was all about; what made the world go round; why she had done those awful things . . . because they had been awful. But they were justified now, surely they were. Len had said once that being with Jennifer was like coming into the sun. That must mean that Lucy had been cold. Jennifer had known that Lucy was a virgin when they married, so perhaps it wasn't surprising that she had found sex difficult. And then losing the baby . . . she had not wanted to go through that again. Probably she thought that Jennifer had done her a favour. Jennifer bit her lip at this point, knowing she was fooling herself. But then she returned to what Len had said: she had never had such a compliment before; even when she thought of it, she felt wonderful. And Lucy was so happy with her mother. Reports came from Linda who was in touch with Mrs Rector. They appeared to have made a career out of Lucy's illness. Martha was nursing her assiduously and Lucy was responding. Truda Goodwin told Linda that "a minor miracle was happening at the Old Rectory". Well, that was good; that was marvellous. It absolved Jennifer from a lot of her guilt. And the other absolution was the immediate success of her plan for her mother. The very day Linda left the hotel and went back to the cottage, the ghastly Bill Tatham had contacted her and offered her a job! So the sticky interview Jennifer had had in that little house in Pittville had obviously paid off.

Jennifer grinned to herself at the thought. There was something about Bill Tatham that was very like herself. The way he had talked over the situation, blunt to the point of brutality, and then the way he had acted upon his decision. He must have kept in contact with the hotel and the moment he heard Linda was leaving he had made his move. Jennifer admired that. Len had been like that. He'd lost some of his decisiveness during the abortive marriage with Lucy, but it was coming back. Jennifer was good for him.

The business about the trip to Roscoff was an example. He had twenty-four hours to accept the assignment.

"It's not enough time," he had said to her that night. "I ought to keep in touch with Toto . . . and it will mean I don't know when I can see Lucy."

"Len, you can't pass this one up! It'll be on the national network —"

"I know. But it needs preparation. And an assistant who knows me —"

She thought he was going to add "like Lucy knew me", and she said quickly, "I'll come, Len. I always wanted the job, you know. When Luce used to talk about it, I knew I would have done it better than she ever could. Please say yes, darling. I don't want to be separated from you for however long it takes. I can cover the woman's

260

angle — you know, the little woman at home, waiting and wondering. Please, darling, please . . ."

"Jen! You've got a job! You'd have to work out a period of notice."

"Or forfeit the money. Come on, Len. You're not going to let a little thing like that stop you, are you?"

Her dark eyes blazed into his, her gypsy hair tickled his nose as she leaned over him. She saw his own eyes kindle with her enthusiasm; she could do this for him — she could do so much for him. They were the perfect pair.

They went to France and interviewed the disgruntled lorry-drivers and the furious farmers and although she was only too aware of her shortcomings, nevertheless there was a time when she appeared on film with him talking to two frightened hitch-hikers who only wanted to get back home after an unsuccessful backpacking holiday. They might not have talked to Len but to this woman, who, quite obviously, was capable of using her sexuality to get a lift in one of the Continental lorries, they could open their hearts.

"We knew we'd have one man to contend with." The girl who did most of the talking was clearly the one who had got the lift in the first place. She wore hot pants and had tied her shirt beneath her small breasts so that her midriff was exposed. "But this is different. There must be over a hundred lorries here. Over a hundred men."

"And that bothers you?" Jennifer asked.

"Well, yes. It increases the risk. My parents would go spare — we're not on camera, are we?"

"I'm not sure." Jennifer smiled. "I'm new at this game. I've come with my boyfriend." And the girl smiled back and went on talking.

Len was delighted and made his second comparison between Jennifer and Lucy. "She would have been so disapproving. Worried that it might upset the parents, worried for the girls . . . Oh God, she was hedged with inhibitions. And you just get it in the can!" He kissed her exultantly. "Darling, you've got the job!"

"Oh Len!"

Yes. She was happy. And she would be even happier if she could take that tiny doubt from inside his head. She knew it was there. There was not much she did not know about Len Travers.

It was one of the reasons she visited George and Toto on her own. For one thing, Len had made no suggestion of taking her to meet his parents and before it could become a hiccup in their relationship, she decided to go it alone. She presented herself at the Tewkesbury house while Len was making his August visit to the Old Rectory.

George answered the door about one second after her ring. He was out of breath.

She said, "You remember me, George? I came to supper here last year. Before Len and Lucy got married. Jennifer Moreton."

The skin on George's face tightened but he said, "I saw the car. Recognized it from the wedding. I didn't want my wife to answer the door."

"But I hoped to see you both." She did not have to feign dismay. Surely they weren't going to go all

Victorian on her? "There's so much I should explain. Can't we sit down and talk properly?"

George steadied his breathing. "I'm not sure. My wife is terribly upset about this whole business. I don't think you can possibly understand what you have done —"

She interrupted sharply, "It takes two, remember, George!"

He did not like her calling him by his first name, but forced himself to use hers. How could he call her Mrs Moreton, anyway? "You were in control, Jennifer. You could have kept your distance."

"I don't think *you* understand, George!" Her voice was still sharp. "Len and I were in love before the wedding, you know! On the way here — to that supper — he asked me to sleep with him!"

George Travers was not Bill Tatham. He flinched, shut his eyes, opened them wide and said, "My God!" Behind him Toto arrived in the hall, heard Jennifer's last words and stopped dead in her tracks.

"You! How have you got the sheer nerve to come here? Close the door, George. We don't want her and her insinuations —"

"I am not making insinuations, Mrs Travers." Jennifer knew better than to use Toto's pet name. "Please listen to me. Len and I fell in love when Lucy introduced us. Len was already committed to Lucy —"

"And still is!" Toto interrupted furiously.

George said slowly, "That's not entirely true, my love. Lucy is living with her mother and Len is living with . . . this young lady."

"Lucy's best friend!" Toto said with deep bitterness.

Jennifer spoke with sudden passion. "D'you think that doesn't hurt me too? I've always loved Martha and Lucy. Always. I am praying that in time we can be friends again! But Len was unhappy and lonely and Lucy asked me to keep an eye on him — get him some food and see to the laundry — and we were thrown together and — and —"

George said, "You'd better come in." He stood aside. "Toto, let's hear what she has to say. Whether we like it or not all this has happened. It has happened, Toto. And the only sure thing about any of it is that Len is still our son." He looked at Jennifer as she passed him and said straightly, "And he is not happy."

She stopped and made a little sound and George held his look and nodded slowly. Toto turned with what was nearly a flounce and led the way into the dining room. She pulled out a chair and sat on it. After a moment's hesitation Jennifer did the same. George sat next to Toto and took her hand. There was a silence.

Jennifer could have wept. She was not going to sweep all before her as she'd done with Bill Tatham. She had bent the truth such a small way: Len had not actually proposed to Lucy before he met Jennifer, but it was true that their mutual attraction had been instant. And anyway the man who had made an objective decision to marry Lucy because she would make a suitable wife was not the man who had returned from the Dominican Republic, made uncertain by grief and anxiety. Len needed her.

She swallowed and said, "He is happy when he is with me. That's all I can say. He was not happy with Lucy. She had turned from him . . . I swear this is true —"

264

"She was ill!" Toto practically spat.

"So was he in his way. He needed love and comfort—"

"Sex, d'you mean?" Toto did spit this time.

Jennifer's temper rose. "Yes, all right! Sex! He had mighty little of that in the last few months with Lucy!"

"How dare you!" Toto half rose from her chair as if to lean over and strike Jennifer. George pressed her down.

"We don't know what went on." He took her other hand but looked across at Jennifer. "And neither do you, young lady. Lucy was pregnant, if you remember. And we know now that things were wrong. I think you have possibly misinterpreted what Len has said to you." He turned and looked into his wife's eyes. "Be still, sweetheart. We must hear her out."

For a moment it looked as if Toto would rebel; she pushed her chair back and freed her hands angrily but then, as George continued to look at her, she subsided. She ignored Jennifer and spoke to him. "They were both devastated. When they came home, she was ill and he was grief-stricken. To do what Jennifer did at that moment was unforgivable. I will listen to what she has to say, George, but you must know that they should have been left to sort out their feelings properly. And to — to — come between them was simply . . . *unforgivable*."

He slid one of his hands around her till he was almost cradling her. "I know, darling. I know. But it has happened. And from what she says, it would have happened later. We must listen. We must try to understand. For our own sakes as well as for Len's."

Jennifer clenched her hands, still very close to tears. They had excluded her more effectively than any other way.

She said shakily, "I'm sorry. I have nothing else to say really. Just that . . . I loved him. And I knew I could make things better for him. And so . . . I did."

She could not have said anything better. She watched them slowly part and sit facing her again, and knew that she had somehow struck a chord. Then George glanced sideways at Toto and she returned the look; something passed between them. Jennifer wondered if it would ever be like that for her and Len. That silent exchange of agreement.

Toto took an enormous breath and let it go slowly. Then she said, "Well. We could sit here all afternoon talking, couldn't we? But in the end, what good would it do? I remember when they came back home in March, Len told me that Lucy hardly ever cried over Dominic because all it did was to leave her with a headache. I think that's all we shall be left with." She glanced again at George and lifted her shoulders. "I rather think that if you had loved him properly you would have kept away. But that is another matter for fruitless debate. You did not. You comforted him. I cannot thank you for that, but I accept it."

Jennifer felt the tears gather in her eyes; she let them fall. Neither George nor Toto made a move towards her.

Toto said steadily, "Crying over spilt milk, girl? You came here to mop it up, did you? We've done that. But it always leaves a sour smell. That's what we've got to live with. Don't forget it."

266

Jennifer said, "I don't want forgiveness for myself. But if you could forgive Len. He is unhappy at . . . how you are."

George spoke suddenly. "Then he must be unhappy, Jennifer. You tell us he is happy when he is with you. There is a price to be paid for that. He must pay it."

She swallowed. She knew it was time to go, but this limited victory was not what she had had in mind. She said in a small voice, "May I come with him sometimes? To see you?"

Toto opened her mouth to reply but George got there first. "Not yet. Can't you see that if we did that — accepted you as a couple — we risk hurting Lucy?"

"She wouldn't mind," Jennifer said eagerly. "Surely you've spoken to her and know that she is happy —"

"And Martha," he concluded inexorably. "We'll see how things are next year."

"In five months then?" Jennifer said, like a child pestering.

Toto could be quiet no longer. "Even then is too soon —"

"We'll think about it again then," George interrupted.

By mid-August, Linda had slept with Bill Tatham twice. She should have felt some kind of positive emotion; if not happiness then an enormous relief, maybe a little triumph. She felt none of those things. All her old enthusiasm had gone for Bill Tatham, for the job, for just about everything. He knew it too and had made love to her carefully, tenderly, as if she were an invalid.

They had set up the marquee by the river at Evesham and the "extraneosities", as Bill called them, were selling like hot cakes. The smaller marquee had been booked for a wedding on August Bank Holiday and Linda was to be in charge of the catering for that. She must be good at it because she was planning and making lists automatically. That day she had been demonstrating a new hamburger griddle and had turned out at least a hundred burgers as free samples. She could make a timetable and keep to it and make sure other people kept to it also. She could sympathize with women who were looking for a certain type of cooker, as well as jolly along the men who thought they were suddenly macho because they could put up a tent. But it no longer gave her a kick. She wanted something more. She had thought that Bill could supply that. Now she knew he could not. Not any more.

They closed down at sunset; she could see him giving instructions to the security patrol, edging away from the Alsatian. She smiled to herself; Bill was a bit like a bulldog himself, it had been strange to discover he was terrified of dogs.

She waited by the car and at last he joined her and opened up. She stood by the open door until he had opened all the windows and the sun roof, then slid in beside him, fanning herself ineffectually with her bag. He said, "All right, Lin?"

"Fine. It's been a good day. Plenty of sales. I made hamburgers till I looked like one!" She laughed. "They'll all go for them eventually."

"Well done." He drove carefully onto the road and turned south. "D'you want to stay with me tonight?"

She bit her lip. In a way she did simply because it was worse being on her own; but only if he really wanted her. She said slowly, testing him, "No. No, I don't think so, Bill. I need to sort out my bed-sit. Wash my hair. Soak in a bath. You know."

"I do." Was he sounding relieved? "Shall we eat first? That pub along the Evesham Road —"

"I've sampled too many of my own hamburgers!" She forced a laugh. What was the matter with her? She was turning down everything she had wanted most. "A sandwich when I go to bed. Maybe."

"Well, mind you do. You haven't put that weight back on yet."

That was one of the things; he was so damned . . . avuncular.

"I was too fat, Bill."

"Never fat," he said gallantly.

"Chubby then. I'm better as I am."

They drove in silence for some way then he said with his usual directness, "Are you all right, Lin? Really?"

"I think so. It's all . . . a bit much, Bill, isn't it? Jennifer sort of pitchforked everyone about as if they were bales of hay. It's as if we had our will-power taken away temporarily."

He laughed. "I think you're right. But Lin, that day I went to see Martha and Lucy, they were OK, you know. They were not just OK, they were positively OK*ay*." He laughed at his own words and she laughed too. They could still laugh together.

"Actually, that's very reassuring. Sometimes I think that guilt will poison the rest of my life."

"It's nothing to do with you, my dear."

"Well . . . that's a moot point." She smiled sideways at him. "I don't quite know what to do, Bill. I don't know what I want any more. Can you understand that?"

"Yes. Only too well." He took his left hand off the steering wheel and patted her knee. It was avuncular again. "Something will happen to show you. Meanwhile, why don't you go and see Martha? Talk to her again. Patch things up."

"And say nothing about us?" Her smile became wry. "Not a very good beginning for a patch-up job."

He shrugged. "Don't keep silent for my sake, Lin. Tell her the whole thing. At least she'll be able to justify herself and her decision then. She'll probably say to you that she always knew I couldn't keep faith."

She murmured, "Keep faith. Ah Bill, I think you've always kept faith." That's what it was, of course. He was still "keeping faith" in his own way.

He said, "We're just coming to that pub. Your last chance . . . ?"

"No thanks, Bill. I'd like to get back to my own place as soon as possible."

It was strange that Archie should phone her that night. She could easily have been in the Pittville house.

He said, "Linda? It's Archie Evans."

"Archie. How nice. I meant to ring you — you know how I am, my dear. This job is proving very time-consuming and —"

"Are you free, Linda?"

"Well, I told you about the job, didn't I? It will last most of the summer I expect. Probably into the autumn too."

"I meant: Are you free in yourself? Are you . . . involved with anyone?"

"No, Archie. But it's a question of getting time off, my dear. As I said —"

He blurted, "May is dead, Lin. She was killed. In a car. With someone else. She's been seeing someone else for years."

She was genuinely shocked. May had been the shadow wife-figure for so long. And now she was gone. And unfaithful too. It was obvious that Archie would always be unfaithful to his wife, but that his wife was also unfaithful was . . . shocking.

She said, "Oh Archie. I am so sorry. I can't take it in just like that . . . Do you want to come to Cheltenham? You've got my address. I'll try and get tomorrow off, shall I?"

"No good. Funeral. Listen, Lin. Will you marry me?"

She looked down at the receiver in sheer astonishment. "Marry you, Archie? But why?"

"Because we get on so well. Because I'm fond of you. And because . . . it will show people. She's not the only one who had a bit on the side! If she were alive I'd divorce her and marry you. Why not now she's dead?"

"Archie, I don't know what to say." She looked wildly around the bed-sit. It was so unlike the cottage; so unlike any kind of home. "This is . . . so sudden!"

She started to laugh at her own words and after a while she heard him laugh too. And then he stopped laughing and said, "That's it, you see, Lin. You make me laugh. I've been angry and bitter and bloody fed up ever since

271

this happened. And here I am, talking to you on the phone and laughing!"

"Oh Archie." She felt helpless. In a wonderful way. "This is the first time anyone has asked me to marry him."

"Really? Then there are a lot of men around who are blind fools." He paused, then said, "Lin, never mind what May has done or not done. Marry me. Let's give it a try. If it doesn't work, what have we lost?"

"Oh Archie," she said for about the fifth time. But now it was almost a whimper. "Oh Archie . . . shall we? Shall I?"

"Give me one reason why not."

There were none. Certainly Bill Tatham was no longer a reason. He had let her stay in the Pittville house because she needed him so badly; not because he needed her. No . . . there was not one reason for turning down Archie's offer.

Jennifer decided, long before she got back to the flat, that the afternoon had been an unqualified success. She had breached the defensive wall put up by George and Toto and they had promised that there would be a grand reconciliation next year. It was an occasion for a celebration, so she booked a meal at her favourite restaurant and asked for a roof table. She imagined her and Len sitting there in the smoky twilight. The sky would still have an orange glow when they arrived and then gradually the stars would reveal themselves and the moon would look close enough to touch and the Chinese lanterns would move gently as the concrete roads below gave off their heat. She had bought a green silk mandarin-collared dress last week and she would wear that with a flower in her hair, and Len would look at her with that dark avid expression that she loved best of all, and he would reassure her that Lucy and Martha were "all right", and then she'd tell him about George and Toto. She would edit the interview as carefully as he edited his film. *They were angry at first — your mother is so much like you, fiery . . . I think, later, we shall be friends. Your father took control. Calmed her down. I tried to tell them how happy we were, and that was all that mattered to them in the end, Len. They want you to be happy. Properly happy. Not chained to a sterile relationship. That's what it would have been — you know that, don't you, my darling? I think they'd like us to visit them together fairly soon. Perhaps we'll leave it till after Christmas. Yes, keep away for a few weeks, Len. Let them think over what we talked about. Then we'll go together. Take some Christmas presents . . .*

Yes, that would be splendid. If she could talk Len out of seeing them for a while, they might get the message. *If you want Len, you've got to take Jennifer . . .*

She ran a tepid bath and soaked luxuriously until she heard his key in the door. "I'm in here, darling one," she called. "Waiting for you. Come and join me. Cool down. Or warm up. Whichever you need."

He came through the living room slowly. She heard him go to the window and then there was silence. He must be standing there staring through into the street. It had been tricky with Lucy, perhaps. She called again.

"Len. Sweetheart. Whatever has happened, forget it. Come and join me. I've got loads to tell you but I want to save it till later. Len!"

There was no sound. She felt a flutter of panic, scrambled out of the bath and drew a towel around herself. She went through the chaotic bedroom and into the living room. She was right, he was standing by the window, his back to her.

"Len?" He turned. His face was stretched; jaw rigid; his open-necked shirt showing his neck as a series of cords. "Whatever has happened?" And then, because he obviously didn't know how to tell her, she said on a high note of panic, "Is it Ma? Is it my mother?"

He shook his head. Then he came to her at last. There was a look on his face, as if he expected her to make everything all right again.

"It's Lucy," he said. "Jen . . . she's pregnant. Oh my God, Jen. We're having another baby!"

CHAPTER
FOURTEEN

Martha walked slowly across the churchyard carrying a milk jelly for Miss Darcy. It was carefully lodged in the base of a plastic carrier bag, but as Miss Darcy liked her "shapes", as she called them, slightly under-set, there was a risk it might slide out of its mould if tipped too far. Martha did not mind the slow walk; it gave her time to look around at the leaves already changing colour and to notice that the prickly-coated horse-chestnuts were beginning to litter the church path. Since last February she had come this way to avoid walking past Linda's cottage. And the news that Linda had returned to work for Tatham's Tents had . . . shocked her. When Miss Darcy told her about it, she worked out that Billy Tatham must have gone straight from the Old Rectory to Linda's cottage that scorching afternoon last May. It was the speed of the volte-face that had shocked Martha. And — and the evidence of Billy's pettiness. She had realized that Lucy made him feel inferior, but to practically run across the road to someone who made him feel so superior was somehow demeaning.

She had accepted it now, of course. In fact Billy Tatham had run true to type; she had known that's how he was from the beginning. It was simply that she had needed someone and she had imagined him to be . . . someone.

She sighed sharply and stopped to rest the base of the carrier on a convenient tombstone. Above her, the church clock boomed twice. How had Jennifer described it? A resonating cow? She remembered laughing inordinately. Clem had said, "That girl is too clever for her own good!" And he had been proved right.

She looked into the bag and the lemon "shape" trembled up at her. She wished she'd put a cover on it but it had not seemed worth struggling with the intractable roll of cling-film for this short journey. Miss Darcy would want to eat the pale yellow delicacy immediately, using a teaspoon and sipping it like a bird. Martha wondered how much longer the old lady could stay in her cottage; this winter would be the testing time surely? Though Truda had been saying that for the past four years at least. And winter still seemed a long way off anyway. It was still amazingly warm for September but there were the chestnuts and the golden leaves and the smell of one of Albert's bonfires. And the baby would be with them in two months. She felt a surge of joy rise in her at that thought. She had already climbed into the attic and brought down the cot and Linda's lovely cot sets. She smiled involuntarily, lifted the bag carefully off the tombstone and began threading her way towards the far gate. She had a full hour before Lucy's midwife arrived, but she wanted to be in good time to hear whether the blood pressure had gone down after a week of bed-rest. Besides, after the check-ups they always had a cup of tea together, and she and Lucy would listen avidly as

Mrs Rowe explained the procedures for "going in" and the variable lengths of stay in the maternity unit. Mrs Rowe knew the situation and had told them several times that as a family for the baby, the grandmother and daughter set-up was an excellent substitute for the conventional mother and father. "In fact," she confided, rolling her eyes, "when I think of some of my poor mothers, married to totally selfish men who won't take a scrap of interest in Baby, your arrangement is far better!" They'd smiled congratulatory smiles at each other. Martha knew there was something askew with this thinking, but it did not matter. That was how things were, so it was as well Mrs Rowe considered it a good arrangement. Apparently there were places in China and the Far East where it was the norm anyway.

Martha came to the gate and paused again to glance over to her left. Miss Darcy's cottage was the end one of the terrace so she could approach it without being seen from others once she had crossed the road. No-one was about but she saw that there were "For Sale" signs outside Linda's cottage and the one next door where the Terrible Twins lived. She frowned and forced herself to cross the road to Miss Darcy's but her mind jumped with possibilities. She was not interested in the Venableses, but if Linda was selling up it must mean that she was throwing in her lot with Billy Tatham . . . And there was Jennifer to consider too . . . What had happened? It was amazing that Albert or his wife or Miss Darcy had not told her all about it.

Miss Darcy was sitting in her small front room, obviously waiting for Martha's arrival. She was almost agog yet at the same time smug with her soon-to-be-imparted news.

"I saw you looking. You noticed the signs? My dear, it is all happening, as they say! Has Truda Goodwin been round to see you? No? I hoped she wouldn't. After all, I knew first."

Martha hovered by the door clutching the carrier. "Shall I —?"

"Oh. A lemon shape? My dear, how delightful! Would you mind fetching one of the sundae dishes from the sideboard, and a teaspoon? I do like to savour each mouthful, you know. And I can tell you about it in between!" Miss Darcy actually laughed, then called out, "Don't bother with the kettle yet, dear Mrs Moreton! We'll have tea later."

Martha could have groaned. She glanced at her watch. Forty-five minutes before Mrs Rowe's arrival.

Miss Darcy took her first teaspoonful and closed her eyes appreciatively. "Just right for this weather? Not too sweet. Not in the slightest bit rubbery. Not too wet . . . there is no-one does a shape like you do, that's for certain." She began to explain about Truda's brightly coloured blancmanges. "She thinks a blancmange is a shape! I tried to tell her the difference, so she made a milk jelly that separated — of course." She paused then added irrelevantly, "If the Davises come to live in one of the cottages, Mrs Davis would be able to bring me round a lunch. Then I could cancel meals on wheels."

Martha refused to enter into that particular discussion. Miss Darcy had never liked meals on wheels. She said

278

conclusively, "Albert won't leave his cottage. It was his father's home."

"It would be ideal for Mrs Davis. Her other cleaning jobs are in the village. I haven't spoken to her yet. Mrs Bowles was going to call at the new Rectory after she left me. She didn't mention the Davises. I'll be able to tell Mrs Davis when she comes to clean. What's today?"

Martha said, "Wednesday. The seventeenth. September."

"She won't be here till Friday. Someone else will have told her by then."

"Never mind. You're going to tell me — aren't you?"

"Yes." Miss Darcy brightened and scooped out the last of the shape. "Well, of course, the first thing was the fight."

She paused and Martha echoed obediently, "Fight?"

Miss Darcy smiled complacently. "Exactly. In Nortons Heath! But I'd seen it coming. Mr Venables told me once they had an open marriage. I said to him: There's no such thing. Making vows — marriage vows, any kind of vows — closes doors. Secures things. How can they be secure and open? Doesn't add up, does it?"

"No," said Martha.

"Those girls. I haven't told you the half, my dear, because you had enough to contend with and I didn't want to make things worse for you. But they were wild. Completely out of hand. I had to ask Mrs Goodwin to stop them coming here."

Martha, remembering the tea tin, merely nodded.

Miss Darcy took a deep breath. "It was just getting dark. Saturday night I suppose it was. Yes, that's right because it was the day after that when Mrs Bowles came round. Only I mustn't call her that now, must I?" She giggled significantly. Martha moistened her lips. "And that was definitely Sunday." Miss Darcy arrived at the conclusion of that piece of deduction triumphantly. "Yes. Saturday evening. Beautiful day again. Lovely sunset. I looked out and said, Red sky at night, and then their door opened and Mrs Venables came out at a run. Pushed out, I'd say. She was yelling like a banshee."

"Oh my Lord," Martha said, startled at last.

"Quite." Miss Darcy sat back. "I had to go into the bathroom and stand in the bath so that I could lean out and see exactly what was happening."

"What about the other houses? Mr Norman and the Franks?"

"Drew their curtains and bolted their doors, I imagine. Not a soul saw a thing. Of course it was Saturday. They may well have been out and about."

"Poor Mrs Venables," Martha said. She wanted to move on to Linda's visit. But then . . . perhaps she didn't want that at all.

"Poor Mrs Venables indeed! She turned round, picked up a very big stone from the rockery and threw it at the window. That's when the children started to scream." She paused to allow Martha to gasp. "Quite," she said again, repressively.

"What did you do?"

"I didn't know what to do. I was taught never to interfere between man and wife. But then he shot out of the front door too and he was bleeding from his head and he grabbed Mrs Venables and hit her and the twins ran

280

out and tried to pull him away — I had to interfere then, didn't I?"

Martha nodded.

"I nearly phoned you. Then I thought: What could you do? So I phoned the Rector, but he was at choir practice so Mrs Goodwin came down."

"Truda?" Martha wanted to laugh.

"She was wonderful, Mrs Moreton. She got between the two of them and I think one of his blows actually struck her! Anyway she did something — I couldn't see what it was — and he doubled up and sort of staggered back into the porch and she just marched the three females back to the Rectory."

Martha was amazed. She could picture it vividly. Truda's knee jerking upwards and Mr Venables retching in the porch.

"Are they still there?" she asked.

"No. That's the worst of it. They've gone to live in Birmingham. With her mother."

"Well, that would seem to be —"

"*Together,* Mrs Moreton! He went to see them the next day and a lorry came and took their stuff and then they had a taxi and went off together! Mrs Goodwin says it's not the first time it has happened. They thrive on it, she says. Anyway the agents came this morning with two 'For Sale' signs."

"Well!" Martha looked suitably amazed at the vagaries of human behaviour and Miss Darcy nodded sympathetically.

"It takes some getting used to, doesn't it? And then the very next day, just after Mrs Goodwin had popped in to tell me this, Mrs Bowles arrived at the door and tells me *she* is selling up too. Came to say goodbye. She'll be living in Birmingham — some big place up on the Lickey Hills."

"Not Cheltenham?"

"No. That's where she worked. This is practically a mansion. She had a small reception there — brought a few photographs. That Jennifer looks thinner than ever. I don't think she can be happy, Mrs Moreton. Neither of them — Jennifer or your son-in-law — looked a bit happy, and when you think they were at a wedding not a funeral . . ."

"They're married? A wedding?"

"Oh yes, my dear. Very small do. Of course. Jennifer and her . . . your son-in-law. Both looking miserable as sin."

"It will take time."

"It's been four months."

"Yes." Martha moistened her lips again. "And Linda? How did she look?"

"I don't know how to describe it really. She looked . . . not radiant. Serene. That's the word. She looked serene. In the photograph and in herself." Miss Darcy glanced up. "She asked after you, Mrs Moreton. She said this was the best thing that could have happened and it would mean that eventually you and she might be friends again."

Martha had no right to be angry but she tasted bile in her mouth.

Miss Darcy said, "Well, she's always looked for respectability, hasn't she? Now perhaps . . . I think this man must be Jennifer's father so she's done right in the end, hasn't she?"

Martha said nothing. That, at any rate, could not be true.

"He looked nice enough. Older than her. Bluff. One of those plump, pink men. Do you know what I mean? Good food and plenty of it but still not satisfied. Maybe he'll be satisfied now. He lost his wife last month and got married this month. He must have been waiting for her all these years. Romantic when you think of it, isn't it?"

Martha's mouth was dry again. She said, "And what will her name be now then? Mrs . . . ?"

"Mrs Evans. He owns a quarry. In Warwickshire somewhere. His father started it up. Evans. I've heard of Evans. Have you?"

Martha remembered that Linda had been with Archie Evans on the day of Lucy's wedding. She smiled. "Oh yes. I've heard of Evans," she said.

In the end she missed Mrs Rowe completely. She would see her next week after all, and Miss Darcy had needed time to talk over the excitement of last weekend. And then Martha had called on Truda to hear exactly what went on with the Venableses. When Truda answered the door sporting a shiner of a black eye, Martha almost laughed, but she mentally told herself off and made more tea in yet another kitchen while she listened to Truda's grim account of last Saturday's events.

"I wouldn't have minded, not really, but when he came round the very next day and she absolutely fell into his arms — well, my dear, I nearly wept! It's not often I want to weep — the last time was at your husband's funeral, and that was from grief. This, though I hate to admit it, was from sheer anger. If she hadn't gone with him then and there I would have shown her the door anyway!"

"Well, the alternative might have been far worse. Supposing they had become lodgers for the next few weeks, or even months?"

"I might have got used to it." Truda swivelled her bloodshot eye. "After all, I've never had a family and I might have been able to exert some influence for good on those two girls. Who knows?"

Martha could have hugged her. Truda Goodwin had cried for Clem and she had seen the plight of the Venableses as a chance to have a family.

She tried to bring a smile to the gaunt face. "You might also have lost your family silver," she said.

But Truda shook her head. "It might have been worth that too."

Martha wondered if there could be any more surprises that day. She left the new Rectory at four-thirty, thankful that tea-time with Mrs Rowe would be over; she had drunk enough tea to last her for today and anyway could hardly wait to have Lucy to herself and tell her the news. She took the path at the back of the church, looked around her surreptitiously and scrambled over the wall into the garden of the Old Rectory. Already she was rehearsing — as Miss Darcy must have rehearsed — just how she was going to tell Lucy what had happened. She was smiling as she went to the back of the house and through the kitchen door. It would be like old times when Clem and Lucy had vied with each other to imitate Marcus and Truda doing one of their dialogues: the Rector echoing every other word of Truda's firm narrative. After the low September sun outside, the kitchen was almost dark. She was conscious of Lucy, standing by the table, indefinably defensive. Another figure was sitting at the table. For a moment she thought it was Len. And then she saw it was Billy Tatham.

Linda found, to her great surprise, that she could tell Archie everything. That first evening after he had proposed and been accepted, he had arrived within an hour armed with flowers, and, incredibly, a sapphire and diamond ring.

"How on earth —?" She had been overwhelmed, laughing suddenly, her mood completely reversed.

"Stopped for flowers along the Evesham Road. Asked the feller if he knew a jeweller's that might be open and he sold me the ring! I knew then it was going to be all right. Oh Linda-love, you did mean it, didn't you?"

"I did. Did you?" The ring fitted; she held out her hand and the light from the single bulb overhead glinted blue. She had never had an engagement ring before.

"God yes. It's been awful. For ages. After your Jennifer's wedding the girl at the hotel told me you were ill and I couldn't see you and I thought it was just an excuse. And then, last night, it just popped into my head. Getting married. To someone like you. Being with you all the time . . . it seemed too good to be true. So then I rang that hotel in Worcester and they gave me a number

in Cheltenham. Sounded like you'd found someone . . .
I nearly didn't ring. But then I did and you weren't there.
And this feller said you'd got a bed-sit just off the Prom
and you had a phone —"

"And here you are!" She was delighted by his ardour,
his persistence, the ring, the flowers . . . There were no
uncertainties here. Archie had always wanted her. She
knew exactly where she was with Archie.

But she had to explain Bill although she was
frightened — genuinely frightened — it might mean
losing Archie. Yet she found she could pour it all out.
That first meeting when he had come to her back gate
looking for Martha. His love for Martha and her
awareness of him; her terrible awareness. She confessed
how happy she had been for those few short weeks;
working for him, sleeping with him. And then his
rejection.

"I was just besotted, Archie. And then, when he took
me back, it was all wrong. Being with someone who was
thinking of someone else . . . you wouldn't understand
how awful that is."

"Well, I understand now, girl. I know I had you —
quite often in the old days, eh, Lin? But I always kept up
a front with May. And it turns out she had this other chap
all the time! She had no fondness for me at all, Lin. She
married me because my father owned a quarry and had
money. That's how it was with our May. Always." He
sighed sharply, then said, "So what if he wants you back,
this chap? Will it all be off between us? Be honest with
me, Lin."

286

"No." She could be sure of that. "I'm fed up with being a doormat, Archie. Everyone wipes their feet on me. Jennifer, Martha . . . even Bill."

"Not me, girl. Not unless you want me to!" He smirked and she burst out laughing and flung her arms around his neck. He swung her from side to side. "Eh, Linda-love, it's going to be great. The two of us. I'm going to be your husband. And you're going to be my wife."

She leaned back and looked at him, suddenly breathless. "Oh Archie. I've never been married. Is it — is it difficult?"

"Most times it's hell on earth. But when it's you and me, reckon we might have got the keys to the garden."

"The garden?" she asked.

"The garden of Eden. Paradise. A little bit of heaven." He kissed her. "Just for us, Linda-love. Just for us."

She said suddenly, "I wonder if I was in love with you all the time, Archie? And Bill just reminded me of you?"

He hugged her to him. "You're a nice woman, Lin. You're a good woman. I know that. You don't have to try to make it better for me. It couldn't be better anyway."

And after that, somehow, she had been able to chatter away to him like she had chattered in the old days to Martha — only more so. After they were married and she and Jen decided to sell the cottage, she told him all about the Venableses and how Truda had got a black eye and Miss Darcy had had to stand in the bath to get a bird's eye view.

"I thought you said she'd been dying for the past five years?" he asked — which just showed he listened to what she said.

"That's it. She's dying but when she wants to see something badly enough she finds unexpected strength!" She smiled. "That applies to us all, Archie."

"It sure does," he said.

The wedding had been in Birmingham Register Office and she did a little tea party afterwards for Archie's sister and brother-in-law and Jennifer and Len. She and Martha had done many similar spreads: vol-au-vents and sandwiches, cocktail sausages and anchovies, sherry trifles and eclairs. It had touched her that Jennifer brought the wedding cake: a fully iced affair with a tiny bride and groom on its smooth white surface.

"I told you you'd be married, Ma," Jennifer said. "I just got the wrong groom!"

They smiled at each other. Linda said, "So you *didn't* nobble Len for my sake, Jen?"

"Course I didn't. I nobbled Len — as you so elegantly put it because I love him." She pulled her mouth down. "It's not all honey living with him, Ma. Especially since he found out that bloody Lucy is pregnant! But I still love him. And I always will. The snag is, I thought loving someone made you happy."

"I don't think it does." Linda remembered being in thrall to Bill Tatham. "No, being in love can have that effect. For a while. But when it settles into loving — and it must settle into loving otherwise it's not the real thing then you suffer for the person you love."

288

"Oh God. You're not going all wise again, are you?"

"No fear." Linda laughed. "I'm married now. Married people don't have to be wise. They can just relax."

"Sounds great." Jennifer pulled a face. "Never worked like that for me."

Linda sighed. "No. Well, you didn't catch the bouquet, did you? I was obviously meant to be married and you weren't."

"Oh shut up, Ma," Jennifer said. But she said it amiably.

They did not have a honeymoon immediately. She wanted, almost desperately, to get rid of the cottage. It was a symbol of her old unsatisfactory life and before she and Archie went away together, she wanted to be sure that was all gone. That Sunday she had intended calling on Martha and Lucy and trying desperately to heal the breach. Unless village gossip was more efficient than she remembered, they would not know about Linda's marriage. That would be an excuse for calling. She tried to work out a scenario: Martha would answer the door, because apparently she did not let Lucy do a thing, and her eyes would widen at the sight of Linda standing there in one of the outfits Archie had insisted on buying her — a lime-green linen suit with white ruffles at neck and wrists. Linda would immediately begin speaking just in case Martha shut the door in her face; in fact she would blurt out about the wedding and the sale of the cottage and the honeymoon in Monte Carlo . . . which should come first? Of course if Archie were with her that would help. He would be a kind of shield between them. But she had declined Archie's offer because she had wanted to call on Miss Darcy and Truda as well.

In the end she left it. It was just too difficult. Besides she might upset Martha and Martha might upset her and it simply was not worth it. Miss Darcy or Truda would put Martha in the picture much better than she could and time was a great healer, or so they said.

She drove home, changing her scenario to the one where she and Archie had drinks before dinner and she regaled him with news of her afternoon. It was lovely on top of the Lickey Hills. The eighteenth hole of the golf course was in sight of their garden and there was an enormous sky like one of Bill's marquees over the house. And there was Archie who really wanted to be with her; who had said, "How long will you be, Linda-love? It's going to seem a long afternoon without you."

She said aloud into the engine note of the car, which was another of Archie's presents, "I'm happy. I don't know how long for, I don't really understand why. But I'm happy. And so is he. So is my own dear Archie."

Mrs Rowe got up to go and Lucy said, "My mother will be sorry to have missed you. But you know how it is. I expect poor Miss Darcy wanted to talk to her."

"Of course, my dear. Anyway, it's you I need to see. Now please don't get up. You really must rest — feet up! — as much as you can. I'm going to talk to the hospital about your blood pressure and I'll be in touch. Try not to worry about a thing. You promise me you are all right financially? I could set wheels in motion to get some extra for your mother in the way of attendance allowance —"

"Really. My husband is very generous. I think we're better off than we have ever been." Lucy began to stand up automatically. "And you are quite certain that everything else is all right? After the last delivery —"

"Your scan was fine. Just that blood pressure. So that's another thing you need not worry about." Mrs Rowe flashed her reassuring smile. "I can't think of anything else and I'm sure you can't either. So remember the order of the day. Rest and relaxation." She opened the back door. "Oh. You've got another visitor, my dear. May I help? Mrs Moreton is out at the moment."

Billy Tatham's short strong figure blocked out the light momentarily as he stepped inside. "It's Lucy I came to see, actually. May I talk to you for . . . ten minutes, Lucy? I promise you it will be no longer."

For a moment Lucy hesitated, then she saw that Mrs Rowe was prepared to do battle on her behalf and she relaxed. "Do come in. Sit down. It's quite all right, Mrs Rowe. We'll see you next week at the same time?"

"Yes. Fine. I'll have some news from the hospital by then." The smart navy-blue-clad figure stepped into the garden. "I'll leave the door open, my dear. It's warmer out here than it is indoors today." She made a face at Lucy, who gathered that Mrs Rowe would hang around in her car for five minutes in case. Lucy smiled and made another face intended to convey reassurance and closed the door. When she turned back, Billy Tatham had settled himself in one of the ladder-back chairs at the table. She remained standing, one hand next to the teapot, the other cupping her abdomen. He looked slightly more presentable today in a shirt and tie, a jacket over one arm. He had a head of hair not unlike Len's: curls; a lot of them. That did not endear him to her. In fact nothing endeared him to her.

He said, "Stop seeing me as a threat, Lucy. See me as an old friend of your mother's who has no intention of encroaching on your privacy but would like you both to know that he is around if needed."

She said nothing. She remembered how her father had used silence as a weapon. "Clients will often say more than they intend if you just keep looking at them and listening," he had told her.

The Tatham man did not seem unduly disturbed by her lack of response. After looking back at her for about five seconds — it seemed longer than that — he said, "Why don't you sit down? Aren't you supposed to rest?"

She would have liked to ignore that too but there was the baby to consider so she pulled out a chair and sat down. He smiled at her.

"No, thanks. I won't have tea." He reached for the cosy and put it over the teapot. "Just in case your mother comes in and wants a cup." She felt herself flushing and he spotted it and said quickly, "I'm only teasing, lass. I really don't want any tea. And I'd rather not see Martha, so I'll tell you quickly why I'm here. Linda was going to pop in last Sunday but she telephoned me — she funked it at the last minute."

Lucy did not want to keep up the silence, but could think of nothing to say. She made a small sound in her throat.

"Yes. It might be better if the two of them did not see each other for a while. It is sure to be an emotional meeting and I think Martha needs to concentrate on other things just now."

He smiled again. He had a good smile; friendly.

She said, "Perhaps."

"Yes." He took a breath. "But I wanted Martha — and you — to know the position. Cards on the table. That sort of thing."

She knew suddenly what he had come to say. He was going to marry Linda. She felt a sudden pang for her mother; how would it affect her?

The Tatham man said briskly, "She got married, you know. To an old friend. He was at Jennifer's wedding apparently — gave her away. Archie Evans. Perhaps you know him?"

Lucy felt her face open with surprise. "Yes. I've never met him but he bought the cottage for Jen and Linda . . . I thought he was married."

"He was. His wife died. It wasn't a happy marriage and he immediately got in touch with Linda and I'm glad to say she doesn't let pride or anything else stand in her way." He was looking across the table very steadily. "She is quite a character, is Linda. Archie has loved her for a long time. He appreciates her. And she recognizes all that. I think she will be very happy."

"I'm sure." Lucy thought of Linda Bowles: hopeless, hapless, generous, loving. She said suddenly, "She deserves this. I'm so glad. Can you tell her that I'm really pleased?"

"Yes. I'll let her know." He hesitated. "It would be . . . nice . . . if Martha could send a card or something. Just a little something."

"Yes. I'm sure she will. It's a chance to . . . reconnect."

He smiled again, delighted. "Yes. That's it. They should reconnect! It's great that you understand that. Perhaps, one day, you can reconnect with Jennifer?"

Lucy nodded. "Perhaps. It's a bit more difficult." She smiled suddenly. "I expect *you* understand that!"

He took a deep breath. "Yes. I suppose I do." He stood up. "I'd better go. Thank you for listening. Don't forget, if I can ever help — I don't know, drive you somewhere, baby-sit, anything?"

"All right." She put out a hand. "Don't go yet. If you really don't want to see Mummy, well, we shall hear her coming along the gravel and you can leave by the back door." He subsided and she said, "Would you like some lemonade? It's cold. Straight out of the fridge."

"I don't think so. Thanks." He looked at her. "You want to know more about me? You cannot understand why your mother let me sleep with her? Why she came out with me on Christmas Day?"

Lucy made a small sharp sound of shock. The hand that had been cupping her abdomen went to her throat. She had known . . . hadn't she? But to be forced to face the fact, as he was forcing her, was unbearable. She hated him now. She had despised him before, but now she hated him.

He saw her shock but chose to ignore it. He said quietly as if telling her a story, "When I arrived in Littleford in 1942, I was fresh from the Birmingham streets. I was street-wise, as they call it now. I didn't fit in with Littleford and I pretended I didn't want to. I continued to thieve. I was billeted with farmers and I stole eggs and sold them; I hardly ever went to school; I wouldn't wash." He smiled again but she stared back at him, apparently not hearing. He said deliberately, "I was filthy. Lice. When Farmer Giles put me in a bath of warm soapy water, I used it as a lavatory and I loved it when his wife came in with a towel and started to scream the house down."

She made a sound of disgust and he lifted his shoulders. "I want you to know that you were right in your first opinion of me. I called my gang the rat-pack. It sounded a bit like the Desert Rats. We decided to make the lives of the local kids not worth living. So we went to school. Anarchy. That was the name of the game. Except that I'd never heard of the word." He laughed. "I told your mother once that the only way I could find the right thing to do — the right way to behave — was to do it the wrong way first. I think I've done that — learned the hard way — most of my life."

He paused and stared at the teapot. His voice changed. "She was the symbol of everything I wanted and thought I didn't want. That I loved and thought I hated. And it was when I thought she was going to fall off that swing and it was all my fault . . . then I saw the light. I saw the right way."

Lucy swallowed audibly and he looked back at her and grinned.

"Don't worry. I'm not going to lumber you with any more confessions. She was so . . . free. It was a tight, closed world, Lucy. Hard to imagine, these days. And she was free. She could climb trees like Tarzan and do acrobats on the village green. Physically she was free. But mentally too. She never wanted to rebel because she had nothing to rebel against. I remembered her always. Knew I wasn't good enough . . . but held her in my head. I knew when she got married and when you were born. And when your father died." He sighed sharply. "And then she booked a marquee from me. For your wedding. And I thought, I actually thought . . ." He laughed sharply. "And she thought too. For a time. But she was right. It wouldn't have worked." He pushed back his chair. "That shouldn't stop us from keeping some kind of contact, Lucy. Especially now. When the two of you are here on your own. I know my own strength now, you see. I know what I can do as well as what I cannot do. So I might be able to . . . help."

She could not speak; she stared across the table at him. He had slept with her mother. He had slept — often — with Linda Bowles. He was a John Bull figure; laughable in a way; in another way not laughable. But his frankness, his honesty, demanded the same from her.

She whispered, "I don't know what to say. I want to tell you to go. Never to come here again. But it could be . . . that we might need . . . someone. I don't know."

His smile split his face again. "Well. Thank you for that. Thank you for not telling me never to darken your doors again!" He laughed. "Don't look so worried, Lucy. I told you before. See me as your mother's old friend. What I've told you — it doesn't matter any more. Really."

"All right. Yes. All right."

She stood up and was turning towards the door when it opened. Martha stood there. She said almost angrily, "Billy Tatham! What are you doing here!"

He said easily, "I dropped in to tell you something. Lucy will fill you in. I must go. I didn't want to be a nuisance but Lucy said we should hear you on the gravel."

Martha stood there helplessly. She said, "I vaulted the wall."

And in that moment Lucy knew. This was the Martha who had done acrobats on the village green. She was still there underneath the layers of civilization. She was the Martha who might well have loved Billy Tatham.

CHAPTER
FIFTEEN

Martha was in the garden when the phone rang. It was the first day in October and she had been standing there consciously listing the flowers that were still blooming: geraniums, of course; roses and marigolds; love-in-the-mist and nasturtiums — they needed clearing but she could not bear to do it yet. The expected surge of energy from Lucy had not materialized. She had refused so far to go into hospital but Mrs Rowe had forbidden her very firmly to do more than sit in the chair by the window. Martha agreed with her that she would get more rest at home than in hospital but it was still worrying.

She picked up the receiver in the hall. It was Toto, who had been ringing regularly since last August. She started, as usual, apologetically. "I don't want to sound as if I'm staking a claim or something."

Martha shook her head helplessly. It was so difficult for Toto and George and there was no way to make it less so.

"Neither Lucy nor I think that, Toto. We'd hate it if you didn't keep in touch."

"Oh, Martha . . . How is she?"

"The same. It's just the blood pressure they don't like. But she's doing exactly what they've told her to do. And she's got some tablets. She had a scan and the baby is fine. She was right. It is a girl."

"Oh, how wonderful." Martha knew Toto was crying. She nearly always was. "I haven't seen anything of Len but I always phone him and give him the news."

"He hasn't called."

"No. I think *she* is making sure he sees no-one from his old life. They've been to stay with Linda and her husband — they're back from their honeymoon."

"Oh. Yes. Of course." Martha had forgotten about the delayed honeymoon.

Toto said suddenly, passionately, "Martha, unless I have them here as a pair — as a couple — she won't let him come! We're his parents and she won't let him come to see us!"

Martha felt the outside world seeping across the telephone wires. She closed her eyes: it was such a mess and if she wasn't very careful Lucy would be embroiled. She said quietly, "Try not to be upset. Why don't you do what Jennifer wants? Invite them round, Toto. A proper invitation. To supper or Sunday lunch. Is it worth standing on your principles? Len is your son and once all the legalities have been sorted out, I rather think Jennifer will be your daughter-in-law."

Toto's cry was despairing. "I — we — don't want her, Martha! Lucy is our daughter-in-law and the mother of our grandchildren — I include Dominic though Len appears to have forgotten him!"

"Oh, my dear. I don't think so. That day in August when Lucy told him about the new baby, his first words were: 'Another baby, another baby'. He certainly hasn't forgotten his first born."

Toto tried to pull herself together. "It's just so awful. I don't remember being so unhappy. Ever."

"That's why you have to do something. Invite them round, Toto. It might make things better. It seems to me it can't make them worse."

"I don't know. I am so . . . gutted. Literally. It's awful, I wake up every morning with this dread inside me. And then I think: How on earth are Martha and Lucy managing?"

Martha felt guilty that in fact she and Lucy were happy. She made some deprecating noises and Toto said, "Has Lucy changed her mind about seeing us?"

Martha tried to explain. "She would see you at any time, you know that. But the best thing for both of us is to keep ourselves to ourselves. And now, it's essential. I don't know whether to worry about this blood pressure thing or not. Lucy is quite right: she is getting better rest and care here than in hospital, but it does mean that I have to keep visitors at bay. I'm terribly sorry, Toto."

"I do understand. It's just that . . . it's as if no-one wants to see us any more. We've become . . . pariahs!" She sobbed the last word and Martha almost smiled because she sounded like a child. Then she said, "Listen, I won't keep you on the phone. You must be up to your eyes. But if I can do anything — anything at all, Martha. Washing, ironing . . . I'm going to send over some frozen meals. George will simply deliver them — leave them in the porch if you like — and go."

"Toto, my dear, please don't. As soon as the baby is born you'll be coming over. What's that — another six weeks or so?"

"Really? D'you mean that? Will Lucy be able to bear to see us?"

"Of course. I've told you, it's simply that she must be quiet —"

"I wondered. You know. If that might be an excuse. She must hate Len and she must hate us for being Len's parents."

"That's just not true! She doesn't hate Len. And she certainly doesn't hate you." Martha hesitated. "She is sorry. As I am. They shouldn't have married, I suppose. But then, there wouldn't be Clemmie."

"Clemmie?"

"That's what she wants to call the baby. After her father."

"Oh my God. It's Gampy's name. Florence Clementina. Didn't she know that? Oh Martha. You had better not tell her." The tears were flowing properly. "How wonderful . . . That's a link with — with — Dominic too. Clemmie."

After Martha replaced the phone she stood in the hall looking through the open front door at the array of flowers. It was beautiful but it was an overgrown mess and would have to be cleared out. Just like their lives. So much happiness and beauty, yet, through it all . . . She bit her lip, almost unwilling to admit to herself how very happy she had been these past few months. She said quietly, "We're split into so many pieces. Yet we're connected too." And the connection, the link in the chain that held them together, was Clemmie.

The fog rolled in at the beginning of the next week. It came from Worcester and the river and lay heavily on top of the trees around the church and pressed against the living-room window so that Lucy had the light on most of the day. It made the house cold and Martha switched on the central heating and lit a small fire in the little-used grate.

"I feel like one of the Brontë girls," Lucy said. "Cut off from the world, living in a vicarage, doing my sewing." She smiled at her mother. "Isn't it wonderful?"

"Yes." Martha smiled back. "Yes. It really is. I only hope poor George doesn't drive over with those frozen meals."

"If he does, let's make him welcome, Mummy." Lucy laid down the tiny dress she was sewing. "I'd like to see him. He and Toto — it's rotten for them, and it's my fault."

"Oh Luce. Don't be silly. Len didn't have to go off with Jennifer."

"But I was glad he did. Don't you remember? I told you how relieved I was." She looked down at her lap. "I'm like Daddy. I'm old-fashioned. In a lot of ways I'm very like Daddy." She held up the dress. "See? Smocking. No-one does smocking these days. It's out of fashion."

Martha stirred the fire gently with the poker. "Well, your father didn't do it either." She looked up anticipating a smile but Lucy was staring at the needlework as if expecting to find something within the pleated material. "Come on, Luce. No introspection. We're warm and cosy and happy. We can't ask for more than that. And I, for one, refuse to feel guilty about it."

"Good. I'm glad." Lucy looked round at last. "I don't want you to feel guilty, Mummy. Not about anything. You made the sort of life that Daddy needed. If there's another kind for you — somewhere, sometime — don't feel guilty."

Martha said steadily, "Lucy, I have everything I want, right here in this room."

Lucy seemed to ignore this. She said thoughtfully and with apparent irrelevance, "I wasn't frigid. Perhaps Jen has convinced Len that I was. But I wasn't. It was all wonderful — I promise you that, Mummy. It was wonderful."

Martha frowned slightly; someone else had talked of frigidity and she could not remember who it was. She said, "Darling, I know. Once when I phoned you —"

"But then . . . something happened. I don't even know what it was. I think I sort of . . . did my duty." She laughed. "I — I *suffered* Len's love-making. Put up with it. Made *him* suffer. I was one big reproach. Can you understand that?"

"Of course. Don't think of it, Luce."

"I am almost sure — that night — he was unfaithful. He went out for a long time. It didn't matter to him. Nor to me, really. But it should have done, shouldn't it? I should have made a fuss — we should have had a row or something. So our — our being in love was probably over then. And there was nothing, somehow, to take its

303

place. I realized that after the funeral, on the beach. If we couldn't make love, there was no other way to comfort each other. He was kind — don't think he wasn't kind to me. He got the flight home as soon as he could. And he let me stay in bed . . . but I knew he wanted to . . ." She shook her head. "I *couldn't*, Mummy. It was probably wrong of me, but I couldn't." She focused on her mother again and said, shockingly, "Was Daddy frigid?"

There was that word again. Martha was horrified yet strangely . . . interested. She thought back. If it weren't for that one night with Billy Tatham she could have given Lucy an unequivocal answer. She forced herself to consider the question objectively and said at last, "No. He was . . . fastidious."

"Oh Mummy. Yes. That was how I felt. Fastidious."

Martha said quietly, "Perhaps Len was a good lover but not a good friend?"

"Perhaps." Lucy nodded. "I loved him. I love him still in a way." She put her head back on the cushions. "Funnily enough, I think Jennifer knew. Right from the start. She need not have plotted so hard to get him. They were meant to be together and it would have happened." She smiled at her mother. "I'd like to see her. If she phones, tell her I'd like to see her."

"She won't ring," Martha said thankfully.

The fog stayed for three days then rolled away and let the sun through, then the rain came. Lucy walked around the garden holding an umbrella over her short blonde curls. She was there when George and Toto drove slowly up the drive with an insulated bag of frozen food. They

304

both enfolded her in their arms; Toto wept as usual but Lucy smiled happily and told her everything would be perfect once Clemmie arrived. That seemed to make Toto worse than ever and George refused all offers of hospitality and bundled her back into the car.

On Sunday 19 October, when the rain seemed to have been falling for months, though it had been only two days, Lucy got up very early and took the first of the winter's chrysanthemums to her father's grave. Then she tidied her room meticulously and in the face of Martha's protests stood at the sink peeling potatoes for lunch.

"I feel full of energy. Haven't felt like that for months. Let me do it, Mummy. It's such fun! I'd forgotten what fun it is to peel potatoes!"

"Will you go and sit down immediately you've finished?" bargained Martha.

"I will," Lucy intoned sonorously.

But first she made a telephone call. It was brief and very matter-of-fact.

"Jen? It's Lucy. Are you alone? No, I don't want to talk to Len, not really. But I thought it might help if you know, both of you, that I'm OK. I'm happy with what has happened."

Jennifer made a sort of choking sound. It could have been gratitude, but it could also have been fury.

"I want to tell you this, Jen, because, well, I'm pretty certain that Len will want Clemmie. And she is Mummy's and mine. We're her family. So it's up to you to look after Len. I don't know how . . . your own baby perhaps? You'll know what to do. Try to stop him from making . . . claims."

There was a long silence. Then Jennifer said, "You haven't changed. But, well, that suits me, of course. All right."

"I don't mean to sound . . . awful, Jen."

"Patronizing. That's the word you're looking for."

Lucy smiled at the wallpaper. "Maybe. I've missed you."

There was another pause then Jennifer blurted out, "Dammit! I've missed you too!" And she replaced her receiver gratingly.

That night Lucy's contractions started. She timed them carefully before calling her mother.

She was panting deliberately. "It's too soon, Mummy. If Clemmie dies as well . . . I can't live through it again, Mummy! I can't!"

Martha was checking the suitcase, panting in time with Lucy. She said, "We might have guessed. Peeling potatoes. Walking about in the rain. We should have guessed." She looked up. "Has it gone? Has the pain finished?"

"Yes. But they're every five minutes. Very regular. Is that good?"

"Excellent. Are they strong?"

Lucy sucked in her mouth and said, "A bit. But quite different from Dominic. I know now he was screaming . . . fighting. Clemmie is just . . . insistent." She took a deep breath and said, "Here she goes again!"

Martha took her hands and panted with her again. "Well done. I'll go and phone the ambulance."

"Tell them it's premature. They must get an incubator ready."

Martha said calmly, "It's not too soon. Four weeks perhaps. Certainly no more. Will you be all right if I go to the phone now?"

It took Martha approximately three minutes to get downstairs, make the emergency call, open the front door and go back up again. Her heart was thumping.

"They'll be here soon. Can you get downstairs?"

"No." Lucy was panting again. Martha took her hands.

"Don't worry, darling. It's all right. A little early but not that much."

Lucy's breathing slowed and her hands lost their grip. "I know. It'll be all right." She grimaced. "Everything will be all right if you're around. I love you. More than anyone. Is that wrong?"

"How can love be wrong, Lucy?"

"People — the world — might well think —" The sentence petered out in a gasp that was also a scream. Martha grabbed the flailing hands and held them tightly. Thankfully she heard wheels scrunching on the gravel outside. Lucy was pulling herself up in bed, rearing like a wounded animal, her hold on her mother like a vice. Martha gripped the clawing fingers and pulled her daughter upright against her shoulder. "Hang on!" she said loudly. "I'm here — take my strength — just hang on!"

After that, she did not remember anything else in the right order. Like a series of snapshots she recalled someone pressing a mask over Lucy's face. Someone else fiddling with the paraphernalia of a drip. The words "section" being said. "She must have a section — soon." And then the ambulance . . . Holding Lucy's hand . . . People running. Lucy disappearing through swing doors.

Everyone had to be quick. Quick and efficient. To save Clemmie. Nothing was said about Lucy. She wondered afterwards, much, much later, and then often, like a recurring nightmare, whether Lucy had died that instant in her arms.

She must have phoned Len. He appeared when she was standing by Lucy's body in the recovery room of the operating theatre. He was breathing heavily; he had obviously run along the corridors, asking questions on the way. He said, "They told me — oh God —" He looked at Lucy and then without hesitation he took Martha in his arms and held her so tightly she could scarcely breathe. She knew he wanted to take, as well as give, comfort. But she was beyond giving or receiving any kind of emotion. She was truly bereft; everything had been taken and she was standing in a kind of wasteland that was eternity.

He said into her hair, "Martha. I'm sorry . . . I'm so sorry. How you must hate me."

She waited until she was disengaged from those long arms and said with a touch of surprise, "Of course I don't hate you, Len. I don't hate anyone. Not even myself. They said there was nothing that could be done. Even an earlier Caesarean wouldn't have helped. The haemorrhage was sudden and massive and —"

"She need not have been pregnant! That day — the funeral — we went to the beach — it must have been then —"

"Len. I know. Lucy told me." She could not bear to hear that now. "Please don't torture yourself like this."

"It's selfish, isn't it? I know that. But . . . Martha, I needed Lucy to forgive me. And now she can't!" It was a wail of despair.

"She saw nothing to forgive. You both made a mistake in getting married. That's all. She had forgiven herself. Can't you do the same?" Martha heard her own voice, weary, almost uninterested. She wanted, quite desperately, to be alone with Lucy. She could not give up her protective role yet; who would look after Lucy now? Was she with Clem? Was there really something else, somewhere else beyond sight?

"Toto and George . . ."

Martha took a deep breath and made one last effort. "Clemmie. Clemmie will do all the forgiving." He was weeping copiously, looking so like his mother it was ridiculous. She touched his hair as Lucy must have done so often. It was like Billy Tatham's: dry, curly, close to the head. Lucy's had been the same. Jennifer's was long and flowing.

She said, "Len, could you ask them to bring Clemmie in here? I don't want to leave Lucy yet."

But of course the baby was in an incubator in the special care unit. It had been a ploy to get rid of Len. She told him to go and see her. "And then will you tell your parents for me, Len? And could Jennifer tell her mother?" Martha wondered for a moment whether she would like to see Linda. No. She did not want to see anyone. She whispered, "I will stay here. Until the morning."

At last he went. People came in to see her, offer her tea, suggest she went into the rest room where there was a single bed. She shook her head and said through dry lips, "You will let me stay with her? Just for tonight. Just for one night."

And at last she and Lucy were alone together. As they had been for the last five months. Their small paradise still intact.

"You knew, didn't you?" Martha looked at the small, round, child-like face framed in curls. "Somehow, you knew. Maybe I did too. And maybe that is why we . . . appreciated . . . everything. Oh Luce. The geraniums will go on for a while and the other flowers will come back next spring. And you won't be here to see them. How can I bear to see them without you? How can I bear anything any more?" She knew the answer: she could almost hear Lucy telling her. She would bear everything. Because of Clemmie. The child meant nothing to her now. But she could wait for love to grow. "But it will be so . . . arid, darling. It would have been fun. Everything would have been fun. And now . . ."

Long before dawn, the hospital clattered into life. Someone led her away and there running down the corridor was Toto with George behind her. Toto was keening like a wounded animal. As she reached Martha she managed to slow down slightly, but even so the impact of their two bodies was a shock and they had to cling to each other to stay on their feet. George came behind and enfolded them both. Martha closed her eyes: they were hot and dry and Toto's springy hair tickled her lids and nose so that she wanted to sneeze. Toto's upper arms were big and strong, the way nurses arms used to be. She smelled of soap and toothpaste; George's jacket smelled of yesterday's rain, his shirt of washing powder and fabric conditioner. Martha knew there was comfort to be had here; she felt the temptation to sink into those arms and that jacket and be taken home to share grief and anguish and, later, the anger which she knew was there too. But she resisted it. To accept human comfort was to be taken just slightly away from that figure on the high bed in the room behind her. Lucy was beyond human comfort. Martha wanted that apartness for herself. That distance which she had worked hard to maintain for Lucy . . . she wanted that back.

She waited until the arms loosened a little and the keening abated, then very gently she disengaged herself. "I'm going to see Clemmie," she said. "Are you coming too?"

Toto glanced at George. Her expression was pitiful. She looked completely helpless, completely vulnerable.

George nodded slowly. "Yes. Yes, we're coming too." He drew Toto towards him. "Then we must find the cafeteria. A hot drink. We must eat something."

Martha said nothing. She knew she was walking badly, like an old lady, but it was only because she had been sitting with Lucy for so long. She ignored George's proffered arm and walked towards the sign that said "Special Care Baby Unit' and then a nurse appeared. It was the same one who had cleared the room the night before. She said something cheerful and smiled at them and led the way and helped them with masks and coats and then they were by a high bed encased in clear plastic, looking in at an incredibly tiny baby, red and too small for its skin which lay in folds and wrinkles at every joint. The baby was sleeping. Her eyes were deep, trapped between a large forehead and high cheeks, her nose was a flattened button, her lips withdrawn and disapproving.

Behind her mask Toto began again to weep. Martha bent her knees slightly so that her face was on a level with the baby's. She looked at her objectively. She recognized Len's black hair that was going to curl into little rosettes all over the neat head. Len's ears too, flat and slightly pointed like a pixie's. But she had Lucy's round schoolgirl's face; her indrawn lips reminded Martha poignantly of Lucy's expression of disgust when she described school dinners.

Martha smiled. This was Lucy again; it would be possible to reconstruct everything. Again.

Toto saw the smile and stopped crying abruptly. Martha straightened and turned to George.

"Shall we try to find something for breakfast now?" she suggested. "And then we ought to talk to a doctor. Discover how long Clemmie has to stay here. What sort of professional care she will need once I take her home."

Again Toto looked at her husband. There was a wild question in her dark eyes this time.

George went out into the corridor and turned to the women as he removed his mask.

"Let's find breakfast first then, shall we?" he said.

CHAPTER
SIXTEEN

Clementina Travers came home to the Old Rectory on Friday 14 November, three weeks and five days after her birth. She weighed six pounds seven ounces and Mrs Rowe said she was the most beautiful baby she had ever seen. Martha did not believe her; she knew that Lucy had been more beautiful than Clemmie. But Clemmie had a way of studying her grandmother that was unique. Everyone said she was too young to focus properly, but when Martha was alone with her that first day, she focused completely and with deep concentration as if she knew that she was now with the person who would look after her and she needed to imprint the face on her brain. Her eyes, which had proved to be blue-grey at birth, were already changing to Len's deep brown which intensified the considering look into a searching stare. At first Martha had difficulty in holding the look and needed to break it up by smiling, blinking, talking to the child.

"Hello, Clemmie. I'm Grandma. We're going to be together now."

By the end of that first day she no longer needed to divert herself from the brown eyes. She leaned towards them and let her own expression remain unsmiling, steady, like a book that Clemmie might indeed be able to read. And perhaps she did because when she cried so passionately, extending her tiny legs and arms, pointing her toes, stretching her fingers in trembling supplication, Martha only had to bend over her and lock her gaze into Clemmie's and the baby would hiccough herself into a soothing silence and wait for the expected feed.

No-one else could read Martha any more. George and Toto had tried in vain to talk to her. She went to the hospital every day, spending hours sitting masked and gowned by the baby. When she emerged she agreed they must talk, but she did very little of the talking and appeared to be barely listening.

At the end of Clemmie's second week of life, Toto said tentatively, "Len thinks she is beautiful too, Martha. He realizes . . . Clemmie will live a great deal of the time with you. But perhaps, sometimes, he can have her? For a day at first. And then . . . who knows . . . a weekend?"

"He is her father," Martha said, nodding.

"And she could stay with us too. Couldn't she? That would make Len's . . . access . . . easier. George and I would so love to be with her. You know."

"Of course," Martha said, rolling up her gown and putting it into the laundry trolley.

George cleared his throat. "Shall we go and have tea and discuss what will happen when Clemmie is ready to leave the hospital?"

"Actually, George, I have promised the Rector's wife I'll do the flowers for a wedding tomorrow. The beech leaves are so pretty now. I thought a really autumnal display around the pulpit and those rowan berries at the pew ends. And vases and vases of Michaelmas daisies."

314

She shrugged into her coat and fished gloves out of the pocket.

"Nice." He coughed again. "Listen, Martha. You can't be solely responsible for Clemmie. We were thinking how great it would be if you came to stay with us for the rest of the winter. The house is warmer and there will be three of us to keep an eye on her. What do you say?"

She drew down her mouth. "Too many cooks, George." She smiled absent-mindedly. "Mrs Rowe has said she will come in every day. Daphne Coupland — the curate's wife, you know — is going to sleep in the spare room for the first two weeks. She's young — three children. Mrs Davis, Albert's wife, is doing some cleaning for me. Really, I am totally spoiled." She thought for a moment and added, "I always have been. So much love. And now . . . Clemmie."

Toto said passionately, "Yes but — Clemmie is our granddaughter too, Martha! And George is — is a man!" It sounded ridiculous and her eyes filled with tears. "And Len would be popping in every day."

Martha said mildly, "I doubt that. Jennifer would not like it."

"Jennifer's gone! That's the one good thing to come out of all this . . ." Toto swept her hand around the hospital corridor. "She felt responsible. She was in a terrible state. Rambled on about losing you and then Lucy. I think she went a bit potty. Didn't her mother have some kind of a breakdown? Probably runs in the family."

For the first time Martha showed an interest in the outside world, her face stretched with horror. "Oh! Poor

Jen. Oh, that poor girl!" She began to walk towards the exit. "What a mess. Where is she now?"

"Gone to stay with her mother and the new husband. Somewhere near Stratford, isn't it?"

"Yes. Yes. That's good." Martha stopped and seemed consciously to relax. Then she started walking again and the automatic doors slid open. It was almost dark and a fine rain blew into the big porch outside. "I do hope the weather will be better for Bonfire Night," she commented, putting up her umbrella. "So disappointing — the local children have made a huge pyre outside Miss Darcy's. Nice for her to be able to see the jollifications."

Toto said, "Martha, you can't do this. You can't shut yourself away with Clemmie like you did with Lucy. It's not fair!"

Martha looked around. Her face was blank with surprise. A drop of rain fell from one of the umbrella spokes on to her face and she blinked.

George said quickly, "Where's your car? Give me the keys. Let me bring it round for you."

She transferred her wide gaze to his face. "No thank you, George. I can manage." She braced herself against a gust of wind that threatened Toto's hat and repeated, "I can manage." Then she turned and hurried to the parking space reserved for the doctors. They had offered it to her the first day and she had accepted gladly. George and Toto watched her unlock, shake and close her umbrella, get in and fasten her seat belt. She reversed out carefully and waved through the window.

"She is so me*thod*ical!" sobbed Toto. "Anyone would think she was completely cold!"

George put his arm right around Toto and held her tightly. "We know otherwise, dearest girl. Don't we?"

"Yes." Toto sobbed into his shoulder. "And we've got each other, George. We've got each other." She sniffed. "I do nothing but cry these days. Will it get better, George?"

"I think so. Ask yourself this, Toto. Do you trust Martha?"

"Completely."

"Then, for now, that must be enough."

At first the house seemed full of extra and unnecessary bodies. Daphne Coupland was a dear but she hung on after breakfast wanting to watch Clemmie being bathed and then put down with milk still dribbling from one side of the indrawn mouth. Mrs Davis seemed always to be underfoot. Martha would ask her to do one room while she and Clemmie were in another, but Mrs Davis either did not hear or could not keep away from the tiny cot. Mrs Rowe was as bad, chatting away about this time next year when Clemmie would be old enough to go to the Mothers and Toddlers group being held over in Littleford's old Methodist church.

"It's a grand room. They can crawl around to their heart's content. And Littleford is less than three miles away."

"I was born there," Martha said. "Actually my father was the Methodist minister."

"Well! My dear life!" Mrs Rowe couldn't get over it. "It's obviously all meant. Isn't it? Meant to be." She raised her eyes significantly. "Someone higher than us

317

arranging things again." She avoided Martha's eyes and said quickly, "Well. Perhaps you could actually take it on? They need someone — older perhaps — to administer it. Keep a register. Make sure the heating is on and the toys put out. You know the sort of thing."

"We'll see. That's all a year off."

"But we must bear it in mind. We must make sure Clemmie socializes with other children from the earliest possible age."

"To compensate her for living with me?" Martha asked.

"Oh no, my dear. Not at all. That is a definite plus. But these little groups, they do help children to share, you know. Prepare them for the hurly-burly of school."

Toto sang the same tune. She came armed with disposable nappies, tins of strained carrots and apples, a music box. "It will lull her to sleep," she explained. "Keep her company. Actually, when she comes to stay in Tewkesbury, I wondered about asking my neighbour to leave her baby with us. Get Clemmie used to seeing other children."

Martha looked through the window. "Lucy and Jennifer were just about eight months old when they met. Linda and I parked the prams outside the Post Office and we could hear them gurgling to each other. I asked Linda to come back for tea so that they could play."

"There you are!" Toto said triumphantly.

"After Christmas and when the evenings begin to draw out, I should go to see Linda and Jennifer. Perhaps you would have Clemmie then?"

"Not till then?" Toto swallowed the protest and nodded. "Of course we will. George would love it. And perhaps Len will come and stay too."

"He telephones every day."

"But he hasn't been round?"

"No." Suddenly, unexpectedly, Martha smiled. "He is the only one who knows I would never harm a hair of Clemmie's head."

Toto was aghast. "Martha, you didn't imagine that I — that we — ever mistrusted you? We've always said, George and I, that we trust you utterly! I swear to you —"

"I know. I'm sorry, Toto. Forgive me. It's just that what with Daphne and Mrs Davis and Mrs Rowe . . ."

"Oh my dear." Tears welled in Toto's eyes and Martha patted her briefly.

"Please don't cry, Toto. This is the first time for ages that you haven't cried when you see me or Clemmie."

"And I'm not going to now!" Toto squeezed her eyes tightly and then smiled. "George said it would get better."

Martha watched her drive away and thought how little she knew. Because of course, it would never get better. It would be different. But never better.

And then the winds came. They rattled the windows and doors and screamed into the chimneys but the old house stood firm and secure while everyone else lost tiles and slates and the Couplands' garage roof blew away and Miss Darcy had to be taken by ambulance to the nursing home while her roof was repaired. Mrs Davis couldn't stand up against it and Mrs Rowe was frightened to drive her small mini. The Old Rectory belonged to Martha and Clemmie. Martha was certain that Clemmie felt as she did. She built a big fire in the living room and laid the little form on a blanket and played with her as she had played with Lucy.

All the old rhymes came into her head without difficulty. "Leg over leg as the dog went to Dover . . ." she sang, crossing the tiny legs in the air. "Roly-poly pudding and pie . . ." She moved the plump shoulders from side to side and was rewarded with a proper baby gurgle. When Clemmie slept, she lay down on the floor by her side and closed her eyes. A gust of wind shook the house and the baby murmured and flung out an arm. Martha caught it and held it warmly. She felt a kind of animal content; she told herself that Lucy was with them. When the telephone rang into their somnolence she was angry and snatched up the receiver and then replaced it without speaking. Clemmie cried out and pointed her toes and Martha scooped her up, singing, "Ride a cock horse . . ." and it rang again. And suddenly she knew who it was. It was Lucy. It was Lucy's way of being there.

She picked up the receiver, Clemmie in her see arm. No-one spoke. It was as if the world held its breath. Clemmie was completely and suddenly silent, staring at the telephone intently. Martha said breathlessly, "Is it you? Is it you? You don't have to say anything — I know — I know . . . Oh Lucy, thank you. Thank you, my darling."

And a male voice said strongly, "Marty. It's me. Bill. Bill Tatham."

320

She cried out with disappointment and then said angrily, "Why don't you — all of you — leave us alone! We're all right! Can't you understand that? We're all right!" And she slammed down the receiver.

It immediately rang again. He said urgently, "Don't cut off. Not just yet. Can I come and see you? Just for an hour? Please."

"Of course not!" She replaced the receiver then unplugged the telephone.

She tried to play with Clemmie again, to re-establish that hour when they had been cut off from the world and Lucy had been there . . . somewhere near.

But Clemmie cried for her feed. And then her nappy needed to be changed. And then Martha thought perhaps she should eat something herself. If only the gales would keep blowing she might well be able to create another moment in time. Put the clock back to somewhere else. And Lucy might stay with them longer this time.

Martha said no more about visiting Linda. Christmas came and went with George and Toto in attendance. When the snowdrops appeared, Martha took Clemmie for afternoon walks in the pram she had bought for Dominic in another life. The little girl was doing well; she tried to sit up by herself but would quite suddenly collapse over her own knees. She enjoyed being propped on pillows for an hour and wheeled around the country lanes. It was during one of these walks that Martha realized the "For Sale" signs had disappeared from Miss Darcy's terrace. Curtains were up in Linda's old house and on the front room window ledge was a box overflowing with snowdrops. She wondered whether there was a baby there and hardly knew how she felt about that possibility. Could history repeat itself? Could there be a friend for Clemmie as there had been for Lucy?

She tapped on Miss Darcy's door then let herself in. Miss Darcy was downstairs, her electric fire six inches from her feet.

"Oh, my dear Mrs Moreton! Bring her in! Let me see her! Has she put on weight?"

Martha swathed Clemmie in shawls and took her into the cottage.

"I think she will have doubled her birth weight next month," she said. "She's doing very well."

"I wish you looked better," Miss Darcy said mournfully. "You do remember to eat something yourself, don't you?"

"Of course. Will you hold her while I put the kettle on?"

"There's some of Mrs Goodwin's cake left." Miss Darcy took Clemmie on to her knee delightedly. "No wonder. It's as tough as old boots. Not a bit like you make."

"I will start baking again one of these days." Martha thought about the prospect as she had thought of visiting Linda. Without conviction. "And who has moved in to Mrs Bowles's cottage?"

"A very nice gentleman." Miss Darcy bounced Clemmie experimentally and the child gurgled. "Oh you little sweetheart!"

"No children?"

"Oh no. Too old. He must be about your age. He bought the place long before Christmas. Moved in last month. January the fifth. It was a Monday because Mrs Goodwin collected my laundry just as the pantechnicon arrived. Not much furniture. It's a weekend place for him." She bounced Clemmie again and laughed aloud. Then said, "He makes tents. Funny job for a man."

She thought he would call. She kept darting to the living-room window to see who was coming up the gravel drive. At weekends she kept herself very much to herself, rarely going for a walk. When she took Clemmie in to see Miss Darcy during the week, she was told that "that nice Mr Tatham always pops in on Sunday mornings"; he made coffee and took in a "treat": doughnuts, hot cross buns. Miss Darcy really enjoyed Sundays now. "He likes to hear what is happening in the village. Always asks after you, my dear. You didn't mention that you'd gone to school together." Miss Darcy looked over her glasses coyly. "Is he the man who took you out the Christmas before last? I remember there was some gossip. So much has happened since then that the details have slipped my mind." She waited expectantly.

Martha felt an unaccustomed prick of annoyance. Village life . . . so petty. She said, "Yes, we attended the same primary school. Actually, Mrs Bowles worked for him. He called a couple of times. I had to ask him not to come any more. Lucy did not care for him."

Miss Darcy was surprised. "Did she not? What a shame! He is such a kind man. And so capable. If there is any little thing . . . I know the dear Rector is helpful and Mr Coupland the same. But they're not *practical* men, are they? Mr Tatham can turn his hand to anything. He took me round to see the garden. It's an absolute picture, my dear. You remember what it was like in Mrs Bowles's time. A washing line and a row of petunias. He's landscaped it. A sunken garden in the middle with a seat — of course absolutely sheltered from the winds. He's designing a kind of canopy for the summer and he says he'll take me round." Miss Darcy's eyes sparkled and her cheeks were flushed. Martha made sure that the next weekend she locked all the doors, drew the kitchen curtains so that no-one could peer in and removed the washing from the clothes line. It was unnecessary because no-one called, not even Daphne Coupland. Even so, Martha informed Miss Darcy during the next week that she intended to spend weekends with George and Toto Travers in Tewkesbury.

It was strange, when she had protected Lucy from unwanted callers she had felt in complete control. Now that control had gone and she felt on the defensive. She thought with longing of castles with moats and drawbridges.

Toto went to see Len on her own. She had a key to the flat and she let herself in, immediately wrinkling her nose at the stuffiness. But the flat was tidy and fairly clean. She opened all the windows, put the kettle on and looked around for a tablecloth. She found one: she remembered it had been a wedding present, perhaps never used. It was still immaculately folded and lay across the table as if it had been starched. She spoke

324

loudly and tremblingly: "I am not going to cry! D'you hear me, Thomasina Travers? I am not going to cry!" And she banged mugs and plates and cutlery onto the table as if emphasizing her own words.

When Len arrived she had laid up an old-fashioned tea: ham sandwiches and cake. She had found out how to light the grill and she was toasting some hot cross buns. It was good to see him smile; she hugged him and was conscious as always that his bones were sticking through his flesh. The tears threatened again and had to be fiercely controlled.

He said, "I think the buns are burning." He leaned past her head and pulled out the grill. "No, they're just how I like them."

"Charred," she said turning from him with downbent head. "I thought they might warm you up. This lovely sun is deceptive. Someone was saying that there's snow further north."

"March is always cold." He went to the window and looked out. The sunshine highlighted everything. He said, "How ugly those dustbins are. I wonder if it looked like this last year."

"I doubt it has changed much."

"No. She hated it here, didn't she? She was always looking out of this window. As if she wanted to escape. Well . . . she did."

Toto opened her mouth and closed her eyes and concentrated on breathing.

He went on musingly. "Just about a year since Jennifer instigated her little plan." He turned. "I'm not blaming her, Ma. I'm to blame, I know that." He came

325

and sat down at the table, suddenly and deliberately cheerful. "Well. What are you doing here? Where's Dad? It's unusual to see you without him these days."

Toto was breathing normally again. She picked up the teapot and began to pour. "We . . . do rather cling to each other, I suppose. It's reaction."

"It's love," he said simply with another smile. "You two are in love — always have been. You're lucky and you know it."

"Yes. We are." She buttered the blackened tea cakes as if her life depended on it. "That's why it's so difficult for us to be, well, firm with Martha. But Clemmie is our granddaughter and we have to see her sometimes. You do understand, don't you, Len?"

"Martha has never stopped you seeing her, surely?"

"No. Never. But it is getting more and more difficult to turn up there, Len. She never invites us. We just have to phone and go and . . . it's awkward. She's not exactly unwelcoming, but she's always . . . sort of waiting for us to leave."

He said nothing. She put a tea cake on his plate and he rotated it slowly as if he had never seen one before.

"I know you telephone Martha. I know she telephones you sometimes. After all, you are Clemmie's father. You are her next of kin."

"Am I?" He glanced up. "I never thought of it like that. After all, she belongs to Martha."

Toto said, "She does not! She does not *belong* to Martha or your father and me. Legally, as far as anyone belongs to anyone else, she belongs to you!"

He raised his brows at her then picked up the tea cake and bit into it. She did the same as if determined to say nothing else.

After a while he spoke. "Come on. What's all this about, Ma?"

"It's about you seeing your daughter! Not phoning about her. Seeing her. Holding her and bathing her and talking to her and *knowing* her!" Tears spouted uncontrollably. "She is part of you, Len! She looks like you! She won't remind you of Lucy if that is what is worrying you!"

He leaned across the table and took her hands; they were shaking crazily. "Listen, Ma. Be sensible. I'm cooking up a new project at the moment. It will involve going up and down the country interviewing, investigating. Isn't it more sensible to leave things as they are?"

"Sensible? Who is talking about being sensible?"

"All right. Let's talk about emotions. I'm going to remind Martha that Lucy is dead. What have you got to say about that?"

"She doesn't need reminding of that!" Tears ran down Toto's face like twin rivers.

"No. Quite. She has managed to find a way to live. If I interfere —"

"Len! She is trying to live in the past! And Clemmie is the future — your future as well as Martha's and George's and mine!" She snatched back a hand and scrubbed furiously at her face. "And I know what you're going to say next. That it's early days. That we must give her time." She choked and went on somehow. "Clemmie will be six months old on Easter Sunday. Half a year, Len! Do you realize that?"

He obviously did not; he paused and thought about it. Then said, "Yes. Well, it's the eleventh of March now. Almost six weeks until Easter Sunday."

"And then? Will you ask Martha if Clemmie can come to us then? And you take a week off and be with her? Will you do that, Len?"

He hesitated. She started to weep again and he said, "All right. I'll give her a ring and put it to her."

"In good time. Tonight. Will you ring her tonight?"

"I'm not sure, Ma. Perhaps this weekend would be better."

Toto retrieved her other hand and pulled one of George's large handkerchiefs from her pocket. She wiped her face and blew her nose.

"I'm using these all the time," she said unhappily. "Tissues are no good and as for those silly little hankies people give you at Christmastime . . ."

"Oh Ma," Len said.

"I know. It's just awful. But it will get better. Your father says it will get better and he is never wrong." She put the handkerchief away. "Come on. We're going to have another bun and then start on these sandwiches. If you don't put some weight on soon, you'll blow away."

He smiled obediently and took another tea cake.

Martha did not know what to do. It was Saturday evening and had been another lovely day but now there

328

was a nasty little wind blowing the daffodils almost flat and the sky seemed to be darkly fluid. Len's phone call had been so unexpected; like a bombshell. She had been stunned, holding the receiver slightly away from her ear as if she could not believe what it was delivering. Len was always so kind, so undemanding. He invariably asked how she was before he asked after Clemmie. And if she did not actually see him, she could feel a certain detached fondness for him simply because he was Clemmie's father. But now, everything had changed.

She went slowly upstairs and looked into the nursery. Clemmie lay asleep, arms upflung, the musical box still slowly chiming out its nursery rhymes. Toto had been quite right, Clemmie loved the musical box. She would love Toto too because Toto was lovable. And . . . Len must be lovable. Lucy had loved him once.

She stood in the doorway until the last notes died away then she leaned over the cot and gently put Clemmie's arms beneath the blanket. She had an electric convector heater in the room, but it still felt cold. Toto had said once that the Tewkesbury house would be warmer for Clemmie. She was right about that too.

The front-door bell buzzed briefly and she jumped, although she was expecting Truda that evening to sort out the parish magazines. Truda was trying to rope her into all kinds of church work again; she had agreed to helping with the magazines as being the least intrusive of all the jobs on offer. She hurried down to answer the bell and there was the person she had dreaded to see. Billy Tatham.

She stood there, holding on to the door for support, not slamming it in his face, not speaking, not knowing how she felt, how she should react.

He was nervous too. His smile was diffident, almost pleading, as he said, "I swam the moat. It was difficult and dangerous. I deserve something for courage."

She never wept but, unaccountably, she felt her throat constricting. She took a step back, opening the door wider, and he came in and stood in the darkening hall. He must have walked over from Linda's cottage because he was without coat or hat; she got the impression that had he worn a hat he would be turning it in his hands. They were clasped among the folds of an enormous and garish sweater and his locked arms revealed an overall tension.

She said, "I heard you had bought Linda's place as a weekend cottage. I half expected to see you before now."

"When I phoned you, you were so angry. And the Rector's wife warned me off. You needed time alone with the baby, she said."

She could have laughed had it not been for the lump in her throat. "They all think I'm going dotty, do they?"

"They think you are dotty and will get better soon."

"I see." She took a breath and turned for the living room. "You'd better come in here and tell me about it." She clicked on the light. The fire had settled into its own cinders and she knelt before it, making it up carefully. Behind her she heard him picking up Clemmie's rattle and her big plastic bricks. "Put them in the toy box, will you? I'll wash them later."

"I don't know how you're coping, Marty. She's so little. There's so much to do."

She said steadily, "Well, I certainly couldn't cope without her."

He was stacking the bricks in a corner of the box and he paused just as she left the fire and stood up again. Their eyes met. He said, "Ah. So your son-in-law has telephoned, has he? Just this evening?"

"You read minds as well as swim moats," she commented.

"I went to see Mr and Mrs Travers last week. They told me that their son was going to ask you if he could take the baby to his parents' house for Easter. They told me he had promised he would phone this weekend."

She was outraged. "How dare you interfere in my family affairs! What have my domestic arrangements got to do with you?"

"You know . . ." He made a helpless gesture. "You know why I have to concern myself, Marty. If everything had been all right, Lucy here, the baby . . . everything . . . you would not have seen me again. But it's not like that, is it?"

She too waved her hands. "It's still nothing to do with you! You are a complete outsider! Why can't you see that? Accept it?"

His hands fell to his sides. He took three breaths. Then he said, "That fire has gone out, Marty. Let's go into the kitchen. I really do want to say something and it's important. Hear me out. Please."

She stared at him tensely for another two seconds, then turned and walked from the room. He followed and clicked off the light. When they got into the kitchen she saw he was carrying the box of toys. He went immediately to the sink and began to draw a bowl of water to which he added the sterilizer that was on the shelf. He plunged the toys into the water.

She said, "Kindly leave that. Say what you have to say. And go."

He leaned on the sink, watching the toys float around the warm water. She wondered, horrified, whether he was weeping.

He said at last, "That time I spoke to Lucy. I've thought of it so often. I have wondered whether she might have had some premonition that day." She gasped audibly and he put out a hand and waved it again. "Sorry. Sorry, Marty. I know I shouldn't speak like that, it's just that . . . well, she didn't like me, did she? She thought I was a jumped-up opportunist. She compared me with her dad and found me sadly lacking." He waved his hand again as she started to choke some protestation at him. She saw the turned-back sleeve of his sweater was dripping with water. He said, "But then, as we talked, I felt her relaxing. And since then, I've wondered . . . God, it sounds so pretentious . . . but she sort of gave me her blessing." He turned. His eyes were full of tears. "I'm sorry, Marty. I don't want to push in or be offensive. I can only be myself. And you liked me. You know you did. And I think she would have done too. But she knew there was no time. She had no time. Forgive me. I didn't intend to say this. Forgive me."

He was speaking the things she had thought herself. She had blocked off the memory of Lucy telling her to get in touch with Billy Tatham; but she had thought, often, that Lucy might have had some premonition of her own death.

She hung her head, unwilling to see his ravaged face and the sleeves of his sweater wet with the washing water.

He waited, audibly recovering himself. Then he came to the table and sat down and put his hands in front of him.

"I have interfered. I know that. Buying Linda's cottage — that was interference. But I had to know how you were. Linda phoned and told me about Lucy and about Jennifer leaving your son-in-law and taking all the blame. So I've been phoning to ask how Jennifer is doing. Not well." He was staring down at his hands. "She's not working. She's not eating. And Linda knows what it is like to lose your own self-respect. So she is . . . anxious." He glanced up. "Couldn't you . . . sit down, Marty?"

She drew out a chair and sat at the table. It was impossible to imagine Jennifer as thinner than she was already; she had never had — or wanted — much flesh on her bones. And that glorious gypsy hair would not be tamed, surely?

He sighed. "So then I bought Linda's house. And I found something I wanted to do . . . besides find out about you, of course." He tried to smile and failed. "I'm making the cottage into my home, Marty. Linda hasn't been able to cope with it for years and it's pretty run down. I've replastered a couple of rooms and had some new windows and I've revamped the garden completely." She wanted to tell him that Miss Darcy had loved it all but she still could not trust herself to speak. So she placed her hands on the table too. They were red from bathing Clemmie; two of her nails were broken and had torn down to the quick; her wedding ring rode loosely around the knuckle of her finger.

He took a breath and went on. "You know what village gossip is like. I didn't take too much notice. It was enough that you were coping so well. You had some help — I know all that. But at the end of the day, it was down to you." He let his breath go with a puff and said, "I was showing that little Miss Darcy round my new garden and the Rector's wife appeared and said something about you and I let her have it. Told her she should be applauding the way you are managing. And d'you know what she said? She said — sadly, Marty — she said, "Yes, Mr Tatham, but she ought not to be managing so well. Think about it." She didn't mean it critically, Marty. She is really fond of you — and you know what an old battleaxe she is. And she is worried about you. So that was when I decided to go and see Mr and Mrs Travers."

Martha interlaced her fingers. The pattern they made reminded her of another rhyme for Clemmie: "Here's the church, here's the steeple . . ."

Billy Tatham said, "Are you listening, Marty? I really did interfere. I went to see Lucy's in-laws."

She looked up. She felt calmer now. They could worry all they liked; she was all right. She and Clemmie were all right. Just so long as they were left alone.

He said, "I knew how you would feel when your son-in-law asked for Clemmie. There's no way you can stop him, is there? He is the child's father and whatever went on between him and Lucy makes no difference to that." She felt her heart jump. Had she forgotten Len's diffident voice on the phone? The way he had said, "Why don't you come as well, Martha? The baby is used to you and you could show us the sort of things she likes . . ."

Billy Tatham said, "You feel beleaguered, don't you, Marty? The drawbridge is up but I've swum the moat and there will be others. And I have no rights, but they will have."

She looked at him, her eyes burning. "Stop it!" she said hoarsely.

He reached across suddenly and covered one of her hands with both of his. She jerked back but he would not release her.

"Listen to me. Then I will go. I've thought about this until my head aches. Lucy wanted you to have Clemmie. Everyone knows that. But they're all unhappy. They're all in a muddle. You're the only one who seems to know what the hell is going on. You can sort it out, Marty. You can make them live again. Will you do it?"

"I don't know . . ."

"It's a logistics problem. What comes first, Marty? It's the same when we start erecting one of our really big marquees. We've got the manpower, we've got all the equipment. But we need to know what happens first. Then the rest usually follows. Automatically." He sounded excited. "I think we start with Jennifer."

She stared at him, frowning, angry, frightened.

"Yes, I know. It sounds crazy, doesn't it? But don't forget I am an outsider. I can see things objectively. And

I've had time to think this one out. Jennifer needs to come back to life. She needs to be forgiven. Then she and Len can make a proper match of it. Maybe have their own children . . . who knows?" He paused and then added, "And you need to forgive Jennifer. Don't you, Marty?"

She felt the warmth of his fingers on hers but it did not penetrate into her hand. She said in an unexpectedly loud voice, "She is alive. And Lucy is dead."

And he said quietly, "Yes." He gripped her hands. "That is what she hates too."

"Oh God!" She gave a dry sob. "I can't do it. You are asking for the one thing I cannot do."

"You are blaming everyone for Lucy's death. Yourself included. This one thing would iron all that out." He frowned, trying to find words. "Literally, Marty. You know, when you have something you are pressing, something creased, and you smooth it with the iron —"

She ripped her hands away. "Oh stop it, stop it! Your parables, your metaphors — they're ridiculous! Logistics! The only logistics is how to get through each day! Can't you see that?" She spread her hands out before him. "Do the washing, the ironing, keep people away — if only people would keep away, I could do it so easily —"

"No. You could try to go back. This way is a way forward." He stood up and his chair almost fell backwards and then righted itself with a clatter. "Listen. Marty. When they come for Clemmie at Easter, don't sit around and think. Get out the car and drive to Stratford and see Linda and Jennifer."

"No!" she said decisively.

"You've got five weeks to get used to the idea. Try to do it, Marty. Not for Lucy's sake, nor first and foremost for Jennifer's sake. For your own. Do this for you, Marty. You'll find you'll be able to swing standing up again . . . I promise. If you look after Jennifer you will be able to go to Montpelier Gardens late at night when no-one else is around and you'll sit on the swing first of all. And then you'll stand up."

She dropped her head. "Go away," she whispered.

"Will you be all right? Shall I make some tea?"

"Just go."

"All right. But I shall telephone in an hour's time and if you don't answer I shall come back and break down the door if I have to."

"I'm not going to kill myself, if that's what you're thinking."

"Then all you have to do to keep me at bay is to lift the phone."

She said nothing and after a while she heard him open the front door and then close it. His footsteps on the gravel were purposely loud.

CHAPTER
SEVENTEEN

Jennifer watched the yellow curtains in the guest room as they turned from ochre at six o'clock that morning, to brilliant gold by eight. It was going to be another hot day. She closed her eyes wearily and inside her head a voice spoke as it so often did: "Who was it said April is the cruellest month . . ." Of course *that* April, last year's April, had been bitterly cold. But this one, unseasonably warm, glorious with late daffodils and tulips, camellia and magnolia blossom, was just as cruel. Perhaps more so. The sunshine was unfeeling, uncaring. At least the wind and rain wept with some kind of objective universal sympathy. The sunshine was simply heartless. From beneath the other window, she heard the clatter of teacups on the terrace. Her mother made such a ceremony of meals. Just as she had clung to the ritual of coffee and tea in the conservatory at Worcester, so now she loved it when they could have meals on the terrace. Especially breakfast. Archie would have gone to the golf course at dawn and would be back home soon, hugging everyone in sight, drinking orange juice because Linda said it was good for him, then settling down to crisp, grilled bacon and tomatoes and gallons of tea. His face would shine like a full moon with sheer happiness. Jennifer knew that he had to make a conscious effort not to show this happiness when she appeared. Probably that was another reason she stayed in bed half the day.

She swung her wrist in front of her face. Eight-thirty. She had had two hours sleep; less than the night before, more than the night before that. Her head ached permanently these days, but it was worse between eight in the morning and midday. It was so unfair; she had always craved to lie in. Her idea of luxury was to get up in time for lunch. Now that she could do that, all it gave her was a headache. Lucy had said that crying made her head ache, so she never cried. Jennifer seemed to have no option but to stay in bed in the mornings. There was nothing else she wanted to do anyway, and it gave her mother and Archie time to relish this unlikely — ludicrous — romance of theirs. It must be a romance because Jennifer felt like a gooseberry every time she was in the room with the two of them. It wouldn't have been like that if Linda had married Bill Tatham. Jennifer could imagine his reaction to her presence. It would be either, "Come on in and be comforted, you poor old girl." Or, "Clear off, Jen. Your mother and I want to be alone." Archie tried to be tactful. And the time for tact had long gone.

She hauled herself up in the bed and punched the pillows into a propping position. Her head throbbed warningly as if she had a hangover. She must have whimpered slightly because from the terrace her mother's voice floated upwards.

"Is that you, Jen? Are you all right?"

If she called back it was more than possible that her eyes would fall out, so she stumbled out of bed and stuck her head through the open window.

"Fine, Ma. Is Archie back yet?"

"No. He's having brekkers at the clubhouse with someone from the quarry. I had mine in the kitchen. I'm making coffee now. Shall I bring some up?"

"No thanks. I might come down in a minute."

She looked at the bed — almost smiling because her mother had said "brekkers", one of Archie's silly words — and wondered whether she could go back to sleep for an hour. Then knew she could not bear to get between the sheets again.

Linda said, "You know, darling, you don't have to keep out of Archie's way. He just loves having you here. Makes him feel like a proper dad."

"Well, he's not my proper dad, Ma. As far as I'm concerned he's your new husband."

"Well, I'm not sure about that. I mean — I know he's my husband and I'm absolutely chuffed about that . . ." First "brekkers" now "chuffed". ". . . but of course, darling, there is a *chance* he's your father."

"There's no chance and you know it. My father was probably a gypsy you met in a wood somewhere." Jennifer tried to summon some of her old spirit into the suggestion. Linda laughed but looked troubled and said something about Jennifer never having a real family or a real chance in life.

"Trying to make excuses for me, Ma?" Suddenly Jennifer put a hand over Linda's ringed fingers. "I had you. You've always been on my side." She gave a wry grin. "Believe it or not, I've been on yours too."

"Oh God, Jen." Linda's eyes filled. "Oh God . . . I want something good to happen to you. And I don't even know what that is any more!"

Jennifer's grin died and she leaned back in the plastic garden chair. "Nor me. But I hope it happens soon. For Archie's sake as well as mine."

Linda started on her usual line. "You mustn't blame yourself, Jen. That's the trouble — you're taking everything on your shoulders and, after all, we know now that Lucy wanted to go home — nothing to do with you and Len. That was the excuse she used. But she wanted, all the time, to go home."

"Yes." Jennifer spoke dully, conscious again of her headache. "Yes. She and Martha . . . Well, never mind. It's no good going over and over it, Ma. You know as well as I do that if she were alive and could tell me herself it might make it a bit better. But she's not. And that's that."

And suddenly the impact of Lucy's non-existence hit Jennifer like a body blow. It happened every so often. She would be Jennifer Bowles one minute, full of a confidence based mainly on sex, certain she would "get over" whatever ailment she had. And then she slid into being Jennifer Moreton, Martha's niece by marriage and Lucy's cousin and a kind of Universal Cheat. The blow — it was physical — always hit her solar plexus so that she doubled over with it. This morning the sudden change in balance forced her headache to her eyes; it was as if she was splitting in half. The pain was so intense she thought for a moment she was having a stroke. There was a bursting sensation; she tasted salt, then knew she was crying. Not the kind of controlled lump-in-throat attacks she had had before. This was a flood, an agony, a screaming protest and plea at the same time.

Linda came to her, crouching on her knees, holding her head.

"What is it? Oh my darling, oh Jen, please don't — please don't —"

"I can't — can't — can't — can't . . ." Her lungs were empty and collapsing. She took a huge shuddering breath and expelled it with the words: "bear it!"

She clung to her mother; Linda was so small, so insubstantial. She thought of Len: they said he was thin now, but he was still comfortably big, surely? She wanted to hold him. But more than that she wanted him to hold her. Not that he would any more. He knew her now. And in any case her scraggy body was practically sexless.

"Don't let me go, Ma! Don't let me go!"

"Darling, I'm here. You're all right. I'm here."

"I killed her, Ma. I killed Lucy. I loved her — and I killed her!"

"Don't be silly, Jen. You know that's not true. Hang on to me . . . This will pass. Just hang on and let it all out."

They both heard Archie cone onto the terrace. Linda half turned, trying by her expression to show that perhaps he should make himself scarce. Jennifer clung harder, thinking her mother was leaving her.

Archie's big face registered shock and then sudden distress. For a moment he hesitated. Then he lunged forward between the two women and scooped Jennifer up into his arms and held her like a baby, tucking her face into his red neck, rocking her. "Come to your daddy, my darling. Let Daddy make it better. There, there, there. Nothing is that bad, Jenny Wren. Nothing in this world is that bad."

Jennifer, shocked, was caught between sobs. Willy-nilly she held his shoulders and over his left ear she looked into her mother's eyes. And there she saw a naked plea.

Archie, encouraged by her silence, continued in his crooning tone. "Let's go indoors, sweetheart. Sit on the sofa and let this gale blow away." He turned to the big patio windows. "My goodness, you're as light as a feather. D'you know, I remember when you were just a baby and Mummy let me carry you from the car over to Willersey pond to see the ducks. I swear you don't weigh much more now than you did then!"

He deposited her oh so gently on the sofa and, without taking his arm from her shoulders, sat by her side.

"There, my lovely. Put your head on my shoulder and tell me all about it. Mummy, come and sit down. Our girl needs us."

Jennifer wept again. She wondered whose need was the greatest. Archie who wanted a daughter and a family so much. Or herself, who wanted . . . what? Archie's shoulder was wide and through his extra-large Fred

Perry shirt she could smell soap and the cologne Linda had given him last Christmas.

She could never call him Daddy, but then she never called Linda Mummy. She pushed herself into the cushions so that their bodies almost enclosed her. "Oh Archie . . ." she sobbed. "Oh Linda . . ."

It was while they were all weeping together that the telephone rang. Mrs Dorrell, who did the cleaning and was not supposed to be there because it was Good Friday, glanced in at them and picked up the telephone in the hall.

"Another Mrs Moreton on the telephone," she reported back, rolling her eyes to cover the embarrassment of their grief and her bewilderment at there being another Moreton in the world. "Good job I did pop in today, innit? Kitchen floor a disgrace and the lot of you gone deaf it seems!"

Linda said, "Oh God. It's Martha."

Archie, definitely head of this little household now, said, "I'll deal with it. Mrs Dorrell, as you're here, can you make some coffee?" He swept her ahead of him and picked up the dangling receiver. Linda and Jennifer looked at each other. Linda said, "Don't worry. She wouldn't ring to be horrid."

Jennifer said frantically, "But what can she want! God Ma . . . I can't talk to her. I just can't!"

"You need not. If Archie can't deal with it, then I'll have a word. Don't worry." She touched her daughter's hand gently. "Darling. Thank you. For going along with Archie. He — he loves you, you know. Always did. I know I should have told him firmly that you were not

344

his. But I've never been much good at being decisive." She smiled tentatively and Jennifer's weeping gentled. She nodded, but not a bit censoriously. Suddenly all Linda's weaknesses were precious to her. They both listened to Archie's voice being non-committal in the hall.

Jennifer took a shuddering breath. "I'll tell you something, Ma. He's great father material. And I could do with a father . . . Oh Ma, what a mess. What a terrible mess."

Archie appeared in the doorway. "She'd like a word with you, Jen. I told her you're not well. She said could I ask you whether she can come and see you. Easter Sunday or Monday."

Jennifer breathed consciously. She whispered, "I don't think I could stand it."

Archie said masterfully, "I'll be here."

Linda clutched her hand. "She must want to see you quite badly, Jen. She wouldn't be asking to make a social call."

"What about the baby? Will she bring the baby?"

Archie shrugged. "I don't know. She didn't say."

Linda stood up. "Let me talk to her, Archie. I'll be able to tell whether Jen can deal with it or not." And when she came back she said, "Martha is taking Clemmie to Tewkesbury. This afternoon. It's going to be terribly hard for her to do that. It's going to be terribly hard for her to come here. But that's what she wants to do."

Jennifer looked up at the two of them. She said pitifully, "She's got to come, hasn't she? I've got to see her."

Linda spoke gently, "I think you must, Jen."

Martha did indeed find everything hard. She had not seen Billy Tatham since he had called five weeks previously. Having talked to her as if he was the managing director of a company and she was the new typist, he removed himself from her life completely. Miss Darcy told her that he was not coming down to the cottage until after the Easter weekend: a big camping exhibition somewhere. The weather was ideal for it. He had to strike while the iron was hot.

"He's full of little sayings," the old lady confided delightedly. "When he calls he always says: 'Cards on the table, Miss Darcy, is it convenient or not, I can go or stay.'" She gave Martha one of her looks and said, "I appreciate his direct approach, Mrs Moreton. At my age, tact can be a two-edged sword."

Martha wondered where tact ended and guile began. She was certain that Billy Tatham's absence was planned most carefully. He had come to see her that evening in March, shot his bolt, and was now leaving it to do its own work. And it was strange how it was working. More like yeast than a bolt. Fermenting and growing. She kept telling herself that there was no way she was going to drive to Barnt Green to see Jennifer Bowles. Or Moreton. But really, she did have to take Clemmie over to Tewkesbury on Good Friday and then what would she do? They wanted her to stay, be part of the family — Clemmie's family. But she knew that though she might do so later, this first visit belonged to Toto and George and Len. So she would come back to the Old Rectory and be on her own. And that was no bad thing either; she had been on her own there before. She could do some gardening and put a coat of emulsion on the kitchen walls. She could even do some baking for poor old Miss Darcy.

She told herself that that was exactly what she would do. Yet all the time, she knew with another part of her mind that she was going to see Jennifer. In the end there was no way out of it.

It was strange to hear Archie Evans's voice. She recalled him from Jennifer's wedding to Simon Moreton: a big, red-necked sort of chap, very protective of Jennifer. And then Linda's voice. Oh God, how she missed Linda. How good it was that Linda was married at last: had some kind of status at last; had a proper family too. Which she would never have had if Jennifer hadn't left Len. If Lucy hadn't died. If Clemmie hadn't been born.

Martha shook her head to clear it. It was Good Friday. Clemmie would be six months old on Sunday. The sun was shining. She was taking Clemmie to stay with her other grandparents. She must go to Tewkesbury. Now.

They were all there to meet her. It was also six months since she had seen Len and she was appalled at his boniness. His face was all planes and burning sunken eyes. She cut through the pleasantries and put her arms around him.

"Lucy would hate all this unhappiness," she said to him, holding him close. "Somehow it's got to end, Len. Did you know I'm going to see Jennifer on Sunday?"

She felt him stiffen in her arms.

"How could I know that?" he asked hoarsely.

"Billy Tatham." She withdrew and smiled up at him ruefully. "It seems he runs a kind of fifth column. Perhaps he's retired now."

Toto, who had been bending over the carrycot talking gibberish, looked up.

"He came to see us, Martha. He's nice, isn't he? So kind. He kept apologizing for coming, but we were only too glad to talk to him. He felt he'd come between you and Linda Bowles in some way. It made him feel responsible. For a lot of things."

Martha said, "It was his suggestion. About me going to see Jennifer. He would like Linda and me to be friends again too. But Jennifer was his main concern."

Nothing more was said then; Martha had to see Clemmie's nursery and then Clemmie had to be taken to the hedge where the baby next door was waiting to be introduced. There was a grand tea laid in the dining room and a plate of rusks shaped like zoo animals for Clemmie. She fingered them to her mouth delicately and solemnly. "She is so . . . wonderful!" Toto said, her eyes suspiciously bright. George said warningly, "Now, Toto!" And she laughed and sniffed and said, "I promised. Remember?"

Len sat next to his father. His eyes rarely left Clemmie and when she looked up at him he leaned forward slightly and smiled and after a while she smiled back.

It was so different from what she was used to at the Old Rectory. Martha watched it all and knew that Clemmie would be happy here: the love in the sunny room was palpable. Well, it was what she wanted,

348

wasn't it? For Clemmie to be happy. Especially with the man who was her father.

Strangely, when the moment to leave arrived, it was not hard. She held Clemmie's head between her hands, kissed her, exchanged one of their special "looks" and left the room. She had to stop herself from telling Toto what time she had her bath and which of the plastic animals in her box she liked to play with and what to do if she woke in the night. Toto must not think she was interfering in any way. And Clemmie must know that when she went to Tewkesbury life would be slightly different from when she was at Nortons Heath. Children picked up things like that quickly.

But however she felt about leaving Clemmie, the Old Rectory seemed enormous and echoing without her. She fed Snowie and then found herself walking around looking under beds and in cupboards as she had done when Lucy and Len were first married. She looked at the wedding dress, swathed in tissue paper and plastic, then pulled down the big box containing the veil and headdress. It was as if she were deliberately wallowing in sentiment; as if she wanted to weep and hold the dress to her and become utterly maudlin. Would there be some relief in conscious melancholy? She carried the dress to the window and stared down at the garden. The marks of the marquee had long gone. And in any case all that particular memory did for her was to remind her of Billy Tatham. Involuntarily she smiled. The way he had accosted her that day of the wedding! So confident . . . so cocky. Like a little bantam. Of course he had thought she had hired the marquee from him because of old associations. Billy Tatham. Those old, old days in Littleford when they had collected shrapnel . . . He had changed so much . . . Cards on the table: he had definitely "bettered himself". And what had she done in those intervening years? Nothing much. Become staid and probably narrow-minded. And . . . pious, and . . . Linda had called her hypocritical. Was she hypocritical? Had she fastened Lucy to her with apron strings of steel? Was she doing the same with Clemmie?

She replaced the wedding dress, went downstairs and as the spring evening faded she made sandwiches and cocoa and looked at the *Radio Times*. Melancholy was not for her; that much she did know. She had Clemmie, she must remember that. She wasn't possessive — surely she wasn't possessive — but Lucy had left Clemmie to her. Her legacy.

Linda heard the car and came down the steps to meet her.

The house was beautiful: solid, four-square with an old-fashioned verandah along the south side looking over the golf course.

"We thought you'd like everything to be as it usually is here." Linda reached up determinedly and pecked Martha's cheek. "So Archie is playing golf and Jennifer is getting up slowly. She's in the bath at the moment."

"Oh yes." Martha smiled. Linda had been practically spitting the last time they had been together. It was good that she had not found it necessary to hedge herself around with Jennifer and the new husband. "I dreaded a reception committee actually."

"Oh . . . Martha. I'm so sorry. The things I said . . . I don't remember half of them, you know. I must have been mad. I think I was for a time. When Lucy was at the hotel with me, we were like a pair of invalids." She bit her lip. "I didn't mean to mention that."

"Mention everything. Don't let's be afraid to open our mouths." Martha stopped at the top of the steps. "This is lovely. A feeling of being on top of the world."

"It is, isn't it?" Linda was eagerly pleased. "I'll show you around later. I've got coffee here. I love sitting out on this terrace." She drew out two chairs. "Martha, I am so lucky. D'you know, all these years, Archie loved me. He really, really loved me!" She laughed incredulously. "And I think I probably loved him! I certainly do now!"

Martha very nearly wept at that. She smiled. "Linda, you don't realize how lovable you are! I'm so pleased it's worked out."

"Yes. It wouldn't have done with Bill, you know. Whatever happened, I would always have been second best. I thought that didn't matter. But it did." She hesitated then said, "It matters for him too. He can't settle for being second best. That was why he came over to see me last May. I expect it seemed odd to you, but he felt terrible that day. Definitely second best. And I came to the gate and he just crossed the road to see me."

"Linda, you don't have to explain. Anything. Not any more." Martha accepted a cup of coffee and said with some difficulty, "That's what Lucy's death did for all of us. Explanations are not necessary." She controlled her mouth and added firmly, "Acceptance is."

Linda said with the same eagerness as before, "I know what you mean, of course. It was so awful, so cataclysmic, it made everything else seem . . . irrelevant."

"Except Clemmie. Clemmie has been the one relevant thing to come out of it."

"Oh Martha . . ."

"I know. That sounded . . . pious!" Martha took a sip of coffee. "I say these things and I don't always mean them, Linda. You know that better than most." She shook her head. "No, that's wrong. I do mean them. But I can't . . . live them." She smiled above the rim of her cup. "It's this theory and practice thing, isn't it? Sounds good. But when I see Toto, nearly always crying, and George looking always anxious, and poor Len so thin and so intense, and Jennifer desperately unhappy, then . . . words are just words."

"Yes. But they're important. Like . . ." Linda waved her hands. "Like little lifebelts you can grab when things are bad!"

Martha laughed. "I've missed you," she said. "Get Archie to drive you over this summer. See Clemmie. Will you?"

"Oh yes. I'd love that."

They both smiled and then by tacit consent began to talk of other things. Linda pointed out her herb garden. "I was never much of a cook. There was no call to be. But Archie loves food, often the wrong kind. So I'm going in for healthy cooking. And fresh herbs are so useful."

Martha thought how odd it was that Bill Tatham was also finding a new joy in gardening; and in Linda's garden too.

352

It was almost midday when Jennifer put in an appearance. By that time a wind had driven them indoors and they were in the kitchen washing up and apparently completely at ease again. Jennifer stood in the doorway, unobserved for a few seconds. When Martha turned to put a cup on the dresser she was shocked not only by Jennifer's appearance, but by her unaccustomed diffidence. Jennifer had always believed in making an entrance and the fact that she had come down so late had seemed a deliberate ploy. Martha saw instantly that this time it was not. Jennifer was afraid of meeting her.

"Jen." Martha stood still, the tea-towel drooping from one hand. "My dear. Hello."

She wondered whether she should open her arms; sweep everything away with one enormous hug. But Jennifer did not move either.

"Hello, Martha." She forced a smile. "You've lost a lot of weight. But I suppose we all have."

"Yes. Len particularly."

Jennifer flinched visibly and Martha said quickly, "Sorry. I saw him on Friday. First time since Lucy died. I was rather shocked."

Jennifer took a short breath. "Is this your idea of throwing me a lifebelt?" Martha stared. Jennifer said, "I was listening. When Ma said that words were like little lifebelts. I thought you might have some for me. I didn't think you'd throw rocks."

Martha forced herself to stay still; she had after all, known this was going to be difficult.

"You don't find Len's name is anything like a lifebelt?"

"No. Nor Lucy's."

"We've got to talk about them, Jen. That's why I'm here."

"Yes. Acceptance. I told you, I was listening. We've got to accept what happened — is that it?"

Martha turned and hung the towel on the rail then put her hand on Linda's arm as if asking her not to interrupt.

Jennifer said, "Ma can do that. Accept. What happened . . . wasn't her fault. And anyway, she's got Archie now." Jennifer tried to stand away from the door-jamb. She propped herself with her hand. Martha saw the wedding ring had gone. "You seem to be able to accept it too, Martha. You have behaved beautifully all the time. And anyway, you've got the baby. Lucy's baby." She swayed suddenly so that Martha thought she was going to fall to the ground. She said, "I can never do that. Don't you see? If I hadn't taken Lucy's husband, she would still be alive now. I'll never be able to accept that, will I?" She rubbed her forehead. "I know I've got Ma. And Archie is so . . . kind. So kind. But I have to be alone now . . . I'm not really fit to be with anyone. Can't you see that?"

Martha shook her head. "There was nothing they could do to save Lucy. I thought you knew that, Jen. She had a massive haemorrhage. If I'd insisted on her going into hospital . . . but even then . . . and the midwife came regularly." Martha frowned, looking inwards, remembering. "I'm not sure what happened really. I mean . . . I don't think about it if I can help it. But sometimes . . . There was a point when she sat up and I held her. The paramedics arrived at the same time so I can never be sure about this. But I think she might have died then." There was a cry of distress from Linda. Jennifer was silent, staring with burning eyes at Martha. Linda made a move and Jennifer gestured to her to be still.

Martha said, "Hindsight gives wrong perspectives. Sometimes I think she knew. It was strange. The five months we were together, we were so *happy*. It was like a dream world. And for Lucy it was recapturing her childhood. Storing it up in some way. Storing it up for me too. For later. Like — like — a bequest."

Linda moaned, "Oh dear God . . ."

Martha heard her and turned, smiling. "Don't be sad about it, Linda. I haven't let myself remember all that before. I block things out. You know that." She turned the smile on Jennifer. "These words, if they're lifebelts, are for me. Because I just spent that time looking after her, not seeing, not doing anything."

Jennifer nodded slowly. "Makes you realize that in fact you gave her a unique gift. I can see that."

Martha nodded. "There may have been other gifts other people could have given her. Len, for instance. But I'm so thankful it was me." Her tentative smile widened. "You see? If it hadn't been for you I wouldn't have had that opportunity." The smile became a grin. "What have you got, to say to that, Jen? Am I still being pious?" She glanced at Linda. "Am I still being hypocritical? I need to know. You're the only ones who can tell me."

Jennifer said, "I don't know. But I do know that you cannot make something wrong into something right. What I did was wrong, Martha."

Linda came and stood by Martha. Her small face was flushed but determined. "We've all done wrong things, Jen! I certainly have. And Martha has too. We've just got to live with it."

"But I can't. Don't you see that? I just can't!"

Martha said quietly, "If you have to punish yourself, then stop punishing Len. Go back to him. Look after him. He needs you so badly, Jen. And, eventually, Clemmie will need you too."

"Me?" The girl's voice rose incredulously. "Don't be ridiculous, Martha. I am the very last person Lucy's baby will need!"

Martha shrugged. "If you go back to Len, make a home . . . get married . . . you will be her stepmother, Jen."

Jennifer stared for another moment, then pushed against the door-frame, turned herself round and disappeared. They could hear her going upstairs.

Linda said, "Martha, thank you . . . thank you so much." She hugged Martha. "That was a wonderful thing to say."

"Jennifer doesn't think so." Martha closed her eyes above Linda's head. She felt terribly tired. What, in fact, had she said? Had she made some dreadful bargain? Had she told Jennifer that if she went back to Len she could have Clemmie? Was that why she had come here? Was that what Bill Tatham expected of her?

"Give her time. She has to think about what you've said. If someone gave you their winning lottery ticket, wouldn't you need time to think about it?"

"Oh Linda." Martha looked around the pristine

kitchen. "It's lovely here. But could we sit down again?"

"Come into the sitting room. And I'll put the fire on. You're really cold." She patted Martha's hand and led the way. Martha noticed that the sky through the kitchen window was gun-metal grey. She sat staring at it while Linda "did something" about lunch. She heard Archie come in and their low voices while Linda told him what had happened. And then he appeared and leaned over to kiss her cheek.

"Welcome, welcome!" He beamed at her. "May I call you Martha? How are you? Linda said you've all had a good talk." Martha nodded; she hoped she wasn't going to cry. His smile softened sentimentally. "Anything you can do to help our girl we shall appreciate. No good beating about the bush, Martha, we're worried. We'd get in a doctor but that means pills and potions and if we can do something without drugs, we'd rather."

Martha nodded again, not trusting her voice. She had said too much already. She must get away as soon as she could and go straight to Tewkesbury and get Clemmie back. Clemmie was Lucy's legacy.

They went into the dining room; green velvet curtains, reproduction Queen Anne table, chairs and sideboard. Linda had made mushroom stroganoff with pasta. They picked mushrooms every morning from the golf course. Archie told her all about it. "If you stay, you must come out with us, Martha. You're a country girl and you'll love it. If I'm not playing golf, we come back and grill them with bacon. Nothing quite like it." He glanced at Linda. "Shall I give Jen a shout?"

But she was there, holding on to the door again, smiling then edging around the chair backs to the place that was laid for her.

"Sorry to be late." She sat down and looked at Martha. "I had to get away for a while. Think." She glanced at Archie. "Has Linda filled you in? Yes? Then you know what Martha said. I mean . . . what she *said*." She shook her head as if to clear it again. "She said a lot of things. Words. Ma called them . . . what was it. Ma? Little lifebelts?" Her gaze went back to Martha and she smiled slightly. "I didn't think much of your lifebelts until that last one!" Her smile widened and Martha knew a moment of sheer panic. Jennifer was going to take Clemmie from her. She was going to use Clemmie as a means of getting back together with Len. She hadn't really changed. She was still a prime manipulator. She saw Clemmie as a pawn in some unholy game she was playing.

Jennifer said, "I knew what it must be costing you, Martha. You were giving me . . . well, you were giving me Lucy in a way, weren't you?" She picked up a spoon and looked at the big casserole of mushrooms. "But what you don't know is that Lucy phoned me. The day that Clemmie was born." She was trying desperately to behave normally; she spooned some pasta onto her plate and only just stopped it skidding onto the table. "She made it quite clear that she did not want Len making any claims on Clemmie. That was my job — to make certain he didn't." Her voice went up a note and she cleared her throat and went on doggedly. "So I can't accept . . . what you were offering. But that you offered it, is enough. Thank you."

The sudden release of tension made Martha feel faint. She stared down at her plate while Linda exclaimed. She heard Jennifer enlarge on the telephone call.

"We didn't exactly patch anything up. But we spoke. That's been part of the awfulness. That we actually spoke a few hours before . . . it happened." Jennifer moved her food around the plate with her fork. "I didn't tell you because . . . there was nothing to tell. But we made contact and it was good. It was awful but it was good. You know."

Archie said something about Lucy wanting to be friends again in the future and Jennifer shook her head. "I don't know, Archie. That's what is awful. I won't ever know."

Martha heard herself say with quiet certainty, "You'd have been friends again, Jen. And Lucy would have let you and Len take Clemmie occasionally. Then, you might not have wanted to take the responsibility. But now . . . now everything is different. I think you need Clemmie." She began to eat her pasta. She could not believe what she was saying; it was as if someone else was speaking.

Jennifer tucked her wiry hair behind her ears. "You can't know how Lucy would have felt in the future, Martha. What she said was Clemmie was yours. Hers and yours. Anyway" — she stuck her fork into a mushroom — "I'm not fit to be a mother."

Linda and Archie spoke at once. Martha continued to eat her lunch. Her heart was beating hard and slow, like a church bell. When the babble of reassurance died down she spoke slowly.

"You could be right. No-one knows till they've tried. There's no training for motherhood. Linda and I know that." She smiled across the table. "But it's certain that Len will need some help during the times he has her." She turned the smile towards Jennifer. "Why don't you go back to him? Look after each other for a bit? See how it goes. Can't we take all this slowly, step by step? Do we have to look ahead and see endless problems?"

Jennifer said, "I left him because I knew he wouldn't be able to bear to look at me again. Nothing has changed."

"Oh it has. It's changing all the time. Would you like me to mention this visit? When I pick Clemmie up?"

"I don't know. I'm not sure."

Martha looked at her. This girl had been Lucy's best friend. But she had betrayed the friendship over and over again. Perhaps that was why Martha was suddenly so sure she would never betray a trust again.

"Think about it. Let me know before I leave."

When she did leave there were still no hugs, no rush of tears, no explicit universal understanding. Martha hardly knew what they had decided except that she would tell Len she had seen Jennifer. She said, "Is there a message or something?"

Jennifer shook her head slowly. "Tell him whatever you think best. If you change your mind, don't say anything."

Martha made no protestations. "All right."

CHAPTER
EIGHTEEN

That first night Toto bathed Clemmie and George hovered nearby holding a warm towel, leaning over it to perambulate a plastic duck nearer the outstretched hands. Len had said he would join them when he had cleared away this afternoon's toys but there was no sign of him.

"Isn't she just beautiful?" Toto was kneeling by the side of the bath crooning the words above the top of the dark fuzz of hair. "She reminds me so much of our Lennie when he was a baby. D'you remember his hands? Opening and shutting all the time —"

"Clutching at life?" George hazarded with untypical whimsy.

Toto looked up, surprised. "Are you joking? No, you're not. Perhaps that was it. Perhaps that is why all this . . . has happened."

George said, "Clemmie is after something else, I think." Just at that moment the baby reached beyond the duck and grabbed his hand. He discarded the towel and leaned closer. "Is that what you wanted, Clemmie? A hand?"

Toto had to begin the process of self-control again, biting her lip and speaking oddly through a constricted throat. "Not any old hand, George. Your hand."

He smiled delightedly and offered the other hand. Immediately Clemmie grabbed it and tried to haul herself up. Her tiny feet slipped on the enamelled surface and she skidded towards him. She gurgled her laugh.

He held her firmly and rocked her and said over his shoulder, "Go on, my darling. You've been so good all day. Have a cry now."

"I mustn't!" But she was already sobbing. "I really mustn't! It's ridiculous!"

"Well, I'm going to. We're entitled. This is our grand-daughter, Toto. And she's the best thing we've ever had."

So it was that Len came upon his daughter swimming on her back with the aid of her grandfather, laughing like a crazy thing, while both his parents laughed and wept copiously at the same time.

He stood for a moment, unnoticed, watching them, thinking that this was Lucy's legacy, but not to him. The only way he could be with Clemmie was here, with his parents. Perhaps when she was older he could take her out and they could be by themselves. But would she want that? Would the bond between her and Martha strangle all other relationships?

Toto wiped her eyes on the corner of the towel and noticed him standing there.

"Lennie! I'm glad you've come. Just look at this."

He stepped forward, nodding. "I've been looking. She is so like Lucy."

Toto was amazed. "Is she? We were just saying that she reminded us of you."

"I can see that. Of course. But she has Lucy's nature. She is naturally happy." He shook his head. "Lucy was a happy . . . girl. I put an end to that. How did I do that, Ma? Will someone do it to Clemmie?"

Toto stared at him, wide-eyed, shocked but no longer tearful.

"It was Dominic, Lennie. Losing Dominic."

"It happened before then. When she was still pregnant. It happened when I . . . pushed her away."

George tried to look round but Clemmie was taking all his attention. Toto made a sound of distress and Len went on quickly, "Not literally, of course. It was Christmas Day. D'you remember? She couldn't get hold of her mother and she was worried. It made me angry. I couldn't . . . reach her. So I spent the night . . . somewhere else."

There was a long pause. George knelt by the side of the bath and very gently righted Clemmie, freed one of his hands and began to line the ducks up around her. Toto gave a dry sob. "Why do people always start these kinds of conversations on the landing or in the bathroom or somewhere equally . . . unsuitable!" She changed the sob into a laugh. Then there was silence again while Clemmie chased the ducks around the water.

George said very quietly, "I'm glad you told us, Len. We might — eventually — have blamed Lucy and Martha for a lot of things."

Len watched Clemmie scatter the ducks with a thrust of her plump leg. He said, "You mean their close relationship? Yes. I blamed that too. It was so . . . exclusive."

Toto was still silent, watching Clemmie as if her life depended on it.

George said, "It had to be. Then. And we don't know how it would have changed with Clemmie around." He pushed the ducks towards Clemmie's legs so that she could launch them off again and gurgle her laugh.

Len said, "Yes. You're right. It had to be precious and private. And . . ." His voice shook slightly. "Lucy had every right to leave Martha in charge. Of course. It's how it should be and I have to accept that."

At last Toto spoke and she spoke with her usual passion. "No! That is not how it should be, Len. What happened between you and Lucy should not affect Clemmie. And Martha is a good and just woman. She will see that. You must talk to her — come to some arrangement. Clemmie is your daughter, my dear." She reached for the towel. "Here. You take her out. Dry her. Put her to bed."

Len grabbed the towel as his mother threw it upwards and held it against him like a shield. "I think you should do it, Ma. She's used to you. She's never had a man around her, after all."

"Look how she adores your father." Toto got to her feet and touched George on the shoulder. "Come on, George. Let's leave father and daughter alone for a bit."

George rested the small dark head against the bath pillow and stood up.

Len bleated suddenly, "I don't know how to do a nappy!"

"They're disposable. You follow the instructions. On the chest of drawers by the cot. The stretchy thing she wears is on the radiator." Toto was already drawing

George out of the bathroom. "Martha brought that musical toy we gave her. She likes that when she's settling down."

They left and Len looked down into the dark eyes of his daughter. For a long moment they stared at each other, and then Clemmie hit the water with the flat of her hand and laughed at the splash. Len took his mother's place by the bath edge.

"Hello, Clemmie," he said quietly. "Are you really happy like your mummy? I wonder if you can teach the rest of us how to be happy again?"

There was another long exchange of looks, then the small girl raised both her arms to be lifted out. Len gathered her into the towel and held her close into his neck. She seemed to fit against his shoulder perfectly and be content to be held for a few minutes. Len carried her into the small bedroom which George and Toto had so lovingly fitted out for her. He sat in the chair next to the chest of drawers and began to towel her gently. On the table was a changing mat; creams and powders were nearby. He began to talk himself through some kind of a routine. He did not once think of Dominic or Lucy as being dead. The weight of their death was lifted from him. When Clemmie was snug in her Babygro, he laid her gently in the cot and wound up the musical toy while she crowed in time to it. His parents came into the room to say their goodnights but he sat by the cot until Clemmie was asleep. His thoughts were all quiet. And, strangely enough, they gradually centred on the most unquiet person he knew. Jennifer.

Martha drove home slowly. The glorious Good Friday weather had gone, the wind was strong enough to shake the car now and then but she felt curiously relaxed. She drove slowly, savouring the tiredness that would make her bed-time routine so welcome. A little scud of rain made her switch on the windscreen wipers and she smiled, thinking that she would be able to sleep right through without disturbance from Clemmie. Bromsgrove and Kidderminster were Sunday-empty, already darkening. By the time she reached Nortons Heath the lights were on and the church bell was tolling for the last Easter service. Miss Darcy's bedroom curtains glowed. Bill Tatham was back; the light in the parlour revealed Linda's Sanderson prints were still being used. She went past very slowly. Then she braked and stopped, put the gear stick into reverse and backed up to the gate.

When he answered her knock, his face registered the kind of shocked fear she understood very well. In that split second she realized many things; they all added up to his love for her which extended through every tentacle of her family. She said quickly, "It's all right. Nothing has happened. Clemmie is with Len in Tewkesbury. I thought you'd like to know that I've been to see Linda and Jennifer. And Archie Evans, of course. I thought about what you said and I went. I've just come back." She gestured behind her. "It took about an hour. Less than that actually. I had lunch and then a cup of tea and then . . ." She was still waving her hand and she put it firmly into the pocket of her cardigan. "And then I came away." She laughed suddenly. "I've talked such a lot today. And now I can't stop. It's all nonsense. That's the trouble. It's all such utter nonsense!"

He said sturdily, "I bet it's not." He drew her inside, backing down the passage ahead of her. "The trouble with this hall is it's so narrow. Can you close the door and come on in? Please, Marty."

She did so and followed him into Linda's front room. It was all quite different, quite changed. He had knocked down the wall between the two small rooms and the clutter had gone; there was space and comfort. She stopped and exclaimed. "It's lovely, Billy! Oh, it's so much better." She went past a small table and looked out into the garden. "Miss Darcy said you'd done wonders outside too. You must have worked so hard."

"Yes. It helps me. I'm not much good at thinking. As you know."

She leaned on the window ledge. Dimly she could see a gravelled area and a wooden seat. She said, "Wrong. Absolutely wrong. You told me once about all the wrong turnings you'd taken. Well, I think you've learned about the right ones." She looked round. "Billy, I think I've lost Clemmie. I think when I have time to think about it, I might go mad. I said that if Len and Jennifer could make a go of it, Jennifer would be Clemmie's mother." Her eyes filled with tears. "Which is true, isn't it? All her life she has wanted to be a member of the family. She couldn't get much closer than being a mother to my granddaughter, could she?"

His arms came around her. They were the same height. It made it so easy for her to use his shoulder. She felt an enormous sense of surrender. It was something she had guarded against ever since that terrible night when she had kept vigil by Lucy's side. She had known she must not give in because of Clemmie. Clemmie had been her reason for living and now . . . She put her forehead down and began to cry. He led her to an armchair, sat her down, sat himself on the arm and held her head.

"I haven't cried before, you know." It was difficult to distinguish her words but after a moment's hesitation he nodded.

"Yes, I do know," he said.

She sobbed helplessly. "I'm so sorry, Billy. You have taken our worries on your shoulders and not been thanked once for all your help. I shouldn't be here now, crying, telling you how awful it all is . . ."

"Where else should you be? I was the one who wanted you to see Jennifer." He smoothed her curls behind her ears. "And actually, my dear darling girl, I haven't taken any worries from you. Think about it. I've given you extra worries."

"No. No, that's not true, Billy. I've said some awful things . . . I've called you interfering . . . awful things." She hiccoughed like a child. "All the time, I knew you were trying to help. All the time I knew that I needed your — your directness, your simplicity —"

"Oh, I'm simple too, am I?" He laughed and after; a while she bubbled damply in return. Then she fumbled for a tissue in her sleeve and dried her face as best she could.

He said, "Don't get up. Don't go. Try to tell me about it. Tell me what happened. Start with how you felt when you left Clemmie in Tewkesbury. Don't leave anything out this time, Mar."

She smiled ruefully at her truncated name. "Cards on the table?" she said.

"Definitely cards on the table," he said, kissing the top of her head as if they were an old married couple.

So she began to talk. She wasn't a great talker and he had to stop her now and then and go back over things. He wanted to know whether Linda was happy — really happy. She loved him for that. He wanted to know about the house in Barnt Green and especially about Archie.

"He's a dear. And don't forget, she's known him for ages. The thing is, Billy . . ." She did not look up at him. "The thing is, he adores her. And she deserves that."

"She does. She is . . . lovable. I love her still in a way."

Martha covered his hand with hers. "Oh Billy." And before she knew it she said, "You are so good. So honest. I love you too."

He was quiet for a moment and she thought he would slide off the arm of her chair and kiss her. But he did not. Instead he said, "Go on, Mar. Tell me how you are feeling after what you said to Jennifer."

She bit her lip, then took a little breath and went on. "I don't know what I think about her. My heart went out to her. But I couldn't — couldn't *show* it! She was still *there* and Lucy wasn't! She's thin and ill and so unhappy — desperate really. Something made me — made me trust her! Jennifer Bowles was Lucy's friend. Jennifer Moreton was not. Perhaps Jennifer Travers . . ."

Suddenly she broke down again and this time he gathered her against him, whispering, "I'm sorry, Marty. I'm so, so sorry."

She said, "Not that . . . it's not that. It's . . ." She snivelled helplessly into his shoulder.

He said, "Come on, girl. Cards on table, remember. You offered to let Jennifer and Len take Clemmie? That's what it is, all right. It was an enormous suggestion. OK, she turned it down, but it's there. It could happen. And it's because of you. You've done something magnificent, Mar. Something that perhaps not even Lucy could have done. It's no wonder you're shattered. Go on, cry it out."

She controlled herself with difficulty and looked at him. His face too was running with tears but whether they were hers or his own, she did not know.

She said, "I don't know about all that. But I do know . . . Oh Billy, somehow, for Lucy's sake, I've got to make something better from all this. Clemmie must always know that though she is loved she is free."

"Yes." He sniffed, tried to smile, and repeated, "Yes."

Martha changed her position so that she could look at him properly. He looked his age, his dry brittle hair was grey and his face lined. Tears ran down the furrows. She must be looking the same.

She said, "But it's still not that. I can't do anything about Jennifer and Len. I suggested they should meet but I can't do more. And maybe one day I'll stop resenting Jennifer. I just don't know. But it's not that."

"Mar, you're not making sense. You're still crying."

She drew a deep breath. "Billy Tatham, I'm in love with you. That's why I'm crying."

His eyes opened wide. "Oh Mar . . . Oh Martha. Oh Martha. I thought you'd never realize it! Don't be sad about it. I know how things are for you and I won't be a nuisance —"

She said loudly, "Shut up, Billy! You couldn't be a nuisance! Not if you tried." She took a breath. "Billy. Will you marry me?"

At last he slid off the arm of the chair and knelt before her. He held her hands in her lap and looked up at her.

"Oh yes, my darling. But . . . are you sure?"

"Yes," she whispered.

"There will still be talk. People might say I am not a suitable grandfather for Clemmie."

"We know differently, don't we?" Her voice was very steady. She could see his throat moving convulsively as he fought tears. For a long time he watched her intently.

At last he said, "When we talked, Lucy and me, that day in the kitchen — d'you remember?"

"Yes," she said. "I remember."

"Well, that day she stopped despising me . . ." He paused as she made a sound of protest and went on very deliberately. "Of course it mattered, Mar. I could fight her dislike of me, but she hadn't considered me worth disliking. The time before — when I arrived and it was so hot — she almost laughed at me. How could I fight that? But this time, in the kitchen, we talked. I told her about Littleford in 1942. She stopped despising me. She listened. She didn't know the Martha that I knew and she was interested. And then I told her that we had slept together . . ." He waited for another protest but it did not come.

Martha said slowly, "I thought she knew."

He nodded. "I think she did, but she didn't like it — she hated me mentioning it. She didn't like the way I put my cards on the table!" He gave a wan smile but Martha nodded slowly. She and Lucy: they had talked about everything under the sun. But had they ever really put their cards on the table?

Billy tightened his hold on her hands. "She hated me then, Mar. But it was a normal, natural hate. And she wasn't a person who could hate for long. The hate would have become a kind of respect — she was already trying to understand me, she was making that effort. And we would have been friends, Marty. I promise you that I'm not saying it to — to advance my case. She had agreed to contact me if you needed any help. She was listening to me, Marty. I told her about Littleford and you being free and happy and she was listening. Do you believe me?"

"Of course. But it wouldn't have mattered, Billy. Lucy and I — we trusted each other. In a way you're right, we didn't thrash things out much. But we didn't need to. What she did was all right by me. And what I did . . . But I'm glad you made some sort of connection —"

"We talked about making connections!"

"Oh Billy." She reached into her pocket and produced a tissue and began to dry his face. "You are an honourable man." She kissed him quickly. "Please don't cry again. I can't bear it. We're going to be happy, Billy, aren't we?"

When he could speak he said, "I think so, Mar. We'll have a jolly good shot at it, anyway."

She took the soggy tissue and blew her nose. "I have to go home. I shut Snowie into the kitchen. Will you come with me?"

"Yes. Oh yes." He tried to smile. "I don't want your car parked outside the cottage all night!"

Jennifer was in Archie's house on her own. It was something that had not happened before because Linda was so anxious about her she made sure she was never alone. But Linda was under the impression that Mrs Dorrell was "doing" the bedrooms so she had agreed to lunch at the clubhouse and meet Archie's old friends. He was intensely proud of his new wife but also intensely anxious about her. He knew she needed a break from the apparently insoluble problem of Jennifer.

Jennifer felt as if she had a day off herself. She got rid of Mrs Dorrell as soon as possible and wandered around the house like an inquisitive child, looking at everything properly for the first time. Archie had removed every possible trace of May, his first wife, but Jennifer discovered things he had missed: some towels in the airing cupboard were still monogrammed and a chocolate box behind some books contained various certificates — for typewriting and shorthand speeds, for swimming half a mile. It made May Evans a real person: she had been Archie's father's secretary way back at the end of the War. She had married her boss's son. Jennifer thought bleakly it must have been a marriage like hers and Simon's. No real love anywhere. May had wanted

Archie's money, Archie's prospects. Probably, at first, she had wanted the sex. But no children. No real tenderness. A barren marriage.

Jennifer went to the window and stared down the long drive. Was she doomed to be good at sex all her life? She had never seen it before as a curse but perhaps that was what it was. And if she stopped being good at sex — and she was pretty sure she had done that already — then was there anything else she could offer?

She thought suddenly of Martha Moreton and the offer she had made on Easter Sunday. She groaned at the sheer enormity of the suggestion. Clemmie. Clemmie would come with Len and with Lucy and with part of Martha herself. What was Martha trying to do? Shrive her own soul? Or punish Jennifer still more? How could anyone — any human being — give away so much?

She blinked and saw that a car had turned into the drive and was scrunching its way up to the front door. It wasn't Len's car but when it stopped Len got out of it. She put a hand to her mouth and groaned through it; her other hand clutched at the window-sill. Len rang the bell but she could not move. She stared at him in profile. She had left him six months ago, running from him as if she could run away from Lucy's death. She had thought Len and she were in the past. Finished. She knew now that that was not so. She knew that if she let go of the window-sill she would fall down. Because of Len.

He rang again and then looked around him helplessly. He was so thin; his face was longer, his hair already grey above his ears. She felt her eyes devouring him; she wanted him again just as she had always wanted him.

374

But now, there was more. There was a terrible concern for him. It was like the physical pain of Lucy's death which she felt so often these days. There was a stupid song she had heard recently, about love hurting. She knew now that it was true. She loved Len. And it hurt. She groaned and bent as the spasm hit her.

Len's glance caught her movement and he focused on her behind the glass. For a moment he seemed to forget what had happened; his dark eyes lit and she could see his mouth shaping her name. It was too much. She put both hands on the window-sill and leaned on them, head down, tears threatening to drown her just like the ones she had wept on Good Friday morning.

She never knew how he got into the house, probably he ran round the patio and found the back door open. She simply knew that his arms were lifting her and carrying her to the sofa and that somehow they were concertinaed together, holding on to each other with a kind of desperation. It was some time afterwards that words were possible and even then they were disjointed, almost rhetorical. "How could you leave me?" "Thought you hated me . . . couldn't bear it." "We can bear anything if we're together." "Except Lucy's death, oh God . . . Lucy's death . . ." "She left us with each other, don't you see?" "To remind each other, always remind each other "No — no. To be another reason for her life." "I can't, Len, I can't. Lucy was like Martha. They are good and I am not." "Neither am I. And I'm not sure about Martha . . ." "It's such a battle, such a battle, Len, and I'm tired." "I am too. Let's try to find some peace. Please Jen. Please. Let's just try."

She hung on to him and remembered what Martha had said about trying. Could she bear it? Could all her stormy relationships find harbours? The kind of harbour that Lucy found in the Old Rectory with Martha?

She whispered, "Do you want to try, Len? Really? After all that has happened?"

"Oh yes. And I want to see something of Clemmie too, and the only way I can do that is if you will be with me to help."

"I couldn't change a nappy to save my life!" she protested, alarmed.

"Oh yes you could. And you will. Lucy left a legacy, Jen. For you as well as for me. Are you going to turn your back on that too?"

She relaxed her hold slightly and leaned against his shoulder. He waited, watching her dark, gypsy face, knowing that he had done her many injustices.

After a long time she said, "Len. The pain is going. The pain of loving you. I don't mean I've stopped loving you. But it's going."

"That's because you're going to come back. We're going to make a home, a proper family home." He swallowed. "That's why it's going. Isn't it, Jen? Isn't it?"

She said slowly, "I don't know. But I will try. Oh Len, I have missed you . . . I thought I was strong, independent. I'm not."

"Neither am I." He grinned suddenly. "We shall still have turmoils. You know that. But, for now, let us be gentle together, Jen."

"Gentle." She liked that. She had never been gentle in her life and it was very appealing. Lucy had been gentle.

She kissed Len's cheek. "Oh yes. Let us be gentle together, Len."

Bill Tatham married Martha Moreton in June of that year. Practically the whole village turned out for the occasion. Toto carried Clemmie and continued to cry copiously. "I don't think I shall ever be able to turn off this blasted tap again!" she wailed, passing Clemmie to George while she fumbled for a handkerchief. But George was as bad and passed Clemmie on to Jennifer while he too dabbed at his face. Toto glared at him. They had made a pact before they came that they would both — and both meant Toto as well as George — be nice to Jennifer. Most of the time that was not difficult; she was not the Jennifer they remembered. Her thinness made her seem small; her eyes were huge under her ridiculous flyaway hair and she spoke very little. When George put Clemmie into her arms she looked terrified and held the child slightly away from her plain linen suit, turning to look for Len in the crowd of guests. But Clemmie was in a party mood: she crowed, made a grab for the hair that was so like her own and butted Jennifer's face with pursed lips which was her version of a kiss. For a moment, sheer bewilderment was added to Jennifer's terror, then she laughed tentatively and Clemmie laughed back. It was as if they became friends. George said, *sotto voce*, "Move away, over to the drinks. Leave them together." And, almost against her will, Toto allowed herself to be drawn away. Jennifer joggled the baby experimentally and Clemmie laughed louder. And suddenly Len was there, hugging both of them. "You

377

see?" he said. "It'll be all right. Won't it?" He waited, apparently holding his breath. Jennifer said wanderingly, "I think it will. I really think it will. Oh Len . . ."

The two of them had a very quiet wedding in the Registrar's office as soon as Jennifer's divorce came through. It was winter and Len had an assignment in Liverpool; Jennifer was going with him. It was better than a conventional honeymoon: it was a return to life.

The two sets of grandparents had decided to take the opportunity to introduce Clemmie to her great-grandparents in Barbados. At fifteen months, she was walking and beginning to talk. She called Billy "Gampy" which delighted Toto. "Have you noticed?" she asked Martha as they emerged from the register office into the winter sunshine. "I haven't cried once today!"

Martha smiled congratulations as Len took his mother's arm.

"Thanks for everything, Ma. Thanks to you all. And Ma, if you do any island hopping, could you . . . just look in on Dominic?" He hugged his mother's plump shoulders. "I'm sorry, Ma. How stupid of me — please don't cry!"

She said, "It's only because I'm so happy. I'm so pleased you can . . . talk about him."

Jennifer was hugging Archie and Linda. "We'll come and stay, of course. As soon as the Liverpool thing is filmed. Yes, I promise. I love you both . . . so much."

And later, Linda said to Martha, "D'you remember Lucy throwing her bouquet? And now, we're both married, Martha. She'd be so pleased, so pleased."

Martha nodded certainly. "She is. I know it."

When Clemmie was two and a half, Len became news-reader for the Midland Television Company, and he and Jennifer bought the Old Rectory from Martha and moved in with Clemmie. Martha and Billy lived in Pittville. Martha loved it; she loved the Park with its trees and walks; she loved shopping in the Promenade and meeting Billy for lunch and going to the theatre. Sometimes in the summer they spent time in Linda's old cottage and had picnics on the lawn of the Old Rectory. Clemmie started school in Cheltenham and stayed with her grandparents during term-time, and that was better still. George and Toto were often with them and at Christmas time Archie and Linda had them all up to the big house in Barnt Green. They were a large family and they took the trouble to be gentle with one another. If Jennifer and Len sometimes forgot that, it was put down to artistic temperament. They might argue over a camera shot; Jennifer had been known to throw things. And then Clemmie would come into the room and they would both collapse with laughter and apologies.

When Clemmie was ten, Jennifer tried to talk to her about Lucy. Clemmie nodded sagely.

"I know you were best friends," she said. "Like me and Tessa."

"You don't resent . . . feel cross because I married your daddy?"

Clemmie made a sound of disgust. "Listen. If Tessa married . . ." She thought around their limited male acquaintances. "Jeremy Denniforth" — she giggled

379

because he was one of the few boys at their dancing class — "and they had a little girl and then Tess died, well, I would marry Jeremy and look after the little girl because of Tess." She thought about it. "Although I don't like Jeremy Denniforth very much and he always steps on my toes when we're dancing."

Jennifer took a breath to explain further, then let it go. "Well, I like Daddy very much," she said. "And he never steps on my toes."

"Well, he does in a way," Clemmie said thoughtfully. "And that's when you shout at him." She smiled. "I'd like to shout at Jeremy. And throw something at him."

Jennifer smiled too. "I don't think you would," she said. "It's not in your nature to get angry."

And Clemmie thought again and then said, "I think your way is best. Because afterwards you're so nice!"

And Jennifer — as she did so often now — laughed.

It was Clemmie's twelfth-birthday and as Len and Jennifer were making one of their documentaries, all the grand-parents had combined to give her a birthday treat. They had taken all the girls in Clemmie's class to the theatre: a proper grown-up outing. It had been a successful evening but, for Clemmie, something of a relief when the parents of all her other friends were waiting outside to collect their offspring. In a way she wished her very, very best friend, Tessa, was going home too. She had shared her birthday with all of them quite happily but now it would be good to have the last little bit with her family.

Grandma Toto was describing to Tessa her life in Barbados. Gran was smiling and nodding. Tess said, "Can you still surf-ride, Mrs Travers?"

Grandad George rolled his eyes and said, "Can she surf-ride!"

Grandma Toto punched him on the shoulder. "Course I can, child! I'm no expert any more but I can take out a board and ride back into the shore. But only when the weather is hot and I mean *hot*!"

Clemmie grinned. She always enjoyed watching George and Toto sparring together. They were so open; they disapproved of Jennifer and thought she did not look after their Len properly. Grandma Toto would often ask Clemmie what she had for dinner; which meant what did their *Len* have for dinner. Sometimes Clemmie made up nourishing menus, especially in the winter, because she felt sorry for Jennifer.

Gampy took her hand. "Well, Clemmie? What did you think of the show?"

"I liked the songs. It was a bit old-fashioned though."

"Yes. It was written a long time ago. But I noticed one or two of your lot having a quiet sniffle so it still rings a few bells."

"Oh, it was so sad. The bit at the end, when they met after they were dead . . . Do you think that might happen, Gampy? I mean, if you die before Gran, will you be there to welcome her when she dies?"

"I might. I don't know, honey."

"You're thinking that Grandad Moreton might be there too?"

He laughed. "I wasn't. actually. But that could happen, couldn't it? And anyway, I think there might be quite a crowd waiting for Gran."

She said soberly, "My mother, you mean."

"And Gran's parents. Grandparents."

There was a little silence then Clemmie said, "I know that's why you took us to see that musical play. To make me feel better about my birthday."

They crossed the High Street and went down Winchcombe Street. The night sky was full of stars. Clemmie found its vastness rather frightening and she held Gampy's hand harder. Ahead of them, Tessa screeched one of her laughs and Gran said, "Tess! Hush!"

Tess said, "Oh, Mrs *Tatham*, that was only a tiny little swear-word. You should hear Jennifer sometimes!"

And Toto said frigidly, "You shouldn't take any notice of my daughter-in-law, child. I'll have a word with her. Talking like that in front of children!"

Gampy laughed quietly. "Poor old Jen. I don't think Toto will ever get used to her!"

Clemmie said, "But Jennifer is so kind, Gampy. When I told her how I felt about my birthday, she said I had to enjoy it twice over. Once for myself and once for Mummy. She always understands things like that."

"How *do* you feel about your birthday, baby?"

"Well . . . it's the day my mummy died, isn't it?" Clemmie avoided a line in the paving stones with a little skip. "I know it's the day that makes Gran unhappy." She looked up into his comfortable square face. "Is that why you chose this play? Because you want us both to know that Mummy is waiting for us?"

They walked in silence for a moment or two. Then Gampy said, "We didn't choose that play actually, Clemmie, there was nothing else on. And it was colourful and romantic . . . Gran thought the girls would like it."

"They did. Oh they did. So did I. When I said it was old-fashioned I didn't mean I didn't enjoy it. But I just thought . . ."

"Listen. You're twelve now. Right?"

She nodded.

"And you're worried about Gran being unhappy on your birthday and Jennifer not getting on with Toto and George. And me being a step-grandad. And your dad still grieving for your baby brother dying a long way away. You're almost afraid to be happy. Right?"

It sounded wet but in the end she had to nod again.

He was smiling, she could tell from his voice. "That's because you're twelve. Next year when you're a teenager, you'll stop worrying about the past. You won't be tied to it any more. Listen. Sometimes, Gran and me, we wake up very early. And we go for a walk. We'll probably do it tomorrow morning. If you're awake — don't set an alarm or anything — come with us. I'll look in on you. All right?"

She nodded again. And then, suddenly, with a thrill of horror, wondered if the walk was to the cemetery. Her mother was not buried in Cheltenham cemetery at all, her ashes had been put in the dear little graveyard next door to the Old Rectory. But perhaps someone else had a grave in Cheltenham, someone she didn't know about . . . and did not want to know about. There were so many dead people and she hated it. She knew she would not be awake when Gampy opened her door.

But he must have disturbed her because as the door closed so she was wide awake. It was still very dark, probably about two or three o'clock, and she lay on her back, listening to Tessa's steady breathing and waiting to go to sleep again. Sleep did not come. Through the two floors she heard the front door close; then the house settled into its silence again.

She thought of how it must have been twelve years ago. Gran had been on her own then, no Gampy to help her. Quite alone with a new baby she probably did not want at all. Daddy had told Clemmie that she was named for her real grandfather and his own grandmother. It made everything even harder to bear. As if she were dragging a heavy weight around with her. She felt the back of her eyes pressing with tears. Poor Daddy, poor Jennifer, poor everyone . . . but mostly poor Gran.

She slid out of bed sideways, thrust her feet into slippers and took her jeans and jacket on to the landing to pull on over her pyjamas. Grandad George's gentle snores sounded from the top floor; she fastened her jeans and fought her arms into the sleeves of her jacket as she went downstairs. She took the key from the hall table and fitted it into the lock to close the door quietly and as she did so the clock from the dining room chimed six. So it really was morning although it felt much earlier.

They were on the other side of the Circus. So they were not going to the cemetery and they were not going to "perambulate" — as Gran put it — the perimeter of Pittville Park. They must be making for town. She did not want to catch them up so she hung back and then ran through the leaves across the central island and hovered by a wall until she saw them turn to make for Winchcombe Street and then the High Street. What on earth were they going to do in town at this hour of the morning — window shop?

With a sense of disappointment she scurried from corner to corner. They crossed the High Street and turned right and then left and entered the Promenade. She hovered, watching them stride purposefully past Cavendish House without so much as a glance at the windows. By the time they reached Oriel Road they were swinging their linked hands like two children on an outing. She began to feel guilty: a spy, an eavesdropper.

She stood with her back to a tree and wondered about going quietly back home, then when she peered around the trunk they'd disappeared and she knew a moment of sheer panic. It was exactly like the time when she was about four and for a ghastly five minutes lost sight of Gran as they were shopping in Birmingham's Rackhams. She ran up past Imperial Gardens and they weren't there. She rounded the Queens Hotel, crossed the road and made for the Rotunda, dodging past the statues in Armless Row. And then there was a movement over to her left and she saw them. They were in the children's playground standing by the swings. She thought she heard laughter. Gran? Laughing? As she stood by the swings at six o'clock on a cold October morning twelve years after the worst day in her life?

A single car approached from Lansdown Road; it paused at the roundabout and then headed down towards town. The headlights picked out the swings and Clemmie saw that Gran was sitting on one of them, swinging gently, saying something to Gampy as he leaned over her.

The public lavatories were the only cover now. They were too far away from the swings for Clemmie to hear what was said, so she was able to tell herself that though she was spying she was not eavesdropping. She stood in their deep shadow, shivering and watching so intensely that her eyes felt dry and she had to blink deliberately. Gampy was now on the swing next to Gran and seemed to be encouraging her. Gran was swaying gently, her feet not leaving the ground; she was laughing still, the kind of laugh that was telling him she had no intention of doing whatever it was he suggested.

He lifted his short strong legs and began to swing. She sat still, swaying, watching him. He was making sounds of encouragement. Clemmie heard her say suddenly on a high note, "I'm sixty-three, for goodness' sake!"

Gampy slowed when she said that. He scuffed his feet on the ground and stopped the swing and clearly through the lifting darkness she heard him say, "And Clemmie is twelve."

There was a silence; a stillness. Clemmie wondered what on earth that simple statement of fact had meant to Gran. It had meant something, that was certain. Clemmie was sufficiently in tune with her grandmother to know that significant things made her pause, just like she was pausing now.

She seemed to make up her mind all at once and she got off the swing quickly as if she dared not delay

386

longer. Gampy got up too and stood by her with that protective attitude Clemmie had seen so often. With some difficulty she raised her right leg and put it on the seat of the swing. With her left leg she pushed herself into motion and then stood, both legs firmly in place. She sang out, "I can do it! Look, Billy, I can still do it!" And she began to pull on the chains of the swing, propelling it forwards, leaning as it swung back, pushing again. She was laughing.

Gampy said, "Careful now, Mar — for goodness' sake, you don't have to go quite mad!"

"I can't turn upside-down, Billy. But I'm doing this bit!" The swing was at the limit of its arc and she relaxed and let it go with its own impetus.

When he was certain she was not going to fall, Gampy turned slightly and called out, "Come on, Clemmie. We know you're there. Come and swing with us!"

She ran to them, half laughing, half crying. "How did you know? Right from when I closed the door? You tricked me — you tricked me!" He put an arm around her and held her tightly as she got her breath; they watched as the swing slowed and stopped.

"Well?" he asked. "Put your cards on the table! What do you think now about your birthday? Does it make Gran unhappy?"

She looked up at her mother's mother; the grey hair curled crisply from beneath a knitted hat, the small sturdy figure was lithe, almost vibrant. It was easy to imagine Gran as a girl. Gampy had called her a tomboy. Yes, that was possible too.

She choked, "No. But why? Why this?"

Martha stepped off the swing carefully. "I used to be particularly good at swinging." She smiled, cupped Clemmie's face and kissed her nose. "Walking here — late at night when no-one was about — it became a sort of symbol for Gampy and me. It's silly, isn't it?"

"Oh no." Clemmie knew for sure it wasn't silly, but she was glad that Tessa wasn't here. "It — it's fun! It stops things from being . . . heavy!"

"Good. That's what we think too." Gran folded Clemmie into her coat and scolded, "You're wearing your slippers! And it's cold!"

Gampy folded both of them in his big sheepskin jacket. "Let's go back and cook bacon and tomatoes and fried bread."

They stayed where they were for a little while and then opened out and walked back through the town as it began to wake up. Clemmie said wonderingly, "I'm twelve. I know I am because everything looks different. It's as if I'm seeing it properly. Does that happen every birthday as you get old?"

Above her head Martha smiled at Billy Tatham. She said, "Yes. I think it does. It's like a bit of knitting when you've dropped a stitch. It looks a mess, then you see where you've gone wrong and it makes sense."

Clemmie thought how like Gran that was. Nothing about the stars or Lucy waiting at the gates of heaven like last night's play. Just . . . knitting. And a dropped stitch.

And then she remembered Martha standing on the swing in the darkness of pre-dawn; swinging her way to . . . who could tell?

388

She butted her dark curls into Gampy's shoulder. Suddenly she was hungry. She thought about the scent of bacon cooking and the way Gampy's cat, who was called Snowcem after dear old Snowball, would appear from nowhere and ask for his share. She thought about her thirteenth birthday and the one after that and after that . . . Time reeled ahead of her and behind her like Gran's knitting wool.

Then she thought again of bacon. And her father coming back home soon with dear, crazy Jennifer. And Gran and Gampy on the swings. She hoped there was a great deal of wool still to be unwound. It was all very . . . interesting.

The publishers hope that this large print book has brought you pleasurable reading. Each title is designed to make the text as easy to read as possible.

For further information on backlist or forthcoming titles please write or telephone:

In the British Isles and its territories, customers should contact:

ISIS Publishing Ltd
7 Centremead
Osney Mead
Oxford OX2 0ES
England
Telephone: (01865) 250 333 Fax: (01865) 790 358

In Australia and New Zealand, customers should contact:

Bolinda Publishing Pty Ltd
17 Mohr Street
Tullamarine Victoria 3043
Australia
Telephone: (03) 9338 0666 Fax: (03) 9335 1903
Toll Free Telephone: 1800 335 364
Toll Free Fax: 1800 671 4111

In New Zealand:
Toll Free Telephone: 0800 44 5788
Toll Free Fax: 0800 44 5789